Fatal
Memories

The MEG

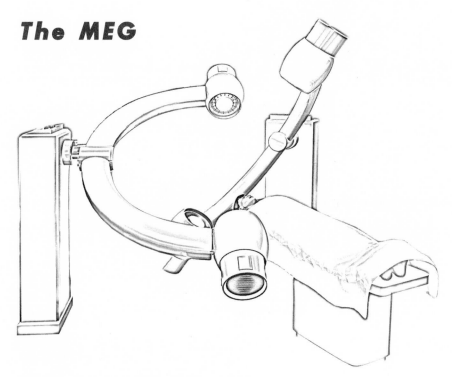

Magneto-encephalograph

Fatal Memories

A NOVEL

Vladimir Lange

RED SQUARE

Moscow • Los Angeles

F

This is a work of fiction. The events, characters and institutions portrayed are imaginary. Their resemblance, if any, to real-life counterparts is entirely coincidental.

A RED SQUARE Press Book / March 2005
Moscow • Los Angeles

Book design by Emily Stankovich

Library of Congress Cataloging-in-Publication Data

Lange, Vladimir.
    Fatal memories : a novel / Vladimir Lange.—1st ed.
        p.   cm.
    ISBN   0-9760398-1-8
    I. Title.

                                        2004092857

Published simultaneously in the United States and Canada

Red Square Books are published by Red Square Press, a division of Knigy Krasny Kvadrat. Its trademark, consisting of the words "Red Square" and the portrayal of the square, is registered with the U.S. Patent and Trademark Office and in other countries. Marca Registrada. Red Square Press, 7661 Curson Terrace, Los Angeles, CA 90046.

PRINTED IN THE UNITED STATES OF AMERICA

10 9 8 7 6 5 4 3 2 1

Dedicated to my family —
past, present and future

Acknowledgments

"Thank you" is not enough to convey the depth of my gratitude to friends and relatives who helped me through the metamorphosis from physician to fiction writer. Without you it would have been impossible.

To my parents, Anatol and Vera Lange, my love and affection for showing me the world, and for nurturing my Russian heritage.

Many friends helped me make *Fatal Memories* a better book. Thanks to Dr. Sue Hall and to Anne Larson for the insightful input; to Lynn Casella, Jane Fisher, Betsy Mullen, Carol Reed and Kathleen Winslow for your skillful reading; to Cindi Beckwith, Candace Moorman, Kathy Root and Susan Toth for your relentlessly enthusiastic encouragement; and to Robyn Shriber for your heartfelt commitment.

Thank you, Amy, for your love, support and patience during the lengthy birthing of this book. And Mandy—thank you for the advice, encouragement and unconditional love from the moment that this book was nothing but a glimmer in my mind's eye.

"Evolution, genetics, psychological experiences and even smells can trigger romantic reactions to another person."

—Anastasia Toufexis, TIME Magazine

"Love is our ancestors whispering in our ears."

—Michael Mills, Loyola-Marymount University

"We are what we were."

—Sasha Levko, Pavlov Institute, Moscow

TECHNOLOGIES COLLIDE

At the start of the third millennium, the field of medicine was enjoying tremendous progress, fueled by titanic improvements in data-processing capabilities of the new supercomputers.

In particular, two specialties were benefiting from this climate of unbridled innovation: radiology, which had become dependent on data-intensive color 3-D images and genetics, which required complex, ultra-high-speed gene sequencers.

Radiology was celebrating the 100th anniversary of the day when Dr. Wilhelm Roentgen discovered X-rays. Barely a month after the discovery, X-rays had been put to good use, diagnosing a broken wrist.

After that, new milestones accumulated at an ever-increasing tempo: fluoroscopy (to search the intestines for cancer), angiography (to find blocked arteries), CT and MRI (to identify tiny defects), PET and fMRI (to study organ function in real time) and a host of innovative combinations of these new technologies.

Genetics was growing at an even faster pace. It was only fifty years earlier that Watson and Crick unraveled the double-helix mystery of DNA. By the time all 30,000 genes of the human genome were identified in 2003, hordes of companies were rushing into the field, convinced that molecular genetics was the gateway to phenomenally profitable pharmaceutical ventures.

Other roles of DNA—for example, its capability for storing memory records—were deemed to have no significant profit potential and were left unexplored.

Advances in imaging and in genetics translated into progress in other medical specialties as well, spawning new technologies ranging from minimally invasive surgery to stem-cell transplants.

But psychiatry seemed to lag. Prozac, and the designer drugs that followed, had been a boost to the field but their results often seemed unpredictable.

In attempts to improve their therapeutic success rate, several research centers began using tests like functional MRI, or fMRI, to pinpoint the areas in the brain where the drugs where active. In 2003, Joy Hirsch, the director of Columbia University's Functional MRI Center, predicted "a future time when psychiatrists will routinely send their patients to radiologists for imaging in order to make appropriate treatment plans."

But the price of an average MRI installation, including the suite with the mandatory radio-magnetic shielding, hovered around the four-million-dollar mark. So most medical centers were reluctant to tie up such expensive equipment in pursuit of esoteric applications that were not seen as profitable.

In response to the marketplace, manufacturing giants like General Electric, Siemens and Toshiba committed the lion's share of their resources to the production of mainstream equipment.

That is how tiny, Massachusetts-based, Sidens Medical Systems, Inc. was able to secure a contract for the development of the MEG—an obscure brain scanning device, with modest psychotherapeutic applications, that was being championed by a young visionary at North Boston Medical Center.

It was a roll of the dice. But if all had gone well, a huge return on the investment could have been expected. Absolutely no one, least of all the researcher or Sidens, could have anticipated that the MEG was on a collision course with another, equally obscure project. Of all places, in the genetic memory research laboratory of Moscow's Pavlov Institute.

Fatal
Memories

1

The small wooden barn smelled of horses and hay. Mournful sounds of a Russian Orthodox choir drifted in from outside. The flickering light of an oil lamp caressed the outlines of two nude bodies lying on the dirt floor: a young woman and a young man locked in a fierce embrace. The lovers seemed oblivious to the straw and gravel that ground into the rope burns and bleeding gashes on the man's body.

He spoke in Old Russian. "I am not afraid to die. It's the thought of leaving you with him that I cannot bear."

The woman clung tighter to him and kissed his cracked lips.

He sighed. "What have we done to deserve this *sudbah*?"

Slowly, the woman disengaged herself from his arms and sat up. "I will not be with him. My *sudbah* is to be your lover—in this life and in the next. Forever."

Her hand trembling, she picked up the oil lamp.

"May God forgive us for what we have done." She crossed herself, Russian style. Three fingers pressed together. "May God forgive me for what I'm about to do."

The tears in her eyes blurred the golden flame. "*Proschay, moe solnychko.* "Farewell, my sunshine," she whispered. "Perhaps, beyond the grave …"

She stood up and flung the oil lamp at the haystacks. With a deafening roar, a raging fire engulfed everything.

Anne Powell bolted upright and pried her eyes open. Her heart was racing, the beats uneven. The odor of burning wood filled her nostrils. She heard flames crackling. *Or was it the phone ringing?* She looked around, struggling to get oriented.

The room was in perfect order. Her computer was in front of her, its oversized screen glowing with multicolored brain sections. The desk, covered with neat stacks of medical journals, the bookcase, shelves sagging slightly under rows of textbooks, the credenza with an empty crystal bud vase and two Russian black lacquer boxes—everything was in its proper place. Medical diplomas, two Kandinsky prints, a cluster of photographs of flowers, and a few pictures of her mother and father hung on the walls.

The fire in the fireplace had burned out, the logs now black and cold. Tchaikovsky's *Swan Lake* was on its last few chords. Her orange tabby cat, Miles, slept peacefully on the windowsill next to her.

She heard the crackling again. It *was* the phone. She glanced at the clock—3:00 a.m.—and reached for the receiver.

"Hello," she managed, forcing herself to concentrate.

"Dr. Powell?" It was the monotone voice of the male operator. "I have Dr. Ross for you."

As Anne listened, the last traces of her nightmare vanished.

"I'll be there in fifteen, Misty," she said, hanging up.

As she stood up, steadying herself against the desk, a prickly pain shot down her left leg. Chastising herself for falling asleep at the computer, she leaned over the keyboard and tapped a few keys, scanning the screen. *What if her head had landed on the "delete" button?* Her work was safe. She breathed a sigh of relief.

Miles leaped softly onto the desk, arched his back and yawned.

"My feelings precisely, Miles," Anne mumbled, running her fingers through his long fur.

Her leg still asleep, she limped into the bedroom, bending down on the way to straighten the edge of the small Bukhara rug. Shedding her jeans, she pulled on surgical scrubs. Getting suited up now would save a few minutes changing clothes again at the hospital. She cinched the drawstring around her firm midriff.

She liked the feeling of soft cotton against her skin. She liked hiding the outlines of her body even more. The shapeless scrubs understated the curves of her breasts and waist, partially concealing a body that often was the object of either lust or envy for her co-workers and a magnet for all sorts of characters she would rather avoid.

She stepped briskly into the bathroom and glanced in the mirror. *Ugh!* The outlines of the keyboard were still imprinted on her right cheek. She must have been asleep on it for hours, hours she needed to analyze the MEG data in preparation for the Feds.

She forced a brush through her honey-blond hair, letting the slight curls settle down evenly on her shoulders. The green scrubs enhanced her green eyes, large and sparkling even though barely awake.

She opened the medicine cabinet, its neat rows of bottles and jars precisely positioned in their places, one finger-breath apart for easy handling. Without even a glance, she located the skin toner and dabbed her cheek impatiently. The imprint lingered. *Oh well,* she thought, *they'd seen me worse.*

With the ultrasonic toothbrush humming in her mouth, Anne swung her right foot onto the sink and leaned forward. A painful pull shot from the heel up through her back, as her cold tendons reminded her that it was too early for her morning stretch.

Three minutes later, Anne slipped into her well-worn down parka, shoved a couple of KitKat bars into her pocket, grabbed her car keys off the hook next to the door and hurried out.

The security lights came on as she padded cautiously down the icy stairs leading to the driveway behind her duplex. By the time she reached her car, the chill of the New England winter night found its way past her parka and sent a shiver through her body.

She coaxed open the frozen door lock of her Volvo, grabbed a plastic scraper and attacked the thick layer of ice covering the windshield.

Clouds of crystals shimmered in the light of the street lamp as she ripped through the ice with even, methodical strokes. The harsh scraping sound reminded her of the crackling of the fire in her nightmare. She smelled the smoke again and shuddered.

She'd had nightmares about fires in the past, but none recently. She thought she was over them. And now the haunting dream was back. Then she remembered the date: February 14, the twenty-second anniversary of her mother's death.

Anne was sixteen when her mother died. Thick smoke clouded the flashing red lights of the fire engines as ...

Stop it! Don't think about it!

She forced herself to take three slow breaths. All the way in, filling her chest 'til it ached, then all the way out. *Nice and easy.* The cold air seared her nostrils. Gradually, the stench of smoke subsided.

The sheets of ice exploding under the tires, she eased the Volvo out of the driveway and headed toward Boston. Her mind switched to battle mode. Misty rarely called for her help. This was not going to be an easy case.

2

Ten miles away in a glass-enclosed cubicle in the Emergency Room of NBMC, North Boston Medical Center, Misty Ross, the thirty-something redheaded psychiatrist, hung up the phone and turned to her patient.

Frank Miller was an emaciated man in his late twenties. He sat perched on the edge of a gurney, his face drawn and in need of a shave. His shoulders stooped and his head jerked rhythmically to one side as if he were trying to look back but was afraid to turn. His wife, Peggy, a petite brunette with gentle brown eyes, stood nearby, nervously chewing on her lower lip.

Frank had been in the ER for several hours. Misty ran him through a battery of tests, searching for an explanation of his latest psychotic episode. On his arrival, he was "oriented times three"—able to state his name, the date, and where he was. But he was rapidly becoming more confused and Misty wanted to do another check.

"Mr. Miller, can you tell me where you are?"

The man's deep-set eyes drilled through her.

"You think I'm crazy, don't you? But I'm not crazy. I want this straight, for the record, OK?" He glanced at the two policemen who had brought him in and were now leaning against the doorway just outside the cubicle. "I kept notes, you know." He turned to his wife.

"Show her the notes ... It's all there." He clasped his hands and squeezed them between his knees, drawing his head deep between his shoulders. "The voices were very clear ..."

Peggy moved tentatively toward him. "Frankie, these people are here to help you."

"Screw their help!" Frank shouted. "I don't need help. I want them to know ..."

Misty had ample experience in dealing with irrational patients. Her short stint at Bellevue Psychiatric on the post-9/11 intervention team had served her well. She knew that distraction often had a calming effect. "Tell me what you had for breakfast, Mr. Miller," she tried.

He exploded. "It was my son, in the water, in my hands ... and you're talking breakfast, you stupid bitch!"

The policemen stopped talking, casually readjusted their service belts and inched closer.

"I ... It was so ... Oh, God!" Frank crushed his hands over his ears. "The voices are back!"

"Mr. Miller ..."

"Get away," he screamed. "Don't touch me!"

Misty glanced outside and tapped gently on the glass. A nurse at the central station nodded and hurried to the medicine cabinet.

The patient slid off the gurney. "Stop the voices!"

"Mr. Miller ..."

Suddenly, with a loud groan, Frank rammed past Misty and hurled himself at the glass wall of the cubicle.

Misty ducked as glass shards rained all around her.

3

By the time Anne walked into the emergency room, the bloody mess had been swept away and Frank lay on a gurney, restrained by leather straps and sedated.

Chad and Kristy, the two medical students Misty borrowed from the surgical service, were painstakingly stitching up the myriad lacerations on the patient's arms and face.

A nurse was hovering attentively at the vital signs monitor.

"About time, Powell," Misty joked with a sigh of relief.

"Got your hands full, Ross?" Anne deadpanned back.

Anne and Misty were childhood friends, their paths crisscrossing as they scaled academic ladders. They attended the same high school, in upscale Newton, in the suburbs of Boston. After graduation, Misty went on to the prestigious Manhattanville College in New York. Anne, by then an orphan, chose the more affordable Boston University.

They were both accepted to Harvard Medical School, graduating one year apart. They lost touch briefly while Misty studied psychiatry at Stanford and Anne stayed in Boston for a residency in neurology. They reconnected instantly when Misty returned to practice in Boston, where Anne was working on her Ph.D. in bioengineering at MIT.

Outside academia, the two women couldn't be more different. Misty's pleasantly plump figure, red hair, contagious smile and unabashed sexuality contrasted with Anne's lean and stunning looks, sultry demeanor and remarkable aloofness toward men.

Anne considered Misty to be one of the most astute diagnosticians and caring clinicians she had ever known. And she loved listening to Misty's graphic descriptions of her amorous escapades, vicariously enjoying adventures she herself wouldn't dare pursue, even in her dreams. When Misty digressed to astrology, karma, channeling, manifesting, or anything else that wasn't in the science books, Anne simply rolled her eyes.

Misty idolized Anne as a medical genius, Anne's successes with the MEG serving as a constant inspiration. But in personal life choices, Misty saw her friend as dismally inadequate and had made it her personal quest to pair Anne up with a man who could draw her out of her emotional shell.

Misty thanked her stars that Anne was in town, rather than lecturing in some far away city. After eight years of managing some of the worst cases that ever walked, staggered or were dragged through the emergency room doors, Misty knew when to ask for help.

Anne surveyed the scene. The case looked more like a car accident than a neurological consultation. She glanced at the monitors and, satisfied with the tracings, peeked over the medical students' shoulders. "I'd let you do my face lift any day," she nodded approvingly.

The students beamed.

The patient gasped. "Air … Ah … Can't breathe!"

"Shouldn't he be on O-two?" Anne asked.

Misty shook her head. "Gases were normal. It's all anxiety."

"Mr. Miller?" Anne said quietly, gently touching the patient's hand.

Frank jerked his hand away as far as the restraints would let him, and stared past Anne, a wild look in his eyes.

"No use," Misty sighed. "He checked out a while ago."

"What's his story?" Anne was in her familiar milieu now, her confident, poised self taking over, her nightmare forgotten.

"I've been following him in the clinic for about a year. Multiple personality disorder. Had him on everything in the book at some time or other. Nothing worked. The guy is totally non-compliant. Wife says half of the time he dumps the pills out. But there's no telling which half, so I'm afraid to keep upping his dose."

As she listened to Misty, Anne did a quick assessment, checking the patient's heart, flashing a light at his pupils, running the pointed handle of her reflex hammer along Frank's foot. The toes responded appropriately by curving down. *Not a localized lesion.*

"What happened tonight?" Anne asked as she rapped on Frank's knees for reflexes.

"Oh, he filled the bathtub and tried to drown his two-year-old son."

Anne winced. "Jeez." She leafed through Frank's medical record. "There isn't much you haven't tried, is there?"

"Every drug in the book."

"Any luck with a combination of Trazodone and Lithium? Wolford has reported …"

"I read his stuff. And I did try."

"And … ?"

"He started beating his wife twice a day instead of just once."

Frank screamed something incomprehensible and lunged toward Kristy's face. She jumped back, knocking the metal suture tray to the floor. The instruments scattered with a loud crash.

Misty turned to one of the nurses. "Debbie, I think he could use another squirt of Ketamine."

The nurse took a pre-filled syringe and reached for the injection port on the IV tubing.

Anne intercepted the nurse's hand. "Hold on for a second." She looked at Misty. "Danger to himself and others, failure to respond to drug therapy and psychotherapy …"

"A classic case for the MEG," Misty completed the sentence. "Which is why I called you. I have him on the schedule first thing in the morning."

"I think we should do him right now."

"You jest! It's four a.m."

"So?"

"And he's smack in the middle of an acute episode."

"Best time to find his locus," Anne retorted.

"While he's thrashing?"

"Not in the clamps, he won't."

Misty saw the familiar twinkle of excitement in Anne's eyes. *There would be no stopping her now.* "He could stroke out on us," she continued to protest.

"He's young. He won't."

"Let's wait. It's just another three hours. The day crew will be in. We'll have all the help we need ..."

Anne had to admit that generally any complications would be best handled during the day. *It might be more peaceful to wait.* But she hadn't gone into her field in search of "peaceful." And as far as danger—there was always danger, in any procedure. One had to balance risks against benefits. In this case, moving fast had definite advantages for the patient.

"In three hours you may not be able to find his locus," Anne said, starting to disconnect the patient from the wall-mounted monitors. "If we do him now, we'll save him and his family from a lot of grief."

"And if he's too agitated for us to find his locus?"

"Then you'll put him on a hold, get his chemistries squared away and try MEGing him later."

Misty hesitated.

"It's what he needs and you know it," Anne said. "Which is why you called me, right?"

"I just wanted you to see him while he was in the acute phase. I didn't expect you to go crazy and rush him downstairs."

"Nothing crazy about it."

The women stared at each other for a moment.

"Come on, Misty, we can do it," Anne smiled.

Misty exhaled noisily through her full lips. "I swear, I've no idea why I let you talk me into these things!"

"Did somebody come with him?" Anne asked, knowing that the

battle was won.

"His wife. She's in the consult room."

"Let me talk to her."

Misty rolled her eyes in mock desperation. Then she turned to the nurses. "You heard the good doctor. Let's mobilize. We're taking Mr. M. for a ride in the remembering machine."

4

"Mrs. Miller? I'm Dr. Powell," Anne said, walking into the tiny consultation room. "Dr. Ross asked me to see your husband."

Peggy sprang to her feet. "How is he?"

"Here, Mrs. Miller, let's sit down," Anne said, taking Peggy by the arm and guiding her to the couch. "We've just finished taking care of his wounds."

The young woman let out a quick sigh of relief, then tensed again. "Good. Now I want him gone."

"What do you mean, gone?"

"Committed. Sent away. Out of our lives. Whatever you people do! I was afraid to say something, you know, with him listening … "Her eyes filled with tears. "I love him, but I just can't stand it no more."

"You've been through a lot tonight, haven't you?"

"And last night, and last month … ," Peggy sobbed.

"I know how you feel," Anne said softly.

"No, you don't," Peggy snapped back. "You've got no idea. One minute he's so loving, and then he up and beats the crap outta me, and I can't do nothing to …" She choked on her tears and coughed, a wet smoker's cough.

Anne's heart went out to this woman. She wanted to tell her that she knew exactly what she was going through. Her mother lived the same horror for years, and there seemed to be no way out until …

Anne put her hand on Peggy's. "He's a sick man, Peggy. We could continue with drugs …"

"I can't go on like this! Look what he tried to do to our Mikey!" the young woman exclaimed, jumping up again. "I want him gone. You understand? Gone!"

Anne nodded. "I know you're scared. But it'd be good for your son to have a father around."

"So he gets drownded or gets his head bashed in?"

"There's one more thing we can do."

"Yeah, that's what you all been telling me. Four freaking years. Let's try this. Let's try that. Well, it ain't working. And I'm telling you, Doc, I've had it!"

Anne wanted to give Peggy a hug, to tell her that everything would work out. But, in medicine, things didn't always work out.

Much of psychiatry was based on a simple principle: We are what we were. Regression psychoanalysis, to bring patients face to face with past issues, often helped them resolve their current problems.

Often, but not always. Those who did not respond were treated with drugs. But no matter how much Prozac and its successors were improved, they all had side effects that sometimes were as bad as the conditions they treated. If they worked at all.

Now Anne was on the verge of introducing a technology that was an effective shortcut to accessing old memories, and a tool for erasing the harmful ones. Without drugs. Without years on the psychiatrist's couch. A technology that would return patients like Frank to their families and to a normal life.

Anne looked into Peggy's deep-set eyes. "I know you're at the end of your rope," she said. "But I wouldn't ask you to try one more thing if I didn't think there was a good chance."

"What, another fancy new drug?"

"No. This is a different treatment altogether. We're conducting clinical studies—scientific testing—on a new device. It's like an MRI …"

"Dr. Ross said something about some machine." Peggy sniffled and wiped her tears. "You do what you want, long as you know I won't have him around unless he's fixed."

"I know we can help him," Anne said confidently.

"If he's not better, he's not coming home," Peggy said again, glancing anxiously at Anne.

Anne stood up. "If the MEG doesn't work, we'll commit him. I promise."

5

Anne caught up with the convoy—Misty, the medical students and two nurses pushing Frank's gurney—as they rounded the corner to the neurophysiology department. The group stopped in front of a vault-like door with a stern warning:

MEG—MAINTAIN MAGNETIC FIELD PRECAUTIONS

The technologist, Pablo, a compact Peruvian man sporting a tiny diamond stud on his right front tooth, stopped them at the door. He grinned as he recognized Anne. She was his favorite doctor. She always seemed to know what she wanted and never had a harsh word for the staff or the patients.

"Buenos dias, Pablito!" Anne greeted him cheerfully.

"Teese ees a holdup," Pablo said with a mock Spanish accent, faking a gun with one hand and holding a basket with the other.

Everyone dutifully relinquished anything that could be damaged or wrenched loose by the enormous magnetic field of the MEG—watches, credit cards, pens.

"And to what do we owe the pleasure of this pre-dawn visit?" asked Pablo, his accent now barely perceptible.

"Because nothing else worked," Misty answered.

"Enter the sancta sanctorum!" Pablo intoned in a fake baritone, pulling the gurney in. "We will open your minds, and you will be healed."

The students hesitated at the door, visibly awed. The suite was more complex and intimidating than anything that they had seen in this hospital, or any other.

A wall-sized bank of TV monitors glowing a mysterious indigo blue covered one side of the dimly lit area. On the other side was a control console—about the size of a large desk, shielded from the rest of the room by a leaded glass partition.

In the center loomed the austere outline of the MEG—the magneto-encephalograph. The most striking features of the slick gray unit were the C-arms—twin semi-circular structures, about eight feet across, each supported at the center by a pivot attached to a pedestal. The pedestals were positioned in such a way that the open ends of the C-arms overlapped like the blades of an eggbeater.

Under the C-arm assembly there was a patient table that fit tightly into the space between the C-arms, allowing them room to rotate around the point where the patient's head would be located, without colliding with either the patient or each other.

Each tip of a C-arm was equipped with an emitting pod—a device shaped like a small beer keg, with a beam lens at the end that would be pointed at the patient.

"That's a hell of a gizmo," Chad whispered.

Misty turned to the students. "Thanks for your help. I'll have the nurses page you for the wound check tomorrow."

The students started to leave, visibly disappointed.

"Do you have time to stay and see the procedure?" Anne asked.

"Yes!" Chad and Kristy exclaimed in unison.

"You can watch from there." Anne pointed to the door leading to the gallery overlooking the MEG. "I'll explain everything over the intercom as I go."

Moving rapidly to take advantage of the lull between the patient's outbursts, Pablo and the nurses transferred him to the table and hooked him up to a bank of vital signs monitors. The quiet staccato beeps of his heartbeat filled the room.

Reaching under the edge of the table, Pablo pushed a button. Two large clamshell grips closed around the patient's head, and smaller restraints grasped his ankles and wrists. Frank was immobilized.

Using two red laser beams for guidance, Pablo quickly aligned the patient's head under the overhanging C-arms.

Frank opened his eyes and looked around, confused. Suddenly, he started to struggle. "Let me die!" he cried. "I want to die!" The veins on his forehead bulged as he strained to break loose.

Anne leaned over him. "Mr. Miller!" she said firmly, squeezing one of his arms. "Listen to me. I know you're scared. But we have to make sure you stay absolutely still for the procedure. Do you understand?"

Her authoritative voice seemed to calm him down. "Don't hurt me," he mumbled.

"We won't, I promise." She smiled. "Try to relax. You'll feel better very soon."

Anne strode briskly to the control console. Her fingers raced over the familiar panel as she booted up the system. The room lights dimmed. As they stood at the control panel, Anne's and Misty's silhouettes appeared dwarfed against the full wall display as it flashed with an electric blue, then dissolved into an image of the patient's brain.

The nurse's voice reported out of the darkness. "BP 135 over 85. Rate 86."

"Thank you. That's how we like it," said Anne. "What do you figure he weighs, Pablo? About 68 or 69 kilos?"

That was around 150 pounds. The exact weight did not really matter, but Anne and Pablo had an unspoken contest as to who could guess the closest. Peeking into the patient's chart beforehand was not allowed.

"Nah, doc. I'd say 67. Look at his arms. Skinny."

"Sixty-seven," the nurse confirmed, consulting the chart.

"I guess I owe you another *latte grande*, Pablito," Anne laughed. "OK, so let's say 67 times point four … Give him about 25 cc."

"Twenty-five it is, Doc." Pablo stuck a syringe into a large vial of contrast medium and drew up the necessary amount.

Anne leaned toward the mike built into the console and looked up at the gallery where Chad and Kristy watched, faces pressed against the glass, like kids in a toy store.

"That's a solution of glucose labeled with Carbon 14." The faces on the other side of the glass looked blank. "Radioactive glucose. That's how we find which part of the brain is active." Anne turned to Misty, covered the microphone with her hand and sighed. "They don't teach these kids much nowadays, do they?"

"Infusion starting, Dr. Powell," Pablo called out.

The giant 3-D image of the patient's brain began a slow metamorphosis. Waves of bright colors swept across the cortex in psychedelic patterns.

"He's holding steady at 140 over 90. Pulse 90," the nurse announced.

"OK, here we go." Anne's voice was steady. But even with hundreds of procedures under her belt, no MEG session was ever routine for her. She pushed a button. Beams of intense blue light flared from the pods on the tips of the C-arms. A low rumble filled the room as the C-arms began to rotate around the patient's head, gradually gathering speed. The blue beams crisscrossed like light sabers, casting bizarre patterns on Frank's face.

Anne raised her voice so Frank could hear her. "Mr. Miller, I want you to remember what you did today."

The patient jerked slightly but kept his eyes closed and said nothing.

"Try to remember."

"Home. I was home …"

"What were you doing?"

"I … I don't know …"

He jerked, but the restraints limited his movements.

"Bathing my son … Water. Lots of water."

"And then?"

"I heard them …"

"What?"

"Loud. I had to obey …"

"What?"

"Voices."

"What did the voices say?"

He was panting.

"Think back, Frank."

The giant monitor registered a yellow flare of activity deep in Frank's left temporal lobe—Frank was beginning to remember.

"I don't want to ..."

"What did the voice tell you to do?"

"Voices ..."

"About your son ..."

The diffuse yellow flare on the screen coalesced into a definite orange spot about an inch in diameter.

"Bingo," Anne mumbled.

"I think we just found the cave where his demons live," Misty whispered.

Anne glanced up at the students. "See the locus?" she asked softly into the mike as Chad and Kristy watched, mesmerized, from the gallery. "This is the exact point in his brain where his memory of the event is located."

"I can't ... Please don't make ..." Frank moaned.

"150 over 100, pulse 120," the nurse said.

"Shit," said Misty.

Anne shook her head. "Don't worry, we'll make it." Her eyes were racing over the monitor screen.

Frank stared wildly at the C-arms spinning above his head like a giant eggbeater.

"Oh, my throat!" Frank screamed.

Anne and Misty were glued to the screen where the hot locus flared like a beacon. Anne probed further. "Frank! Is something hurting your throat?"

"Let go!"

"Talk to us!"

"No, please!" Frank writhed in pain.

"180 over 110 and climbing."

"We should have waited," Misty said.

"Don't worry," Anne replied calmly.

"Sometimes I wonder who the nuts are around here," Misty mumbled.

Bundles of multicolored lines danced on the wall display.

Anne continued. "Where are you, Frank?"

"I can't see! It's all black." He gave a giant heave against the restraints.

Anne glanced at a monitor and cringed. The image of the brain had shifted by several millimeters from its original position.

"Damn, he's out of alignment."

"See? It's no good, we should stop," Misty chimed in.

"210 over 112." The nurse's voice was shrill.

Misty was losing it. "Let's just shut down, before he strokes."

"I can fix it!" Anne stepped out from behind the glass partition, ran up to the MEG, paused for a moment to adjust her timing, then ducked between the rotating C-arms, like a matador sidestepping a charging bull.

A stray metal pen flew out of her pocket and stuck to one of the magnetic pods. As Anne leaned over the patient, the electronic image of her own head flashed on the wall display.

"Anne! Watch out! You just got blasted with …"

Before Misty could finish, Anne had repositioned Frank's head in the restraints, snatched her errant pen off the C-arm, and slipped back into her place behind the glass shield.

"Real smooth, Doc, getting your brains fried!" Misty whispered angrily.

"Just a short blast. No harm done."

"Last time you got zapped, you had nightmares for a week."

More like a month, but so what? "No demons in my caves," Anne shrugged.

"Right. And I'm a virgin," Misty shot back.

"That's treatable," Anne replied with a twinkle in her eyes. Then she turned back toward the MEG. "Frank, what do you see now?"

The patient's voice became very thin, like a child's. "Can't … God!

No, please! He's choking me!"

"Who, Frank?"

"Argh …" Frank gurgled, thrashing against his restraints.

"Breathe slowly, Frank. In and out … Who is choking you?"

"A man … my … my daddy. It's my daddy."

The brain waves converged into a single, bright, angry knot. The MEG had done what years of psychotherapy, bucketfuls of drugs and dozens of sessions with a hypnotist had failed to do. Frank remembered.

"His father?" Misty leaned toward Anne. "That's incredible! His father died when he was barely two and a half years old! You just took him eight months further back than any other patient we've ever had!"

Anne flashed a triumphant smile.

"180 over 120." The nurse's voice cracked with anxiety.

"We'd better stop now!" There was a thinly disguised panic in Misty's voice.

The nurse was frantic. "His T-waves are way up, Dr. Powell …"

"Anne! Don't you think it's safer …"

But Misty knew that when Anne had a goal, there was no reasoning with her.

"We can debate this 'til we miss the whole thing …" Anne mumbled, turning to the control panel. "Or we can get in there and do what he needs done." She keyed in a password. M-E-M-O-R-I-E-S. The unit beeped.

Anne grabbed the joystick in the middle of the console. Two red index lines appeared across the image of the brain, near the flaring locus. Anne heard herself humming a few chords from the soundtrack of *Rocky*.

Misty was tapping her foot impatiently. "OK, just zap it and let's get out."

"We've got to be exactly on the locus." Anne worked the joystick with the precision of a surgeon, but her tongue stuck out like a schoolgirl's concentrating on her homework.

The red lines on the monitor drifted closer to the locus. But not close enough.

"Come on, Anne."

"Hang on."

A high-pitched shriek pierced through the hum of the MEG. It was the blood pressure alarm.

"Dr. Powell! He's 220 over 140!"

The patient started gasping. Even in subdued lighting, they could see that his skin was turning beet red. Misty was beside herself.

"Dammit, Anne! Shut it down!"

I need to make this work, Anne wanted to say. *I promised the wife this would be the last try. It has to work!* "Give me five seconds."

"You don't have time …"

Anne twisted the joystick.

"Three seconds!" Misty's voice was shrill.

"He's not breathing!"

"Two …"

The lines converged.

"Stop!"

"I'm there!" Anne flipped the guard off a large red button and punched it.

The blue beams turned red. A penetrating hum filled the room, as two powerful beams from the C-arms converged on the patient's locus. The patient's back arched off the table. On the TV display, the bright spot convulsed one final time, then collapsed to a pinpoint and vanished.

"Jeez …"

Misty, the nurse and Pablo let out simultaneous sighs of relief. The C-arms ground to a halt. Frank took a noisy breath and opened his eyes. Slowly, his lips spread into a thin smile.

"Where am I?" he asked quietly.

Misty turned toward Anne. "The iron maiden does it again."

"Teamwork," Anne said modestly.

Then she turned away, clenched her fist, punched the air and whispered, "Yes!"

She was ready to face the final obstacle.

6

The employees' cafeteria was deserted. It was that quiet moment when the graveyard shift folks were busy on the wards finishing their chores, while their daytime replacements were still snoring at home.

Humming cheerful bars from Bizet's *Carmen*, Anne went behind the counter and poured herself a large cup of coffee. She took a sip and closed her eyes, enjoying the warmth of the cup as much as the aroma of the thick brew.

She extracted a KitKat from her pocket. With ritual precision, she slid the bar out of the paper sleeve, carefully unfolded the foil wrap, and inhaled the scent. Gently, she broke off one of the segments along the score line and placed it in her mouth, the chocolate covering, softened by her body heat, exploding in a burst of flavors. She closed her eyes and rolled it around with her tongue. Then she bit into the bar, relishing the delicate crunching. She snapped off another segment and forced herself to rewrap the rest. Half a KitKat meant running an extra mile, but it was worth every calorie.

She glanced at her watch. It was too early to make rounds, too late to go home, and her adrenaline level was too high to catch a nap. She headed for the stairwell and sprinted three flights up, two steps at a time. Unlocking her office door, she walked past her assistant Lucia's desk and entered her own office.

The space was a bit cramped, but neat. Stacks of journals and patient charts for review. A glass display box with a scale model of the first MEG. A small cactus that Misty had brought for her from an Arizona spa. Somehow Lucia had managed to keep it alive despite the Boston weather. The young woman came to her from Sidens, the company that manufactured the MEG, only a year ago, but already she had proven to be indispensable.

Through the double-pane window, beyond the two new medical buildings that obscured most of the view, Anne could see a patch of sky beginning to turn a beautiful pink.

She pulled off her scrubs and took off her bra, her skin breaking out in goose bumps from the overnight chill of the office. Opening the bottom drawer of her file cabinet, she found her jogging bra and a Lycra running suit and quickly slipped them on.

Moments later she emerged in the alley behind the hospital. Bracing herself against the chilling wind, she jogged down the narrow alley between the buildings, past the liquid oxygen storage tank, past the trash trailers and onto Brookline Avenue.

She didn't play tennis, golf, or dance. She ran. Usually she ran after work before going home, to avoid the nightmarish Boston outbound traffic. Running in the early morning, when no one was out and the world was hers, was a real treat.

She turned off Brookline Avenue, relishing the soft patches of new snow under her feet, and headed up Longwood Avenue through the Medical Area. Here, almost a dozen major hospitals were clustered around one of the most revered teaching institutions: Harvard Medical School, her alma mater. The austere Greek façades of the four teaching buildings loomed in the twilight around the quadrangle, like temples on the Acropolis.

A delivery truck slowed to let her pass. The driver eyed her and grinned. She responded with her standard emotionless smile. No matter how she dressed when she jogged, her long legs and confident stride never failed to attract attention. It made her feel more in control to respond positively and move on, rather than to get irritated.

She continued past Beth Israel Hospital. She had warm memories about this place, where she had worked part-time throughout medical school as an autopsy assistant. She didn't mind her classmates teasing her about the gruesome job. Five bucks an hour wasn't much but back then it covered pocket expenses.

She was lucky to land the job as soon as she started medical school. Working quietly, she listened to the deceased patients' internists or surgeons when they come down to observe the autopsies and debate the causes of death.

The psychiatrists never came. As she held the brains—soft corrugated globes of white and gray matter—in her hands, weighed them, dropped them into jars of formalin and filed them on shelves, Anne thought that the shrinks were missing a valuable chance to learn what had actually happened in their dead patients' heads.

Why don't they look beyond the couch, she wondered. There were imaging techniques, like MRI and CAT scans, that could reveal minute details of brain anatomy. Other techniques, like PET, could provide glimpses into brain function. *If the two could be combined to shed light on the patient's psyche before the patient wound up on the autopsy table,* Anne mused.

That's how her idea of the MEG was born.

She crossed Beacon Street, took a shortcut through the narrow strip of grass and buildings that passed for the Boston University campus, and crossed the pedestrian bridge spanning Storrow Drive.

This was the beginning of her pre-measured five-mile loop along the Charles River. Her usual time was around forty-two minutes. Very respectable for a thirty-something sedentary worker. Today she felt in top form. Maybe she could shave a few seconds off her best time …

Just relax and run, she chastised herself.

She bounded down the steps of the overpass onto the running path along the river, slowing briefly to admire a lone rowboat gliding silently on the glassy surface. Long, even ripples fanned out behind the slender craft, like a peacock's tail. Or like magnetic lines …

Her senior high school science project was an ambitious attempt to duplicate the well-known experiments that proved that homing pigeons used the earth's magnetic field to navigate, presumably by sensing the magnetic pull on microscopic metal particles imbedded in their nostrils.

She had no problem securing a few pigeons. For magnetic fields she resorted to an ingenious solution—a junkyard on the outskirts of town, where there was an electromagnet strong enough to lift cars. The experiment failed to yield the expected results: the birds cheerfully scattered in all directions when she released them. But Anne became hooked on science.

During one medical school summer she worked as assistant to a professor who was perfecting three-dimensional MRI—magnetic resonance imaging. MRI provided accurate 3-D images that could be rotated to any angle for closer examination.

In the last year of the four-year neurology residency, Anne figured out how to combine an MRI scan, which provided information about brain anatomy, with a PET scan, which showed the brain's biochemical activity in real time. That work earned her the admiration of her colleagues, and the publication of several articles in prestigious journals.

A shaft of sunlight cut between the naked tree branches, illuminating the clouds of steam billowing from her mouth with each breath. Endorphins now racing through her body, she picked up the pace. Her feet struck the cement path with metronomic precision. Her breathing was deep and steady. *In and out.* Four steps to a breath. Concentrating on form. *Heel, knee, hip.* A bicycling motion.

The next building block for her MEG idea came from a discovery by a group at Beth Israel Hospital, just down the hall from the autopsy room where Anne had worked, that magnetic waves applied to the skull (rTMS, for Repetitive Transcranial Stimulation) could be used to treat various conditions, including depression, schizophrenia and epilepsy.

Very elegant, Anne thought. All that remained to be figured out was how to make the currents go exactly where they were needed. The solution came to her in a flash, during a run, six years ago.

Her strides smooth and powerful, she cruised past the boathouse on the Charles. *One mile.* She glanced at her watch. *Eight seconds ahead.* It was going to be a good day. The rest of the KitKat bar awaited her in the office.

She raced up the stairs leading to the pedestrian path on Longfellow Bridge. Morning traffic was thickening. The golden eastern sky was ready to burst into sunshine.

Two miles. Twenty-two seconds ahead. Feeling great, she came off the bridge on the Cambridge side of the river and tore down the sidewalk along the quay. In another mile, she approached MIT.

When she had completed her residency, instead of hanging out her neurologist shingle, Anne enrolled in the bioengineering program at MIT. Within two years she figured out how to focus magnetic fields on a small area of the brain and earned a Ph.D. in the process.

The MEG prototype was rolled out on her thirty-fourth birthday. That was four years ago. Now she was awaiting final approval from the FDA. If all went well at the FDA review scheduled for the end of the month, the MEG would be cleared for commercial distribution. Her dream would finally become reality.

She pushed faster and faster. The exertion made her feel light-headed. Runner's euphoria. She glanced at the dome of the MIT library, sidelit by the rising sun, its shadow reaching almost across the river.

Suddenly she saw Peter's face.

But today it wasn't a memory. The image of the face was so real and so close she thought she could touch it. Her visions were always more vivid whenever she accidentally entered the MEG beam. With as much work as she did on this project, an occasional exposure was practically unavoidable. *No harm.* Unlike CT scans, which used X-rays, MRI relied on magnetic and radio waves and was considered harm-

less—"non-invasive." She knew her brain would soon return to normal.

The image of Peter's face lingered. She could see his sparkling
eyes, feel the touch of his hands on her face, smell his scent.

Peter Morrison was the closest relationship she had ever had with a
man. Her only love. Or at least as close to love as she had ever gotten.

They had met in that very library, the first month that Anne
entered MIT. One afternoon, Peter, sitting in one of the carrels, was
watching her as she went back and forth into the stacks, carrying armfuls of obscure journals. Finally, he walked up to her and said, "Let's
go for a walk. It's too nice to be inside."

It was the most beautiful walk she had ever had. To this day, the
strongest memory she had of that first encounter was his scent—the
faint aroma of candle wax.

In the ensuing months, they discovered that they shared many
interests, both personal and scientific. He offered to help her with her
research on magnetic beams and they wound up spending endless
hours together. "It must've been the smell thing," Peter often teased
her. "Who knew that using candle wax to seal my test tubes would get
me in so much trouble!"

As Peter and she grew closer, Anne began to experience a feeling
of comfort and belonging. This was much to her surprise, since in the
past all her relationships ended the same way: As soon as she felt anything that was even close to love, some door in her mind slammed
closed and she ran.

But now the door remained open. And for the first time in her
life, she began to enjoy physical intimacy. The soft touch of his lips,
the feel of sweaty bodies sliding against each other, the peace of lying
in his arms afterwards, the whispered "I love you"—they all swept
over her like warm waves on the beach.

She tripped while staring at the flat spot between the river and the
concrete embankment. One summer five years ago, that spot had
been covered with grass. She and Peter sat there side-by-side, cross-

legged, finishing a couple of submarine sandwiches they brought for their weekend picnic. Peter peeled an orange. Holding a slice between his teeth, he leaned toward Anne and gently pushed her down on the grass. Very slowly, he brought his lips next to hers. She could smell his warm, sensuous scent mixed with the aroma of the orange. He pressed the orange against her mouth. Her lips parted. As he bit into it, the fruit exploded in her mouth, filling it with sweetness, the juice flowing, running down her neck, his tongue licking it as the sweet stream oozed down her chest and between her breasts, where her heart was pounding against his, their bodies pressed together, all barriers between them collapsing.

She couldn't stop smiling the rest of the day. She and Peter were one, and he had been part of her, all her life and longer, and she wanted to be with him forever.

But that night she had a terrifying nightmare. She woke up drenched in cold sweat, screaming, "Don't touch me, don't love me."

"What happened? What happened?" Peter kept asking, trying to comfort her in his arms.

"Blood, blood everywhere," she cried, pushing him away.

"What did you dream?"

"I don't know. I can't remember."

"Try."

"I don't want you to love me."

"But why, for God's sake?"

"It will be horrible. Horrible," she repeated, clutching her arms around her head.

"What are you talking about?"

"If I love you ... I feel ... Peter, I can't explain."

"Deep breaths, slowly now."

"I'm scared, Peter."

"Everything will be fine ... I love you."

"No! You mustn't," she exclaimed, dashing across the room.

"Anne, darling, come back to bed."

"Leave me alone!" she screamed. "Please."

She paced, sobbing, until morning. The love that was so sweet had changed to a deep, unexplainable fear. A chasm had opened between them, never to be bridged.

After Peter left reluctantly for his lecture at MIT, she rushed around the house, methodically packing her belongings. Part of her kept screaming, *Where are you going, what are you doing?* while the other part urged her to move faster and faster, as if the house were on fire and she had to flee.

Her parting note to Peter was brief: "I can't love you. If I do, something terrible will happen. Please don't ask why, or how I know it. I just feel it. Maybe some day I'll figure it out ..."

There had been no one like Peter since.

To this day she remembered the gripping, paralyzing fear she felt that night. But try as she might, she could never recall the nightmare itself.

She picked up her pace, whipping around the corner onto the Massachusetts Avenue Bridge with such speed that she almost fell.

She pushed harder and harder, her chest ready to burst, her legs burning. *Faster, faster. Don't think. Don't remember. Just breathe.*

She raced across the bridge, away from MIT, away from her memories, toward the hospital that was now in sight.

Toward the safety of *not* being in love.

7

Ten time zones away, in Kemerovo, one of the most desolate coal mine towns in Siberia, Vissarion Yossifovich Namordin was delivering his standard campaign speech.

Despite the gloomy skies and cold drizzle, the crowd around him had grown from a dozen blue-collar workers to a sea of coal dust-covered faces that filled the town square and spilled into adjacent streets. It was a typical political rally crowd, except for the many red banners that glowed prominently against the bluish mist. Some of the banners were decorated with a hammer and sickle, others with pictures of Lenin and even Stalin. It was an unusual sight, even by the new free-speech standards.

Fragments of Namordin's words boomed from loudspeakers. "Fix the damage done by the economic collapse…make Mother Russia a mighty nation again … this would not have happened if my grandfather Yossif Stalin were in power …"

The crowd nodded approvingly, cheered and waved the red banners. The man was right. Things weren't so bad back then, under Communism. At least everyone was guaranteed a job, and bread, when available, was affordable. But now Russian oligarchs—overnight billionaires—continued to thrive, making fortunes at the expense of those who actually worked for a living. It wasn't fair. Changes were in order. Drastic changes. Perhaps the country needed another iron-fisted leader like Stalin. Perhaps Stalin's grandson, Namordin, was the man who could make those changes, reunite the country and lead it once again to the glory that it deserved.

Red banners fluttered. Hats flew into the air. They loved his message. And his heritage.

In the hotel overlooking the square, a gaggle of Namordin's handlers watched the local coverage on a small black-and-white TV and grinned. In this political climate, being the grandson of Stalin practically guaranteed Namordin's success in the elections that were a mere two months away.

Campaign Chief Vassin stared at the screen and nodded pensively. *If only Namordin's energy would last. If only the hallucinations that haunted the man, turning him into a mental cripple at the most inopportune times, would leave him alone.*

A few hours later Namordin was snoring in a luxurious leather seat of a Tupolev TU-134 military transport aircraft, modified to serve as his mobile headquarters. An aide walked in with a glass of steaming tea, and gently tapped Namordin on the shoulder.

"Comrade Namordin! We'll be landing in Krasnoyarsk in 15 minutes."

Namordin did not respond. The aide gave him a firm shake.

"Wake up, sir! It's time."

Namordin opened his eyes and stared. Suddenly he seemed to remember something. He backed into the corner, flailing his arms as if fending off an attack of killer bees.

"Get away, leave me alone!" he shouted in a high-pitched voice.

"Vissarion Yossifovich, it's me, Andrei …"

"Go away, I'm afraid of you," Namordin whimpered. Then, turning toward the window, he curled into a fetal position, pulled the blanket over his head and started singing softly. It was a sad, melancholy song. *"Suliko, gde ty moya Suliko … "*

The aide walked toward the front of the aircraft and whispered something to Vassin.

The campaign chief sat up and winced. "Not again!" He turned to the aide. "No one must know about this, understand?"

Punching a button, Vassin spoke into the intercom. "Petya. Change of plans. Reroute to Moscow."

"Yes, sir. Direct Moscow," the pilot's even voice came back.

Vassin thought for a while, then picked up a telephone and dialed the number for the Pavlov Neuropsychiatric Institute in Moscow.

At the Institute the call was rapidly transferred up the chain of command to Professor Baldyuk himself.

"I understand. But we did warn you when comrade Namordin was being treated here ..." Baldyuk wanted to make it clear that he wasn't to blame. "All I can recommend is that we readmit him for additional treatment ... A month, perhaps longer ... Yes, I'm aware that he needs to be on the road ... but I see no alternative." Heaven knows, Baldyuk thought, some of the best people spent months treating this man. Conventional psychotherapy, regression hypnosis, countless sessions with Aphanasy, the phenomenally successful faith healer. They even consulted psychiatrists in Germany and America.

America ...

"There's one more approach," Baldyuk said into the telephone. "But it will be expensive."

"Our backers have always been very generous with your Institute," Vassin replied dryly.

"It's not just the Institute. I might need to get personally involved," Baldyuk said, the hint thinly disguised.

"We'll make it worth your while."

"I'll get back to you," Baldyuk said, hanging up.

He knew exactly what to do next.

8

"Girlfriend, that was a sweet case!" Misty said as she and Anne walked across the hospital lobby that evening. "We're getting there," Anne replied modestly.

"What's wrong with you, girl? When will you ever say, 'Yeah, that was good'?"

Anne shrugged. "We can do better."

A fine snow was falling. As they hurried across the slippery walkway to the parking lot, Misty held her briefcase over her head to protect her red curls.

"Can't we do this another time?" Anne asked, trudging up the stairs of the parking structure. "I'm bushed."

"Here, give me the keys. I'll drive. You sleep," Misty said cheerfully. "I caught a nap after lunch, so I'm OK."

"You sly fox. How'd you manage a nap?"

"In the psych residents' room."

"Oh? Sure it was just a nap?"

"Yes, smarty-pants. Just a nap."

Misty eased herself behind the steering wheel of Anne's Volvo and adjusted the seat. The car groaned plaintively as Misty gunned the engine and dove into the thick traffic on Longwood Avenue.

"Hey, easy," Anne exclaimed.

Misty glanced at her, an amused twinkle in her eyes. "You sure are braver in the MEG room." She patted Anne's hand. "Lie down and go to sleep. I'll get us there in no time."

"In one piece, please."

Anne reclined the seat and forced herself to close her eyes. Her shoulders ached and her mind was still racing after the long day. She rolled her head from side to side trying to ease the tension.

It made her think of Frank's head, shifting during the scan. She made a mental note to talk to the folks at Sidens. *Perhaps if the clamps were more steeply contoured near the edges, like a deeper spoon ... Of course, that would mean retooling. New molds. Expenses. Delays. Jack would protest.*

"You know something?" Misty's voice brought her back. "You don't look good."

"You're so sweet."

"No, really. You've these big black circles under your eyes ... And your face, it's all like tied up in knots."

"It's been a long day."

"It's not just today. You need a vacation."

"Vacation? What's that?"

"My point precisely."

"I hate vacations," Anne said.

"That's because you don't know how to take them."

"Maybe I should take a course in it," Anne said sarcastically.

"Come to Canyon Ranch with me."

"What's Canyon Ranch?" Anne asked without enthusiasm.

"A spa. You know, a place people go to relax? First week in May. It's fabulous. Incredible food, all the personal services you can stand."

"Excuse me?" Anne opened one eye and glanced at her friend.

"Get your mind out of the gutter. Massages, facials ... those kinds of personal services."

"I never know with you," Anne said, and they both giggled.

"And plenty of trails to run for those who can't sit still," Misty added.

"Maybe next year."

"Annie, you've got to lighten up. Dedication is fine, but how about some balance in your life?"

Anne turned demonstratively toward the window. "I thought you were going to let me sleep."

Misty rolled her eyes. "Fine, sleep."

Anne twisted her body into a more comfortable position.

"Anne?"

"Now what?"

"Before you check out. You got any music? I'll play it quietly."

"Blast away all you want. It won't bother me." Without opening her eyes, Anne found the stereo controls and punched a button. The soft sounds of a Russian church choir filled the car.

"What the hell is that?" Misty exclaimed, turning down the volume.

"The Easter Liturgy at the St. Petersburg Cathedral of the Transfiguration, Pyotr Ilyanov conducting."

"Of course it is!" Misty retorted. "But why?"

"It's uplifting. Just listen to those voices," Anne protested, as male and female voices blended into a rich melody.

"And you understand this stuff?" Misty asked skeptically.

"No, but doesn't it just grab your soul?"

"Hmm-m," Misty pretended to listen attentively. "No, not exactly. But it does grab my guts," she added pantomiming a bellyache.

"Peasant."

"Snob. Where did you get this, anyway?"

"Jack brought it from Russia."

"Figures," Misty mumbled.

"What's that supposed to mean?" Anne shot back.

Misty pretended to be concentrating on traffic. "Nothing. Go to sleep. I'll listen to the radio."

Steadying the steering wheel with her knees, Misty reached for her briefcase, pulled out her iPod, and tuned the car radio to the iPod's iTrip frequency. The St. Petersburg Choir was replaced by jazz.

Anne considered pursuing the remark about Jack, but bit her lip and closed her eyes. Misty never agreed with her on the issue of Jack.

Anne met Jack Halden four years ago. Jack was the Director of New Product Acquisitions for Sidens Medical Systems, a small but respected medical device manufacturer based just outside Boston.

They met during a site visit arranged by the Medical Center to help Anne forge an agreement with Sidens to develop the MEG for commercial use. Jack was a reserved man in his late forties—Anne's senior by at least ten years. His closely cropped salt-and-pepper hair set off a sallow patrician face. He smiled rarely, and never with his eyes, which were set so deep it was hard to determine whether or not he was making eye contact.

During the first meeting his questions to Anne were short and to the point. He asked her about patent ownership, projected development milestones, competitive products, and expected market penetration. Anne was not used to dealing with business issues and felt flustered.

"It's not important if you do not know all the answers, Dr. Powell," he said calmly. "That's one area where we can help you." To Anne the voice sounded instantly reassuring—not for its emotional warmth, of which there was none, but for its steely determination.

To her surprise, Sidens not only picked up the MEG, but also put it on the fast track, at the sacrifice of several other products then in development. In a record eighteen months, they manufactured a prototype and negotiated the necessary FDA permits to begin clinical testing.

Jack was promoted to Vice-President, attached exclusively to the MEG project. In the course of the development of the MEG, Halden and Anne had to meet frequently. They talked for hours on end about how the device could be improved and what the production models should look like. She loved arguing fine technical and manufacturing points with him, winning as often as not. She also sensed that the success of the MEG was nearly as important to him as it was to her. *Halden is someone I can count on to ensure the survival of my brainchild,* she thought.

On a personal level, getting to know Jack was a slow process. He was a widower. His wife had shot herself in the head in front of him, ten years ago. He never remarried, and he never spoke of anything having to do with love or relationships. His life seemed to be his work at Sidens. And that was just fine with Anne.

As work on the MEG progressed, their long days often extended into evenings. They began dining together after work, then going out socially.

Anne remembered the first night with Halden. They had flown together to a trade show in Chicago. After walking the exhibit at McCormick Hall for ten hours, they returned, exhausted, to the hotel. He stopped in her room to review the literature they picked up. They ordered room service. Too tired to eat, they relaxed on the adjacent twin beds.

Next morning they woke up in the same bed, fully dressed. Both were mortified, but the barrier was broken. Eventually, they started to spend nights together and became lovers.

Anne appreciated the companionship of someone who did not push for emotional intimacy. Someone for whom the idea of being in love was as foreign as it was for her suited her fine.

As Anne dozed off, lulled by Misty's smooth driving and the hum of the Volvo, Jack's face suddenly appeared before her. Slowly, it metamorphosed into a bearded stranger. The man crossed himself, and she heard the St. Petersburg choir singing. It sounded like a funeral dirge. The scraggly face leaned forward, the cracked lips pressing against her mouth. The man tasted of smoked fish. The weight of his body pushed her toward the ground. Lower, lower. Her spine strained painfully. She was on her back, twisted. Her pelvic sphincters went into searing cramps.

"Wake up, sleepy head," Misty was saying. "It's show time."

Anne opened her eyes. The red neon sign of the Lexus dealership loomed above her window, the light diffused by falling snowflakes.

Anne wiped her mouth with the back of her hand, and uncrossed her legs, painfully cramped against the dashboard. Her bladder felt ready to burst. "You go ahead, I'll wait," she said groggily, still trying to shake off the nightmare.

"No way, you're going with me. And here, you need this." Misty shoved a comb into Anne's hands. "And your lipstick is all smudged."

"Wait a sec, why do I need to prim ..."

"The guy we're meeting is Terry Adkinson. He owns eight dealerships in New England," Misty said cheerfully, getting out of the car. "Be nice and smile, and maybe he'll give you a good deal on a Volvo trade-in."

Twenty minutes later they were back in the Volvo. "I can't believe you did that!" Anne fumed as they drove back. "You're a real shit."

"I just wanted you to meet him," Misty protested sheepishly from the passenger seat.

"You tried to fix me up! Admit it!"

"No, really ..."

"I don't need this."

"Anne, listen. I don't know if you realize this, but you scare the shit out of most men."

"No, I don't."

"M.D., Ph.D., drop-dead gorgeous and soon to be rich and famous? Nah, I'm sure most men are completely comfortable with that," Misty said sarcastically. "Terry is one of the few guys I know that could possibly match ..."

"I'm not looking for a match," Anne interrupted. "Look, I know we'll never see eye-to-eye on Jack, but I am happy with him, so just let it be, OK?"

"I can't. You're my best friend. And I know he's not the one for you," Misty protested.

"I'll be the judge."

"I think the world of you, Annie, but in matters of love you're a lousy judge. The guy has no passion ..."

"Not everything is about passion."

"Granted. But what does he have?"

"Lots of things ..." Anne said vaguely.

"I'm all ears."

Anne hesitated for a moment, organizing her thoughts. "He's one of the most intelligent men I know," she said finally. "He's good company. He's not demanding. We like the same music. He's not pushy about the relationship thing. And he's as committed to the MEG as I am."

"I didn't hear 'love'."

"What makes you think I don't love him?"

Misty grabbed her friend's hand and turned to her. "Because your eyes don't sparkle when you talk about him, and your face doesn't glow when you're together, and your hand doesn't run through his hair when you are next to him …"

"Enough," Anne said quietly. She pretended to be checking the traffic in the side mirror to hide the tears forming in the corners of her eyes. She started humming random chords from the *Easter Mass Liturgy*.

"I'm sorry, but he gives me the creeps, Annie. There's something very cold and calculating about him."

"I'd take 'cold' over 'flaming' any day."

"Tombstone cold. I-have-no-feelings cold. You're-just-a-convenience cold."

"Misty, don't."

"Don't you want someone who will make you laugh, and blush, and do crazy things?"

"I don't need crazy. I need sane."

"Don't you miss the chemistry?"

"It's fine the way it is."

"Sorry, but as your best friend …"

"Stop, damn it," Anne shouted, her knuckles blanching as she gripped the wheel. "Just stop it."

Misty's lips froze in mid-sentence. They drove in silence for a few minutes.

"You're still not over Peter, are you?" Misty asked suddenly, refusing to drop the subject. "Is that why you're with Jack?"

The wheels screeched as Anne slammed on the brakes just short of the rear end of a garbage truck. Right there, in the middle of the heavy traffic on Route 128, she put the car in "park" and turned to Misty.

"Yes, I'm sorry about Peter, and about all my other relationships that went nowhere. And I'm tired of having my hopes dashed to pieces every time I get close to a man. No, Jack doesn't make my heart go pitter-patter. And that's just fine with me, because right now that's all the loving I can muster. So, please, don't rock my little boat, OK?"

She punched on the Russian choir on the CD player, rammed the gearshift into "drive" and floored the gas pedal.

Love. She had given up on love a long time ago. Right now it was best to focus all her attention on tomorrow's meeting. The big day was finally here.

9

"Upon review of your documentation we find sufficient evidence to recommend approval ..." an FDA inspector droned.

Anne, Misty, the hospital administrator, the chief of staff and Jack Halden sat in the hospital conference room, facing three FDA representatives who arrived with great pomp to deliver their decision about the MEG.

"Your device demonstrated effectiveness ..."

Here it comes. The culmination of years of work, the vindication of endless battles with skeptics. The MEG was about to become a recognized, approved, commercially successful and medically useful device. Anne's heart was beating so hard, she was afraid everyone would hear it. *So what? Let them.* If the FDA guys were the least bit more human, she might have jumped up and hugged them.

The Fed continued in the same monotone. "Moreover, in reviewing your report of the procedure you performed on ..." He checked his notes. "Miller, Frank. We found that Miller, Frank was regressed to age two years..."

"Twenty-two months," Anne corrected him with ill-concealed pride.

The main inspector glanced at her over the rim of his glasses and continued without missing a beat. "… which corresponds to an age six months younger than any of the other patients …"

Where is he going with this? Small variations among patients were to be expected.

"In light of this, we are recommending that final approval of the device be delayed until additional data …" the Fed recited mechanically.

A steel vise gripped Anne's throat. A cold, steady pressure. Tightening. Suffocating.

"Unexpected development … insufficient evidence …"

Anne listened as if in a dream. Suddenly she could hear her father's voice. *Not good enough. You can do better.* She grasped the edge of the console to conceal the fine tremor in her hands.

When she was a little girl her father never rewarded her with whole-hearted praise, no matter how well she did. "That was good, Anne," he would say coldly, staring at a report card full of A's. "But don't you think that you could have …" and she would stop listening, because the pain of realizing that she had disappointed him, that she was a failure, was unbearable. After her father turned into an abusive monster to her mother and lost all interest in Anne, she found herself longing even more for the approval she never had.

"Ambiguous results …"

She had failed. She shouldn't have treated Frank. Should have let him go. Listened to Misty. Postponed. So what if the locus couldn't be found later? What's one patient? Now everything was ruined.

"Due diligence …"

I really tried, Daddy, Anne wanted to scream. *I did good work. It was the right thing to do. I …*

No, damn it. This was not about her father, or his approval, or validation of her worth as a scientist. Her research had been impeccable, her findings consistent. Frank's outcome was compatible with previous work. And, in human terms, highly successful. This was nothing but a blatant bureaucratic block.

Anne lowered her voice to keep her fury under control.

"Mr. Schleiker, I was under the impression that you indicated that the data was acceptable. So why is it …?"

She forced herself to stop. Contradicting the FDA was worse than challenging the IRS. With the IRS, all you had to lose was money and you could appeal the decision. With the FDA, you were likely to find your life's work put on permanent hold. And the decision was final.

"We will require additional data …"

You're just stalling, you moron, Anne wanted to scream. Instead, she lowered her voice even more. "Could you be more specific?"

"Follow-up studies on patients regressed to the same age. A small series. Perhaps a hundred …"

Anne couldn't believe her ears. "But that could take two or three years!" she exclaimed before she could contain herself.

The FDA investigator shrugged his shoulders and gave Anne a "that's-your-problem" look.

A barely perceptible wince registered on Halden's face. The original series had taken eighteen months of painstaking search through thousands of records to find 340 suitable cases that could be regressed ten or fifteen years back. A hundred cases that could be regressed to the much younger age demanded by the Feds meant a very long delay indeed.

Anne sat still, her fingernails almost cracking as she dug into the edge of the table. *Deep breaths. Nice and easy. Don't blow it. Don't make it worse than it already is.*

"That concludes our recommendations," the chief investigator announced. Like a drill team, the FDA men dropped their papers into their briefcases, slammed them closed and stood up. "We're looking forward to talking with you again, Dr. Powell," said the chief. "Best of luck to you."

Halden forced a smile. "Thank you for your time, gentlemen."

The FDA men shook hands with everyone and filed out.

For a moment, they sat in stunned silence.

"Well, that's one thing we didn't need," the hospital administrator mumbled, slumping into his chair.

Misty walked over and put her arms around Anne's shoulders. "I'm so sorry, Annie."

"They're wrong. Just like they were on the previous patient selection issues," Anne protested. "Regression to twenty-two months is completely compatible with the variations we've been seeing."

"You know it and I know it," said the chief of staff, scraping his chair back and rising to his feet. "But these guys have only one goal in mind—to cover their asses. And looks like we're stuck doing the covering."

"Now what?" Anne asked Halden after everyone else left.

Halden's mind was churning. The MEG was his key to personal success. His chance to prove his worth to the board of directors and undermine the current CEO, who had been opposed to this project since the beginning. The setback to the MEG threatened to derail Halden's bid for the top post at Sidens. With that went a fortune in stock options, a seven-figure salary and a severance package worth around six million. The success story was turning into a train wreck. He had to figure out how to solve the problem or cut his losses.

"It doesn't look like we'll be ready to go into full production anytime soon," he said slowly.

Anne glanced at him, fearing what was coming.

"As the one in charge, I have to make a decision about keeping the assembly line going, or ..." he paused.

"Or?"

"Shutting down for a few months. A year, at most. Just 'til you complete the new cases they want," he added quickly, trying to sound encouraging.

Anne felt a lump forming in her throat.

"It's hard to explain to the board why we have ten-million dollars in manufacturing equipment tied up in a device that ..." He stopped abruptly.

"A device that's dead in the water? Say it!"

"Not dead. Just delayed. Look, it's a cash flow problem. We had two scanners in development that we sidelined for the MEG. The board will demand that we reactivate those projects so Sidens can generate revenue. Much needed revenue, I might add."

"Do what you have to do," said Anne flatly.

"Believe me, if it were up to me …" He felt genuinely sorry for Anne. *The poor woman must be devastated. But what could he do?*

"Hey, you don't have to explain."

"Anne, I'll do whatever is necessary to keep your unit at the hospital fully functional. And we'll complete work on the one at the factory so it can be on standby. Then, as soon as you have the Feds' blessing," he snapped his fingers, "we'll be right back up again." His voice sounded hollow.

"*If* I find enough patients, *if* the Feds approve, *if* the money is there. And *if* somebody doesn't rip the idea off in the meantime!" She almost choked on the words.

He squeezed her hand. "We'll just have to hope for the best."

His fingers were cold and not at all reassuring.

The evening run, which normally did so much to clear her head and restore her energies, degenerated into a walk full of anger, disappointment and self-doubt.

Anne stumbled back into her house, yanked off her running shoes without unlacing them, turned on *Madama Butterfly* and headed straight for the refrigerator.

The family-pack of KitKats was empty. So was the little box of Godiva truffles. The rich Russian milk chocolates with creamy filling that Halden brought back from his last trip to St. Petersburg tasted rancid. She rummaged through the cupboard until she found a package of Gummy Bears. The package was old and the bears were matted into a multicolored rubbery mass. It would have to do.

Miles arched his back, rubbed along her leg, and meowed expectantly, hoping Anne would toss the toy mouse across the room a few times.

"Sorry, Miles. I can't play fetch with you tonight," she said, dishing out a bowl of Kibbles. "Maybe tomorrow will be a better day."

But she knew the setback would be long-lasting. She pulled off her clothes and climbed under the covers. The bed was cold and empty. She felt the acid in her stomach as the Gummy Bears began to dissolve.

Inadequate data … The Fed's words cracked like a whiplash. *She failed. She disappointed. She didn't measure up.*

She longed to have someone to lean on, to talk to. She longed to be held. There was no one to wrap her in his arms.

Halden's response was understandable. He had to protect Sidens. She would do the same in his shoes.

We cannot recommend the MEG for approval at this time …

She curled up in a ball, drawing her knees against her chest, and with the FDA ruling echoing in her mind, she slipped into a fitful slumber.

She dreamed that she was a young woman. She was in a long white dress and was dashing through a burning building. Flaming beams were crashing all around her. But she was not afraid of the fire. She was running from something else.

Suddenly a handsome blond man on a black horse galloped out of the flames. Moments later, she was in his arms and the man's lips were kissing hers. An uncontrollable longing engulfed her body. She wanted him to hold her forever. But a gruesome gray-bearded stranger grabbed her arms and ripped her clothes off. A searing pain tore through her groin, her womb …

Anne screamed and woke up.

10

Two days after his treatment, Frank was showing signs of remarkable improvement. During evening rounds Anne found him in his bedside chair, cuddling his son and wife, smiling and lucid. Another unequivocal success, in a string of many.

For nothing.

Her pager went off. It was for extension 2664. The MEG room. Anne frowned. No one was scheduled to be there. She dialed the number. To her surprise, she heard Halden's voice.

"Anne? I wonder if you could come down for a minute. There's someone I want you to meet."

"Ah, the inventor herself!" Halden exclaimed as Anne entered the MEG room a few minutes later. Gesturing toward three men standing next to him, he said, "Dr. Powell, I would like you to meet Drs. Baldyuk, Ivanov and Yulin."

Ivanov and Yulin were short, broad-faced men wearing hopelessly mismatched outfits. They had the "disheveled-academic" look common to researchers the world over.

Baldyuk was a corpulent man in his sixties, with bulldog-like jowls and cavernous nostrils that wheezed with every breath. His face reminded her of the evil czar in the fairy tale that was painted on one of the lacquer boxes that Halden brought her from Moscow. All this man lacked was the crown and the gray beard to complete the image.

Baldyuk's broad frame was stuffed into an ill-fitting Armani suit. A bright red tie strangled his neck. This was a Communist bureaucrat in capitalist businessman disguise. Anne detected a hint of alcohol on his breath.

"Actually, Dr. Powell is part Russian herself," Halden said cheerfully. "Isn't that right, Dr. Powell?"

Anne shot Halden an angry look. Yes, her great-uncle's relatives were from Russia, but that didn't make her "part Russian." It only meant that a small portion of her genes had come from a man who was Russian. Considering the boorish behavior of some of the recently arrived citizens of the former Soviet Union, being "part Russian" was not something to be proud of.

Baldyuk took her hand and, raising it to his lips, kissed it lightly, European style. "It is honor and pleasure," he said, pronouncing each word with care.

There was something deeply disturbing in his eyes as they locked into hers. They were wolf-like gray, bloodshot and tearing at the corners. And they made Anne feel naked. He had that look of overbearing dominance that always made Anne recoil, and sometimes sent her pelvic sphincters into spasm. It was like a Pavlovian reflex. She had had it since childhood, and she couldn't explain or prevent it.

Unconsciously, she jerked her hand out of his grasp. Much more quickly than would have been polite.

Baldyuk's smile chilled. "Your success with MEG is very ... very interesting," he said with a steel edge in his voice.

"Thank you," she replied, stepping back. "It's been a challenging project." She glanced at Jack, wondering about the purpose of this visit.

"Professor Baldyuk and his colleagues are from the Pavlov Institute in Moscow," Halden explained.

"Really?" Anne said, her eyebrows raising slightly. She had heard of the Pavlov. Their scientists had published a number of articles on hypnotherapy in prestigious European journals, but the concepts were too esoteric for the American medical community.

"The Pavlov Institute is our most esteemed client," Halden said to Anne, smiling in the direction of the Russians. "Over the past four years, they've been kind enough to place orders for many MRI and CT scanners," he added, with deliberate emphasis on "many." "And they're very interested in your work with the MEG." He punched up "very."

"Your MEG can make less problem with too much crowds in our institutes," interjected one of the physicians. "Many thousand patients need treatment, but no place for them. And no money for medicines."

"A tough problem," Anne agreed cautiously. One of her worst fears was that inappropriate use of the MEG would undermine its credibility. "I must emphasize that MEG was intended only for patients who have failed to improve with conventional therapy and ..."

"Our colleagues understand that," Halden interrupted quickly.

"Russia is big country, Dr. Powell," Baldyuk smiled condescendingly, "and we have much mental illness. Enough to make work for ten machines, morning to evening. Only patients who are meeting your very strict standards, of course," he added sarcastically.

Halden turned to Anne. "I was hoping you'd give our visitors a quick tour of the MEG. Just the highlights."

Anne looked at him, then at the Russians. "I'd love to," she replied, "but I've a ward full of patients. Besides, Mr. Halden can do a better job," she added forcing a more cordial smile. "So if you gentlemen will excuse me ..."

"Please, is no problem. You will come back, yes, Dr. Powell?" asked Baldyuk.

"I'm afraid I'll be tied up for the rest of the evening. It was a pleasure," Anne said coldly, heading for the door.

Halden winced. "I'll be right back," he said to the Russians, following her out.

"What was that about?" Anne snapped as Halden caught up to her in the hallway.

"Cash," he answered, lowering his voice and walking closer to her. "About two-point-five mil. And they want to place an order."

Anne's eyebrows shot up. "So?"

"I think we should do it."

"No way!" The words just slipped out of her mouth.

"Why, no way?"

She searched for a plausible reason, but all she could think of was her visceral aversion to Baldyuk's handshake.

"Did you tell them we're in 'FDA-approval limbo'?" she asked.

"They're Russian! They know about red tape."

"And the Feds are just going to stand by and let us sell them a unit?"

"The FDA has jurisdiction only over U.S. sales. They could care less what we do abroad," said Halden.

"And the Federal Trade Commission? They could tie up the export permit for years …"

"Come on, Anne. The MEG has no strategic value whatsoever. Besides, the White House has been bending over backwards to keep Russia happy."

"Who's going to teach them about patient selection, about positioning, about scan interpretation? If they screw up and get bad results, the Feds will use it as an excuse for another delay. We may never get licensed!"

"The Pavlov is one of the most prestigious institutions in Europe. They do have a reputation to uphold. "

Anne leaned against the wall and tapped her fingernails on the railing. "I can't stand the thought of somebody we hardly know, ten thousand miles away, using a device that isn't even ready for our own market."

"It was the Feds who said it wasn't ready. You did over 300 cases without a single glitch. Do you think it's ready?" Halden asked, emphasizing the 'you' as if it were the only thing that mattered.

"There are improvements we could make …"

"Perfection is the enemy of progress. Is it ready or not?"

She wanted to yell, *Yes!* But something was holding her back. *Was she afraid of the void that would remain if she let go of the one central passion around which her life revolved?*

"It's time to let the baby go, Anne," Halden said quietly, as if reading her thoughts.

"Maybe we should hold off 'til we place a few units in the U.S." she suggested hopefully, knowing what the answer would be.

"Anne!" There was a steely edge in his voice. "We just had a huge setback. I don't know if I can persuade the board to sink more money into your project, even after it's approved …"

"Oh, now it's *my* project?" Anne said sarcastically. "I thought Sidens considered it a *joint* project."

"It's going to be *nobody's* project if it doesn't get a cash infusion. Quickly."

Anne said nothing, her mind in turmoil.

"It's not just one unit for Moscow," Halden was saying. "We could sell dozens to the Russians alone. To say nothing of the entire Eastern European market. And China … Once we sell one or two, it'll snowball." Halden tried to sound more conciliatory. "It's going to be big, Anne."

She bit her lip. "I'll think about it," she said, disappearing up the stairwell.

That evening, as she wove through the heavy traffic on the outbound Brookline Avenue, heading home to Newton, her brain was racing. The Russian doctor said they would need ten MEGs for Moscow alone. Anne visualized whole wards of patients waiting for treatment. *Patients. Lots of patients who needed help.*

She punched a button on her car phone autodial and said "Jack Halden."

He picked up on the first ring.

"Will the Feds accept patient studies from abroad?" Anne asked without introduction.

"I don't see why not …" *Why was she asking that*, he wondered.

She took a deep breath. "OK, then, here's the deal. Sell them the unit, with the condition that I'll have final say in patient selection for the duration of the study."

"And how do you propose to do that from ten thousand miles away?"

"I'll go there with the MEG."

"Why in God's name would you want to do that?" Halden exclaimed.

"That way the Russians get the MEG, Sidens gets the cash, and I get to collect the data I need and make sure the Russians won't do anything ... shall we say, inappropriate." She smiled at the thought of completing all the cases dictated by the FDA in record time.

There was no answer from Halden. She could practically hear him agonizing over the choice. "Are you there?" she asked.

He tensed at the thought that with Anne in Moscow, dealing directly with the Russians, he could easily lose control of the project.

"They'll never go for it," he said firmly, trying to blame the Russians as a cover up for his insecurity. "I think you need to reconsider, Anne."

"If I don't go, the MEG doesn't go."

Halden forced himself to count to ten before answering.

"I'll run it past them first thing in the morning," he said flatly. The MEG was his passport to corporate and financial success, and way too important to leave it in Anne's inexperienced hands. He had to assure himself of a more permanent control of the situation.

"Anne? How about dinner tomorrow night?"

"That sounds great."

Taking a deep breath, he added, "There's something I want to discuss with you ..."

11

The valet let his eyes linger on her long legs as Anne stepped out of the car in front of the Four Seasons Hotel. She looked stunning in an ankle-length black dress, slit to her mid-thigh.

Halden was already waiting when she walked into the plush, quiet and very dignified dining room of the restaurant. He wore one of the dark suits that were his usual uniform for special occasions and meetings with the corporate brass. The only embellishment he permitted himself was an Italian silk tie, a one-of-a-kind $300 piece of neckwear, a sure indication to Anne that something was up.

"You look nice," Anne commented.

He kissed her on the cheek. "So do you," he replied mechanically.

As soon as they sat down, a waiter materialized with a bottle of champagne. A '54 Veuve Clicquot. Personally, he would have opted for a dry Martini, but this evening was for Anne.

"What's to celebrate, after the Feds' ruling?" Anne asked.

"Let's hope the Russians say, 'yes'," he said, raising his glass. "To the Pavlov!"

"To the Pavlov," she echoed half-heartedly.

They let the bubbles percolate in their mouths, then made small talk about local politics and world events—another bus bombing in Moscow by Chechen terrorists, the recent capture of one of Russia's notorious multi-billionaires on his way to deposit his loot in a Swiss bank, the continuing debate over human cloning.

"And now, with Putin's second term coming to an end, there is no telling what will happen over there. So, of course, they're paying us in dollars, instead of rubles," Halden said, as if the sale of the MEG were a done deal.

The waiter brought menus, recited the specials, offered several suggestions and made a show of taking their entire order without writing it down.

They sat in silence for a few moments. Halden toyed nervously with the amber bracelet on Anne's wrist that he had bought for her in Russia the year before. Finally, he took another sip of champagne and got to the point.

"It's been a bit awkward, keeping our relationship … hmm … to ourselves." He wanted to say "secret." "For both of us, I'm sure," he added hastily.

"Actually, I don't care who knows that we …"

"Wait, hear me out. With you being the principal investigator, Sidens funding the project, and me as the vice-president …" he trailed off, knowing that he didn't need to spell out the potential for gossip, for accusations of conflict of interest, even for the arousal of the FDA's curiosity.

"Should we stop seeing each other?" Anne asked.

"My God, no!" Halden exclaimed. "Anne, we've had a great working relationship for four years. And we've enjoyed each other's company outside of work for—what?—over two years now, right?"

Anne nodded. "About that long." The relationship just slowly grew on them, and there was no anniversary date that either of them could pinpoint.

"Maybe it's time to make our relationship … official."

Her jaw dropped. "Jack …"

The waiter arrived with the appetizers. "Your Portabella mushrooms in a red wine reduction served over grilled polenta, madam."

She welcomed the interruption.

Time to make our relationship official … What was the relationship?

She liked him as a friend, admired him as colleague, appreciated him as a companion ... But she wasn't in love. The thought of being in love sent shivers down her spine.

Anne forced a forkful of polenta into her mouth. The succulent corn puree stuck to her palate like dry crackers.

Being in love isn't for me. The relationship she had had with Peter proved it, once and for all. Her life was safely structured around her work, and she was happy with that.

"Anne?" she heard Halden ask, "do you like it?"

"What?"

She noticed the ring he held in front of her—a beautiful, brilliant-cut diamond, surrounded by a row of small emeralds.

"Jack, I ..." She gently pushed his hand away. "I'm sorry ... I don't know what to say," she stammered. "I didn't expect ..."

"We would be good together, Anne."

He truly believed that. After his wife's suicide his heart was dead. And while Anne had never shared the detail of her past with him, he suspected there was something that made her equally afraid to love. Emotionally, they were a good match. The common goal of making the MEG a success made the relationship even better.

He leaned forward and slipped the ring on her finger. It fit perfectly. Lucia, his former assistant whom he had transferred to Anne, had given him the right measurements. The woman was worth her weight in gold.

"It reflects your eyes," he said, turning Anne's hand so the light played off the facets of the beautiful stones.

She looked at the ring for a few moments, then gently withdrew her hand out of his. "Let me think about it, Jack," she said, sliding the ring off.

He drew a seething inhalation, but remained speechless. He hadn't anticipated rejection. He took an angry sip of champagne, then gulped down the rest.

Anne slipped the ring into the box and handed it back.

"Baby steps, Jack. I need to move in baby steps. Please."

He pocketed the box, stone-faced.

The waiter brought the main course. The duck *a l'orange*, its skin crisped to perfection, the aroma of thinly sliced oranges floating over it, was deliciously prepared and beautifully presented, but neither of them could enjoy it. They made conversation through the main course, but felt like two strangers at a wake.

The waiter appeared and inquired about dessert.

"I'd better not," Anne said, glancing at her watch.

Halden nodded and asked for the check.

"Shall I follow you home? Perhaps we can have a nightcap," he suggested coldly, as if expecting rejection again.

She didn't have the heart to turn him down twice. "As long as we make it short."

12

She pulled into the driveway and went into the house, leaving the door unlocked. Jack came in soon afterwards.

"Grand Marnier?" Anne asked, opening the cupboard.

"Sure." As Halden sat down, Miles jumped off the couch and bolted out the door.

Anne poured Halden a shot and went to the bedroom to take her shoes off. Moments later, he came in behind her. Before Anne could turn, she felt his arms wrap around her.

"I want you," he whispered.

In pitch black darkness, he pushed her down onto the bed and groped with her underwear. She winced at the pain as he pushed himself into her, oblivious to her dryness.

"I want you," he mumbled, moving back and forth inside her, faster and faster. Moments later, his head arched back and he climaxed.

He stood up, mumbling, "I'm so sorry. I don't know what came over me." He sounded embarrassed.

"It's OK," Anne said, sitting up and pulling her blouse down over her breasts. She tried to smile, but tears welled in her eyes.

Halden skulked back into the living room. By the time Anne joined him, he had finished his drink. Soon afterwards he left, citing the long drive home and an early morning meeting.

Anne took a bath, lingering in the water, pensively poking at the soap bubbles as plaintive strains of Tchaikovsky's *Romeo and Juliet* drifted in from the living room.

She reminded herself that usually Jack was more considerate in their sexual encounters. She had never been able to reach an orgasm with him, but neither had she with any other man. The only exception was Peter, just before she left him.

She dried herself off and climbed into bed. Her thoughts drifted to the disturbing dinner. She was angry with Halden. He had no right to disturb their fragile status quo, to breach their tacit agreement. *Why didn't he just accept things the way they were?* Whatever intimacy they had was difficult enough for her. Asking for a lifetime commitment was asking for the impossible.

Outside, the wind was picking up. She felt cold air drafting through the gaps in the windows. *She should make a trip to Home Depot to buy new weather stripping…*

Her anger changed to sadness. *What was wrong with her?* Men flocked to her, attracted by her looks. The shallow ones retreated rapidly, intimidated by her accomplishments. Others persevered drawn to her brain, not just to her beauty. A few of them she liked, but even with them she had never let her guard down.

"I wish I could pierce that armor of yours," one of them said once.

"I don't know what you're talking about," she had answered. But she did know.

Her mind flashed to the emptiness she felt when she ran away from Peter, five years ago. Why didn't she stay with him? Why couldn't she let the love she felt sweep her away?

She wished he were with her now. She longed to feel his arms around her, to hear him whisper, "Everything will be all right, honey."

Instead, there was only the rumble of the wind scraping a tree branch against the windowsill.

She was awakened by the banging of dishes in the kitchen and a man's voice, yelling angrily. Her heart racing, she opened her eyes.

The house was empty. It was 2:00 a.m. The wind was blowing harder. The branch was still banging against the window. *Must remem-*

ber to trim it, Anne thought, forcing her eyes closed again.

She tried to think of nothing and will herself back to sleep.

More thumping. A dull thud. A high pitched noise. *Was that a woman screaming?*

3:00 a.m. *Sleep, Anne, sleep.* That's what she used to tell herself when she was a young girl, lying in bed and hearing her father come home late at night. *Sleep, so you don't have to hear it.* Anne felt the familiar, sickening tightness beginning to build in her pelvic area.

She tried to curl up into a fetal position but somebody grabbed her legs and forced them apart. A searing pain tore through her groin.

Anne screamed and opened her eyes. It was the sheet, tangled around her legs. But the feeling of being attacked had been so vivid, so real, that she had to get up and turn on the lights.

She paced for a while, then crawled back into bed.

A fire siren approached, went by.

4:00 a.m. She was afraid to close her eyes again, lest the vision return.

She had tried to work out the rape nightmares with several analysts. None could find a plausible cause for them. Childhood molestation was at the root of many problems in adult life, but it seemed to have no bearing on hers. Her father, a high-strung executive at the Boston branch of British Petrol, had been demanding but he had never abused her physically, sexually or otherwise.

Instead, he abused her mother. As far back as Anne could remember, her life was plagued by her father's shouts during the night, sounds of furniture shattering, soft thuds of fists slamming into flesh. Cowering in her bed, Anne would roll up into a bundle and feel a sickening cramp in her pelvic area.

Much later in life, when both her parents were already dead, Anne learned in anatomy class that the feeling was an involuntary tightening of her pelvic sphincters. A few times the spasm had been so severe that she was unable to move her bowels or urinate for days. On one occasion, she even had to go to an emergency room and have a catheter inserted into her urethra so her bladder wouldn't burst. She experienced these involuntary spasms even now, in moments of extreme stress, or with men who were in some way threatening to her.

In her childhood, she had ample reason to have these episodes frequently—her father took his frustrations out on her mother almost nightly.

As Anne became older, she would venture out into the kitchen and try to intercede on her mother's behalf. But the sight of her raving father made her sphincters tighten up even more and she would stand like a fawn caught in the headlights of a speeding truck. Paralyzed, hypnotized, compliant, unable to help her mother or herself. Memories of these episodes of complete helplessness tortured her even more than outright physical abuse ever could. Particularly the last time it happened.

It was a few days before her sixteenth birthday. Anne awoke to the sounds of a brutal fight. Gripped with a sickening anticipation, she rushed into the kitchen. Her father had pinned her mother against the sink from behind. Her nightgown was ripped, bloody. Her father's pants were down at his knees

"What are you looking at?" he bellowed when he saw Anne in the doorway. "Get out of here!"

Her mother turned away, her bruised face distorted with shame.

Anne took a few tentative steps toward the telephone. *She was going to call the police. She was going to put this man away …*

But she couldn't move. She imagined police cruisers racing up to the house, her father being lead away handcuffed as she clung to him, sobbing, "I'm sorry, Daddy, I'm so sorry." She would never forgive herself. Despite her deep loathing for the man, she still longed for his love and approval. After an eternity of doubt, she vomited on the kitchen floor, dashed to her room and dove into her bed, sobbing uncontrollably.

Anne shuddered, remembering the fire … Smoke billowing, sirens wailing … Fatal memories that would haunt her for the rest of her life.

The alarm clock shrieked. Anne opened her eyes. It was 6:00 a.m. Slowly, she crawled out of bed, completely exhausted.

Her nostrils still burned with the acrid smell of smoke.

13

Considering the potential bureaucratic pitfalls in a transaction of this magnitude, the sale of the MEG went remarkably smoothly. The Russians seemed delighted by the prospect of contributing their patients to Anne's research. The FDA saw no problem in accepting data gathered in Moscow, as long as strict research conditions were observed. And the full two-and-a-half-million-dollar payment in U.S. currency, on which Halden had insisted in view of recent instability of the Russian ruble, was transferred to Sidens' bank the day the deal was signed.

The only moment of friction occurred when the Russians demanded shipment within ten days or sooner.

"I have no idea why," Halden said. "Allegedly some politician wants to enhance his image as a do-gooder before elections."

"The former Communists sure learned from our democratic ways, didn't they? What's next? Miscounting ballots?" quipped Anne. "*Can* we deliver in ten days?" she asked, frowning.

"I'll put an extra shift on the unit we have at the factory. All it needs is final tuning of the cryocircuits. We'll finish by the end of next week."

"*Otchen khorosho,*" Anne said.

"'Very good' is right. When did you learn that?"

"Didn't you know, I'm part Russian," she smiled, referring to his recent comment about her to Baldyuk.

In reality, she had picked up a Russian language CD the day the sale went through. "How can you visit people without at least trying to communicate with them in their own language?" she told Misty. Russian was a hard language, but she was surprised that it came to her a lot easier than she had expected. *Maybe it was the Russian genes that she had inherited, after all.*

Two days before Anne's departure the MEG was moved to Bedford Airfield, just outside Boston. Anne and Halden stood on the tarmac and watched as the gigantic Russian Air Force Tupolev TU-214 carrying the MEG lumbered down the runway, lifted off slowly and disappeared into the low-lying clouds, bound for Moscow.

"Four months is a long time," Halden said suddenly. "I'll miss you."

"I'll miss you too," Anne replied. "Why don't you come visit?"

"Of course I will." He cleared his throat. "I've been wondering," he said carefully, "whether you gave any thought to … to that question. At the restaurant …"

She put her hand on his arm. "Baby steps, Jack. I need to move in baby steps."

"If you're not ready, how would you feel about moving in with me?" *If she wanted baby steps, he'd give her baby steps.* He was sure that eventually she'd come around.

Anne studied his face. Halden lived in a lakeside house located in very blue-blood Winchester—an imposing building dating back to the mid-1800s. The place had been modernized several times, and part of it was set up as an ultra-modern home office with a wireless network that rivaled many corporate installations. Moving in with him would give her personal life some semblance of stability, and she could devote her full attention to analyzing the results that she would bring back from Russia. Maybe they could discuss this when Jack came to visit her in Moscow …

"How about setting a tentative date?" she heard him ask.

"To visit?"

"No, to move in! It'd give us something to look forward to while you're gone."

Anne didn't answer. She had stood her ground on the engagement issue, probably at no small pain to Jack. There was no reason not to compromise on the question of moving in with him. *As long as he respected her emotional involvement boundaries.*

"July is a slow month at the plant," Halden continued. "If we planned, let's say, for the fourteenth—it's a Sunday—we could move you in, take a week or two off, go someplace nice and still be back before the August rush at the factory."

"July fourteenth sounds nice," she said, leaning forward and kissing him lightly on the cheek.

He allowed himself a sigh of relief. It wasn't as firm as an engagement, but it was a baby step toward making sure that Anne didn't drift away while she was in Russia. Now he could concentrate on insuring the success of the MEG transaction. Success that hinged on a single test case.

14

Eight time zones away, in the basement of the Pavlov Institute, Igor, a white mouse, sat in the starting gate of a maze. Three Cyrillic letters were inscribed on his back in black ink.

Volodya Verkhov pushed a button. A buzzer sounded. Igor took off like a race horse. Volodya mentally crossed himself and held his breath.

The laboratory was a cavernous room decorated in early-Communist style: exposed air ducts, wooden shelves, walls painted whatever color was available that week. Several long workbenches piled high with cages made the room itself look like a giant maze.

Volodya's assistant, Lena, a pleasant young blond Belorussian, was scrubbing the same sink for the twentieth time just so she could keep her eyes on Volodya. Even the ever-present stench of the tiny rodents in cages was a small price to pay for being around him. In fact, half the women at the Pavlov would have gladly traded places with her any day. Or night.

Volodya was in his early forties, but his weathered skin made him look older. His robust frame would have been more fit for a farm hand than a scientist, but he moved with the elegant ease of a ballet dancer. His blue eyes could reassure or ravish at will. A stray lock of wavy blond hair seemed to always hang over his forehead, covering the deep worry lines. He sometimes flung it back with a boyish toss of his head.

Lena's washrag slid up and down in slow motion along a water spigot as she admired Volodya's firm behind. It looked just like two beautiful, hard soccer balls, she thought with a sigh.

Left. Right. Right. Home run. Igor the mouse dashed through the end gate, ran to a small container filled with fluid and buried his nose in it. Gently, Volodya picked Igor up and brought him to his face, the animal's whiskers tickling his nose. He could practically read the question in the tiny red eyes. *Noo, kak? How did I do?*

"*Molodetz!*" Volodya said out loud. Good boy.

Parking Igor on his shoulder, he fed him a pinch of food pellets. With a single finger he stroked Igor's back while the mouse chewed away.

Igor was his favorite. Of the ten carefully matched mice in the experimental group, Igor had been the most difficult to train. But Volodya persevered, teaching him the maze in small segments, working patiently as a parent would with an uncooperative child. Now Igor could run the complex course as if it were his home, and Volodya was ready to start phase two of his work.

Lena inched up to him from behind.

"Volodychka," she said using the affectionate form of his name, "Do you think you could give me a ride home when you're done?" She grimaced. "My ankle's killing me …"

"It is?" He smiled, glancing at her feet. "I thought I saw you running earlier."

"No, really, right here." She swung her leg onto the lab bench, revealing a generous portion of a smooth white thigh. She took his hand and placed it on her ankle. "See? I think it's swollen …"

"Lena, Lena …" Volodya chided her gently.

He started to take his hand away, but Lena held it in place.

"Feel, right here." She slid his hand further up her leg.

Women found Volodya's face handsome and his body irresistible, but it was his hands that they remembered most. There was something in those rugged yet supple fingers that made Volodya's touch as tender, as intimate, as electrifying as the most sensuous kiss.

Lena felt a warm rush spreading from his fingers up her leg.

"Listen, come home with me. I'll heat up some borscht," she said persuasively. "I made it the way you like it. With big red beets."

Lena was sweet and she was a real joy in bed, but he didn't want their occasional encounters to become a habit. Women were allowed in his life only as transit passengers. He made no exceptions. It was the safest way not to get hurt.

He eased away from Lena. "Lenotchka, you need somebody who can give you real love. Somebody who can take care of you ..."

"Why can't you take care of me?" she asked, pouting. "You don't like me?"

"I think you're wonderful. But I'm not the right man for you."

"Yes, you are!" She leaned against him. "You're exactly what I want." Touching his face, she whispered, "I could make you so happy, if only you'd let me. I could ..."

She was interrupted by the ringing of the phone.

Volodya grimaced. He hated the phones. He resented being saddled with the task of answering after-hours calls for the entire division, just because he was usually the only one working late and secretarial staff were not in the budget, even at the prestigious Pavlov. "Let it ring," Lena suggested.

"It's the outside line. I have to answer."

Disappointed, Lena reached for the receiver and handed it to him.

"*Da, slushayu*," he snapped into the phone.

"Dr. Balldyke? This is Lucia, Dr. Anne Powell's secretary."

"Not Balldyke. Bal-dyUK. Pro-fes-sor Bal-dyUK," Volodya said in passable English. He took a bit of perverse pleasure in correcting Lucia's pronunciation.

"Oh, I'm sorry."

Volodya drummed his fingers, waiting for her to get to the point. "Dr. Bal-dyUK, right?" Lucia struggled with the pronunciation.

"Right. Baldyuk."

"I'm calling for Dr. Powell. She asked me to ..."

"But this is not Professor Baldyuk. He is sleeping at home already."

"Oh. Well, could you please let the Professor know that Dr. Powell will be arriving the day after tomorrow, at 3:00 p.m., and she will ..."

"Yes, yes, we know already." *The whole department was painfully aware that the new device was arriving with a baby-sitter.* "We shall meet her at Sheremetevo."

"That won't be necessary. She plans to take a taxi."

Right, take a taxi, Volodya thought. Taxis were one of the Russian Mafia's favorite enterprises. They charged five times more than the ride was worth—when they didn't actually rob the passengers. And they loved preying on foreigners. Particularly Americans. Particularly women. Without an escort, she wouldn't make it past the airport gate.

"We already make plans for meet her," Volodya said firmly.

Baldyuk had been very specific about treating the woman like royalty. Without going as far as being there himself, he insisted that someone from the department take four hours from work and be there when she landed. By default, the task fell to Volodya. He spoke fair English, he had a car, and his research was considered to be optional. *After all, it was only basic science. No glory in that. And certainly no money.* Sometimes he wondered if Baldyuk wouldn't be happier if Volodya were gone altogether.

"I shall meet her," he said with finality.

"Thank you. How will she recognize you?"

That one he didn't catch. "Sorry, what?"

"How do you look? So she can find you."

I will find her, Volodya thought. Spotting an American woman arriving alone would be quite easy.

"If you tell me who she should look for …" said Lucia.

It seemed that this woman needed to do things the American way. He shrugged his shoulders. "You have fax?"

"Uh, yes we do." *Apparently, Russia hadn't joined the twenty-first century and gone to e-mail yet,* Lucia thought.

He scribbled the number down and hung up.

"Give me a minute," he said to Lena. "Then I'll drive you home."

Her eyes lit up.

"But only to the door," he added, pulling out a set of keys and walking away.

He crossed the hall and went into the office where the department's only copier and fax machine were kept. He unlocked a metal cabinet, took out a piece of white paper and carefully re-locked the door.

His budget was spartan and most of it had gone toward a Kronos gene sequencer—his pride and joy, the only high-speed gene sequencer in all of Moscow. It had to be high speed. There was no other way to measure the genetic changes in his mice from generation to generation. The pleasure of working with the Kronos more than made up for the inconvenience of putting up with an ancient copier and an always limited supply of paper.

He fed the sheet into the tray of the old East German photocopy machine, lifted the cover, bent down and placed his face on the glass. The beam swiped his cheek. The machine whirred and delivered a grotesquely distorted image of the right side of his face. He walked over to the fax machine, fed the picture in and dialed Lucia's number, smiling in anticipation of her reaction.

As he waited for the paper to go through, he felt a hand run across his buttocks and reach between his legs.

"Lena, don't!" Volodya said, moving away.

"Lena?" said a sultry voice.

He spun around and found himself staring into a pair of black eyes: Sasha. Short black hair. Full, juicy red lips. Almond-shaped eyes. An exotic blend of Russian and Mongol features. The kind of woman that probably inspired the gypsy song "Dark Eyes."

Her small but compact frame was clad in a loose white blouse tucked into tight jeans, a Moschino belt draped elegantly over her well-rounded hips. At 42 she looked younger and sexier than any Pavlov woman ten years her junior.

"Lena?" Sasha teased, her hand still exploring him. "Did that feel like Lena?"

She rose on her tiptoes so her mouth was in line with Volodya's. He felt her hot breath as she inched closer. Her nails dug playfully into the back of his neck.

"And where is Lena tonight?"

Before he could answer, Sasha clamped her mouth over his. Volodya felt her tongue exploring, then tasted the metallic taste of his own blood as her teeth sunk into his lower lip.

He tried to pull back but she held him. He drove his thumb into the sensitive spot at the front of her shoulder joint, and she let go with a hiss of pain.

"What was that for?" He wiped his mouth, smearing a streak of blood on his sleeve.

"That was for Lena," she smiled.

"What are you doing here at this hour, anyway?"

"I was bored," she said mischievously, her hand slipping into his jeans.

Lena's voice came from the other room. "Volodya, are you ready?" She appeared in the doorway and froze.

"I think he's definitely ready," Sasha said, her hand still in Volodya's pants.

"I … Excuse me!" Lena stammered. "I just wanted to tell Dr. Verkhov that I finished."

Lena was petrified of Sasha. She knew that in a battle for Volodya she would be an instant loser. Not because Sasha was any prettier or any more desirable. Not because Sasha, as the acting head of the Neuropsychiatry Department, far outranked her, and could make Lena's life miserable. Her fear stemmed from knowing that Sasha was utterly ruthless, and would stop at nothing to get what she wanted—be it a promotion or a man.

Her gut in a knot, Lena backed out the door. "Good night, Professor Lefko. Good night, Dr. Verkhov," she mumbled, and hurried down the hallway.

Sasha turned to Volodya. "I hope I didn't spoil any plans," she said sweetly. "Are you almost done here?"

"I need another hour."

"You and your stupid rats," she sighed. She sniffed his shirt and made a face. "You even smell like them."

"Mice, Sasha, mice," Volodya corrected her. "And they're not stupid."

"Whatever you say, Dr. *Pavlov*," she said, not missing the opportunity to tease him about his scientific idol.

"You're jealous because you have to work with nuts."

"At least my patients respond."

"Mine do too." He tried to extricate himself from her grip. "Come on, let me show you something."

"In a second," she answered, her hand still on him. "So, do you like making love to her?" she asked, her voice husky.

"Who?"

"Don't play dumb."

"I don't sleep with her anymore."

Sasha rolled her eyes. "Right!" She raked her hard nails through his blond curls. "It's all right, you can tell me," she murmured seductively.

"Nothing to tell."

Sasha slid the tip of her tongue along his upper lip. "Are her nipples as hard as mine?" He felt one of her nipples rub against his chest. Her hand was massaging him again. "Does she get as wet as I do?"

He felt the hardness returning, despite himself.

"Does she scream when she comes?"

"I don't want to talk about her," he tried to break loose, but she pressed harder against him.

"I want to know what she's like!"

"She's not like you. There's nobody like you. You're the best."

That was the truth. When it came to sex, they were good together. Her insatiable appetite matched his patience, stroke for stroke. She had no inhibitions. No place was too public or too inappropriate for a passionate encounter. Sex with Sasha was always an adventure, no matter how long or brief.

Best of all, Sasha was not looking for a relationship. She was perfectly happy to see him only occasionally and had no long-range plans, for love or for family. Actually, she had a puzzling aversion even to the mere thought of having children. So much so, that she had a tubal ligation in her early twenties.

Sasha's casual approach to relationships suited Volodya just fine. The last time he was seriously involved with a woman was twenty years ago. He liked it that way. Or at least he thought he did.

"Am I really the best?" Sasha breathed into his ear.

"Yes."

"Prove it."

"Not here."

"Yes, here. Now. I want it now." Her hand tightened around his testicles, the pain shooting into his belly.

He reached for her nipples, finding them under her blouse, already engorged. She gasped as he squeezed them, the pain forcing her to relax her grip.

"I'm going to fuck you," she hissed, shoving him against the bench.

"Only if I let you," he whispered back, collecting both of her small firm breasts into a single handful.

There was nothing Sasha liked more than to wrestle with him. There was nothing he liked more than to please her. Or any woman he was with.

She let go of his testicles and grabbed his pants. Her other hand grasped his shirt at the collar. Her muscles tightened as she braced herself.

"What are …?"

With one smooth practiced motion, she pulled up on his pants and sideways on his shirt. Volodya felt himself being lifted off the floor, losing his balance, leaning out of control. The next moment he was flat on his back. Sasha straddled him, fumbling with his belt buckle.

"I'm going to …" Sasha hissed.

Recovering, he grabbed her arms and pushed them together, his strong hand encircled her wrists like a pair of handcuffs.

Sasha leaned forward and tried to bite. He let her teeth graze the shirt over his nipple then pushed her away again, teasing.

His free hand slid under her T-shirt, found the bra hook and sprung it with a flick.

"Damn you," she panted, struggling to free herself.

Slowly he released the two ends of her bra, easing her breasts out.

He toppled her on her back, pinning her legs with one of his, stretching her arms above her head.

"No, no, no," she grunted, bucking like a Mongolian pony.

His fingers traveled down her chest, over her belly, feeling her rock-hard muscles.

He reached her belt buckle and undid it.

Suddenly she was absolutely still, her black eyes daring him, her parted lips wet and inviting.

He unzipped her jeans. Slowly, so she could feel the zipper opening, tooth by tooth.

She lay motionless. His concentration wandered and his grip on her wrists loosened momentarily.

Lightning fast, she jerked away, extricated one arm, sat up, and sunk her teeth into his neck.

Gasping in pain, he broke loose, twisted her arm and rolled her face down. The weight of his leg fell across her thighs. Once again, she lay subdued.

His free hand pulled on her jeans. Inch by inch, he worked them down to the middle of her buttocks and paused to admire the firm roundness.

She felt his breath on the back of her neck, the heat racing along her spine down to her toes like an electrical shock, paralyzing her. This time her whole body went completely limp against her will.

His lips slid slowly down her spine. The touch was so light, she wasn't sure if it was his lips or the warm air coming out of them in long, even breaths.

She felt a warm fullness building in her groin.

Releasing her wrists, Volodya knelt next astride her, his mouth slowly working its way down to the little tuft of soft fuzz in the small of her back.

She lay still, frustrated and excited by his tantalizingly slow progress. *Would he ever get there? Damn him!*

Finally she felt his tongue, soft, wet and delicious, caressing the crack between her cheeks.

She arched her buttocks up toward him, moaning "Yes, yes, yes!"

But he changed course. His mouth, now nibbling rather than licking, began moving sideways across her hip.

Limp with excitement and anticipation, she let him gradually roll her over on her side, then onto her back, the nibbling continuing uninterrupted.

He lingered along her flank, finding that sensitive area of her belly just in front of the hip.

"Damn you, do it. Now!" she groaned.

The wetness between her legs gushed out as she tightened her muscles. She heard him moan quietly as he reached her bushy hair and inhaled her scent.

"I want you inside," she whispered.

She felt his head rock side to side. *No.* His tongue continued to explore her.

"Volodya, please ..."

He straightened up.

"Don't move," he ordered.

His eyes locked with hers, he undid his shirt button by button and slipped it off, his muscular body towering above her.

He reached under her buttocks and eased her jeans off, lifting her legs one at a time then letting them down slowly, as if she were made of fine china.

Finally he unzipped his pants and allowed her hand to reach his hardness. She shuddered, feeling a drop of wetness already formed on him. She opened her legs to receive him, enjoying the feel of his pants on her naked legs, the roughness of his hairy chest against her nipples.

They moaned in unison as Volodya, ever so slowly, started to slide into her.

Anne was in her office at her computer, struggling to concentrate. She had only a few hours of sleep in the last three nights, working until the wee hours to complete the preparations for her trip. Fatigue was taking its toll. This morning she could hardly keep her eyes open, and caught herself nodding off several times. She was on the verge of falling asleep again when Lucia's voice startled her.

"Meet your date, Dr. Powell." The secretary placed a piece of paper on Anne's desk.

Anne looked down. Even with one cheek distorted by the pressure of the glass, the man's face was strikingly handsome. But it was the haunting look of the eyes that sent a chill through her. She barely heard Lucia's next words.

"Now, that's a face that'll make your head spin!"

Anne's eyes closed. A rumble filled the room. Horses. Galloping. Closer. Faster. She saw hooves flashing by in clouds of dust. She tried to open her eyes. The fax wasn't there. Only fragments of a vision. A grassy field. Patches of dirt. Then something rolled up to her feet.

A man's head. It had been torn off at the neck. The head laid on its side, its features grotesquely distorted. One of the eyes blinked slowly, then glassed over. She knelt down and stroked the familiar features.

Somewhere in the distance Lucia was saying, "Dr. Powell! Are you all right?"

Anne opened her eyes. Her hands were stroking the fax, smoothing it out.

"What? Oh …" Anne took a deep breath and wiped her face with her hand. "I'm fine, Lucia. I must've dozed off."

The vision was gone. The rumble she heard was nothing but the noise of a steel file cabinet two workers were moving across the hall.

Lucia eyed her suspiciously. "You sure? You look kinda green to me." Over the past week she had wondered if she should share her concerns about Anne's health with Halden. After all, her former boss wanted to be kept appraised of everything in the department. *She should definitely call him.* "How about I fix you a nice cup of tea?" she offered.

"That would be nice, Lucia," Anne admitted. Falling asleep and having nightmares while sitting at her desk in the middle of the morning was bordering on the ridiculous. "I guess I must be really tired."

"Amen! That's what I've been trying to tell you for weeks. You're going to kill yourself if you keep this kind of schedule."

"I'll rest when I get to Moscow," Anne said, forcing a smile. "I hear their nights are long and cold. Plenty of time to catch up on my sleep."

"Not if you have to work with guys that look like this one," Lucia grinned.

15

The evening before Anne's departure, Halden threw a *bon voyage* party. Close to a hundred people, both from the hospital and from the manufacturing plant, came to wish Anne a good trip and celebrate the sale of the first MEG.

Halden congratulated everyone and gave a glowing summation of the bright prospects for the new product. The crowd broke into applause, and then animated conversation and laughter filled the room as the guests moved toward the bar.

Later in the evening, Anne, Misty and several members of the hospital staff stood in a circle, chatting and sipping champagne. Halden approached them, and casually placed his hand on Anne's shoulder. "Incidentally, there's another event I'd like to celebrate with you today," he said casually, raising his glass in Anne's direction. "When Anne comes back, she and I ... How shall I put it? We'll be sharing home offices."

Anne couldn't believe her ears. The announcement was so inappropriate, so unnecessary. He hadn't even discussed breaking the news with her. She felt violated.

Halden pretended not to notice Anne's reaction. She was justified, of course, but he hoped that bringing things out in the open would make this baby step less reversible.

At the end of the soirée, a line of well-wishers paraded past Halden and Anne. Everyone had a handshake, a hug or a good word to offer on her forthcoming venture to Russia.

"Best of luck to you, Dr. Powell," said Pablo, giving her a long hug. "I know your trip will be a great success." Avoiding her eyes, he hurried away, and Anne saw him pulling out a handkerchief from his pocket.

Misty hugged and held her.

"Have a great time in Russia," she whispered. "I hope you find somebody there to knock some sense into you, before you set up housekeeping with Halden."

One of the last people to come by was an elderly, stooped, white-haired woman. A black skirt, black blouse, black scarf tied with a double knot, and plain black shoes gave her a monastic appearance. Anne thought the woman looked familiar, but couldn't quite place her. *Probably one of the ladies from the hospital's charity group,* Anne decided.

"Good luck, Dr. Powell," the woman said in a quiet, soothing voice, pressing something into Anne's hand. "May God be with you on this journey."

Anne glanced down and saw a tiny cross with two short extra crossbars, one of them at an angle to the main shaft. She recognized the traditional Russian Orthodox cross that she had seen in pictures. A glint from a ceiling light bounced off the delicate silver work.

"It's beautiful," Anne gasped, looking up.

But the woman had already vanished into the crowd.

16

Misty and Halden accompanied Anne in the limo to Logan Airport.

The security line at the international check-in area reached halfway across the lobby. Misty and Halden stood next to her until the last minute, making small talk.

"I hope your pantyhose doesn't have runs, in case they want to search more than your shoes," Misty teased to lighten the tension.

The last thing Anne remembered was Halden's quick hug and kiss. "Take care, Anne. Call when you get settled in. And good luck," he called out to her as she was walking through the security portal.

He knew she would need it. Before Baldyuk returned to Russia, he confided in Halden that the MEG was more than a pre-election gesture. The success of the deal depended solely on one thing: the rehabilitation of one person whose time was running out.

Delta's Flight 52, a Boeing 777, slammed down on the runway, jerking Anne awake. Tentatively she uncurled her stiffened body and peeked out the window.

The squat gray terminal emerged out of the fog. Patches of uneven tarmac peered through dirty snow. Ancient army-green service vehicles waited patiently on the motorways as the plane lumbered past them, bouncing precariously through potholes.

Anne rubbed her eyes and tugged at her wrinkled clothes, regretting not waking up in time to freshen up in the lavatory before landing.

The plane still taxiing, Russian passengers began getting up and pulling their belongings out of the overhead bins.

"*Uvajaemye passagiri!*" The American flight attendant tried to sound authoritative. "Ladies and gentlemen, please remain seated. We're on an active taxiway!"

The obese man next to Anne gave the attendant a dirty look, mumbled something that might have meant, "*We're in my country now*," then got up and pushed his way down the aisle, oblivious to the attendant's warnings. The closer the plane got to the terminal, the more the offenders pushed and shoved, jockeying for positions at the door. Duffels, satchels, suitcases and electric appliances in unwrapped boxes cluttered the aisle.

The plane jerked to a halt at the gate. Anne watched from her window as the ground crew, in motley parkas and jeans, drifted out of the building and slowly made their way toward the plane, with none of the urgency that ground crews generally displayed. Anne sighed. She was in a country where time and rules had a different meaning.

It took at least forty minutes for her two suitcases to roll off the conveyor belt. Not finding either a luggage cart or a porter, Anne half-carried, half-dragged her belongings to the customs line. It took another half hour to get to the customs area.

The pale, doughy-faced inspector wearing an army green uniform, eyed Anne's possessions. "Cigarettes, whisky, pornographic videos?" he asked checking her out.

"*Oo menya nitchevo nyet,*" Anne replied, trying to remember what she had learned from the Berlitz tapes. "I have nothing to declare."

The man yawned, poked her suitcase with his calloused fingers, and waived her on.

Stepping from the relative quiet and order of the customs area into the main arrival lobby was like entering another world. Familiar airline logos appeared side by side with unreadable signs written in

Cyrillic alphabet. Blond Slavs, dark-skinned Georgians, almond-eyed Khirgiz men scurried under the tall ceiling of the cavernous building, lugging enormous suitcases, cardboard cartons, or sloppy bundles wrapped in plastic and tied with twine. Public address announcements, children's cries and fragments of conversations in a variety of languages mixed into an ear-rattling cacophony. Fatigue-clad soldiers toting AK-47s were everywhere.

Anne, still dazed by the long flight and the eight-hour time change, felt totally lost. *Where was the person who was supposed to meet her, anyway?* She began to make her way through the crowd toward the exit, trying to maintain control of both her luggage and her composure.

Spotting a lone female traveler, porters, taxi drivers and money changers rushed toward Anne like sharks to chum, grabbing her arms, tugging at her clothes, fighting for her bags. Within moments, she found herself completely surrounded.

"Taxi, cheap."

"Good hotel, hot water!"

"Rubles, rubles, rubles. Best rate."

Their faces came closer: young, old, dark, wrinkled, the stench of cigarettes, garlic and vodka overwhelming her.

Suddenly a hand grabbed her arm. She tried to resist, but the hand dragged her inexorably through the crowd, and out into the open.

A ruggedly handsome man stood before her.

"Dr. Powell? I am Volodya Verkhov. Welcome to Moscow."

She looked at him, searching for any similarity to the fax she had received. *The strong nose with a slight crook to one side. The open, honest face, the sensuous lips. The face was so familiar …*

"Volodya Verkhov, from Pavlov Institute," he repeated.

"Yes, I know," she heard herself say.

Volodya was still holding onto her arm. She could feel each fingertip as it pressed into her. There was something comforting yet frightening in that grip. It was a confusing mix of sensations she had never experienced before.

As she stood still, unable to take her eyes off Volodya's face, she felt her heart stumble. Her skin turned cold and clammy as blood slowly drained from her face. Afraid she might lose consciousness at any moment, she glanced around, hoping her suitcase was close enough to sit on.

What was happening to her? Something about the man's face ... Her brain flashed to the fax he had sent. Then a fragment of the dream she was having when the fax arrived. *A decapitated body. A head, rolling up to her feet...* Her knees started to buckle. She took a deep breath and tried to focus. *Jet lag,* she decided, trying to be clinical.

Volodya kept looking at her, mild amusement sparkling in his eyes. He was accustomed to women being smitten by him, but this one seemed ready to faint.

His look angered her, and the anger helped her regain her composure. "How do you do. I'm Anne Powell," she said mustering a modicum of dignity.

"Welcome to Moscow," he replied, releasing his grip on her hand.

She bent down to pick up her bags but Volodya intercepted her. "Please, I shall carry your baggage," he said, snatching both suitcases and the carry-on before she could reach them. "Is big walk to car. Maybe difficult, after long trip? You want to sit, I get car?"

Without replying, Anne spun on her heels and headed for the exit.

They marched out of the terminal and onto the concrete sidewalk, covered with a thin layer of dirty snow. Anne didn't even notice that she had automatically fallen in step with Volodya's long strides. There was a haunting certainty to his gait.

Volodya studied her out of the corner of his eye. *So this was the Dr. Powell whose arrival everyone dreaded.* She was not the old scrawny American woman that he had imagined. In fact, she was rather attractive. Alive, energetic. With a certain unembellished beauty that radiated striking confidence. *Probably very intimidating to most American men. And that stride of hers, so powerful. The hair. Real blond. As pretty as any Russian woman's. And the eyes, so green. Like a spring meadow.*

He took a quick breath. *Yes, a very attractive woman.*

He couldn't help stealing a glance at her breasts as they moved slightly with every firm step. Then he noticed the small cross hanging from a chain around her neck. Three crossbars. Russian. *Nice touch.*

Anne caught his stare. If all Russians were so blatantly lecherous, it was going to be an unpleasant visit. She tried to respond with her usual scathing fake smile, but the sparkle in Volodya's eyes made it difficult to summon enough disdain.

"Car is not far now," Volodya mumbled, trying to cover up the awkwardness of the moment.

Feisty, isn't she, he thought, wondering if she would be friendlier once she had a chance to rest.

They entered a cavernous parking structure. Water dripped from the low ceilings, forming oil stained puddles everywhere. They climbed two flights up a concrete staircase, Volodya and the suitcases barely clearing the narrow passage.

His car was a small, faded-gray domestic compact. The hinges screeched as he pulled the passenger door open. He rummaged in the glove compartment, found a rag, wiped off the vinyl seat and covered a tear with an old blanket.

"Please," he said as he motioned for her to get in. "Sorry car not big. But goes very good," he said, beaming.

She caught herself studying his lips. The smile was so warm, so engaging. She almost smiled back, but her heart started missing beats again. She ducked into the car and pulled the door shut, like a clam retreating into the safety of its shell.

Volodya walked around to the driver's side, perplexed. It wasn't often that a woman did not respond to his smile.

That smile had served him well since childhood. When he was barely four, his mother had vanished on her way home from work. Volodya's father, devastated by grief, made the rounds of the various government establishments, searching for any information on her whereabouts. Having no one with whom to leave young Volodya, he took him along on these pilgrimages. There were few bureaucrats, particularly female, who could resist the young boy's endearing grin. It was this smile, more than his father's efforts, that paved the way past many a bureaucratic road block. "What an adorable little boy!" they would say. "What can we do for you?"

After three years of searching, Volodya's father learned that his wife had been involved in the aborted 1967 anti-government uprising. Those rebels, once they disappeared, were never seen again. Volodya's father gave up the search and turned to vodka for relief.

At the age of seven, Volodya found himself virtually alone, with no one to turn to for advice, consolation, or help with preparing a meal—until he realized that this smile, directed at the right recipient, could work wonders. The smile retained its magic in his adult life: Few women could resist it. But Anne Powell seemed to be an exception.

He got in, started the car, coaxed it into first gear and rolled out of the parking structure. As he checked for traffic, he caught another glimpse of Anne's profile and wondered if he would see this woman again soon.

17

The little gray vehicle groaned along the highway under a lead sky. Anne watched in fascination as the thriving suburbs of Moscow flashed past her window. Clusters of massive apartment buildings, alternate with ultramodern glass-and-concrete structures. Public parks, trees denuded, vacant benches covered with snow. Crowded bus stops. Endless rows of car dealerships. Schools, warmly bundled children racing across soccer fields, or doing calisthenics. Railroad yards, with miles of parked cargo trains. Here and there, churches, old and stylish or simple and functional.

Volodya kept busy pointing out landmarks: the monument to the tank troops of World War II, the largest truck factory in Russia, the site of an old World's Fair.

Pointing to a billboard, Volodya said, "And that is, how you say, propaganda, yes? For elections."

It was a huge billboard featuring a photograph of a middle-aged man with a beefy face and thick mustache, smiling benevolently against a hammer and sickle background.

"I thought the Communist party was dead," Anne exclaimed.

"No, no, no. Communist party is living and can have candidate, same like other parties."

"And do many people belong to it?"

"Communist party?" He shrugged. "Many, not many. Is not sure. This man is Namordin," Volodya continued, referring to the face on the billboard. "He is son of son of Stalin—how do you say, grandson, yes?"

"Really? I'd think that would be a huge liability."

"Sorry, what?"

"Liability. Something that would make it difficult for him to win."

Volodya shook his head. "Who can say? People not happy with regime. Sometimes they say we need strong power. This is very difficult time for mother Russia," he sighed.

Anne wanted to ask him about the Russian views on various political topics: Would Putin attempt to amend the constitution and run for a third term? Would there be another campaign against Chechnya, to avenge the latest suicide bombing on Red Square? Would Russia be friendlier to Americans after oil concessions in Iraq?

But she was struck by the tenderness and passion in his voice when he said "Mother Russia." Clearly, Russia was more than a place of birth for him. It was family. Asking questions felt like prying.

They rode in silence for a few miles.

"I read many good things about your MEG," Volodya announced suddenly.

"Really?" She wondered where a driver would have had a chance to read about the MEG.

"Why you do not worry about effect of alpha resonance on hypothalamus?"

Anne's jaw dropped. *Not your typical taxi driver.*

"Semiglazoff found serious membrane depolarization and ion pump block maybe. In synapses."

"Not really. The Semiglazoff effect has been shown to be of no significance when two perpendicular beams are used. Although the alpha wave amplitude …"

She stopped. How could this man know about alpha waves? He was probably parroting a discussion among Pavlov physicians that he overheard.

"Maybe your technology needs more proving?" he asked.

First he ogles her, then he questions her research. This man certainly knew how to push her buttons.

"I think my technology had enough proving," she snapped, turning toward the window.

Volodya drew a breath to answer, but reconsidered. *Yes, this woman would be definitely intimidating to most men.*

Twenty minutes later they entered Moscow, and their forward progress slowed to a crawl.

"Very sorry is slow," Volodya said. "Tverskey Prospect is like Fifth Avenue for Moscow. Very much traffic."

It was indeed "very much traffic." The Prospect and all the adjacent streets were jammed with cars. The few signal lights were inadequately supplemented by policemen on foot, who bravely waved their batons in futile attempts to control the sea of cars.

Despite the light snow, the sidewalks were packed with shoppers. The storefronts looked opulent, the window displays rivaling the best on New York's Fifth Avenue. Billboards, the Cyrillic words in strange juxtaposition to familiar American images, loomed everywhere. "*Peyte* Coca Cola." "*Gostinitza* Marriott." "*Delay*—Just do it. Nike."

"Kremlin," Volodya said suddenly, pointing to a fragment of red wall visible in the distance between buildings.

Anne felt a shiver of excitement. A month ago Russia wasn't even on her list of places to visit. In her very early childhood she had learned a few details about Russian culture from her Russian greatuncle. Born and raised in Russia, he tried to get Anne interested in Russian traditions, but she was too young to be receptive. Instead, his stories had left her with an unexplainable feeling of fear and foreboding, and no desire to see the country. But here she was. And not just as a visitor, but, in a way, a participant.

Volodya turned right and pulled into a circular driveway in front of a Baroque façade, decorated with a row of foreign flags fluttering in the wind.

"We arrived," he announced. "Hotel National. Best hotel in

Moscow." *It better be good,* he thought to himself. The daily room rate here was more than he made in two weeks at the Pavlov.

Two pompous bellmen stood at the door, attired in ankle-length burgundy coats with gold-and-black trim and top hats. They glanced disdainfully at Volodya's car, wondering how long this eyesore was going to detract from the appearance of their establishment. As soon as they realized that the car brought a hotel guest, they rushed forward and practically wrestled Anne's suitcases out of Volodya's hands.

"Thank you for the ride," Anne said.

"Please, my pleasure," he said smiling. He backed away, his eyes never leaving Anne's face. "If you need …"

His foot slipped off the curb. His arms flailing, he leaned out onto the street.

Brakes screeched. Anne saw a car sliding toward them, out of control.

"Look out!" she yelled.

Volodya tried to recover, but the momentum was carrying him into the path of the oncoming vehicle.

Seizing his wrist, Anne yanked him toward her. The car missed Volodya by a fraction of an inch. The driver regained control and yelled an obscenity. Volodya waved, then turned to Anne.

"You make me distracted," he laughed as if nothing had happened.

"That was close," she said, her heart still racing from the near miss.

"Ah, not worry," Volodya replied nonchalantly. "Cars not problem for me."

"Oh, really?" she shot back, irritated that she was more concerned about his safety than he was.

"Really. I shall not be killed by car. I shall be killed by jealous husband." He paused, looking into her incredulous eyes. "I know, because my babushka—that means grandmother—she see it in tea leaves."

He stood inches from her now. She could feel the warmth of his breath on her cheek. His face was serious but his eyes were smiling.

"Do you have husband, Dr. Powell?"

Her breath caught. "Yes. Yes, I do," she blurted out.

"In such case, I must be very careful," he said, with mock seriousness.

Flashing another smile, he climbed into his car, cut across six lanes of traffic and disappeared.

18

In the lobby of the Hotel National, rich oriental carpets alternated with exquisitely inlaid parquet floors. Massive baroque vases were filled with even more massive arrangements of freshly cut exotic flowers. A pale-cheeked woman wearing a billowing pink dress was playing a harp, her delicate profile turned toward a ceiling decorated with frescoes of peaceful seascapes and a crystal chandelier bigger than Volodya's car.

In bizarre contrast to this idyllic setting, a group of swarthy, stocky men were obstructing much of the registration desk, arguing loudly and smoking.

The bellmen deposited her luggage with deliberate politeness, but looked disdainfully at the five-dollar tip.

A young woman clerk approached Anne from behind the counter. "May I help you?"

Anne reached into her purse. "My name is Anne Powell. I have a reservation ..."

"Oh, Dr. Powell," the woman smiled. "Welcome to Hotel National. I am Natalia. Your room is ready. Let me show you. You must be tired. We will record your passport later."

Natalia was full-figured, but moved with the elegant poise of a woman comfortable with her size. She spoke with a clean all-

American, accent. *Rather surprising,* Anne thought, *in a country where Americans were the enemy until just recently.* On the left lapel of her impeccably ironed uniform, Natalia wore tiny Russian, British, French and German flags, and Anne wondered if her control of all these languages was as good as her control of English.

"I will be your hostess while you stay with us," Natalia announced as she filled out the forms, imprinted the card key, and stepped out from behind the counter, all in one smooth motion. "Follow me please."

"The hotel was built for visiting dignitaries in the last few years of the reign of Nicholas II," Natalia recited as they rode in the elevator. "Under the Communist regime, the building served as a residence for party members from the other republics. It was converted back to a hotel when the Communist government decided to welcome foreigner tourists. And foreign currency," she added in a conspiratorial whisper that instantly dispelled the stiff corporate image. "Now the National is owned and operated by a Finnish company."

They stopped in front of a set of tall double doors, with ground-glass inserts depicting flying cranes.

"Number 1675. This is your suite," Natalia said, inserting the card key into the door lock and holding the door open for Anne.

The suite was luxurious beyond her expectations. The main part of the complex consisted of a large room with a queen size bed, covered by a pale-green silk bedspread with a faint floral pattern. The pattern was repeated in the carved cherry wood headboard.

Off to the right, a set of three hardwood stairs led down to a smaller room that contained an elegant cherry wood desk, a small couch and a counter with a built-in refrigerator. On top of the counter were four cut-crystal glasses and two large bottles of water.

"Please drink only bottled water," Natalia admonished. "In our city water purification is not the best."

So much for modern conveniences, Anne thought. "Anything else I should know?"

"Change money in hotels or banks only. The black marketeers will often give you counterfeit rubles, and you don't want to be in a

Russian jail. They're not like yours. Do not use taxis from street. They can be … well, not safe. Use hotel car, or if you are away in town, just stick your hand out, and any private car will stop."

"You're kidding?"

"No. Private individuals give rides to earn extra money. And they're safe. Just be sure to agree on the rate beforehand. I always travel this way," she added, in response to Anne's raised eyebrows. "Or use the Metro. Also, I'll give you a card for public phones until we can get you a cell phone. Welcome to Russia, Dr. Powell," Natalia added with a warm smile, as she headed toward the door. "If you need anything, just ask for me."

Anne unpacked rapidly, methodically hanging her clothes in the closet and arranging her toiletries on the pink marble bathroom sink. Electric toothbrush in the right corner. Next to it, a tube of Crest tooth paste, neatly squeezed from the bottom up. A bottle of Hand and Nail Treatment Cream. HydraFresh skin toner. Two tubes of lipstick, peach and pink. A jar of Sea Kelp Night Cream. All items a finger-breath apart, in the same positions as she kept them at home.

Satisfied, she walked over to the desk, admiring its elegant Louis XIV design, the beautiful wood inlays of flowers on the mirror-smooth lacquered surface.

She set up her laptop, but couldn't get the internet connection. She couldn't blame it on the hotel. It was a frequent occurrence even at home. She sighed, thankful that e-mailing was not her favorite way of communicating.

She sorted through her papers, organizing them in neat stacks, and made a mental note to order a filing cabinet as soon as possible. She came across Volodya's face fax, crumpled it, and tossed it into the trashcan. Deciding it would make a quaint opening page for her journal for this trip, she retrieved the fax and placed it on top of one of the stacks. Her new lodgings organized to her satisfaction, she drew back the curtains and stepped out on the balcony.

The view was exquisite. Sprawling Red Square, dusted with freshly fallen snow. The brick-red walls of the Kremlin, its towers topped with enormous red stars and white-blue-red Russian flags. The candy-colored domes of Saint Basil's, each playfully different in size, shape and color. Everywhere, onion-shaped church domes, topped by Russian-style crosses with three crossbars, glistened in the sun.

Many of the churches in front of her dated back to the thirteen- and fourteen-hundreds. She found it mind boggling that Moscow was already a prosperous cultural center when Boston was nothing but thick forests, and Columbus wasn't even born yet.

Surrounding the Kremlin were starkly angular high-rises, emblazoned with gaudy neon signs. The din of rush-hour traffic from the main thoroughfare just around the corner barely reached her sixteenth floor balcony.

She heard distant church bells playing the same motif over and over, as if someone were practicing. A complicated mix of low-pitched and high-pitched notes intertwined into a haunting melody with a syncopated beat.

Oblivious to the cold Moscow air, Anne leaned against the railing, admiring the scenery and listening to the bells. Squinting, she made the colorful patterns of the domes of St. Basil's dissolve into a multi-colored kaleidoscopic image. She took a slow deep breath of cold air and, for the first time in months, she relaxed. Her new home away from home felt right.

Now it was time to put the MEG to work.

19

W ith a loud screech, the crowbar ripped a thick board from the side of a huge wooden crate, exposing the shiny surface of one of the MEG's C-rams.

"Very careful. *Otchen ostorojno*," Anne exclaimed protectively. The six burly workmen who were uncrating the MEG in the basement of the Pavlov smelled of sweat and vodka, and inspired no confidence whatsoever.

"You have to hold this up … Up!" Anne gestured at the support brace. "Before you pull the unit out! Do you understand? *Ponimaesh?*" If the C-arms were not properly supported while the unit was moved, their delicate gimbals could be damaged.

The workmen glared at her and continued to rip the boards.

Anne pushed her way past them and maneuvered her body to get better leverage against the C-arm. Her muscles burned as she strained to hold it up by herself.

"Like this. Do it, now," she yelled at the workmen.

Reluctantly, they complied.

"*Spasibo.* Thank you."

Gradually, like a baby dinosaur breaking out of its egg, the MEG emerged from the remainders of the crate.

"*Gde … gde …* hmm, *emergencia svitch?*" Anne tried to come up with a best guess for the word "emergency" as the workmen connected the unit's wiring to a junction box on the wall.

The foreman shrugged his shoulders. "*Ne ponimayu.*"

"You know, switch. Power cutoff." Anne moved her fingers up and down, imitating flipping a switch, then made a slicing motion across her neck. "Cutoff switch."

"*Ah, vyklyutchatel! Netoo.* No haff svitch," the forman said.

Great. If she ever needed to make repairs, they would have to open the junction box and physically disconnect the high-voltage wires. "OK, now I need you to …" Anne was about to pantomime turning on the power, but she was interrupted by the foreman's shout.

"*Zakontchelly.*" Done.

Anne watched in bewilderment as the workmen, like a well-rehearsed team, stopped dead in their tracks. The foreman pointed at his wrist watch, then at the door.

"But we're almost done!" She gestured at her own watch and held up two fingers. "*Dve minuty.*" Another two minutes and the unit would have been calibrated and ready. But they were already gathering their tools. It was obvious that here quitting time was a rule that was never broken. Anne dropped her arms in resignation and made her way past the crate debris toward the door.

As soon as she left, a bottle of Vodka appeared.

"*Davai,*" the foreman yelled.

The man with the bottle lobbed it across the room. The bottle bounced off the C-arm dislodging the cork and spilling vodka all over the control panel. To a chorus of groans, the men rushed toward the bottle, trying to salvage the precious contents. One of them tried sucking the liquid that had pooled on the flat surface of the panel. The rest, laughing and cursing, pummeled the clumsy quarterback.

None of them bothered to wipe off the few drops of alcohol that remained on the control buttons.

20

Generally, MRI and CAT scans were performed in basements, in order to facilitate radiation control, and utilize less desirable real estate. But the decision makers at the Pavlov seemed to have gone out of their way to choose the most remote and inhospitable recess of the building for the MEG. Anne had trouble finding the room earlier in the day, and she was having even more trouble finding her way back out now.

She meandered along narrow dim corridors looking for familiar landmarks. Signs in Cyrillic pointed in various directions but she couldn't decipher anything that spelled *vykhod,* Russian for exit. Everywhere there was the whining of electric motors, the hissing of compressed air, and the rumbling of heavy machinery. She thought she even heard dogs yelping.

As she passed a partially open door, she heard a high-pitched squeal. Anne peeked inside, hoping to see someone who could help her. A man's figure, silhouetted against a single light bulb, was hunched over a workbench.

"Hello?" Anne called tentatively from the doorway.

The figure turned.

"Ah, Dr. Powell! This is pleasant surprise!"

She squinted at the light and recognized Volodya.

He grinned, as if he had been expecting her. "Come in, please."

"Actually, I was looking for a way out."

"You are lost?"

"I'm afraid so," she admitted.

"I will show," he said. "Just I do this … Can you please help?" He motioned her toward the chair across from him. "We rapidly finish, and then we go."

It was too late to back out gracefully. Anne stepped into the room. Volodya was holding a white mouse that was squealing plaintively.

"Will be very quick. I am now expert in fertilizing."

"Expert in what?"

"Fertilizing. Take sperm from one animal, put inside other animal …"

"Artificial insemination," Anne laughed, despite herself.

"Yes, yes, yes. Please hold here."

He gently repositioned her hands on the mouse's hind paws. "Carefully, please! Her feet very delicate."

She thought that his fingers lingered on hers moments longer than necessary. The touch felt firm and confident, like his grip on her arm at the airport. But here he seemed to be a different man. His intense gaze was focused on his work, his eyebrows furrowed, his fingers moving with surgical precision. She watched him, realizing that this man was no taxi driver.

He filled a pipette from a vial sitting in a beaker of ice and leaned over the mouse. Even though Anne tried to pull back as much as possible, their faces were close enough to touch. She was intensely aware of his scent—a faint aroma of freshly baked bread mixed with something warmly familiar but tantalizingly unidentifiable.

Suddenly it hit her. It was the scent of bee's wax. Of burning wax candles …

"Pull back legs, a little more please," she heard him saying.

He helped Anne spread the mouse's legs. His hands, so large next to the mouse, moved gracefully. She studied the chiseled contour of his cheeks, the powerful line of his lips, the fine wrinkles in the weathered skin. There was something very masculine and earthy about him.

Volodya glanced up. Anne quickly looked away. She thought he pretended not to notice. *Or was he so engrossed in his work that he wasn't even aware of her?*

"Now please do not move." Volodya leaned closer to the mouse, concentrating. One of his knees pressed against hers. She tried to move but the table leg prevented her.

Anne watched as the tip of the tiny pipette slipped into the animal's vagina.

"Very important to make fertilizing work, or much time will be wasted," Volodya said.

Carefully he thrust the pipette deeper. Anne felt the mouse jerk. She forced herself to concentrate so the animal wouldn't slip out of her fingers.

The spot where his leg was touching hers was burning hot. She felt the heat spreading slowly up her thigh. In a gradual crescendo, she heard the blood begin pulsating in her temples. She knew she was blushing and was sure he would notice if he looked up.

This is ridiculous, she thought. Last time she felt like this was at a drive-in in junior high. She tried to control her breathing, afraid that he would notice that she was breathing faster. Finally, she couldn't stand it any longer. She jerked her leg away, hitting the bench in the process and causing Volodya to dislodge the pipette.

"I'm so sorry," she stammered, now totally flustered.

"Not problem," he answered without even glancing up. He reinserted the pipette and, squeezing the bulb between two fingertips, injected the gelatinous fluid into the mouse.

"Now please hold legs together few minutes."

She looked up at him. He smiled, his face still very close to hers.

"Soon we shall be parents," he announced.

21

Sasha Lefko stood in the doorway, taking in the scene. Anne's presence in Volodya's lab shocked her.

Anne's arrival, or more specifically, the arrival of the MEG—brand new technology, imported from *Amerika*—was a threat to her. She was just beginning to assert her authority as the number one person under Baldyuk. Being subservient to that arrogant, lecherous fool was humiliating enough. But now there was a new expert on the scene and that meant that her own authority could be undermined.

She was relieved to see that Anne was young and pretty. As Sasha knew from first-hand experience, beauty and youth in an institution dominated by old men was a definite disadvantage. Hopefully, this disadvantage would be enough to prevent Anne from usurping any of Sasha's hard-won influence.

Sasha's present position as acting chief of psychiatry at the world-renowned Pavlov Institute was a fortuitous result of the premature retirement, nine months earlier, of the long-time chief, caused by alcoholic cirrhosis of the liver. Not an uncommon occurrence in a land where vodka was cheaper than bottled water.

So far Sasha had done an exceptional job running the department. If she could only hang on for another three or four months, she may have a good shot at keeping the position indefinitely. Which would be an unprecedented achievement for any woman who just recently turned 42—a baby by academic standards. Particularly a woman with Sasha's background.

Her background had two strikes against her.

One was the fact that Sasha was half-Tartar. Tartars, an offshoot of the Mongols, were the horseback riding descendants of Genghis Khan and his "pillaging and raping hordes." Eight centuries ago, the Tartars were the scourge of Russia, raiding villages, killing the men and enslaving the women. Now they had been reduced to a small cluster of Moslem people, confined to the tiny republic of Tatarstan, in the far south of what used to be the Soviet Union. But they were still distrusted and shunned.

Sasha's Russian father, a civil engineer, met her Tartar mother during one of his trips to Tatarstan, where he was working on a hydroelectric dam. Seduced by her exotic looks, delicious cooking and passionate lovemaking, he soon married her, despite her ethnicity.

Sasha's parents moved back to Moscow when Sasha was only three. Her father, who had studied abroad, taught her fluent German and English before she had even started kindergarten. But it was her mother's Tartar culture that dominated her upbringing—the songs, the love of rugged mountains, the passion for life. She loved to hear her mother's folk tales about Tartar battle victories. She enjoyed shocking people by pulling out, in the most inappropriate places, the small curved dagger that she inherited from her maternal grandfather and carried as a talisman. Being half-Tartar was not a social asset, but she was proud of her heritage.

The other strike against her was her lack of connections—political or financial. She had always fought for every enrollment, every promotion. During Soviet times it was the children of party members who were accepted by the better schools and handed the more desirable jobs. When the Soviet regime fell, the meritocracy remained, but now it was based on financial rather than political clout.

Despite her outstanding performance in graduate school, fulfilling her dream of getting a job—any job—at the Pavlov proved impossible. She was passed over, time and again, in favor of applicants who were far less qualified but better connected. After three years of disappointments, she decided that it was time to change tactics.

At that time the chairman of the admissions committee for postgraduate work at the Pavlov was an elderly, happily married biochemist, who, rumor had it, was totally immune to any temptations, except large sums of money. He liked Sasha, whom he recognized as a promising scientist, but not enough to promote her ahead of those who could pay for the favor.

Under the pretext of needing extra cash, Sasha persuaded him to hire her for a few hours a week as a personal assistant. One night, when the professor's wife was away for a long holiday at their beachside dacha on the Black Sea, he asked Sasha to prepare dinner for him and several guests. Rushing through preparations in the kitchen, she spilled borscht on his white shirt. Mortified, she insisted that he take the shirt off immediately, then disappeared into the bathroom to rinse it off. Moments later, she came out, stark naked. Wrapping herself around him, she kissed his bald head, her breasts pressed firmly against his wrinkled, shocked face.

On cue, Sasha's boyfriend burst in through the door that she had left unlocked, wielding a borrowed camera, snapping pictures. The professor stood there in the middle of the kitchen, blinking, shirtless, and dazed. Sasha smiled. "Little man, you're toast!"

It didn't matter that the boyfriend had forgotten to put film in the camera. The professor, fearing for his reputation, agreed to say a few persuasive words to the other members of the committee, and Sasha got her appointment to the Institute.

She was now fiercely determined to protect her hard-won territory, from anyone and anything. Particularly from this Americanka, who appeared to have made herself prematurely comfortable in Volodya's lab.

Sasha smirked. "From rats to foreigners," she said in Russian.

Volodya turned around. "Sasha, *zdrastvooy!*" he greeted her gruffly, irritated by the interruption. He was looking forward to walking with the American doctor.

Sasha moved toward them, placing her feet carefully, like a cat stalking its prey, circling around Volodya.

"And this must be Dr. Powell, I presume?" she said in almost flawless British-accented English. "I'm Sasha Lefko, head of Psychiatry," she added, extending her hand. "I understand you and I will be working together."

"How nice! I'm glad to help in any way I can," Anne replied, startled by Sasha's vise-like handshake.

Still staring directly into Anne's eyes, Sasha planted her hands on Volodya's shoulders. "I see you're getting acquainted with the Pavlov," she said, her fingernails stroking Volodya's neck like little daggers.

"I was totally lost, and I wanted to ask directions ..."

There was something intimidating about this woman. Despite herself, Anne felt guilty, as if she had been caught flirting with another woman's man.

"This place can be overwhelming," Sasha agreed. "But I'm sure you'll learn your way around very soon. In the meantime, is there something I can do for you?"

"Actually, I was hoping to start pre-screening the patients, while the MEG is being setup."

"That's nice of you ... but I've already pre-screened the first dozen or so," Sasha said with a frigid smile. It was bad enough that Baldyuk was forcing her to use new technology, which implied that Sasha had failed. Now the Americanka wanted to check her work!

"You did?" Anne tried to avoid sounding as if she were doubting Sasha's competence.

As if reading Anne's mind, Sasha recited the criteria of the protocol. "Therapeutic failure after three years of psychotherapy, at least two suicidal or homicidal episodes ... I read your articles, Dr. Powell."

Indeed, Baldyuk had insisted that she give him a detailed analysis of the MEG before he made his trip to Boston. There was zero room for error on this project.

"I just checked on the MEG," Sasha continued. "The crew will have it ready by noon tomorrow. I told everyone to be in the auditorium at nine o'clock sharp so you can brief them."

"Excellent. I guess all I need to do is introduce myself to the patients so they'll be more comfortable with me tomorrow." She waited for Sasha's offer to take her to the ward, but none came. "Perhaps you could direct me to the patient floors?"

Sasha's lips tightened. The woman just didn't know when to give up. "I'm afraid tonight is too late. But if you wish, you can see them in the morning just before your presentation."

"How do I get there?"

"Come into the main lobby, turn left, take the second set of elevators up to the fourth floor of the Razdin building. I'll inform them that you'll be there at eight. The nurses will show you which patients I scheduled."

"My Russian isn't very good … *Da, spasibo, nyet,* that's about it. How will I …"

"Don't worry, several of the nurses speak English. They can translate for you."

"Razdin Four?" Volodya asked in Russian. "Without an escort?"

"She'll be fine," Sasha answered in Russian.

"Come on, Sasha. Even you always bring someone when you go up there."

"If you're so worried, why don't you take her?" Sasha snapped.

"Maybe I should!" Volodya snapped back.

Sasha glared at him.

Anne turned from one to the other, wondering what was going on.

"We're debating the best way to get you where you need to go," Sasha said in English.

"Don't worry, I'll find my way," Anne replied standing up. "I'm looking forward to working with you. I'm sure it'll be a great experience for both of us," she added. "Now, how do I get out of here?"

As she walked down the corridor, Anne heard the door slam behind her. She shrugged her shoulders. She was here to treat patients, not to win a popularity contest. In a few months she would have the data she needed and she would be able to go home.

22

Having barely escaped the convoluted labyrinths of the Pavlov, Anne was reluctant to tackle the subway. According to Natalia, hailing a cab was a bad idea. And Anne wasn't about to hitch a ride with a stranger. So she pulled out a map of Moscow that Natalia had given her that morning, and started toward the hotel, staying on the well-lit main streets.

The traffic was denser than in almost any major U.S. metropolis. Shiny black Mercedes intermingled with ungainly domestic subcompacts.

The mix of people on the sidewalks was fascinating. At first sight, the crowd appeared like any other rush-hour crowd in the U.S. But here and there Anne would notice odd details: an old woman bundled in a black scarf, hurrying along, with two live chickens in a knit shopping satchel; an old man leaning against a lamppost, playing an accordion, his thin, worn jacket covered with military medals. Women always walked arm in arm, and men kissed each other on the cheeks. Almost everyone smoked, including children as young as ten or twelve.

Here and there Anne would spot a statuesque blond beauty, her cell phone pinned to her ear, the mink coat carelessly sweeping the dirty snow, sauntering nonchalantly past a young mother holding an infant in one hand and a beggar's cup and a cigarette in the other. It was amazing to see such contrast between rich and poor, between haves and have-nots, just a few years after the collapse of the regime that promoted total social and economic equality.

There seemed to be no lack of merchandise in the stores, and the brightly lit storefronts bore names like Prada, Gucci and Sony. But the prices were outlandish. Anne kept recalculating in her head, refusing to believe that a Benetton sweater could sell for the equivalent of $350—in a country where the average monthly income was half that.

Walking briskly, Anne covered the distance to the hotel in forty-five minutes. When she got to her room, she called Halden.

"How's work?" he asked after a brief greeting, as if she had never left.

She told him about the Pavlov, describing the MEG room and her working conditions in great detail.

"Have you connected with our friend Professor Baldyuk yet?"

"Thankfully, no. I'll be working with another pill in the psych department."

"Anne, I know I don't need to remind you how important it is for them to be happy with the MEG."

"Jack!"

"I'm sorry, I'm sorry. I know you'll do fine," he corrected himself quickly.

There was a pause in the conversation. She wanted to tell him how exciting Moscow was, how at home she felt, how beautiful St. Basil's looked, and how she wished she could share all this with him.

Before she could start, Halden spoke again. "We're sending you a backup PM17, in case one of yours blows, and several image collimators. I don't know why I didn't think of including them."

"Do you miss me?" Anne interrupted.

"Of course I miss you," he answered, a little surprised. It wasn't like Anne to talk about feelings, let alone on the phone. "I have no one to argue with," he said, trying for humor.

"This place is so cold, Jack."

"I told you, you shouldn't have gone."

"It's much colder than Boston."

"Make sure you dress warmly then. Anne, I've another call coming in. Let's talk again soon." He hung up before she had a chance to tell him she wished he were there.

Anne pulled out a bar of chocolate that she bought at a street kiosk on her walk back and held it next to the heating vent for a few moments. You couldn't appreciate the full flavor of chocolate unless it was soft. Then you could knead it with your tongue—chocolate connoisseurs called it pumping—to release the full flavor and appreciate the texture. Frozen, it just crumbled into tasteless pieces that stuck to your teeth.

She peeled back the foil wrapper and bit into the bar. Luna. It was called Luna. Moon, as in lunar. "*Nyet.* Luna. Lu-nah!" the young kid at the kiosk corrected her pronunciation, putting the accent on the last syllable. The Luna was good. Rich, intense chocolate, higher fat content than Swiss. Layered over what was the local equivalent of Rice Crispies, maybe a hint of honey. She savored the sweet, crunchy mixture, chewing slowly, letting the flavor caress her tongue. Orgasmic, as Misty would say. Even the name seemed to just flow off the lips. Lunah. She would have to stock up before going back to Boston. Her favorite KitKats were up against some stiff competition.

She sat down at her desk and rearranged her files. Her eyes fell on Volodya's fax. *A real character.* She was sorry that Sasha's arrival prevented her from finding out more about his research. *Artificial insemination. What was he working on? And what was that about tea leaves and getting killed by a jealous husband?*

She considered dropping by to visit him in the next few days, but put the thought out of her mind. He was obviously a man convinced that all women were smitten with him. She didn't want him to misinterpret her interest. *No visiting.*

Suddenly, she recalled the sensation of the heat of his knee pressing against her thigh. The feeling was so vivid, she reached down and rubbed her leg. The heat persisted, spreading, electrifying.

An image flashed through her mind: she and Volodya riding a horse. Bizarre, because she was terrified of horses. She was behind him, her arms wrapped around his muscular hairy chest, their bodies moving as one as they galloped down a flower-covered mountain slope, the wind blowing, his blond curls caressing her face …

Definitely no visiting.

23

The car ordered by Natalia the night before was waiting when Anne emerged from the hotel lobby. The young driver, a cigarette dangling from his upper lip, swung the door open for her.

"Good morning, Doctor. I am Victor. For your orders," he said with a thick accent, taking one last drag from the cigarette and tossing it carelessly on the sidewalk.

It was an unseasonably warm and clear February morning and as the car sped down the sunlit streets, Anne regretted that she hadn't walked. She rolled down her window and inhaled the crisp morning air. Refreshed and energized, she tried to imagine what her first day at the Pavlov would be like. The first day that her MEG would be used outside the familiar research setting. The grand opening. The true test.

She closed her eyes and smiled.

Ten minutes later, the car pulled up in front of the Institute. Birds were chirping in the barren trees. Huge icicles hung from the façade, their melting tips sparkling in the morning sun. Two elderly women in scarves stooped over their homemade whisker brooms, sweeping the sidewalk.

Anne walked briskly into the entrance, crossed the cavernous black-granite lobby decorated with faded photos of Russian scientists, found her way to the Razdin elevators and rode to the fourth floor.

The hallway was deserted. On the sign taped to the tile wall she recognized the Cyrillic letter "Р," which resembled the universal character "Pi," then the Russian "S," like the English "C." "PSYCH-something," she figured.

She followed the sign to a locked door and rang the bell. Nothing happened. She rang again. On the third try the electronic lock clicked, and the door swung open.

Anne entered a narrow passage that dead-ended at another locked door. As she stood wondering what to do next, a small window in the wall slid open, revealing an overweight woman in a dirty white smock. She stared at Anne.

"*Zdrastvooyte.* I'm Dr. Anne Powell," Anne said. "I have an appointment."

It was ten to eight according to the wall clock, but Anne didn't think that being early would matter. The woman gave her a strange look and asked her something in Russian, glancing at the door through which Anne had just walked in, as if expecting to see someone else.

Anne didn't understand. "*Ne ponimayu,*" she said, smiling apologetically.

The woman tried again, then shrugged her shoulders and pushed a button under the counter. The inner door swung open.

Anne stepped into a wide hallway, lined with thick metal doors on either side, most of them open. Each room had a small wooden bed and a chair, bolted to the floor. Dirty clothes, soiled bed linen and trash were everywhere. Dim fluorescent overhead lighting gave the peeling green paint a sickly tinge.

It was eerily quiet. Her steps echoed off the bare tile floor as she continued down the hall.

Anne opened a metal door, and found herself in an enormous unfurnished room. The noise became overwhelming. She saw twenty or thirty men and women of various ages. A few wore dirty hospital scrub suits. Most had nothing on but patient gowns, the untied back flaps exposing their emaciated bodies.

They sat on chairs or squatted on the floor, gobbling down porridge from their metal plates, dropping globs of the mixture on their laps or on the floor. Two of the women were struggling for control of a spoon.

A gigantic man stood alone in a corner, towering over everyone else like an enormous statue. His red beard was matted and split like a fish tail. He rocked back and forth on his heels, mumbling the same phrase over and over: "*Spassy bojee, spassy bojee, spassy bojee ...*" Periodically, he crossed himself and bowed, swinging his bulk with ease.

Anne looked around, hoping to find a staff person.

An emaciated woman, wearing nothing but a stained, untied, patient gown, ran up to Anne. She seemed to be in her forties, but was probably younger. Her thick blond hair hadn't seen a comb in weeks, her even teeth showed signs of decay and her pink skin was covered with pustules. Only her large blue eyes spoke of happier times.

The woman grabbed Anne's hand and kissed it reverently, then dropped to her knees and started to bow, her head hitting the floor. A male patient with disheveled hair and a deranged look squatted behind the woman, attentively inspecting her bare buttocks.

Anne tried to help the woman up, but she resisted, continuing to bow and kiss Anne's hand.

Anne felt someone tugging at her jacket. She spun around in time to keep one of the men from pulling her pen out of her pocket. Several patients formed a semicircle, egging him on.

Another man ripped the notebook out of her hands with such force that she almost lost her balance. Giggling wildly, he started tearing pages out and folding them into airplanes.

The jeering and laughing intensified. Anne felt cold sweat beading on her forehead as the crowd around her thickened. Paper planes sailed across the room as if in a dream.

Suddenly, the crowd quieted and opened up. The red bearded giant shuffled toward Anne, stiff-legged, his arms outstretched, as if he were blind. He paused and sniffed the air, his nostrils flaring, try-

ing to smell her. Anne made an attempt to slip around him but found
herself pinned against other patients.

The giant came closer and stroked her hair. His thin lips barely
covered his brown, carious teeth. Anne could smell his putrid breath.
She forced herself to stand still, afraid to provoke him.

Behind her, the door swung opened and Baldyuk and Sasha
appeared. They stopped dead and exchanged glances.

"Let's see how she handles it," Baldyuk whispered, an evil grin on
his face.

The man's hands slid down Anne's neck and explored her chest.
The crowd murmured approvingly. Anne could barely control her
urge to vomit.

A faint smile crept across Sasha's lips. She was enjoying the newcomer's predicament. Suddenly, there was commotion at the other
door, and a figure burst through the crowd.

"I think you dropped your pen, Dr. Powell," Volodya said, deftly
slipping between the man and Anne and gently steering her away.
"Nicolai, *poshell.* Go away," he said quietly looking up into the giant's
eyes.

The red-bearded man, at least a head taller that Volodya, grunted
but stood his ground.

"Nicolai," Volodya repeated in a threatening whisper.

Nicolai took a step toward Anne.

With a barely perceptible twist of his body, Volodya jammed his
elbow into Nicolai's ribs. Nicolai gasped and squatted on the floor.
The crowd began to disperse. Nicolai limped away, clutching his
chest.

Anne stood still, shaking violently. "You are too soon," Volodya
muttered, glancing at his watch as if nothing had happened. "Not
eight o'clock yet."

"Thank you," Anne managed to whisper. She felt an urge to lean
against him and bury her face against his chest.

"What are you doing here?" Sasha snapped in Russian at Volodya
as she and Baldyuk approached.

"I came to see you," Volodya said innocently, controlling his anger. He knew Sasha had a mean streak, and Baldyuk was a bastard, but this was going too far. "This is no way to treat a visitor," he added quietly.

"Mind your own business," Sasha hissed back.

"You seem to be lost, Dr. Verkhov," Baldyuk mumbled through his teeth. "The rat farm is in the basement."

Volodya looked straight at Baldyuk. "Yes, Professor. It is. And it's a nicer place, too," he added, heading for the door.

Baldyuk started to say something, but Sasha steered him toward Anne. "Dr. Powell, you've met Professor Baldyuk I believe?" she asked cheerfully in English.

"Welcome to Razdin Four, Dr. Powell," Baldyuk said with exaggerated politeness. "Do our patients meet with your approval?"

24

Her knees still trembling, Anne followed Sasha and Baldyuk to the lecture hall. It was a stark room with a dozen rows of wooden chairs facing a small lectern in front of a blackboard. Next to the lectern was a bank of light-boxes on a wheeled stand, displaying MEG scans.

Most of the seats were already occupied. Younger staff members sat in the front rows, pencils and notebooks at the ready. The big brass settled further back. Anne noticed Volodya sitting off to the side, several attractive young women clustered around him, whispering and giggling quietly.

The crowd fell silent as Sasha, Anne and Baldyuk entered the room. Sasha marched up to the lectern, briskly tapped the microphone, and gave a brief introduction.

When Sasha turned the mike over to Anne, an elegantly dressed young man sprung to his feet and planted himself next to the lectern. "I shall be your interpreter," he said with a British accent.

Anne started with her usual "it's-a-pleasure-to-be-here" opening, followed by a summary of the socioeconomic impact of mental illness in the U.S. and throughout the world. The translator was keeping up, but Anne noted that many in the audience were glancing at their watches or whispering among themselves. She changed the pace.

"Magneto-encephalography is based on technology that has been around for a number of years. I don't know the background of everyone here, so please stop me if my explanations aren't clear."

She thought she saw a smirk on Baldyuk's face: "Don't worry, we can keep up."

She gave a brief overview of how she came up with the MEG, delivering the facts in her usual self-effacing style, crediting her colleagues, emphasizing that she had not discovered anything new, but simply assembled work developed by others. Misty always told her that she was too modest, but Anne felt that she had merely combined existing elements. "Yeah, and Henry Ford merely combined existing elements, too," Misty would smirk. "Give yourself credit, woman."

"Basically, the procedure consists of two parts," Anne said, taking a piece of chalk. "Imaging and ablation." She wrote the two words on the board.

As the translator interpreted, she noted with amusement that many of the technical terms were English words with a Russian twist. "*Elementy, ablatzya ...*"

"First, let's talk about imaging. How do we find the area that we want to treat?" Her voice grew stronger and more animated. She was in her element now.

"What we do is, we inject the patient with a small amount of a glucose solution that contains Carbon-14, which, as you know, is radioactive. We chose C-14 because it's been so successful in PET."

"What is PET? I am not versed in American abbreviations," the interpreter apologized.

"Positron Emission Tomography. *Tomographia positronykh emissyi,*" Baldyuk interjected from the back row. "Pioneered here at the Pavlov in 1983 by Yussupoff," he added pointedly in English, for Anne's benefit.

"Thank you. And a brilliant innovation it was," she said unfazed. "The glucose, which is an energy source, goes to whatever areas of the brain are active at that particular time. For example, if the patient is asked to sing a song, the radioactive glucose will collect in the left temporal lobe."

While the interpreter finished the sentence, Anne snapped a piece of chalk in two and, holding a piece in each hand, turned to the blackboard. Swinging her arms in large elegant arcs, she drew two absolutely perfect mirror images of a cross section of the brain. She looked like a conductor in front of an orchestra as her hands outlined the cortex, the corpus callosum, the cerebellum …

Two-handed drawing was a trick she had learned from one of her neuroanatomy professors. It actually was a lot simpler to do than it looked: the human body was wired for symmetrical movement. But it never failed to impress an audience.

When she turned around, all eyes were on her. As she scanned the faces, she noticed that Volodya, too, was listening intently.

"Singing would show up here." Anne made a small circle on the side of the right cortex. "However, if we show our patient a photograph, the brain activity will be over here instead." She marked an adjacent area. "And if we question her about her childhood memories, the activity will be somewhere in the frontal cortex area. Right here."

Anne paused to make sure the information registered.

"The areas with the most activity will use the greatest number of glucose molecules, including the radioactive C-14 ones. C-14, as you know, releases subatomic particles called positrons. These positrons will be picked up by two gamma cameras built into the pods of the C-arms of the MEG. Because there are two cameras, which look at the patient from two views …" She drew two perfectly straight lines at right angles to each other across the brain cross-section. "… And because the cameras are rotating around the patient, we can generate a three-dimensional view of the patient's brain, in full color."

You could hear a pin drop.

"So that's how we get the image. Now, how do we access the memories? After all, if years of psychoanalysis failed, how can a brief session in the MEG succeed? The answer is simple. Depolarization. Armond's research showed that if we could lower the electrical charge across the neuronal synapses, we could, theoretically, enhance the flow of information from neuron to neuron."

She drew several arrows across the brain. "It's like opening a faucet to help memories flow." She was rewarded with several nods from the audience.

"The question is, how do we do that in a reversible, controllable fashion? Well, the electromagnets built into the pods of the C-arms, right next to the gamma cameras, produce a strong magnetic field. As the C-arms spin around the patient's head, the movement of the magnetic field induces a weak electrical current—a few nanovolts—within the brain. Basically, it's like a generator, a magnetic field moving around a coil of wire."

She paused and looked around. Satisfied that all of them grasped the principle, she proceeded.

"It is this weak current that changes the charge across the synapses, allowing the patient to recall events that are not normally accessible."

She paused again, realizing that several faces in the audience looked confused.

"Think of it as giving someone an injection of Pentothal. Truth serum," she added, resisting the temptation to make a remark about how the Russians might have pioneered the use of this drug as part of their interrogation techniques in the not-so-distant past. "If you open the synapses—whether you use Pentothal or a magnetically-induced electrical current—the memories come back."

They seemed to be with her again.

"How do you make sure that the patient remembers a particular event?" Sasha asked. From the tone, Anne gathered that Sasha knew the answer, and the question was just an attention-getting ploy.

"I was just getting to that. We want a particular event, and not all the memories stored. That would be like reaching for a book and having the whole shelf land in your lap."

A few in the audience smiled politely.

Anne decided to skip the details of her early MEG work. Back then she relied on non-verbal stimuli such as smells. The mother's perfume, grandma's cinnamon buns, or the boyfriend's T-shirt proved to be extremely potent reminders. But they weren't specific enough, so eventually Anne settled on simple questioning. It wasn't as powerful a memory aid as smell, but a lot easier to work with.

"So, how do you access the target memory?"

She paused to make sure everyone understood the problem.

"We ask questions. If we guide the patient, we can point her in the right direction. The recall process will take over and automatically take us where we want to go."

"Like psychoanalysis," someone said skeptically.

"Yes, but with the MEG we can go much faster, and much further back than we can with conventional psychoanalysis."

She loved the "ah-ha" expressions on their faces.

"As the patient's brain focuses, we'll get a concentration of C-14 in the area where the disorder is centered. What we'll see on the image is a 'locus'—a red or orange hot spot which designates an area of high activity in the neurons. Let's say, right here."

She made a large circle in one of the lobes.

The interpreter was barely keeping up. Anne's enthusiasm was spreading to the audience. Upright in their chairs, they took notes furiously. Even Baldyuk and Sasha, sitting side by side in the back of the room, were listening.

"This is where we find out if our choice of patient was correct. The best candidates for MEG therapy are patients with phobias and simple psychoses, because they're going to have just a single small locus. Those who have complex disorders, such as schizophrenia, multiple personality or sub-acute neuroses, will have multiple loci," she drew several partially overlapping circles. "These patients cannot be treated with MEG. Why?" she asked, to preempt the inevitable question that surfaced in every one of her lectures. "You'll see in a second."

She paused to let the translator catch up. She glanced in Volodya's direction. Their eyes met, and she saw him smile approvingly. She felt herself blushing and turned away.

"Now comes the most critical part of the procedure: the ablation phase. We need to destroy the cells where the memory is stored—and only those cells—to cure the patient."

She went to the board again.

"The pods on the C-arms generate RF beams. Ordinary radio frequency. Think of it as a directional microwave."

She saw eyebrows shoot up.

"When the beams intersect, the energy is cumulative. It's the Gamma Knife principle. Incidentally," she said, unable to resist a dig back at Baldyuk, "the technique was pioneered by my colleagues at MIT."

The Gamma Knife was an ingenious tool to destroy tumors in areas of the brain where a surgical knife could not reach. The device looked like a small igloo studded with hundreds of tiny radiation-emitting guns. The patient's head was positioned at the center of the igloo and the guns were aimed in such a way that their pencil-thin beams converged on the tumor. The surface of the brain did get a small dose of radiation, but the effect was cumulative in the one spot where all the beams came together, destroying the cancerous cells.

Anne had applied the same principle to radio frequency waves delivered by rotating beams—minimal exposure harmlessly spread over a large surface, but powerfully concentrated in a chosen spot deep inside the brain.

"By precisely aligning the spinning C-arms with the patient's locus, we get maximum concentration of energy. Right here."

She scribbled over the X with such vigor that she broke the chalk.

"Result—irreversible cell damage." Smiling, she put the chalk down and wiped off her hands. "All traces of the memory, gone."

There was silent scribbling. Then a hand went up. It was Volodya's. "Is danger to destroy areas that have other functions?"

"Very good question. The possibility is remote when you're dealing with a single locus. But in people where there are several loci, there's a definite likelihood of destroying healthy tissue. It's too risky. You never know what you may hit. So we don't touch those cases."

Volodya nodded and went on. "I see, on all your scans, spaces with no color change. Can you please explain."

"We use only ten percent of our brain capacity ..."

"Yes. But one study here at Pavlov shows maybe some persons use twenty percent," Volodya corrected her.

"Interesting ..." Anne said skeptically. The ten percent figure was cited in at least a dozen international studies. Leave it to the Russians to find a twist. "In either case, a large portion of the brain is under-utilized."

"So empty spaces on scans is brain we do not use?" Volodya asked, his curiosity now fully aroused. What this woman was describing had direct parallels to his own work.

"We are not sure," Anne admitted. "They've found bits of the so-called extra-conscious information stored there."

"What means 'extra-conscious'?" Volodya asked.

"Oh, for example, inherited behavior patterns: maternal instincts, territoriality, sex drives, that sort of stuff. Nothing that would show up on a scan."

"Sex drives?"

Anne thought she spotted a twinkle in his eyes. *The bastard, he's teasing me,* she thought.

Sasha stood up. "I think we're drifting off the subject," she said in Russian. "We'll schedule another briefing session later in the month. In the meantime, there will be no unauthorized visits to the MEG room."

Turning to Anne, she added in English, "Dr. Powell, we thank you for the lecture. Now, let's see what your device can do for our patients."

25

The Russians had commandeered one of their existing procedure rooms, already equipped with an observation gallery,
and their MEG setup looked identical to the MEG room in
Boston, including the wall-sized TV monitor. Anne noted two TV
cameras, one aimed at the patient table, the other at the control panel.

"So we can review the procedure later," Sasha explained. "We
don't want to miss any learning opportunities."

For the first few cases, Anne had Sasha translate everything in each
patient's record, making sure that the criteria of her study were being
met. Sasha did it efficiently if not cheerfully, sometimes adding help-
ful details from memory, since she had been personally involved in the
care of most of the patients. As far as questioning the patients during
the induction phase, Anne had no choice but to rely entirely on Sasha,
since there was no time to translate.

Several times during the day, Baldyuk appeared in the observation
gallery above the MEG room and just sat there, his thick arms folded
across the railing, his beefy face inches from the glass. Anne had an
uncomfortable feeling that he was watching not the procedure, but
her. Sometimes she thought she could hear his nasal wheezing over
the intercom. The sound brought back the gripping feeling she felt in
her pelvis when he tried to kiss her hand in Boston.

She forced herself to pretend he wasn't there.

By 4:00 p.m. they had treated five patients—an excellent day, even by the standards of Anne's experienced crew in Boston.

"Good job!" Anne exclaimed to Sasha as they finished the last patient on the schedule. "If you want, we can grab a cup of coffee and review the results," she added, more as a social overture than a teaching necessity.

"In Russia we take tea," Sasha replied dryly. "Besides, we have one more …"

As if on cue, the door flew open and Baldyuk walked in, followed by two swarthy men, their identical black leather jackets barely disguising the outlines of holstered guns.

"Everything is ready," Sasha said in Russian, jumping respectfully to her feet. She turned to the nurses. "You're done for the day. Lock the outside doors on your way out." Then she turned to Anne. "Our last patient."

Two more guards pushed in a seemingly empty gurney, draped on all sides with white sheets that extended almost to the floor. Anne flashed on her days in the autopsy room. That's how corpses were transported through the hospital—the body was stored on a shelf inside the apparently empty gurney, hidden from view by sheets. She spun angrily toward Baldyuk. "Is this some sort of joke?" she snapped.

"Not joke, Dr. Powell. Our client demands privacy."

The bodyguards drew back the sheets, revealing a stocky man in his late forties, a thick mustache covering his entire upper lip. They pulled him up and helped him swing his massive body onto the gurney.

Anne stared, trying to figure out why the man looked so familiar.

"Isn't this the politician …" she whispered to Sasha, suddenly remembering the face on the billboard outside Moscow.

Baldyuk overheard her. "Vissarion Yossifovich Namordin," he announced with ill-concealed pride. "Communist party candidate. The most influential person in Russian politics today."

Anne watched as "the most influential man in Russian politics" sat on the edge of the gurney, staring aimlessly into space, his thumbs counting his fingers.

"He was treated here for recurrent anxiety reactions, manifesting as phobia of crowds," Sasha said, handing Anne a thick file stamped with large red Cyrillic letters. "Obviously, we didn't cure him yet."

"Did you try combination therapy?" Anne asked, scanning a cover sheet typed in misspelled but understandable English.

"Yes, we did. We also had specialists flown in from Vienna and from London to consult."

"And no success?"

"Nothing. He gets better for a few months, then slips back."

"Any suicidal ideation?"

Sasha pointed to three recent entries in the cover sheet. "Once he survived only because his bodyguard was trained in cardiopulmonary resuscitation."

Anne leafed mechanically through the thick file, even though she couldn't read the hand-written Cyrillic entries. The case was obviously complicated.

Sasha pointed to two more entries. "Please note that he is also prone to homicidal tendencies. He has been in countless brawls, including several where guns were involved. Last month he tried to shoot his campaign manager, but the staff managed to subdue him."

"And this is the man who is running for election?" Anne asked skeptically.

"This is the man who must *win* election," Baldyuk snapped. "Elections are in three weeks. We must make him better. Immediately."

Sasha shifted impatiently. "Shall we put him on the table?"

A voice inside Anne told her that she should take the time to really delve into this man's history before proceeding. *Or was she simply having cold feet because of the man's VIP status?*

"Has he signed a consent form?" Anne asked.

Baldyuk stepped forward. "Dr. Powell, everything is approved," he said in a bored monotone, as if addressing a child.

"So the Institute has the power-of-attorney ..."

"Dr. Powell, we have different laws here. And I assure you, everything is … *normalno.*" He used the word "normal," the traditional Russian descriptor for everything that wasn't hopelessly wrong. "His wife signed. Our patient is ready." Baldyuk's emphasis on the fact this was *their* patient could not be missed.

For a moment, Anne was tempted to demand to see the consent form personally, but she reconsidered. *After all, the Institute was a reputable place, the case had tremendous visibility, and they were not likely to jeopardize …*

"He meets your criteria, Dr. Powell," Sasha said, with an edge in her voice. "Do you see any reason not to treat him?"

"I hope your political views are not interfering with your professional judgment, Dr. Powell," Baldyuk added, drilling Anne with his eyes.

Anne glared back, insulted by his challenge to her professionalism. "Please wait outside," she said coldly. "We'll let you know when we're done." Then she turned to Sasha. "Let's put him up."

They moved Namordin to the table. His neck turned out to be so short that Anne had trouble making his head fit into the clamps. Sasha injected him with the radioactive solution. The C-arms rumbled up to speed. The outline of Namordin's brain appeared on the TV wall.

Speaking in Russian, Sasha started the induction.

"Vissarion Yossifovich, please describe how you felt after your last speech?"

Namordin began humming quietly, but continued to stare into space.

"Did the crowd frighten you?"

Anne could tell from the tone of Sasha's voice that she was in awe of this man. She wondered how she herself would feel faced with a presidential candidate back home. *Probably just as nervous,* she decided.

Namordin hummed louder.

"Were you afraid?" Sasha continued her probing.

Namordin wasn't answering. Anne turned up the depolarization field. The patient's humming turned into unintelligible mumbling.

"Vissarion Yossifovich …"

Suddenly Namordin's body arched. Saliva dripping from his lips, he started rambling, gagging on his own words.

"What's he saying?" Anne asked.

"It's confusing …"

His voice grew louder.

"Something about the war." Sasha glanced at the monitor. "Anything?"

Anne shook her head. She turned up the power another quarter-tesla, but saw nothing that could pass for a specific locus.

Namordin continued struggling in his restraints. His muscles bulged and his limbs bent in unnatural directions.

Concerned that he might injure himself, Anne reached for the control panel. "I think that's all we're going to see today." She started to key in the shut down sequence.

"We're stopping?" Sasha exclaimed. This was not the result they had hoped for. Baldyuk had practically staked his career on the success of the project. Sasha's future depended on his. Failure was not an option.

"We'll try again in a few days. Maybe then …"

Baldyuk's voice thundered from the intercom. "Elections are in three weeks! We cannot wait."

"I gave him the maximal safe dose. We'll have to wait."

Baldyuk wasn't giving up. "There is too much at stake!"

"Yes, there is. His life!" Anne snapped.

"What good is his life without his mind?"

"The answer is no, professor. I will not jeopardize …"

Suddenly, Namordin's face contorted, and he gave another heave. To the sound of splitting plastic, the left arm restraint ripped out of its attachment to the MEG. Two bolts flew up, and cracking like gun shots, snapped onto one of the magnetic pods on the spinning C-arms.

"How in the world …" Anne exclaimed. Of all things that could go wrong with a treatment, a mechanical failure was the least likely.

"Tell him not to move!" she yelled, punching the Emergency Stop button.

Her panic changed to horror as the C-arms continued to spin at full speed. She tried again. The control was useless.

She cursed for allowing the workers to hardwire the unit into the power net. Now the only way to stop the arms was to unscrew the panel, reach the main buss bar ...

Namordin, his left arm now free, rose to a semi-sitting position. The massive C-arms whistled like giant wrecking balls within a hair's-breath of his head.

He leaned forward. The edge of one of the pods hit his head, knocking him back down on the table. He groaned and started to sit up again.

Anne had no doubt that a direct hit would crack the man's skull. An image of Namordin's brains splattered on the wall flashed through her mind. She couldn't believe this was happening. She couldn't allow it to happen.

She dashed out from behind the protective glass panel and ran up to the MEG. Pausing only long enough to match the timing of the spin, like a child waiting to step into a game of jump rope, Anne dodged the C-arms and slid up to the table.

Namordin was sitting up. His bulk dwarfed Anne as she hung her full weight on his shoulders, trying to force him down. To no avail. He shrugged her off and continued to struggle with his restraints. It was just a matter of time until he would free himself, then stand up into the path of the C-arms ...

Damn the hardwiring. There was no plug to pull to stop the machine.

She felt her mind wander under the effect of the magnetic field. *A vision of a church service. A wedding.*

She forced herself to focus on Namordin.

Sasha looked on, the horror of the situation slowly dawning on her. *Namordin could be injured. In her department. In her custody.* This would spell an end to her career, or worse. After all, they were dealing with the same Communist party that just a few years ago had the muscle to make people disappear permanently for much smaller issues.

In the background, Baldyuk's voice was bellowing something on the intercom.

A C-arm grazed Anne's head. She cried out and fell. As she willed herself to get up, she saw Sasha running toward the table, as if in slow motion and, like Anne did seconds earlier, ducking between the C-arms.

"No! Get out of the field!" Anne yelled.

Sasha seemed oblivious to the warning. She locked her arm around Namordin's neck, and twisted him to the side, like a cowboy wrestling a heifer. The two women leaned closer to Namordin, seeking better leverage.

Out of the corner of her eye, Anne saw their three heads clearly displayed on the giant screen: Namordin's in the center, Sasha's and her's near the periphery of the screen, where the radiation was strongest. Her trained eye noted the indicator of field intensity: 95%. Well into the danger zone. She and Sasha were right in the thick of the magnetic field and needed to get out. Fast.

The spinning blue lights of the MEG cut through the darkness, strobing glimpses of Sasha's face.

Anne felt a headache building gradually. Her vision blurred.

Suddenly, she became aware of Sasha's smell. It was something metallic, like the odor of a freshly honed steel blade.

"Sasha, get out of the field," Anne repeated, but her words sounded slurred.

Sasha blinked, but hung on to Namordin's neck. Anne's voice seemed to be coming from far away and the garbled words made no sense. Was it English she was speaking?

Sasha felt Namordin straining against her. The struggle was intoxicating. The feeling of wrestling this man into submission was so sweet, so pleasurable.

Then she saw Anne's eyes. Green. Sparkling. Wet. Sasha was overcome by an inexplicable desire to touch the Americanka. *They were teammates. Fellow warriors, battling a common enemy.*

Totally dazed, Sasha kept staring into Anne's eyes.

The look sent a chill down Anne's spine. Her thoughts were now completely jumbled. She tried to remember why she and Sasha were there, but couldn't. All she knew was that something very wrong and very dangerous was happening. And that she was very afraid of … she didn't even know of what. It was a deep fear that paralyzed her body and her brain.

"Step-out-of-the-field," she repeated, sounding like a pre-recorded announcement.

Sasha just stared.

Somehow Anne summoned the coordination to lean as far back as possible, managing to move most of her head out of the magnetic field.

As her brain began to clear, she realized that she was afraid that the C-arms could hit Sasha. Afraid she and Sasha were being exposed to an overdose.

She looked at Namordin. He was beet red, the veins on his scalp bulging, his eyes glazed over. Sasha's arm was still firmly wrapped around his neck.

She's going to strangle him, Anne thought. She pulled on Sasha's arm.

Anne's touch sent an electric jolt through Sasha's body. Smiling a bizarre smile, she relaxed her choke hold on Namordin.

Anne reached for the broken restraint dangling from Namordin's wrist and tried to reconnect it to the MEG. There was nothing to attach it too. The plastic was shredded.

"It's useless," she mumbled, more to herself than to Sasha.

With a grunt, Sasha pulled the restraint out of Anne's hands, shoved it into place, and held it. "Use my belt," she yelled to Anne.

Anne was already taking her own belt off, but it was made of cloth. Sasha's leather belt would be stronger.

Sasha felt the warmth of exposed skin as Anne reached around her and pulled out the belt. The feeling was tantalizing. Unconsciously, Sasha relaxed her grip and lost control of Namordin. But Anne had already wrapped the belt around the arm restraint and secured it to the table, and Namordin stayed in place.

Sasha cinched the belt so tightly that Namordin's fingers turned white. "He won't move now," she mumbled.

The two women ducked the C-arms and ran back to the control panel. Anne felt an instant relief as soon as she cleared the field, and her thought processes began returning to normal. She glanced at Sasha.

"Are you OK?" she asked tentatively.

"That was a little scary," Sasha admitted, panting slightly from the exertion. "How do we stop this thing?"

Anne dug her nails under the Emergency Stop button trying to pry it loose, but her hands were shaking and it wouldn't yield.

Sasha fumbled under her shirt.

Anne recoiled as a curved knife blade came toward her.

Sasha thrust the knife handle into Anne's hand. "Here, try this."

"Oh!" Anne glanced at the knife, with its intricately carved bone handle and glistening blade. Then she forced the tip under the button and pried the button out. A few drops of liquid filled the button well, and Anne smelled alcohol. Without pausing to decipher the mystery, she teased out the exposed wires and short-circuited them. To her relief, the MEG hummed down to a halt.

The room now silent, they heard someone banging on the door. Sasha opened it. Baldyuk shoved past her and stormed up to Anne.

"What is meaning of this?" he screamed, his face inches from hers, distorted with anger. "You could maybe killed him ..."

Blood rushed to Sasha's head at the site of Baldyuk's outburst against Anne. Without even considering her actions, she forced herself between them and started yelling in Russian.

Taken by surprise, Baldyuk stood speechless, listening to Sasha's angry tirade. Moments later, he turned and marched out of the room. Anne wanted to ask Sasha what she said, but words didn't come.

Sinking to the floor, Anne passed out.

When she came to, Namordin and his guards were gone and she was lying on the MEG table. Her temples were throbbing. There was an ice pack on her forehead, where the pod hit her. Baldyuk and Sasha were talking quietly nearby.

"Good morning," Sasha said cheerfully as she saw Anne sit up.

Anne struggled to remember what had happened.

"How do you feel?" Sasha asked. The cold edge that had been in her voice ever since she met Anne was now replaced by friendly concern.

"A little sore, but OK," Anne replied. "Where's our patient?"

"We sent him away. But you, we should probably admit."

"Not a chance. I'm fine!" Anne exclaimed, swinging her legs off the table and sitting up. She couldn't bear the thought of being hospitalized, for a meaningless reason, on her first day here. The entire episode had been embarrassing enough.

"I feel completely normal," Anne lied, easing herself off the edge.

Baldyuk approached. "I will drive you to hotel," he announced.

"Thank you, but I am going to walk," Anne said in a tone that precluded objections.

"But your head …" Sasha argued.

"All I need is fresh air." Anne turned and headed for the door, thankful that her legs were up to the task. It was the images racing through her brain that were deeply disturbing.

26

As Anne passed the front desk she was vaguely aware of nodding to Natalia, the concierge. Her hands shaking, she unlocked the door to her room and staggered in. The noise of the door slamming shut behind her reverberated in her head like a clap of thunder.

She stumbled toward the bed, shedding her clothes along the way, and fell asleep even before her head touched the pillow.

Then she began to dream.

Fire.

She was running through the burning ruins of a huge house. She knew the mansion belonged to her father, a rich landowner in the Novgorod region. And she knew the year was 1431. She was certain of it, because she had just celebrated her sixteenth birthday.

In the dream, her name was Anytchka.

She saw herself dashing out of the burning building, heavy beams collapsing around her, sending showers of sparks flying through the air. She was coughing violently as the acrid smoke filled her lungs. She was terrified that the charred timbers would soil the beautiful silk dress that her father had brought her from Moscow. *A ridiculous worry,* she realized, *at a time like this.* The Tartars had struck like lightning in the dark of the night, and had been methodically ransacking the village for several hours. *They could find her at any instant.* The stories of what Tartars did to the women of the Russian villages they plundered were too horrifying to think about. *It was better to worry about the dress.*

Then she was standing outside in the field behind the main house, on a small hill. The grass was covered by early morning dew. The early sunrise glowed purple on the eastern horizon. Below lay her home village, its thatched-roof shacks burning like giant torches. From this distance the view reminded her of the hundreds of candles that burned in front of the icons in church on holy days.

She could hear the clatter of armor, men groaning, women screaming. She looked around, wondering where to run. *Where were her parents? What happened to the servants?* She knew only that she had to hide somewhere. *Anywhere.*

She circled the main house, the heat of the fire scorching her face, and ran down the back of the hill toward the stables. She had no trouble finding her way, even in darkness. This was where she used to sneak away, to play with the daughters of the peasants that her father owned. He was a good landowner, well liked by all his serfs. He treated everybody with kindness. *Why did God have to inflict this assault on them?*

She kept running, glancing back occasionally. Once she thought she saw the shadow of a Tartar galloping in the same direction, but he soon vanished into the darkness.

She smelled the stables before she saw them. The familiar warm, pungent smell of hay and manure. Circling around to the back, she slipped inside, leaving the doors open. Only when she heard the quiet, even breathing of the horses, punctuated by occasional snorting, did she feel safe. She sighed, and started to cry.

Streaks of bluish moonlight mixed with the orange glow of the fires found their way through the small windows high up under the roof. As Anytchka's eyes became accustomed to the low light, she went from stall to stall, shooing the horses out into the open, where they would have a better chance to escape the fires and the invaders.

She stopped to touch Orlik, her beloved stallion. "What have we done to deserve this, Orlik? What have we done?" she sobbed as she nuzzled him. His snout felt warm, humid and comforting. She clung to him as tears rolled down her face.

Suddenly, she felt Orlik twitch and draw his ears back.

A moment later, she heard footsteps. Coming closer.

She froze.

The footsteps stopped, then continued around the building. She dashed toward the back of the barn, tripped, fell, started running again ... But it was too late.

The squat frame of a Tartar soldier appeared in the doorway. He wore a leather shirt with a fur vest, and baggy bright blue pants made of rough cloth, cinched around his waist with a wide leather belt. A round wooden shield, decorated with small metal plates, hung casually from his left arm. In the right one he held a curved sword, its wide blade streaked with blood. A long bow and a quiver of arrows were slung over his shoulder. Even from this distance she could smell him—a revolting odor of sweat and horsemeat breath.

He spotted her white dress. She heard him grunt—a grunt of pleasure and anticipation—as he inched toward her. She crossed herself and prayed that death would be swift.

He was halfway to her when she heard hoof beats approaching rapidly. The Tartar hesitated, then turned toward the sound.

The figure of a tall man on horseback, brandishing a lance, filled the doorway. Moonlight streaked through his blond curls. His white linen shirt was covered with a protective garment of finely woven metal mesh that made his wide shoulders seem even more powerful. Anytchka knew he was not a Tartar. But he was not from her village, either.

The Tartar spun toward the young newcomer. *This was her chance.* She started to back away slowly, but fell again. Her right hand came to rest on a smooth handle. *A pitchfork*, she realized.

The rider yelled and launched his horse at the Tartar, who stood motionless, as if inviting the horse to crush him. At the last instant, he stepped aside, and, with a barely perceptible flick of the wrist, slashed his sword across the horse's front legs.

Anytchka uttered a muffled scream. The animal cartwheeled, a fan of blood spurting from its wounds, then collapsed, pinning the rider.

The Tartar sauntered up to the Russian. Agony distorted the fallen rider's handsome young face as he struggled to free himself. Grinning savagely, the Tartar lifted his sword. The young man stopped struggling and closed his eyes.

As the curved blade whistled through the air, Anytchka flung herself at the Tartar.

The sword missed. The Tartar fell, gurgling, his throat pierced by Anytchka's pitchfork.

Anytchka knelt by the rider. Their eyes met. She saw his mouth open and close, speechless, as his eyes scanned her face.

"Who are you?" she whispered.

"Vovka Ermakoff," he managed to whisper back. "Lieutenant to his Excellency Knyaz Grudskoy."

"I am Anytchka, daughter of Yury Vassilievitch Feodorov."

He smiled the most beautiful smile she had ever seen. For a blissful eternity, they couldn't take their eyes off each other. Then they spoke simultaneously.

"I saved you," both said to each other in unison.

"But I saved you first," Vovka added proudly. And then he passed out.

Anytchka ran her fingers through his thick curls. Ascertaining that he was breathing, she turned to the horse. She tore a strip off her dress and bandaged the animal's legs, stopping the bleeding. Then she squatted at Vovka's side and waited for him to come to.

Hours later, Anytchka and Vovka were climbing up the hill toward the smoldering house. The Tartars had been driven out. Russian warriors were helping peasants put out the fires, caring for the wounded, hauling away the dead.

As Anytchka and Vovka approached the charred remains of the

mansion, they saw a column of Russian warriors marching in from the opposite direction. Their red and white pennants fluttered in the morning breeze. Several banners had images of the Virgin Mary and Russian-style crosses: three crossbars, the lowest one at an angle.

At the head of the column, an imposing man in his sixties rode a prancing black stallion. The man's face was dark and furrowed. His eyes were metal grey, like the color of the teardrop helmet that partially covered his large head and thick silver mane. A cold sneer danced on his thin lips.

He wore the traditional battle gear of a nobleman: thigh-high leather boots under a red kilt. A *pantzyr,* a protective metal vest, its plates decorated with gold and silver inlays, shimmering in the light of the rising sun with every breath he took. The folds of his *kolchooga* undergarment, made of thousands of tiny interlocking metal rings, draped his broad shoulders and muscular, hairy arms. A battle-ax dangled from his belt, its curved blade and spike still bloody. The oval shield hanging from the saddle was adorned with a coat of arms: a bear standing on hind legs, holding a cross in one paw and a sword in the other. The shield was crisscrossed by deep gouges, witnesses to fierce combats the owner had faced.

Two warriors marched in front of the leader's horse, holding long poles. Impaled on top of each pole was the severed head of a Tartar chief.

"That is His Excellency Alexandr Ivanovitch Grudskoy," Vovka whispered. "Knyaz of the entire Novgorod area."

Anytchka had heard of the man before. Ruthless, powerful and ambitious, he was feared and hated by all his neighbors. His troops were well trained and fearless, and his lands were the only ones the Tartars avoided on their frequent raids.

"I must go now," she heard Vovka say.

And then she was standing between her parents, in the charred remains of the main hall. Her father wore his long linen *kaftan,* finely trimmed with gold thread, that he wore only on holidays. Her mother, her head covered by her best embroidered scarf, her simple linen dress wrapped tightly around her, was holding a tray with a loaf of bread and a small pile of coarse salt. Anytchka stood next to her mother, clutching a heavy icon of the Virgin Mary of Novgorod.

Grudskoy and a dozen of his men marched in, their muddy boots thundering on the wooden floors, their *pantzyrs* and *kolchugas* rattling ominously.

Grudskoy scanned the room, found the icon Anytchka was holding, faced it squarely, and crossed himself three times. His eyes went back to Anytchka's face, lingering over her delicate features. The huge green eyes, rimmed by long eyelashes. The satin-smooth skin, the cherry-red lips. Her young breasts heaving with every breath …

Turning to her father, Grudskoy said, "Greetings, Yury Vassilievitch."

Anytchka's father bowed deeply, his hand touching the floor. Anytchka had seen him bow like that only in church. "God be with you, Your Excellency Alexandr Ivanovitch."

Grudskoy responded with a lofty nod of the head rather than a full bow. He walked up to Anytchka's mother, broke off a piece of bread, dipped it into the salt and swallowed it, almost without chewing.

"Welcome into our home, Your Excellency," Anytchka's father said.

Servants collected the tray of bread and salt and Anytchka's icon, and hurried off.

"We thank God that you arrived in time," Anytchka's father said.

"It is God's will that we fight the infidels wherever we can find them. Someday Mother Russia will be rid of their scourge." He crossed himself again. "But for now, perhaps the time has come to join our lands, my friend."

Anytchka felt the blood draining from her face. She knew what "joining lands" meant. It meant that her once proud and independent father would become a subordinate to the ruthless *knyaz*. In her eyes, death by Tartar sword was a better fate.

"It would be an honor, Your Excellency," she heard her father answer, in a resigned voice that broke her heart.

She knew that standing there among the ruins of his house, he must have felt utterly incapable of protecting his family and his villagers from other Tartar invasions that would inevitably come.

"Good," said Grudskoy. "I will leave a garrison at your disposal, to protect your village."

And to ensure that her father would be forever under Grudskoy's control, Anytchka added mentally. She dared not lift her eyes off the floor for fear that Grudskoy would see her hate.

"This is my brave lieutenant. He will stay here and be in charge," she heard Grudskoy say.

She glanced up. Grudskoy was pointing to Vovka. She met Vovka's eyes again, but hastily looked away, afraid that someone would notice the spark that passed between them.

"All I ask in return," Grudskoy continued, "is that you send me one hundred bushels of wheat every fall harvest, and fifty fox hides every winter."

Her father bowed deeply. A hundred bushels and fifty hides was nothing compared to what his lands yielded yearly.

"And one more favor I ask of you ..."

Anytchka heard Grudskoy move. She continued to stare at the floor. She saw his bloodstained boots coming closer. She heard his wheezing and the metallic clanging of his *pantzhyr.* His smell reached her nostrils. It was a mixture of stale bread and rusty metal.

She felt a sickening feeling in her stomach as he took her hand and raised it to his lips.

"Yury Vassilievitch, you have a lovely daughter," Grudskoy said, kissing Anytchka's fingers. As his hand came down, it brushed against her breast.

Before she could contain herself, she yanked her hand away and slapped his face, the sound exploding through the quiet hall.

There was a collective gasp, then dead silence. Vovka clenched his jaw.

"God have mercy!" her mother breathed.

Her father dropped to his knees. "Forgive her, Your Excellency!"

A crooked smile crept across Grudskoy's lips.

"One more favor ..." he repeated, touching his cheek where Anytchka's hand landed, his eyes locked on hers. "I want your daughter's hand."

Now her mother fell to her knees. "Please, Your Excellency! She is our only treasure ..."

"She's just a child!" her father pleaded. "She is not ready ..."

Grudskoy squared his shoulders. "Then let the Tartars enjoy her," he snapped, turning and walking away.

He was almost at the door when Anytchka heard her father's voice again, hoarse with tears.

"Your Excellency, please wait."

Grudskoy stopped.

"So be it," Anytchka's father whispered.

Grudskoy turned and smiled. "I'll send for her after Easter. She's a spirited woman," he added glancing at Anytchka. "I like that. She'll give me a brave son. A worthy heir to protect my lands."

Anytchka heard her mother's scream. She tried to run, but Grudskoy's hand dug into her shoulder, pinning her down.

Anne opened her eyes. A hand was still gripping her shoulder.

"Anne, wake up! Are you all right?" Sasha was sitting on the edge of the bed, shaking her awake.

"Oh ... sorry, I was dreaming ..." Anne mumbled. "How did you ...? What are you doing here?"

"You didn't come to work and didn't answer the door. I got worried. The concierge let me in."

Anne realized that all she had on was sheer underwear and quickly pulled a sheet around herself.

"What time is it?"

"Eleven."

"But it's light outside."

"Eleven in the morning!"

"Damn!" She had slept for fourteen hours. Anne rubbed her head, trying to focus. Slowly the dream receded. She was in the hotel room, this was Sasha, they worked together ... "Didn't we have cases to do?"

"It's all right, I cancelled them. There were only four anyway." The thought of getting behind schedule so early in the game bothered Anne. "How about this afternoon?" she suggested.

"You're not in any shape. Besides, the restraint is broken."

"Oh, that's right ..." Slowly, the events were coming back. *Namordin. Broken restraint. Being hit on the head.* Anne grimaced as she sat up.

The danger and adventure they had shared the day before had a bonding effect. Sasha's initial resentment toward Anne was replaced by tenderness. "Hurts?" she asked, reaching toward the bruise on Anne's forehead.

Unconsciously protecting her wound, Anne intercepted Sasha's hand. Sasha's fingers were warm and dry. To her astonishment, Anne felt Sasha's hand wrap around hers. And hold.

The women stared at each other, then, almost simultaneously, jerked their hands away.

Sasha stood up quickly and turned toward the door. "I'll see if I can get the unit fixed and get the patients back on the schedule," she said curtly, trying to hide her embarrassment.

"I'll see you at the Institute, then," Anne replied.

When the door closed behind Sasha, Anne got up. Fragments of the dream whirled in her head: the massacre, the revolting old man, the young Russian warrior who saved her.

Fresh air. She needed fresh air to clear her head. As she stepped out on the balcony, she heard an engine roar to a start and saw Sasha's figure speeding off on a large red motorcycle.

On her way back inside, Anne caught a glimpse of herself in the bedroom mirror. She looked as pale as if she had just seen a ghost.

27

Leaning against the MEG, Anne watched apprehensively as a young mechanic hastily patched the ragged opening, drilled a new hole and reattached the broken restraint with a bolt.

"Don't worry, it will hold," Sasha said, as if reading Anne's thoughts.

"And it's not even made in Detroit," Anne smirked, shaking her head.

"Made in Detroit, assembled in Moscow. A deadly combination," Sasha replied.

The women smiled at each other. Sasha let her smile linger, relieved that Anne seemed to have forgotten the embarrassing hand holding episode that morning.

It was bizarre, Sasha mused. It was as if someone had forced her hand. But she was probably blowing the whole thing out of proportion. *An accidental touch, that's all it was.*

The engineer stood up. "*Gotovo.*" Finished.

"You need a lock washer," Anne said, pointing to the new bolt. Without a lock washer, the bolt would loosen over time. She was determined to avoid a repeat performance.

The engineer said something in Russian.

"He doesn't have one now," Sasha translated. "He'll bring it down later."

No lock washer? A simple two-penny item available in any hardware store. Any home mechanic had a dozen of these things just floating around in the toolbox, for heaven's sake.

The engineer mumbled something else.

Sasha laughed. "He says, don't worry. We used to send cosmonauts into space with less than that."

Four patients, four cures. Despite the late start, their second day went smoothly, the two women already working like a well-trained team.

"Professor Baldyuk was wondering what you plan to do about Namordin's next treatment," Sasha said at the end of the day, broaching the subject carefully.

"I usually like waiting five to eight days between treatments."

"It'd really help if we could do him sooner," Sasha remarked as casually as possible, her apprehension barely under control. Just yesterday Baldyuk had a surprise visit by the party representatives to check on Namordin's status. The heat was on, and getting hotter.

Anne thought for a moment. The episode with Namordin weighed heavily on her mind. Not only had the session been a disaster, but she didn't even get a meaningful glimpse at the scan. She was vaguely aware of seeing the telltale double clusters of atypical schizophrenia, but she couldn't be sure. *What if she waited, only to find that he wasn't treatable? It would be a big disappointment for everyone here. No hope was better than false hope.*

"OK," she said finally. "Let's give him three days. Since we didn't complete the scan, he got a smaller dose, so three days will be enough. Then get a blood chem panel on him, and an EEG, so we can be completely sure he has no residual. If both tests are normal, I'll reconsider."

"I'll pre-order everything tonight," Sasha said, relieved. Anne Powell was turning out to be more reasonable than expected. Besides, Sasha had good reason to know the tests would come back normal.

Sasha glanced at Anne. "Listen, Volodya and I are going to a wedding, day after tomorrow. Why don't you join us?"

Anne hesitated. She didn't enjoy big gatherings, even at home—where she knew everyone. Spending hours with people she didn't know and whose language she couldn't understand ...

"Did Volodya tell you that he rings church bells as a hobby? It's worth the trip just to hear him. He's amazing!"

Sasha was trying to be a good hostess. It would be rude to refuse, Anne thought. *Besides, how often would she have an opportunity to see a Russian wedding?*

"Well, if it won't impose on anyone ..."

"Great! I'll give you directions."

When Anne emerged from the institute, it was snowing. A large red *M,* for Metro, glowed just across the street. She decided to give the subway a try instead of risking the slippery streets, and joined the crowd streaming toward the entrance.

The station itself, Teatralnaya, looked like the lobby of a five-star hotel, complete with marble-clad walls, crystal chandeliers and statues of historical figures. Yet the area was filled with old men and women, selling everything from eggs to flowers. They stood on pieces of cardboard to protect their worn shoes from the cold marble floor, stooped, wrapped tightly in their thin coats, occasionally calling something out to the passers-by, peddling individual bottles of milk, armfuls of freshly baked bread, or what appeared to be lottery or theater tickets.

Anne got in line to buy a ticket—a paper card with a magnetic strip that cost less than thirty cents. The turnstile was a very contemporary photoelectric gate that slammed closed with a fierce bang on those who attempted to sneak through without paying.

Anne stopped in front of a map and realized to her delight that she had no trouble figuring out where to go—letter-by-letter, she was mastering the Cyrillic alphabet. She was even able to decipher a few words on billboards, strangely similar to their English counterparts—*komputer, offiss, faks.* She remembered someone in Boston telling her that even the Russian word for "stress" was *stress. The Russians had adopted the entire corporate package.*

She stepped onto an escalator that was faster, steeper and longer than any she had ever seen. Despite the speed, almost everyone around her hurried down the steps, pushing and shoving. Anne noticed that some of the people were giving her dirty looks.

"*Bystro, bystro,*" somebody shouted angrily. It was one of the first words Anne had learned from her Berlitz tapes: "faster, faster." An obese woman in a blue uniform was leaning out of a glass booth at the bottom of the escalator, shaking an accusing finger at her. Anne could barely refrain from laughing: *The woman was an escalator traffic cop!*

A train rolled in within a minute, steel wheels grinding. She squeezed in with the rest of the commuters, wincing at the mixture of smells that filled the cramped car. She was sandwiched between a neatly-uniformed soldier, stiffly clutching a bouquet of roses as if it were a rifle, and a woman in a mink coat and hat, toting a stylish hand bag in one hand and a knit satchel with a whole plucked chicken hanging out of a newspaper in the other.

When Anne emerged on the street, expecting to be just a block from the hotel, nothing looked familiar. Instead, the exit stairs were lined with dozens of people, each holding puppies, kittens, or birds. It was a pet shop without the shop. One orange kitten in particular gave her a twinge of nostalgia. She stopped to pet it, and wondered how Miles was doing without her. Misty was far better with people than she was with animals.

"*Gde Krasnaya Ploshchad?*" Anne asked the old stooped woman holding the kitten. If she could find Red Square, she could find her hotel.

"Dwenty dollars," the woman answered automatically, with a heavy accent, punching up the last syllables and trusting the kitten into Anne's hands. "Dwen-ty doll-ars."

"*Nyet, nyet.* I mean, *gde Krasnaya Ploshchad?*" Anne tried again.

The woman, disappointed and now totally disinterested, pointed vaguely down the street. "*Tooda idi.*"

Anne set off in that direction, bracing herself against the wind, the back wall of the Kremlin slowly becoming more recognizable in the distance.

As she glanced down one of the side streets, she noticed half a dozen youngsters playing soccer in an empty lot. They were running back and forth, laughing and shouting, oblivious to the cold.

A man was playing with them. As Anne got closer, she recognized Volodya's broad shoulders and erect posture. She watched him race the youngsters to the makeshift goal posts, dribbling the ball around them, teasing, laughing, then letting them steal the ball and bursting out in applause when one of them scored.

She was about to call out to him when two of the youngsters collided and fell. As they rolled on the icy concrete crying, Volodya squatted next to them. He hugged each of them, wiped off their tears and talked about something until the kids calmed down. Then he grabbed them by the backs of their thick coats and lifted them up like two buckets, the boys squirming and laughing, their pain and tears forgotten. He raced toward the goal using the boys' feet like hockey sticks to maneuver the ball, the two youngsters squealing in delight, with the rest of the team in close pursuit.

Anne saw Volodya turn toward the street. She lowered her head and hurried off, hoping he hadn't seen her, hoping she didn't disrupt the moment. As she walked toward the hotel, she wondered whether one of the children was his.

The hotel room felt painfully empty, and she wished she at least had Miles to greet her. She wrapped herself in the soft terry cloth robe embroidered with the Hotel National logo, and ordered room service.

Her mind went back to the near disaster with Namordin. She remembered Sasha's deranged smile, her bizarre look of pleasure while she wrestled with Namordin.

She tried to estimate how much magnetic exposure she and Sasha received. Probably a fair amount. She could send the automatic recording to Boston to verify the exact amount, but it probably wasn't worth the effort. The effects were short-lived. Other than the scare and the embarrassment, no harm had been done.

Room service arrived, filling the room with the aroma of garlic and freshly baked bread. Settling cross-legged on the bed, she uncovered the plates: vegetable soup that was listed as *schi* on the menu, and broiled sturgeon *po Moskovsky*, a generous piece of fish smothered in sour cream and surrounded with tiny boiled potatoes sprinkled with parsley.

While finishing her dinner, she called Halden. It was early afternoon in Boston, and at first Halden sounded distracted, as he often did when she talked to him at work.

"Good … Excellent … I'm glad," he interjected periodically, as Anne described yesterday's events, his mind obviously elsewhere.

"Damn it, Jack. Listen to what I'm saying," she blurted out finally. "The restraint broke. We tried to abort, and we couldn't."

There was a brief pause as Halden began paying attention. "Yes, I see. It could've been a serious problem."

"No kidding!"

"Does Baldyuk know about it?"

"Of course. He was hovering over us the entire day."

"How did he take it?" Halden asked, wondering why he hadn't heard from Baldyuk directly.

"Sasha calmed him down. I think he was more scared than angry."

"Can you still use the unit?" Halden asked.

"They patched it up."

"Great. So you can bring Namordin back right away?" It was more of a statement than a question.

"I had them run a chem panel. Maybe we can do him a little sooner."

There was a long silence on Halden's side.

"I know they're in a bit of a rush on this one, Anne."

"That's too bad. They'll have to wait," Anne retorted.

Halden bit his lip.

"The MEG at the Pavlov is supposed to be our showpiece, Anne. It's the reason you went …"

"The reason I went is to gather data."

"Just remember," Halden said, articulating the words carefully. "Right now the Russians are our only hope of keeping the program out of financial trouble."

"I have no intention of getting the program into *any* trouble.

Either by delaying, or by rushing," Anne answered pointedly. She was already deviating from normal protocol by even considering an accelerated treatment schedule. Halden didn't need to belabor the obvious. She wouldn't be doing it were it not for the extreme urgency she sensed from the Russians, and the high expectations they pinned on the case. But she wasn't about to deviate from safe practice.

"On a lighter note, guess where I'm going Saturday?" Anne asked, changing the subject.

"Where?" he answered absentmindedly.

"To a wedding."

"Wedding? Excellent. Maybe it'll get you into the mood."

"For what?"

"For July 14."

July 14? Bastille Day? Oh, the day she had promised to move in with him! How could it have slipped her mind?

"Jack, we're just moving in together, not getting married."

"I know, I know. Where's your sense of humor?"

"Don't have any, I guess. I'm looking forward to it," she added, concerned that she couldn't muster the enthusiasm that the sentence required.

"By the way," Halden said casually, "I've asked my, uh, your secretary, Lucia, to scout out a desk for you. For your new home office."

"Jack, please keep the staff out of this."

"I figured since Lucia knows your tastes …"

"Let's just wait 'til I get back."

"I'm only trying to please you," Halden said defensively. "I wouldn't do anything definitive without checking with you. Listen, I've got to go. Call me soon, OK? I want to hear how Namordin's next treatment goes," he added, hanging up.

She rolled her shoulders and took a deep breath, trying to relax. She dug in her suitcase, found the stash of gummy bears and treated herself to two large fistfuls. Then, turning the thermostat down to fifty, she crawled under the comforter.

As she started to drift off, she realized that she was looking forward more to hearing Volodya's church bells on Saturday than to July 14.

28

"**G**ood morning," Sasha said cheerfully. "Just waiting for you, so we can start." She had already warmed up and calibrated the MEG, the first patient was on the table, and six more were on the schedule. At this rate Anne would have at least three hundred cases by the end of May or early June.

They moved easily from case to case. Sasha had her questioning down to a fine art, like a prosecutor guiding the defendant to a final confession. All Anne had to do was zoom in on the loci and blast them away.

Around five in the evening, two attendants brought in the last patient.

"Marussya was a 33-year-old housekeeper at the Moscovskaya Hotel," Sasha recited. Anne recognized the woman who kneeled in front of her when she was visiting the patients on Razdin. Emaciated, face drawn, matted hair.

Anne smiled and gave Marussya's thin arm a gentle squeeze.

"*Dobry vecher. Ya doctor* Powell." She turned to Sasha. "How was that for 'good evening'?"

"Starting to sound like a native," Sasha smiled approvingly.

Anne watched attentively as the nurses strapped Marussya into the MEG and injected her with the contrast medium.

"And how can we help Marussya?" Anne asked Sasha.

"She thinks she's the lady-in-waiting to the great-grandmother of Princess Anastasia."

"At least she doesn't think she's Anastasia herself," Anne whispered back.

"They did have one of those here ten years ago," Sasha chuckled quietly. "But somehow she slipped out of the lock-up unit, and they never found her."

Anne wondered whether there was a political reason for the alleged escape. Back under a Communist regime on the verge of collapse, someone claiming to be Princess Anastasia, direct descendant to Emperor Nicholas II, with rightful claims to the throne, might well be treated with a "disappearance."

"Let's see what we can do here," Anne said, heading for the MEG panel.

Marussya turned out to be a difficult case. Anne had to keep turning the field up higher and higher as Sasha did the questioning.

"See?" Anne said ten minutes into the procedure, pointing to the fuzzy highlights on the screen.

Sasha leaned closer. "What?"

"Her memories are in two groups, of about equal intensity. One here." Anne circled a cluster. "That's most likely her dominant personality. I think this other one … it's slightly weaker." Anne pointed to a smaller formation, close to the center of the brain. "This one's probably the locus of her lady-in-waiting complex. Unfortunately, it is partially covered by the dominant one."

"I see," Sasha nodded.

"It's a classic atypical schizophrenic pattern. You have two personalities, but they are overlapping. Ablating the delusional one without damaging the main one is next to impossible."

"So what do we do?"

Anne sighed. "Why don't we ablate what we can … here and perhaps a bit here." She pointed to parts of the locus.

"It'll have to do. Go for it," she added, motioning Sasha toward the control panel.

"You want me to do it?" Sasha said, delighted that soon she would be able to run the MEG on her own.

"Time to start learning."

Sasha grasped the joystick and began maneuvering the cross hairs toward the sharp part of the locus. After a few tries and a nudge or two from Anne, Sasha succeeded.

"Right on!" exclaimed Anne.

Sasha flipped a switch. The blue beams of light emanating from the pods changed to red, indicating that the magnetic fields went into ablation mode. One edge of the locus began to fade.

"That's good. A little more ..." Anne coaxed. "Pretend you're carving a statue out of a piece of marble."

Sasha chipped away until only the fuzzy part of the locus remained.

"How's that?"

Anne smiled, amazed at the ease with which Sasha had mastered the technique. "How do you say 'fantastic' in Russian?"

Sasha beamed. "But we haven't cured her, have we?"

"Nope. With CAS cases—Classic Atypical Schizo cases—it's practically impossible to separate the two clusters. We can't cure her, but what you did will help."

As the nurses helped Marussya off the MEG table, Anne heard the young patient say something in what sounded like Russian.

Sasha spun around, surprise on her face.

"*Shto?*" she snapped at the woman.

A brief conversation followed, the surprise on Sasha's face gradually escalating to astonishment.

"What's she saying?" Anne asked.

"It is not what, it is how she is saying it," Sasha retorted.

"Explain."

"It is ..."

Marussya spoke again. Another brief exchange occurred.

Finally, Sasha turned to Anne.

"For a minute she spoke in Old Russian."

"What's Old Russian?"

"It was the language spoken in the 1600s. No one uses it now, except in churches."

Marussya continued babbling to the nurses.

"She's back to normal now," Sasha said.

"Foreign Language Syndrome," Anne said.

"Foreign what syndrome?"

"Foreign Language. There've been a handful of cases. Two were women, same year, I think in '03 or '04. Each had a stroke, and afterwards one spoke with a British accent, the other with a French accent."

"Why?"

"No one knows for sure. A couple of neurologists thought it was because the stroke wiped out the main language centers, so the women reverted to a former language. Except that neither had been abroad. Although one had a French nanny when she was a year old—too young to learn a language. So who knows."

"And Marussya?" Sasha asked.

"Any chance she had heard Old Russian before?"

"Maybe in church as a child?" Sasha suggested.

"That would make sense. So when the beam was close to her dominant speech center, it must have temporarily deactivated it, so she reverted to Old Russian."

"A delicate balance, isn't it!" Sasha exclaimed.

"Now you see why we can't use the MEG on multiple personalities—you never know when you're going to wipe out something important in the dominant!"

"And if we kept going?"

"We would destroy a lot of things that make Marussya 'Marussya.' It would be like amputating the body to save the leg."

"Whatever it takes!" Sasha joked.

"But I see what you mean," she added seriously.

"Sad to say," Anne said, "there is nothing our MEG can do here. I think Marussya will be on drugs and in an institution for the rest of her life."

"Right," Sasha replied absentmindedly. Her mind was racing far beyond Anne's explanations. *If only she could persuade Anne to be a little more adventurous in her research! The opportunities were endless.*

29

Saturday dawned colder than the day before. The crisp snow crunched under Anne's footsteps.

St. Gyorgy's church turned out to be about a twenty-minute walk from her hotel. *The church, surrounded by dull apartment complexes, was much newer than St. Basil's,* Anne guessed. "Newer" was a relative concept in this city that just recently celebrated its 850th anniversary. Here, "newer" meant that instead of being built when Columbus landed in the New World, St. Gyorgy's was constructed when the Declaration of Independence was being drafted.

The building was freshly painted, its white walls elegantly highlighted by light blue trim. Anne admired the two symmetrical belfries, each topped with an onion-shaped dome painted deep blue and decorated with small gold stars.

By the time Anne arrived, mass had already started. The church was packed. As in all Russian churches, there were no benches, and everyone was standing, except a few ancient women perched on rickety wooden chairs in the back of the nave.

The walls, covered with gold-framed icons, reflected rows upon rows of candles and looked like shimmering golden curtains extending from floor to ceiling. The stained-glass windows cast multicolored shafts of light through the clouds of incense that hung in the air.

The choir was better than any recording that Anne owned—a beautiful blend of male and female voices, interrupted occasionally by a solo with the lowest bass Anne had ever heard.

Trying to be unobtrusive, Anne worked her way through the crowd toward the center of the nave until she caught a glimpse of the couple. The beaming bride wore a simple white dress with a modest short clip-on veil. The groom, in an ill-fitting dark suit, stood ramrod straight next to her. Two young men stood behind the couple holding crowns above the newlyweds' heads.

A priest, flanked by two altar boys, made the rounds of the icons, waving an incense burner and mumbling prayers. His long beard, gold-embroidered robe and massive crown encrusted with precious stones gave him the appearance of a medieval king.

Sasha's face lit up when she spotted Anne on the other side of the church. *She was so afraid Anne wouldn't come. It would have ruined Sasha's day. Now that Anne was there, she could enjoy the ceremony.*

The bells began to toll. Slowly at first, then faster, the rhythm becoming more and more complex. Sasha caught Anne's eye and, pointing up in the general direction of the belfries, mouthed "Volodya."

Anne smiled back, "Nice!"

The ceremony lasted almost two hours. Anne hardly noticed, enthralled by the choir, enjoying the ringing of the bells and following every movement of the priest and his entourage.

The couple walked down the church steps after the ceremony, friends showering them with fistfuls of rice. Then they climbed into a large black sedan sporting two platter-sized, gold-colored rings as a hood ornament. The newlywed's parents and grandparents packed into two subcompacts and the procession drove off, everyone else following on foot. The reception took place in the basement of an office building, the institutional coldness overshadowed by the festive attire of the guests, their laughter echoing in the cavernous room, children running around playing hide-and-seek in the hallways.

Anne noticed that besides gifts, each of the guests brought a home-cooked dish. Soon the folding tables set up in the center of the room were sagging under a staggering variety of food. Bowls of potato salad lovingly decorated with flower-cut radishes; enormous trays of finely sliced salamis, cheeses and honey-cured ham artistically interwoven; plates of smoked fish of several kinds, accented with sprigs of parsley; pickled tomatoes and sauerkraut, wild exotic mushrooms and dishes that Anne didn't venture to identify. There was even a grilled piglet with a baked apple stuffed into its mouth. Bottles of vodka and champagne were everywhere.

Anne wandered aimlessly across the room, feeling out of place. Sasha was nowhere to be seen.

Running a gauntlet of kisses and hugs, the newlyweds made their way to the head of the main table. They looked more like brother and sister, with their matching pink cheeks, light blond hair and innocent blue eyes.

As they were about to sit down, a hoarse voice in the crowd shouted "*Gorko.*" Immediately, other voices responded. "*Gorko.*" Soon everyone was chanting, "*Gor-ko! Gor-ko! Gor-ko!*" Anne looked around, wondering if she should join in. There was something mesmerizing about the chant. Something that sent a chill down her spine.

She heard a whisper in her ear, "*Gorko* means ... how do you say? Not sweet."

She turned around. It was Volodya, his face inches from hers.

"Not sweet, as in bitter?" she whispered back, her breath catching, her whole body suddenly aware of his closeness.

"Yes, yes, yes. Bitter. Guests say wine is *gorko*—bitter. So couple must now kiss and make wine sweet."

Indeed, the groom leaned shyly toward the bride and kissed her on the lips. The crowd cheered and downed their glasses.

"Why do they do that?" Anne asked. "Besides, they're drinking vodka, not wine."

Volodya thought for a second, then shrugged. "Is old tradition."

"Interesting tradition."

"We have many, Dr. Powell."

She felt a shiver as he took her by the elbow and gently guided her toward the tables. "Come, you must drink and eat."

Like his first touch at the airport, the contact felt warm and comfortable. And frightening. She wanted to follow him, to compliment him on his bell ringing, to find out where he learned it, to ask what he was doing with the mice, and how he wound up at the Pavlov, and ...

"Can you tell me where the restrooms are?" she asked instead, and, excusing herself, hurried away.

Disappointed, Volodya watched her disappear into the crowd. *How could she be so aloof? And so impervious to him? It was just a shell,* he decided. *If only he could get past it ...* He was convinced that there was more to Dr. Anne Powell than the cold façade.

Anne lingered in the rest room, the chant reverberating in her head. "Gor-ko! Gor-ko! Gor-ko!" Like the fragment of an unfinished tune, she couldn't make it go away. Bitter, bitter, bitter. *Kisses sweeter than wine* she hummed, an old tune her mother used to sing. *Kisses sweeter than wine.*

By the time she ventured back out into the ballroom, everyone was either eating heartily or dancing.

"Where have you been?" exclaimed Sasha. "And where's your food? You have to eat. Come, let me fix you something."

Sasha pulled her toward the tables, and, oblivious to Anne's protests, filled her plate with generous portions of everything within reach.

"Now I need to go back and help," Sasha said, "but let me introduce you to Valya. She worked on a cruise ship, so her English is pretty good."

Valya turned out to be a voluptuous redhead stuffed into a flowery dress three sizes too small. Her eyes lit up when she heard that Anne spoke English, and for the next twenty minutes she delivered a monologue on everything from her prowess as a cook to her opinions on the dating habits of women who went on cruises. She raised her voice gradually to overcome the noise of the dancing crowd. Anne let her ramble on, grateful that she didn't have to answer. Eventually, Valya drifted off in pursuit of an elaborately attired handsome man in his thirties, and Anne was able to retreat to an inconspicuous chair near the dance floor.

The orchestra consisted of six young men playing drums, guitars and string instruments with triangular bodies. Those must be balalaikas, Anne guessed. At first, the tunes seemed to be nothing more than Russian versions of American hits from the Eighties. The older people sat those out. The younger ones danced with energy but without passion.

As the party wore on, the motifs changed to traditional Russian. It was to these melodies that the guests really warmed up. To her surprise, Anne caught herself humming occasionally, or tapping her foot to the rhythm.

Several times she spotted Volodya, always dancing, always with an attractive woman, sometimes with several. Watching him was an amazing experience. He wasn't just dancing. He *was* the dance. His whole body gyrated to the beat, in the moment, fully engaged.

With sweat pouring down his face, his blue shirt soaked, he crisscrossed the room, oblivious to everything. He squatted and leaped in the Russian Cossack dance, his legs propelling him high up in the air, then folding to the ground, like springs. Or he whirled like a gypsy, his arm wrapped around a slim-waisted companion, his body erect, his head high. And then the music would change, and he would glide elegantly across the floor like a ballet dancer, his toes barely touching the floor, his eyes closed in oblivion.

Mesmerized by his ability to yield to pleasure with such abandon, Anne found herself craning her neck to catch a better view of him among the sea of other dancers. Even sitting still, her body was resonating with his, pulsating with him to the beat of the music, to the power of his animal force.

The tempo picked up. Volodya responded, leaping and twisting, suspended in the air in defiance of gravity. A circle opened up around him, clapping, egging him on.

Anne couldn't take her eyes off him. Suddenly he burst through the crowd and stood before her, panting and grinning.

"Dance with me," he exclaimed, holding out his hand.

Her heart missed a beat, and a long moment passed before she could mumble an answer. "Thanks. I'll … I'll just watch."

"Don't watch, Dr. Powell! Live!"

"No, really …" she looked up, pleading. "I can't. I really can't." She would have loved to share the experience with him. But the thought of looking clumsy, of disappointing him, made her knees weak. "Maybe later," she said.

Crestfallen, he retreated into the circle, scooping up two women along the way, and finished the dance with a new burst of energy, to shouts, cheers and applause. He kissed each of his dance partners on the mouth, and, tossing back his blond curls, wiped the sweat off his forehead.

He made his way back to Anne and sat on the floor at her feet, breathing heavily, dripping with sweat, content.

"Hello," he said simply, looking into her eyes.

She couldn't help smiling. "That was breathtaking."

"Is 'bread taking' good?" he asked.

"Yes. Very, very good."

"Then I am happy."

Somebody handed him a shot glass filled to the brim.

"*Eschtye odnoo!* One more!" he exclaimed, grabbing another glass and giving it to Anne. "Here. We drink to living!"

Tentatively, she raised the glass to her lips and sipped.

"No! All at once! Like this." He dispatched the glass with a single swallow.

She hesitated, then did the same. Tears sprung to her eyes as the chilled liquid scorched her mouth, then burned its way down her throat and into her belly. She had to muster all her willpower to stifle a cough.

Volodya laughed. "Not bad, Dr. Powell. For foreigner."

She glanced up at him, pleased that she was able to live up to the challenge. "My friends call me Anne," she said.

"No, no," Volodya exclaimed, leaping to his feet. "In Russia, to change to first name, we have special drinking."

"What kind of special drinking?" she mumbled, already feeling the first rush of the vodka. *Direct absorption through the lining of the mouth and esophagus,* her scientific brain remarked. She remembered how diabetics in a coma responded to a mouthful of orange juice long before it reached the stomach. *In this case, vodka.*

"We say '*vy*' that is, polite 'you,' to people we do not know very well," Volodya was explaining.

The *vy* sounded very much like the *u* in "ugly," Anne noticed. "And we use father's name," Volodya continued. "So, I am Volodya Yurevich Verkhov, because my father's name was Yury. It means 'Volodya who belongs to Yury.' What is yours?"

"What?"

"Name of your father?"

"Andrew."

"Andrew. Like our Andrei, yes? So I call you 'Anna Andreyevna Powell'."

"I see."

"But for friends, we use first name—Anna, and not *vy* but *tu*. Is like English 'thou'."

Her head was starting to spin as the vodka percolated to her brain. She was listening to his words, but her eyes were on his lips.

"But now I cannot say Anne," he was saying. "I must say Anna Andreyevna. To change to first name, we must have special ceremony."

He banged a knife against a bottle. "Attention, attention." With hoots and cheers, the crowd gathered around them. Bottles were passed until everyone, including Anne, had a full glass. Only Sasha stood empty-handed, her jaw tense, anger and confusion registering on her face. Before Volodya could speak to her, she turned and disappeared.

Volodya faced Anne. "First, we cross arms. Like so."

He held his glass to his lips and guided her arm through his, like two links on a chain.

"Now we drink," he announced his eyes locked on hers. "*Za zdorovye*. To your health."

"*Za zdorovye*," yelled the crowd, tossing back the vodka.

"*Za zdorovye*." Anne braced herself, took a deep breath and swallowed. This time the liquid burned less.

"Now say something bad to me," Volodya commanded.

"What do you mean?"

"Bad. Not nice."

"Like what?"

"Anything. Make insult."

"Why?"

"Why, why! I don't know why. Is tradition. Say it."

"OK. You're ugly," Anne blurted out.

The crowd laughed.

"You are fat," Volodya responded solemnly. "Now we must apologize."

Before she could protest, his lips landed on hers. *So soft, so wet, so unexpected.* She tasted the salt of his sweat. She inhaled his scent of bread and beeswax and honey, now so familiar.

The crowd was cheering—but far away, in a different world.

His tongue was gliding along her lips, probing gently. At first, she resisted. Then her lips parted, letting him in. It was a kiss like none she had ever experienced. She felt the soft inner surface of his lips slipping warmly against the softness of hers, their tongues dancing around each other.

Her body went completely limp. She was glad she was sitting, or she would have sunk to the floor.

The kiss lasted forever, but not long enough. By the time they separated, most of the crowd had already drifted back to the dance floor. Barely breathing, Anne looked at Volodya, wondering what just happened.

He smiled affectionately.

Her legs still weak, she forced herself to stand up. "I have to go now." She hurried toward the door leaning on tables and chairs for support along the way.

Near the exit someone tapped her shoulder. Anne turned.

"You lose this," Volodya said, holding up a rose.

"I ... I don't think that's mine," she mumbled, looking away.

He noticed that she had tears in her eyes. "You were crying?" he exclaimed.

"I always cry at weddings," she lied, trying to sound casual as she quickly wiped her eyes.

"Why?" His mind was suddenly racing. *Did he offend her? Did he awaken some painful memory? Did he breach a boundary that should have remained intact?* "Why are you crying?"

"Tradition," she replied, starting toward the exit again. Her head was spinning more and more from the vodka.

"Dr. Powell. Anne. Wait." *The woman was a total enigma.*

She stopped and turned back. "What?"

"Your lips are not lips of happily married woman," he said softly.

"I'm not."

"Not married? Or not happy?"

She didn't answer. He noticed that she was unsteady on her feet.

"May I take you home?"

"I don't think so."

"Does 'don't think so' mean 'maybe'?" he smiled.

"It means 'no'."

"But I feel, how you say, such *chemistry* for you!" The words came out before he could stop them.

"I'm sure you do. Good old C2-H5-OH."

"H5-OH?"

"It's the formula for ethyl alcohol, professor. Vodka."

He stepped back, hurt. "You are like ... like ... long piece of frozen water, how you say?"

"Icicle?" she suggested, her voice now harder.

"Yes, icicle."

"That's me. Icicle." She wanted to tell him the icicle was trying desperately not to melt. "Bye, Volodya," she said, hurrying off.

At the exit, she turned. He waved good-bye. It was just a tiny, tentative flick of the hand. She froze in mid-step.

"Volodya," she started to say, but he had already retreated into the crowd. His image lingered in her head.

The gesture was so terribly familiar that it made her heart ache.

30

Back at the hotel her bed was neatly turned down, the thick down comforter fluffed up, two Russian chocolate mints and a small card with tomorrow's weather forecast on her pillow. The air vents were blasting and the room was unbearably hot.

Anne found the thermostat and turned it down. She undressed, methodically hanging up each item, then sat on the edge of the bed and ate the mints, savoring each small bite, letting the chocolate melt in her mouth.

Her head was spinning from the vodka. The room was still too hot. She turned off the lights and opened the door to the balcony. The blast of cold air made her skin tingle. Goose bumps spread down her arms and legs. She stayed out until the chill penetrated her, then went back in and crawled under the comforter, enjoying its softness and the now welcome warmth.

Soft singing and the plaintive sounds of an accordion came through the open doors. The music reminded her of Volodya. *He is probably still there,* she thought. *Still dancing, women all around him.*

She stared at a thin crack in the ceiling and tried not to think. Suddenly she tasted salt on her lips. *His sweat.* She could feel the kiss again, as vividly as if he were in bed next to her. *His soft wet lips blended with hers.* She closed her eyes.

More music and laughter drifted from outside, surrounding and over-whelming her. Someone was shouting *"Gorko! Gorko! Gorko!"* It sounded like a "Kill! Kill! Kill!" cry at a lynching.

Suddenly she saw Anytchka, her face pale, her lips drawn, her eyes red and swollen. The room filled with bearded men dressed in long tunics embroidered with gold brocade. Many wore tall fur hats. Some had massive gold crosses hanging from their necks on heavy gold chains. Anytchka knew they were important people. She had seen several of them before in the church of the Holy Ascension, when her father had taken her to Moscow during one of his trips.

Blazing torches in the corners of the room cast their flickering light on long oak tables sagging under the weight of huge jugs of wine, whole roasted pigs and loaves of bread the size of cart wheels.

"Gorko! Gorko! Gorko!"

Kill! Kill! Kill! Anytchka stood in the middle of the room, her face now covered by a white veil, her bowed head adorned by a white silk tiara—the *kokoshnik*—embroidered with precious stones. A parting gift from her parents. She was weak from sleepless nights spent crying and had to lean against the table for balance.

Anytchka's father and Grudskoy stood nearby. Grudskoy wore a groom's silk caftan and a long tunic of Persian lamb, cinched with a thick leather belt adorned with gold studs and a gold buckle.

The two men bowed to each other, then kissed three times, alternating cheeks. Grudskoy raised a jug filled with wine, and his voice boomed over the noise of the crowd. "May the union of our lands last as long as the union of our families."

"Gorko! Gorko! Gorko!"

Grudskoy crossed himself. "And, God willing, may your daughter give me the male heir that I want."

"Gorko! Gorko! Gorko!"

Grudskoy turned to Anytchka. He paused for a moment, then tore the veil off her face, thrust her chin up, and crushed his mouth against her lips.

The crowd went wild. *"Gorko! Gorko! Gorko!"*

As Anytchka felt her body forced against Grudskoy's, her mind drifted away. All she could see were the torches. Blurred by her tears, their light shimmered like a solid wall of fire.

Then there was only darkness and the thumping of hooves muffled by deep snow, and the tinkling of the tiny bells slung under the horses' yokes.

The troika of black stallions galloped along the winding road, steam bursting out of the animals' nostrils, clouding up in the icy air. Anytchka felt Grudskoy's bulk slamming against her as the sleigh carriage bounced precariously over snowdrifts.

A few times she caught glimpses of Vovka galloping alongside at the head of the honor guard, staring straight ahead, afraid to look at her.

The carriage made a sharp turn into Grudskoy's estate and came to a halt. Anytchka saw servants with torches running out to greet their master and his new bride.

Vovka's horse reared to a stop. He leaped off, dashed to the carriage, and swung the door open. Grudskoy emerged carrying Anytchka in his arms like a trophy, his boots digging deeply into the fresh snow.

Risking all, Anytchka managed to slide her finger along Vovka's hand as he stood holding the door open. Their eyes met and held, as Grudskoy carried his new possession into the house.

Just when Anytchka was about to disappear from view, Vovka ventured a furtive wave of the hand. A hopeless farewell.

Anytchka heard a voice murmuring reassuringly into her ear, as a comb ran gently through her hair. It was Nyanya, her new lady-in-waiting. She was taller than most women Anytchka had known. Her peasant dress concealed what once may have been an attractive body. Her ageless face looked serene. She moved with the calm, deliberate rhythm of someone whose inner peace could not be shattered by anyone.

Nyanya removed Anytchka's outer garments. "Be brave my child," Nyanya whispered, seeing the fear and despair etched on Anytchka's face. Quickly wiping her own tears with the corner of her caftan, she added, "It's God's will that you be Alexandr Ivanovitch's faithful wife."

"But it is not him that I love," cried Anytchka.

Nyanya placed a finger over the young bride's lips. "*Sterpitza, slyubitza,*" she said, repeating what Anytchka's mother and grandmother were fond of saying. "As you learn to bear it, you'll learn to love it."

Heavy footsteps thundered through the hall, and the door burst open. Grudskoy stepped in, ducking his head under the low doorsill. Nyanya bowed and, holding her head low, hurried out, silently closing the door behind her.

Grudskoy strutted up to Anytchka.

"It's time," he said hoarsely.

Anytchka looked up. Instead of fear, her eyes were full of hatred.

In one swift motion, Grudskoy ripped off her camisole, exposing her body. Anytchka gasped, but kept staring defiantly.

He let his eyes feast on her firm white breasts, her soft flat belly, her round hips and long muscular legs. Then he shoved her, and she fell backwards onto the bed. He grabbed her ankles and pushed her further up, the rough bed sheet scorching her back and buttocks.

As she lay naked and motionless, he slowly unfastened his belt and let his heavy tunic drop to the floor. Wheezing with the effort, he climbed on the bed and straddled her. Anytchka felt his breath, a mixture of vodka and something metallic.

The golden cross on his neck dug into her breast as his body crushed her. Moments later, he rammed himself into her, and her mind went blank.

He moved back and forth a few times, then stopped.

Something was wrong.

He rolled off, grunting. Anytchka felt him spreading her legs, tugging painfully at her hair, probing her with his thick coarse fingers. Moments later, he leaped off the bed.

And then a scream of inhuman rage pierced her ears and echoed through the house. Reverberating, growing, drowning everything.

The rest of the night was a blur. Hunched figures scurried back and forth by candlelight, like ghosts in a nightmare. Anytchka lay on the bed naked, as two old women poked unceremoniously between her legs, shaking their heads and mumbling.

Grudskoy was pacing the length of the small room like a caged animal, a gray-haired monk trotting behind him, prayer book in hand.

An old man-servant limped into the room.

Grudskoy stopped pacing. "What the hell took you so long?" he bellowed.

"I came back as fast as I could, Your Excellency," the old man mumbled, panting and bowing. He opened the ragged folds of his caftan and pulled out a scrawny chicken. "I had to go all the way to ..."

"Shut up and do it, old man!" Grudskoy yelled.

The man pulled out a knife, and with one swift stroke beheaded the chicken. The bird flapped aimlessly as blood spurted out of its severed neck.

"It will look just like the blood from her maidenhood, Your Excellency," the man mumbled, letting the blood spill on the sheets.

Too terrified to move, Anytchka felt the hot sticky liquid squirt on her thighs. The foul smell overwhelmed her.

The sheet properly stained, the old man re-wrapped the dead chicken in his caftan and left. Nyanya and the two old women helped Anytchka off the bed, collected the sheets, then laid her back down on the bare sack cloth covering the straw that served as a mattress.

"We will hang the sheets tomorrow, Your Excellency, so they can all see that she was a proper virgin. No one will suspect," said one of the old women.

"Out, all of you!" Grudskoy bellowed.

Bowing deeply, the staff backed out of the bedroom.

Anytchka opened her eyes and saw Grudskoy's hulk towering above her, his eyes full of fury.

"Who?" he roared.

She turned her head away.

He grabbed her by the hair and pulled her up. "Who deflowered you?"

She glared back defiantly. "Nobody."

"Liar!" He smashed his fist against the bedpost, cracking it. "Tell me who it was. I'll kill him."

Anytchka shuddered. "I was born like this."

"You're lying, bitch."

She tried to shake her head, but his thick fingers were still entwined in her hair.

"Swear to it," he ordered. "On your mother's life!"

"I swear," she whispered, closing her eyes and praying that God would forgive her lie.

He dropped her on the bed. "If you ever look at another man, bitch, you'll regret it." His face was inches from hers. "Forever!" he hissed. "Do you understand? Forever, 'til the end of time! It will haunt you in this life and the next. So help me God!"

He picked up her camisole off the floor and tore it into long strips. Seizing her hair again, he rolled her face down, pinning her with one knee against her back. Anytchka tried to struggle but she was no match against Grudskoy's muscular frame.

"I expected a virgin," he grunted, tying the cloth strips to her wrists and ankles. "You've spoiled it. You'll pay for it."

She felt herself immobilized, spread-eagle, as he cinched the strips to the bedposts. Even petrified at the thought of what he was going to do to her, she still refused to give him the satisfaction of begging or crying.

His full weight knocked the breath out of her.

She felt his hands grabbing her buttocks, pulling them apart. Then a searing pain tore through her body like a branding iron, and she felt her flesh ripping where he penetrated her, her pelvic muscles going into spasm, her bladder contracting, her urine running out against her will, her womb imploding with pain ...

No longer able to control herself, Anytchka let out a gut-wrenching scream and passed out.

Anne leaped out of bed, twisting her ankle. Oblivious to the pain, she stumbled into the bathroom and fell to her knees in front of the toilet bowl. She vomited, the bitterness filling her throat and nostrils.

She felt an unbearable burning pain in her pelvis. Spreading, gripping, paralyzing. The same pain she had in her dream. The same pain that had plagued her for as long as she could remember, this time stronger than ever.

She clung to the cold porcelain, whispering over and over, "Please, stop. No more pain. I can't … Please, no more …"

What seemed like hours later, she struggled up off the bathroom floor. Her whole body was shaking and she had to hold on to the sink to keep from falling. Her heart pounded erratically, and cold sweat was beading on her neck.

Feeling an intense urge to urinate, she sat on the toilet, but could not make herself relax. She ran warm water into the tub and crawled in. Fragments of the dream, mixed with images of her father abusing her mother, flashed through her head in a painfully vivid kaleidoscope.

The bitter taste of vomit lingered in her mouth. *Bitter. Gorko. Grudskoy's lips. Stale, smoky, metallic.* The memory sent another wave of pain through her lower body.

She got out of the tub, turned on the faucets and tried to urinate again. This time she succeeded, welcoming the relief.

Her ankle still throbbing, she limped out of the bathroom, past the bed, and out onto the balcony.

The sounds of the accordion were gone. Everything was quiet. The bells on the Spasky Belfry of the Kremlin struck 3:00 a.m.

She stood still, letting the cold permeate her body, gradually regaining her composure. She heard the bells again. 3:15 a.m. …

She was as cold as an icicle. She stepped back inside and closed the doors. Trying not to look at the bed for fear it would remind her of the dream, she staggered into the bathroom and eased herself back into the tub, letting the still warm water scald her frozen skin.

She lingered in the tub until the water turned cold and her skin wrinkled like an old woman's, and the light of dawn started to seep into the room. Only then was she able to crawl back into bed and close her eyes.

31

Anne woke up at noon to the sound of Sunday church bells. Fragments of the dreadful dream still churned in her mind. Without even thinking, she reached for a Luna candy bar but stopped herself. Instead, she got out of bed, pulled on her running suit, grabbed her hotel key card, the phone card, a few sheets of toilet paper—just in case, and a wad of rubles. Then she ran down the stairs and went outside.

A blast of frigid air burned her cheeks, but the closely fitted Lycra suit held up well. The doorman, cocooned in a thick coat, eyed her appreciatively, then shook his head and wrapped his arms around himself, pantomiming, *Too cold!* Anne tossed her head back and forced a smile. *Nothing can hurt this girl.*

She crossed Manezhnaya Ploschad and broke into a run toward the Kremlin, steam billowing from her mouth and nostrils. She traversed Red Square, dodging tourists who posed, shivering, for the traditional photographs with St. Basil's Cathedral in the background.

After she rounded St. Basil's, at the far end of Red Square, the crowds thinned and she picked up speed. Within a mile, Anne warmed up and started to sweat. She felt the endorphins flowing through her, helping her mind relax.

Funny thing, she thought. The brain can be the source of such intense inner torment one moment, then heal itself the next, sealing off painful events as if they'd never taken place. *It's the only organ in the body that has no nerve endings of its own and feels no pain,* she mused, remembering how shocked she was during the first brain surgery she witnessed: the patient, his skull open, was awake and responding while the surgeon poked around.

Down Armyanskaya, across the Beregovoy Boulevard, and on to the wide tree-lined sidewalk that ran along the Moskva River.

It was a beautiful stretch. The waterfront was deserted. The water, black and sprinkled with broken sheets of ice, reflected the low sun peeking through heavy bulbous clouds. The trees, denuded of foliage, created a tortured frame for the Kremlin walls towering above her. It was so different from her Charles River run, and yet so familiar.

She crossed a massive bridge, its red brick bulk probably dating back several centuries. An hour and eleven minutes later she had completed the loop. Her whole body was steaming like a bowl of freshly boiled vegetables.

Later that day she called Misty.

"I'm so sorry I missed you," Misty's husky voice, doing its sexy best, came from the answering machine. "Tell me who you are and I'll call you right back."

"Hi, it's me. Nothing important. I'll try you …"

"Hello, hello, hello. Don't hang up. I'm here."

"Hi. Screening your calls?"

"In bed."

"It's noon."

"It's Sunday." Anne heard Misty stretching sleepily. "It's good to hear from you. How've you been?"

"Adjusting. Little by little."

"Oh, yeah. I like little by little," Misty mumbled, her voice thick and low. "Little by little."

Anne heard moaning. "What was that?"

"Uh, nothing …" There was giggling in the background.

"Maybe I should call later."

"No, no, it's OK. I'll send him out." There was more giggling, then the sound of a wet kiss, then the door closing.

"Was that Angelo?" Anne asked.

"Oh, God, no. He's history. That was Ramman. I just met him. He's from Morocco."

"You're such a slut," Anne teased.

"Have to be. Making up for you."

They laughed.

"Listen," Anne said more seriously, "have you ever heard a story about a young woman who married a powerful old man ..."

"It's in every issue of *People*."

"No, seriously. Something old, like a fairy tale. Maybe from a movie that you and I might have seen. Or a book."

"Hmm. No, can't say that I do."

"Something with a Russian setting," Anne persisted. "*Brothers Karamazoff, Crime and Punishment, Anna Karenina*?"

"You're the literate one. I read the Cliff's notes."

"Try to think."

There was a pause.

"Talk to me, Annie. You didn't call to discuss literature."

Anne debated what to share.

"It's nothing. I just w..."

"Bullshit. What's up?"

"Well, I had this dream. Actually, two dreams."

Anne gave Misty a brief summary, omitting the more graphic details.

"Girl, what *have* you been drinking?" Misty exclaimed when Anne finished. "Sounds like one of my romance novels!"

"I figured it was something I read."

"Well, be sure to let me know. I want to read it too," Misty laughed. Then she added more seriously, "So now you're wondering where this stuff came from?"

"Exactly. It was too ... too organized for me just to have dreamed it up."

"No pun intended?"

"I figured it was from something I've seen or read, but I couldn't come up with anything. It was definitely in Russia. I know, because I remember seeing those three-piece crosses they have around here. And I remember the name Novgorod."

"Well, you're in Russia. What do you expect?"

Anne sighed. *Misty was going to be of no help.*

"Maybe it was a movie you saw?" Misty suggested, sensing Anne's frustration.

Movie. Period movies were her favorite, but she'd remember a movie. More likely it was from her Eastern European literature class in college. An obscure passage in War and Peace? It'd have to be something that one of the characters was recounting from past history rather than the main story of the book, because the setting was 1431—four centuries before Leo Tolstoy's masterpiece. Or ...

"Pushkin?" Anne asked, more of herself than of Misty.

"Never heard of it."

"Him. Famous Russian poet."

It could've been Pushkin. Killed at the age of thirty-eight in a duel defending his wife's honor, Pushkin's work spanned time periods and styles that rivaled Shakespeare's. Her dreams could be her brain's interpretation of one of Pushkin's fairy tales.

"Or maybe you're remembering stuff that your Russian uncle told you," Misty suggested.

"He was a grand-uncle, not uncle. And I was barely three when he was around. How would I remember anything he said?" Anne felt a shiver of aversion at the mere mention of that relative of her mother's. "That makes no sense, Misty. Why would you even say a thing like that?"

"Take it easy, I'm just trying to help. Listen, if you're so convinced it's something you read, why don't you look it up?"

"That's exactly what I was thinking."

"Why am I not surprised? I know you. If you don't find the answer, you're going to stew for months."

"I guess I need the books."

"Or simpler still, you could ask one of the Russians."

"I could ask Volodya," Anne mused.

"Right. Ask her." Misty's attention was drifting again.

"Volodya is a 'he'."

"Ah, a 'he'." Misty's attention snapped back. "Handsome?"

"He thinks so."

Ask Volodya. Oh, yeah, that would work, Anne thought sarcastically. Excuse me, Dr. Verkhov ... Oh, pardon me. Volodya. I know it's Volodya, because we kissed on it. So, Volodya, do you know any fairy tales about beautiful maidens married to disgusting old men but in love with stunning young warriors?

It sounded like a bad pickup line.

She actually kissed the man! She should have stayed close to Sasha at the wedding and passed on the vodka. The episode with Volodya would never have happened if she were sober. It was obvious that all the man wanted was to be able to brag to his friends—in the gym, or in the sauna, or wherever Russian jocks hang out—about scoring with an Americanka. Well, she wasn't going to become a notch in his belt.

She would ask Sasha.

"Anne, you there?"

"Sorry, just thinking. You'll never believe what this guy did. A colleague invited me to a wedding ..."

She told Misty about the kiss.

"Wow!" Misty exclaimed. "You sure he didn't make it up just so he could kiss you?" she added skeptically.

"It crossed my mind. But the other guests seemed to go with it."

"That's *so* sexy! Maybe I'll start the custom here. 'Hi, my name is Misty. Kiss me.' What a great way to screen your prospects. I love it! Was he a good kisser?"

"Stop it."

"I want to know. I never had a Russian. Good lips?"

Soft, slow, sweet. Anne felt herself blushing. "Sweaty."

"Sweaty could be nice. You going to see him again?"

"Misty!"

"What did I say?"

"I feel guilty enough."

"For what?"

Anne hesitated. "I feel guilty because I didn't feel guilty," she said quietly.

32

"I have Comrade Namordin's results," Sasha announced cheerfully on Monday morning, handing Anne a slip of paper.

Anne studied the printout. Latin-based abbreviations were used the world over. The "K" for potassium, or *kalium,* as it was called in Latin, was 4.5 mg%. Normal. So were the rest of the electrolytes. 'Cr', or creatinine, a product of muscle or brain tissue breakdown, was only slightly elevated, indicating that whatever damage had occurred during treatment was healing rapidly. The EEG showed no evidence of residual cytoplasmic damage—smooth alpha waves, no dielectric dips.

The only value that didn't make sense was the "P." Phosphorus. It was a component of the myelin insulation around neurons, and, in Anne's experience, it always stayed elevated for weeks after a treatment. And yet here it was, 39 mg%, WNL—within normal limits.

"That's strange ..." Anne started to say.

Sasha interrupted. "Yes, the phosphorus should have been higher. I already told them to run it over," she added, seething inside about the slip-up. Her instructions to her contact in the lab were to make the panel look normal for someone who was just MEGed, not textbook-normal.

Anne handed the sheet back to Sasha. "If the phosphorus checks out OK, we can do him again tomorrow." *Mistakes happened. Even at the great North Boston Medical Center. One wrong result shouldn't cast a shadow on the entire panel.*

"If that's acceptable to you," Sasha said politely, mentally congratulating herself. Although delayed by a few days, the project was back on course.

While Sasha went around the room shutting down the video cameras and removing, labeling and storing the tape recordings of the procedures, Anne slipped a disk into the drive at the control panel and punched a few buttons.

"By the way," she asked Sasha, while she waited for the material to download from the main drive, "how well do you know Tolstoy's *War and Peace?*" She figured the thousand-page masterpiece spanning an entire generation of Russian culture was a good place to start looking for Grudskoy and for Novgorod.

"Embarrassing, but I haven't read it. Why do you ask?"

"Oh, I'd love to be able to read all those classics in Russian some day," Anne answered vaguely. Sasha was going to be of no help. *She would have to look things up in the library,* Anne decided. *A good project for the weekend.*

"*War and Peace* didn't do much for me," Sasha continued. "I didn't really care for the 1800s. I was more interested in ancient times. Ivan the Terrible was my favorite," she added with a small giggle. "I took a lot of teasing for that."

"I know about teasing," Anne smiled back. "How do you tell your friends you like magnets better than dolls?"

They exchanged a glance of mutual understanding.

Suddenly Sasha felt closer to Anne than practically any woman she could remember. That puzzled her: just a few days ago Anne was nothing but an unwelcome threat to her authority. And now ...

"What are you doing tonight?" Sasha asked.

"Dinner, reading, phone calls ..."

"A bunch of us are getting together to play soccer."

"In this weather?"

"In Moscow, if we waited for weather, we'd be indoors year

'round. Besides, it's about the only thing most of us can afford. Movies are expensive, theater tickets almost impossible to get ... Why don't you join us?"

"I've never played soccer," Anne said, fishing for excuses.

"Don't worry. If you can walk, you can play. The only one who's any good is Volodya. The rest of us just kick the ball."

Why not, Anne thought. She was going to be in Moscow for months. It would be good to be someplace other than the Pavlov or the National. And it's not like she would be forced to interact with Volodya. There would be plenty of people there. "I guess I can try."

"Good. Let me tell you how to get there. Go two stops past the station where you'd get off to go to the National. Walk back four blocks, turn left ..."

"I think I know where that is. I've been lost there before," Anne remembered. "Actually, I think I even saw Volodya playing there ..."

"You did?" Sasha felt a twinge of jealousy. "What did you do with him?" she blurted out before she could check herself.

"Nothing. I didn't even stop ..."

The computer chimed as the download was completed.

"I need to overnight this to Boston," Anne said, ejecting the disk and placing it in a padded envelope.

"I'll take care of it." Sasha slipped the envelope into her pocket. "What's on it?"

"Sample scans. I like our electronic wizards to run tests once in a while," Anne added vaguely. "To make sure there're no surprises lurking in our little black box."

33

The Pavlov soccer players were a motley crew—a dozen men and women, old and young, many obese, some clumsy, others athletic and experienced—who looked forward to chasing a ball around the dimly lit lot, sliding and shouting and laughing, the stresses of daily life forgotten.

Volodya and Sasha always played on the same team. A perfectly matched pair who communicated with nothing but glances and nods, they effortlessly outmaneuvered, outran and outlasted their opponents.

Today, despite Sasha's recent sleepless nights and several bouts of headaches, the two were as good as ever. Sasha headed the ball to Volodya. He leaped high into the air, bounced the ball off his chest, trapped it with his foot and returned it to her further downfield. With a fake to the side, she sped toward the goal, dribbling past opponents as if they were frozen still. Barely touching the ball with her instep, she passed it back to Volodya. He lunged right, hauled back, and took the shot, drilling the ball between the two trash cans set up as goal posts.

"Go-o-o-o-oal!" the players yelled in unison.

Sasha smiled. They were good. Good on the soccer field, on the dance floor, in bed.

Moments later, as Volodya ran across the lot, the ball again in his control, Sasha spotted Anne. *Yes! Anne made it.* Now Sasha could learn more about her new colleague. *Perhaps teach her a few moves. Chat.*

"Everybody, this is Dr. Powell," she shouted in Russian.

"Hello." "Welcome." "How do you do," responded a chorus of voices. Anne recognized a few faces, including Igor, the cheerful round-faced man who brought patients down from Razdin, his hairy belly now protruding over his belt, and the tall red-headed nurse, Irina, who was in charge of vital-signs monitors and now had a cigarette dangling casually from her thin lips.

Seeing Anne, Volodya stumbled and almost lost the ball to Igor. Recovering, he tapped the ball into the air and headed it toward Anne. Caught by surprise, Anne stepped back awkwardly. The ball bounced off her chest, dropped at her feet and rolled into the gutter.

"Oh, sorry," she stammered. *Nice start. She should have stuck to running.*

Sasha winced. *Anne was her guest, not his. What business did he have passing the ball to her? Next thing you know, he'd ask her to be on their team.*

"Anne, please play our side, yes?" Volodya said, retrieving the ball and rolling it back to her, this time gently.

Sasha felt her lips tightening. *How predictable. How inappropriate. Was he interested in this woman? Stupid question. He was interested in them all. Normally, that was fine. Except in Anne's case. She was a guest. Her guest.*

"I have a better idea," Sasha said icily in Russian. "Anne and I will join Igor's team against Volodya's. So it won't be so one sided." She turned to Anne and pointed out the players on their team. Then she added, "It's like hockey. Just push everybody aside and ram the ball into that goal, and don't worry about anything else. Here we go."

At first Anne felt that her feet were going in all directions on the slippery asphalt. But soon she was kicking competently, if not skillfully, her stamina and long legs compensating for her lack of technique, and her shyness overcome by the thrill of a new game.

Ten minutes into the game Anne was already sweating. She ran to the sidelines and pealed off her down parka. Sasha found herself admiring Anne's tightly fitting green and white Lycra top as it glistened under the fluorescent glow of the street lights, outlining Anne's elegant shape. *Nice shoulders. Nice legs. Most American women probably weren't in such good shape. Certainly very few Russian women were.*

Anne threw the parka on a bench and ran back into the game. And came face to face with Volodya. He was toeing the ball absent-mindedly, watching her.

Anne sensed an opportunity. Looking in the opposite direction and feigning disinterest, she rushed the ball, reaching for it with her leg. But even distracted, Volodya was quicker. Rolling the ball back with the tip of his toe, he tapped it, bounced it off his heel and sent it sailing over their heads. Before Anne could figure out where the ball went, he recaptured it behind her.

"Quit clowning and play!" Sasha yelled in Russian.

Oblivious, Volodya danced around Anne, his toes barely touching the ball, the ball moving obediently back and forth around Anne's feet, tantalizingly out of reach.

He made it seem so easy, so effortless. She was going to get that ball, if it was the last thing ...

Anne made another wild stab, but again Volodya's foot pulled the ball back.

"You must move only very, hmmm, very little ... How you say, like kiss?"

If he means "gently," it's not what he's going to get, Anne thought as their eyes connected. *The bastard was teasing her.*

She stopped dead and dropped her arms by her sides in mock resignation. Then, still looking into his eyes, she suddenly stepped toward him, her body almost touching his, reached her leg as far as she could between his, twisted her foot sideways, connected with the ball ...

"Like this?" she asked innocently, stealing the ball and sending it toward Igor.

Volodya's eyebrows shot up. Several players laughed.

"Americanka is good!" Igor yelled, passing the ball to Sasha.

Moments later, as Volodya ran in front of her, Sasha turned and, as if by accident, rammed her elbow into his ribs.

"Oh, I'm so sorry," she said with a glacial smile.

"What's wrong with you?" Volodya mumbled, rubbing his side.

Sasha shot him a furious look. *Wrong? Absolutely nothing. What could be wrong? She brings Anne down here, wants to teach her soccer, and this bastard steals her. What could be wrong with that?*

Her angry thoughts were interrupted by a bell that rang nearby.

"*Khvorost!*" someone yelled, and, like a beehive, the players abandoned their positions and raced toward the approaching vendor's cart.

Within minutes, everyone was eating. Anne watched as the old man dropped strips of dough into boiling oil, then skillfully fished them out with a homemade ladle, dipped them in a pot of honey and passed them around. *Russian churros*, Anne thought.

"This one is yours," Sasha said, handing Anne a crisp golden brown strip dripping with honey.

Anne bit into it, mentally counting the calories, but pleased to be treated as if she were a member of the team.

"You deserve it. You played great," Sasha added, giving Anne a quick hug.

"Perhaps drink?" Volodya suggested, approaching them with a bottle of vodka. "Make food better."

"At least get a glass for Dr. Powell," Sasha chastised him.

"I am sorry," Volodya mumbled, embarrassed, giving Sasha a perplexed look. *She knew they had no glasses. They always drank from the bottle.*

"Go see if the vendor has one," Sasha said sharply, pleased to be able to embarrass Volodya in front of Anne. *Serves him right for flirting.*

"Forget it," Anne said quickly. "It's no problem." She mouthed the bottle, took a tiny swallow and passed it back. "I can drink from a bottle with the best of them," she lied, suppressing a cough.

Volodya gave her a grateful look and moved on.

"He's such an oaf," Sasha said watching him disappear into the crowd. "But what do you expect from someone who spends his life playing with rats?" She changed the subject. "By the way, you were right."

"About what?"

"I called the lab after you left. The phosphorus on our star patient was really 90, not 40. A lab error, as you expected." She casually took another bite of her pastry.

Anne chewed on her lip. She didn't know why, but she still had an uneasy feeling in her gut. Yet there was no objective reason to delay Namordin's treatment.

"OK, bring him in tomorrow," she said finally.

"Great. I'll put him on the schedule. You've no idea what a relief it's going to be for the professor," Sasha said. *You have no idea what a relief it is for me,* Sasha added mentally.

As for the safety of MEGing Namordin again, even if his brain hadn't completely healed yet, Sasha had no worries. She had done her research. The worst that could happen to the man would be minor damage to the motor cortex. *So what? If Roosevelt could run America from a wheelchair, Namordin could be a Communist party puppet on crutches.*

A bucketful of pastries and a bottle of vodka later, the group resumed the game with the same enthusiasm, if not with the same coordination.

"Anne, to you!" Sasha yelled, sending the ball across the field.

Racing into position, Anne collided with Volodya. She slipped on the wet snow and was headed toward a nasty fall when Volodya's arms wrapped around her waist. Instinctively gripping his shoulder, she regained her footing.

"Very sorry," he exclaimed, his arms still around her. Her body was firmer, more muscular than he expected.

"It's OK," she mumbled back, trying to extricate herself.

"You not hurt, I hope?" he asked, holding on to her a moment longer than necessary, inhaling her scent of soap and clover honey.

Sasha stared at the two, their bodies against each other.

A burst of insane jealousy sent a torrent of blood rushing to her head, the sudden surge sounding like gusts of wind in the trees. Her vision blurred, and she could barely make out the outlines of the couple. Sasha stood speechless and motionless.

Through the haze she saw Volodya wrap his arms around Anne and begin undressing her, the clothes coming off in slow motion ...

Anne pulled off his shirt ...

Soon they were naked, two silhouettes against the shimmering snow, the total silence broken only by the wind still whistling through the forest.

Sasha wanted to dash toward them but her legs wouldn't move. She saw the couple blend into one, as they sunk down in a passionate embrace ...

"Play, Sasha," someone yelled, and she felt something striking her foot. She focused. It was the ball.

The vision vanished.

She swung with her right leg. But she misjudged, and the ball sailed toward Volodya.

Reluctantly, Volodya let go of Anne and ran after the ball. As fast as a hunting predator, Sasha darted toward him, and, sweeping high with her foot, nailed Volodya across the shins. Several players gasped. Anne winced, stunned by the unnecessary roughness.

Volodya groaned, collapsing.

Sasha stood over him as he writhed in pain, rubbing his shins.

"You almost broke my leg," he moaned.

You lecherous son of a bitch, Sasha wanted to scream. I could kill you. She still felt the pressure in her temples. She hauled her leg back, preparing to ram his ribs, anticipating the sweet crunching sound her boot would make ...

But her head was now clear, and she was able to control herself. She smiled sweetly and, imitating his accent and inflection, mumbled, "You not hurt, I hope?"

34

"Dr. Powell, wait!" Natalia, the concierge, was hurrying down the hall, her ample body undulating in rhythm with her steps.

"Somebody left this for you," she said, panting as she caught up to Anne. She held a small bouquet of tiny white flowers, shaped like bells, that reminded Anne of snow drops. A card was taped to the simple white paper wrapped around the stems.

"*Podsnezhniki*," Natalia announced as triumphantly as if she had grown the flowers herself. "The name comes from '*pod snegom*,' which means 'under snow'."

"Thank you, Natalia. It's so nice of you."

"Oh, they're not from me, Dr. Powell."

"From whom then?"

Natalia shrugged. "A messenger dropped them off. Somebody must have gone through a lot of trouble to find these so early in the season."

Anne opened the card. It had two lines written in Russian, followed by the English translation: "When *podsnezhniki* come out, spring and hope are near." There was no signature.

Anne was two blocks from the hotel by the time she realized that she was still clutching the little bouquet. She considered returning, but decided that the flowers would be better off in the cool MEG suite than in the hotel room that the maids insisted on overheating.

Over the years Anne had received her share of extravagantly elaborate bouquets. But there was something especially touching about this tiny handpicked arrangement. A "thank you" was definitely in order.

But what? A note? "Dear Volodya, thank you for the beautiful flowers." *Bland.* "Volodya, I appreciate the effort, but you're wasting your time." *Heartless.*

So it might be heartless, but what did he expect, anyway?

She han't encouraged him in any way. Admittedly, she had almost melted when his leg touched hers in the lab, but there was no way he could have noticed that. And she had kissed him at the wedding, but that was a tradition. There was nothing else between them and never would be. She was in a committed relationship with Jack. There was no room for another man in her life. No matter how appealing he might think he was.

She would stop by his lab, thank him for the flowers in person and tell him his pursuit was futile. He could save his fancy footwork for soccer games.

Down in the now familiar basement, Anne paused briefly in front of the glass case of an exhibit of medical specimens to adjust her hair and touch up her lipstick. Her reflection, superimposed on dozens of human organs floating in formalin jars, stared back at her. The preserved brains reminded her of her time as the autopsy assistant at Beth Israel. It seemed like eons ago. *Boston.* She wasn't even missing it.

She found Volodya's door and knocked, hoping she wouldn't find him with one of his women.

"*Da!*" Volodya's voice was always so cheerful and energetic.

"Good morning."

"Anne! What surprise! Please, come in," he exclaimed, jumping up and pulling a chair for her. "You play football very good. Not football, how you say in American? Soccer. Very good, soccer, big talent you have. Sit down please."

Anne was about to say, "I just wanted to thank you," when

Volodya noticed the flowers and whistled.

"*Podsnezhniki?* Already? I thought minimum one more week before they come. Where did you get?"

Caught by surprise, Anne blurted out the first thing that came to her mind. "The hotel concierge gave them to me."

So the flowers weren't from him. She looked away to hide her confusion. "Actually, I was looking for Sasha. Have you seen her?"

"Probably she is meeting with Professor Baldyuk. Same thing every morning. Shall I call?"

"No, it's OK. I'll just wait for her in the MEG room. Sorry to have disturbed you." Anne quickly turned toward the door, painfully banging her thigh into the corner of a bench in the process.

"Anne?" Volodya called after her.

"Yes?"

"I wish flowers was gift from me. But I was thinking you are angry."

"Angry? Why?" *Just because he was an arrogant son of a bitch who obviously wanted to add her to the stable of women who found him irresistible?*

"I apologize, about wedding," he said quietly.

Anne didn't know what to say. She blushed as their kiss flashed through her mind. *What was the right answer? It's OK? Or, Apology accepted, don't ever try it again?*

"Would you like to visit our patient?" Volodya said before she could answer.

"What patient?"

"Come see," he beckoned her back in.

She followed. He opened one of the cages and gently pulled out a white mouse. Even from far away Anne could see that the little animal's belly was bulging.

"I hope you do not mind. I named her with our names." Volodya pointed to the 'A/B' painted on the mouse's back. "'A' is for Anne. 'B' is Russian 'V', for Volodya."

He put the mouse in her hands. The animal sniffed, then scurried up her arm and settled comfortably on her collar. Anne couldn't help smiling as the tiny whiskers tickled her neck.

She took the mouse down and held it in the palm of her hand. "A, B. A-B. I guess that would be Abby."

"Abby?"

"Short for Abigail. Good American name. So, what's Abby doing here?" The technical question brought things back to safe, familiar turf.

"Oh, just experiment," Volodya answered vaguely.

"Is it something … you can discuss?" Anne was going to say "classified," but that might have sounded too much like a line from a bad spy movie.

Volodya hesitated. "Not secret, but …"

He was tired of defending his theory. And she of all people, cold scientist that she was, would certainly have nothing encouraging to say. "I think is not your piece of cake," he said, trying to sound casual.

"Cup of tea," Anne corrected him, suppressing a smile. "Try me anyway."

He tossed his thick curls back and glanced at her. Tentatively, like a schoolboy about to take an oral exam. "I study memory."

"What about it?"

"How memory is transmitted."

Anne perked up. That was right up her alley. "You mean within the brain, in mice?"

"Yes, brain. And heart, and muscle. Also sperm, and ova."

"Really?" Anne winced. She loved exploring new concepts, but they had to be grounded in reality. In the medical establishments where she trained, discussion of memory storage in sperm and eggs— or anything else besides brain cells—would be considered quackery.

Volodya could read her like a book. "There is much evidence to prove it," he said defensively. "Animal learns skill, then muscles are transplanted to other animal, and new animal can learn skill faster …"

Those experiments were popular a decade ago, but had proven nothing except that muscles retained their original strength in the new host. Was he going to tell her next that feelings of love were stored in the heart?

"Is there a lot of research on this 'extra-cerebral memory' here in

Russia?"

Volodya was stung by her thinly disguised skepticism. "Yes, here. And even in America," he added pointedly.

"Oh?"

"Did you read book, *Changing Heart*?" he asked. "American. Very interesting. About woman who had heart transplanted, donated by man worker who is killed by car, and then she started to like beer."

Anne remembered seeing the book, *A Change of Heart*, on Misty's desk one day, but she assumed it was a romance novel.

"What do you mean, like beer?"

"She did not like beer, and other things, before transplant. Then, after transplant, she like them very much."

"And you figured the change was related to the new heart?"

"Very possible, no?"

"But how?" Storing memory required a complex network of cells that could communicate with each other and form new connections. Muscle and heart cells didn't have that capability. She spoke patiently, as if explaining a simple concept to a child. "Something would have to cause changes in cell structure to retain a memory."

"I think fear, love, other strong feelings, make brain produce chemicals—how do you call, *nevroperedatchiky* …"

"Neurotransmitters. Yes, it does. I'm not arguing with that …"

"… and these neurotransmitting chemicals make changes in cells."

"But how?"

"I don't know," he said simply.

"What do you mean, you don't know? How can you postulate a theory without any concept of the mechanism of action …"

"Some day we know. Now, I have feeling my theory is right."

"A 'feeling'?"

"Yes, feeling. Do you not "feel" you're right sometimes?"

He said it matter-of-factly, but it stung her. *No, maybe she didn't feel things as intensely as some others. Yes, maybe she was a little more cerebral than emotional. What was wrong with that? It kept her out of trouble. It gave her the safety she needed. It protected her from people like him.*

"Personally, I'm more into precise science," she snapped back impulsively. "You know, *facts.*"

"Shame," Volodya said, shaking his head. "You must keep mind open! If not, you're just a … pragmatist."

"I'm not 'just a pragmatist.' I'm a scientist and proud of it." Anne was angry. *He could sure push her buttons.*

"I'm scientist also, Anne. Only not so proud," Volodya said gently. "I think many things we do not understand how they work. First step, find if they are so. Explanation will come later. Sometimes, we must feel."

Anne looked at him for a long moment. "You're right. This is not my cup of tea," she said, handing Abby back.

"Anne?"

"Yes?"

"We make bet. If I prove some memory can be stored in sperm and eggs …"

"Recorded in genes?"

"Yes, in chromosomal DNA in the genes in sperm cells," he agreed patiently, "and passed to next generation, I win."

"Win what?"

He grinned. "You must dance with me."

She looked him up and down, trying to decide if this man's disarming style was insulting or endearing.

"Sure. I'll dance," she said, hanging on to her anger. The odds of him being right were such that she could've said, Sure, I'll fly.

"And you? What will you want if you win?" he asked with a twinkle in his eyes.

"Nothing," she said, walking out.

She hurried down the hall, embarrassed by her rudeness. *But he called her a pragmatist. She was sure he meant it to be an insult. And the flowers … She was such a fool. Why did she even think that the flowers were from him? And why was she disappointed that they weren't?*

His interest in her was flattering. But why? There certainly wasn't anything else appealing about him. Absolutely nothing.

35

When she finally found her way to the MEG room, she put the battered flowers in a paper cup, added water, and placed the cup on the shelf where MEG manuals were kept, wondering who the sender was.

Moments later, the door swung open and Baldyuk walked in.

"Dr. Powell, as always it is pleasure to see you," he said with an exaggerated bow.

"Good morning, Professor," Anne replied, forcing a civil smile.

"How is our famous doctor today?" Baldyuk's arrogant tone made "famous" sound condescending.

Anne turned to the console and tried to look busy. "Very well, thank you."

Pretending to be interested in what she was doing, Baldyuk walked up and positioned himself close behind her. He smelled of stale cigarette smoke and of something strange that Anne could only describe as rusty.

Baldyuk inched closer.

She heard his nasal wheezing, inches away. She was sure he was trying to smell her. A fragment of her recent dream flashed through her head: *Grudskoy leaning over Anytchka, touching her ...*

"Dr. Powell, tomorrow I have dinner. Small party. Few friends.

Please join us, yes? As my special guest."

Suddenly, it hit her. *The flowers were from him!* She felt the beginning of a spasm starting to build, deep inside her pelvis.

"I'm sorry, I can't. I have other plans."

"Other plans? I am very disappointed, Dr. Powell."

The spasm grew stronger.

"What are you disappointed in?" It was Sasha's voice, coming from the doorway. "What?" she repeated in Russian, her eyes drilling into Baldyuk.

What the hell was he doing here, stepping on her turf? It was her project, her department, her relationship with Anne. Why was he standing so close to Anne, anyway? Couldn't he see the disgust on her face?

"What are you doing here?" Sasha asked, trying to sound civil.

"We're discussing treatment for our patient," Baldyuk shot back in Russian. "We are ready to cure comrade Namordin, yes?" he added in English, turning to Anne. His question sounded like an order.

"It's being taken care of," Sasha snapped. "I told you I had it under control."

Anne looked from one to the other, not understanding what was being said, but realizing that tempers were running high. "I reviewed Mr. Namordin's tests," she interrupted the confrontation. "And I decided that it is safe to repeat the treatment." She was determined to make it clear that it was her decision and not Baldyuk's insistence that led her to push up the schedule. "In a day or two."

"Very good, then." Baldyuk looked triumphantly at Sasha.

He had already spent much of the $280,000 advance that the party had given him, on his assurance that the MEG was the answer to their Namordin problem. Not delivering the results could be hazardous to his health. He had to stand his ground against this bitch.

Sasha felt the blood hammering away in her temples. She had an urge to punch his insolent face. She never respected the man, but always managed to treat him politely—a wise career move. But now she was overcome by a visceral, barely controllable anger. The feeling was so intense, it surprised and frightened her. She stood very still, quietly looking into the distance, afraid that if she moved, she would lunge at him.

"Happy we are agreed," he spat, walking out.

Sasha felt a sense of victory as Baldyuk stormed out of the room. She almost did a little victory dance behind his back. Like an alpha male who had successfully defended his harem from an interloper.

She squinted and pressed her fingers against her temples as the pounding in her head increased. *She'd had the same headaches for several days now. At the soccer game, when she got angry at Volodya, and now, with this poor excuse of a director. Probably tension headaches,* she decided. *She should take something for pain before getting started.*

But a patient was already rolling in through the doors. The day had began. Absorbed in her work, Sasha soon forgot about the headache.

As Anne was leaving at the end of the day, Sasha noticed the tiny bouquet. "Oh, you got the flowers already," she said, sounding annoyed.

Anne spun around. "The flowers?"

"That Natalia, she blew it. I wanted her to put them in your room while you were gone so you'd have a surprise when you got back from work."

"Thank you. They're very beautiful," Anne mumbled.

"If you keep them in a cool place, they'll last for a couple of weeks. Perhaps 'til Easter."

"I'll do that," Anne said, hurrying toward the door.

She wasn't sure whether she was more disappointed that the flowers were not from Volodya, relieved that they were not from Baldyuk, or perturbed that they were from Sasha.

Flowers from a woman? Perhaps it was just another Russian custom. After all, in this country men kissed each other in public and women walked arm in arm. Why not flowers?

On her way to the Metro, Anne left the bouquet on a snow-covered windowsill.

36

Within days, Sasha and Anne had the procedure down to a fine art. Anne was delighted. This day in particular was one of the best days yet. Ten patients. Three who would need a few more sessions but would eventually improve. One was not MEG material. But six improved enough to be discharged the following day. And of those, two were regressed beyond age two. *If things continued at this rate, she would blow the Feds away with her results. They wouldn't dare turn her down this time.*

The long day ended again with Namordin, who arrived with the same entourage and the same secrecy as the first time.

Anne triple-checked every step of the positioning and personally tugged on every restraint. No more fiascos on her shift!

As soon as the MEG unit hummed to life and the scan of Namordin's brain appeared on the screen, Anne realized that it wasn't going to be an easy fix: there was no central locus of any kind.

She turned the power up by small increments. The image on the monitor gained details. Sasha began her questions.

Namordin's replies were slurred, but Anne caught two words she understood: Hitler and Leningrad.

"Sasha, what's he saying?"

"I can't figure it out. Something to do with World War II."

"Was that something that came up in therapy before?" Anne asked.

"I don't know, really. I wasn't that involved with his analysis." She scanned his record. "I suppose with Stalin for a grandfather, he must've heard all the war stories a million times. It would give anyone nightmares."

Suddenly, Namordin started singing. His voice sounded different, coarser.

Sasha perked up, trying to make out the words. "*Suliko,*" she whispered after a few moments.

"What?"

"*Suliko.* The song is called *Suliko.* It's about a woman ..." Sasha's voice trailed off.

Anne glanced at the monitor. "Look at that," she exclaimed touching Sasha's shoulder.

The bright loci on the brain scan formed two partially overlapping clusters. One of them included a bright spot that pulsated as the song waxed and waned.

Frowning, Sasha circled the two areas with her finger. "Two different personalities?" It was more a statement than a question.

"Exactly. And one of them is singing."

"Like Marussya, the atypical schizophrenic we did the other day?" Anne nodded.

"Not a good sign?" Sasha concluded, her voice sinking.

"No, not a good sign," Anne agreed. *How was she going to explain to Baldyuk that cases with two or more overlapping entities were not treatable by MEG? One would have to perform the equivalent of an electronic lobotomy on all of them except the dominant personalities. That was certainly out of the question with current technology.*

"Looks like we're in trouble here," she whispered to Sasha.

Sasha felt the blood draining from her face. It was a failure of titanic proportions. She could practically hear the death knoll for her career.

"Maybe we could just ablate one of the areas, leaving the other," Sasha suggested in a weak voice. "He looks easier than Marussya," she added, grasping at straws.

"You know we can't go blasting in there, Sasha. We could wipe out something important," Anne reminded her. Glancing up at the gallery where Baldyuk was listening to every word over the intercom, she couldn't help adding, "We might make him forget he's a Communist, or something!"

Looking back at Sasha, she added quietly, "I'm so sorry, but there's nothing we can do here."

"You must prepare him for campaign. You must ..." Baldyuk yelled over the intercom.

"I'm going to send Mr. Namordin home now," Anne said firmly. "This time around, the Communist party will have to do without him."

"Is not acceptable ..."

"Professor," Sasha snapped into the microphone, her disappointment and frustration now re-directed toward Baldyuk. "I think Dr. Powell made it clear that there is nothing she can do."

"I want results!" Baldyuk bellowed. "We promised ..."

"*Zatknys!*" Sasha blurted out in Russian.

For a moment Baldyuk was speechless. *Had she dared tell him to shut up?* His voice trembling with rage, he growled into the microphone, "I will see you in my office."

"When we're done," Sasha spat back.

Baldyuk vanished from the gallery.

Sasha rammed her foot into the console. The failure with Namordin made her angry. But Baldyuk's attempt to pressure Anne infuriated her even more. "*Sookin sin.* The son of a bitch," Sasha hissed through clenched teeth."

"Easy!" Anne said softly. She put her hand on Sasha's arm. "Let it be." Blowing off steam at your boss wasn't the best way to deal with a treatment failure.

"He can't talk to you like that!" Sasha felt her headache building like the sound of an approaching drum.

"He has trouble understanding that 'no' means 'no.' That's all."

"This is not his little fiefdom. He can't order people around like he owns them."

"Just give it up," Anne repeated. "Think about all the other patients we helped. And there will be many more."

Sasha glanced at her and took a deep breath. *Anne didn't need to know that Sasha had no intention of giving up.*

37

L ate that night Sasha sat alone in the dark and empty MEG room, hunched over a video deck.

"*We must prepare him for campaign,*" Baldyuk's words came from the playback speaker.

She had retrieved the tapes from the video cameras that recorded the procedures and was reviewing Namordin's record for the fifth or sixth time, struggling to find an answer.

Her anger at Baldyuk had given way to gut wrenching fear. Namordin had been in their charge long enough to give the party confidence that rehabilitation was taking place. It was just like Baldyuk to withhold the bad news from his "sponsors." But the later they found out that Namordin was not going to be ready for elections, the fewer the party's options, and the greater their desire to punish somebody—anybody—for the failure.

Since Baldyuk was too highly placed, the most likely "somebody" was Sasha. *And the most likely punishment would be swiftly dispensed in some dark alley when she least expected it.* She had no delusions: the party would never take a chance that a disgruntled former employee wouldn't air their dirty laundry.

Yes, we must fix him, thought Sasha. *But how?* She had taken a questionable shortcut, with Baldyuk's blessing, by asking her connection in the lab to falsify the results so she could convince Anne to move the treatment up. Now that move had proven to have been in vain. The entire project to rehabilitate Namordin in time for elections was crumbling before her eyes.

"Damn it," she muttered under her breath. *The MEG was such a versatile device. It had so much to offer to so many people. How could they have failed with Namordin?*

The wall monitor displayed Namordin's scan. His voice came over the speaker. It had only a hint of the Georgian accent that was so pronounced in both his father and grandfather. The guttural g's, the nasal a's and u's, so characteristic of Georgia, the southern republic best known as Stalin's birthplace, were barely noticeable.

"*Big crowds. I'm scared. I must lead ...*" Namordin was saying.

In the background Sasha heard some comment by Anne. Then her own voice asking Namordin to describe where he was.

Sasha fast-forwarded the tape. More questions.

"*I won't let Hitler take Leningrad,*" Namordin was yelling, his Georgian accent suddenly much thicker. The dual memory clusters scintillated on the wall screen like overlapping constellations.

"*Why are you afraid of Hitler?*" Sasha heard herself asking.

Namordin mumbled something unintelligible that sounded like "*Fascist pig.*"

Stalin's grandson, to the bone, Sasha thought as she rewound the tape and listened again.

She heard Anne's voice, "*Sasha, what's he saying,*" and then her own, answering, "*I can't figure it out. Something to do with World War II.*"

Why did this man have such an obsession with a war that ended when he was still wearing diapers?

"*With Stalin for a grandfather, he must've heard all the war stories a million times. It would give anyone nightmares.*"

That's what she thought at the time, but now she suspected that the explanation wasn't that simple.

She heard the plaintive sounds of Namordin's song in the background. *Suliko.*

The song was about a young man searching for his beloved. Old songs like *Suliko* had long ago given way to Western music. *Suliko* would not have been remembered either, except that it had been Stalin's favorite. Allegedly, when he heard it for the first time on the radio, he ordered the singer flown to Moscow for a private performance. Then he played the recording several times a day, until the day he died. It could have become a topic for jokes, but at the time joking about Stalin was a life-threatening pastime.

So why was Stalin's grandson singing it? He was three when the dictator died. So if he heard the song around the Great Leader's chambers at the Kremlin, it was only in early childhood. And for a short time.

On the recording, Anne was saying, "*If we go blasting randomly, we could wipe out something important. We might make him forget he's a Communist, or something!*" Sasha smirked at the thought of Namordin promoting capitalism.

Suddenly she flashed back to the day when they were MEGing Marussya. *Anne's words: "We would destroy a lot of things that make Marussya—'Marussya.' It'd be like amputating the body to save the leg."*

Sasha sat up and drummed her fingers.

Her pulse quickened as an idea germinated in her head. *It was risky, but there was nothing to lose. If she didn't do something now, in a week Namordin would be useless to the party and Sasha would be in somebody's crosshairs.*

The problem was, Anne would never agree to repeat the treatment. Why did Anne have to be so rigid? If there ever were a perfect case for pushing the limits a little, Namordin was it.

Sasha paced, thinking, analyzing, refusing to give up. Suddenly, she stopped.

Maybe there was a way …

38

Despite the late hour, Sasha found Baldyuk in his office. He barely glanced at her when she marched in.

"I want you out of here, first thing in ..."

Sasha interrupted. "Right now, you'll let me do what I need, or you can kiss the whole project good-bye," she snapped.

"What!" He couldn't believe his ears. "I don't have to do anything ..."

"Yes, you do, because I'm the only one who can help you keep your little bonus."

Baldyuk jerked in his chair, but tried to look unperturbed.

Sasha smirked. "What do you think, I'm stupid? I know you aren't doing Namordin out of civic duty."

Baldyuk tried to say something, but reconsidered.

"Don't worry, your deal is safe," she said disdainfully. "But here's what I want you to do."

It felt strange, saying 'I want' to this man. Sasha wondered where she found the courage to speak to Baldyuk in that tone of voice. *Something had changed in her since Anne started working in the department.*

"Tell Sergey in Engineering that he's to be at my beck and call, day or night, for the next few days. Get him a pager. I may need him on a moment's notice."

"What for?" Baldyuk grunted, making a futile attempt to sound more conciliatory.

Sasha pretended not to hear. "Also, I need two tickets to the Bolshoi Theater for Wednesday night. I think it's *Swan Lake*. Doesn't matter. Get the best seats. I'll pick them up."

She headed for the doorway, then stopped.

"One more thing. If I pull this off—and I know I will—I want a full professorship and an increase in salary to match yours …"

"Dream on!" Baldyuk blurted out.

"And the big office on the sixth floor, the one they'd been renovating," she added, gloating because she knew Baldyuk had his eyes on it. "As far as my share of your bonus, we'll discuss that later," she said casually, walking out.

She strode down the hallway, trembling with the excitement of her idea. *What if it worked? Not if. It was going to work. What would Anne say when she found out? Would she be proud of her? Would they work together? Co-publish a paper?*

What a coup. No one will walk over the new Sasha, she told herself. Soon she could challenge Baldyuk's position, become Director …

A week ago she would have considered these ambitions ludicrous. But today … She relished the bitter taste of an adrenaline surge.

Yes, things were about to change.

39

"The unexplained absence of Vissarion Namordin continues to puzzle everyone in Russia," the CNN broadcast droned on the TV.

Anne pushed the room-service dinner tray away and turned up the volume.

"The odds-on favorite in the upcoming election," the news anchor continued, "has remained incommunicado since his spectacularly successful rally in Kemerovo two weeks ago. There is speculation that he has been hospitalized for an undisclosed malady, but is expected to be released, fully recovered, within the next few days. This could give the Communist party a tremendous boost, as well as undermine the opposition efforts to ..."

CNN's fact checking was getting sloppy, Anne thought. *Mr. Namordin wasn't going to be in any elections anytime soon.* But she could see how the party might want to leak an optimistic report.

She shut off the TV, made herself comfortable in bed, and, skimming through recent issues of the *New England Journal of Medicine* and the *Journal of Neuropathology,* she dozed off.

At 6:00 a.m. the phone rang.

"Anne?"

The connection was distorted by static. "Misty?"

"Oops, did I wake you?"

"It's OK, I'm not awake," Anne mumbled. "I mean, I'm not asleep. Well, I was, but ..."

"I'm sorry. I must've miscalculated the time," Misty said cheerfully. "I wanted to catch you before you went to work. Listen, what's with the disk you sent me? You into group therapy?"

Anne tried to focus. "Good. You got the scan ..."

"Got it, saw it. What happened?"

"The patient ripped out the restraint and tried to get up."

"I heard. Halden was ranting and raving about installing reinforcing plates. But that doesn't explain the other two heads. And from what I see, it looks like the patient is the only one who didn't get treated."

"What did you find?

"He hardly got anything—0.4 tesla."

"And the other two?"

"A fair amount."

"Significant?"

"Oh, I'd say so. About 35 tesla per square centimeter for one of them, around 100 for the other."

Anne winced. Even 35 was five times more than she had ever used in a single dose. She wondered who had gotten the higher dose, she or Sasha.

"But how? It was only a few seconds ..."

"But real close to the source. I mean, real close."

"Still ... That's a lot ..."

"Do the math: square of the distance ..."

Anne was calculating, now wide-awake. *The intensity varied inversely with the square of the distance from the source. Twice as close meant four times as much exposure. Real close meant a whopping dose.*

"No wonder you've been having weird dreams," Misty said.

"What're you talking about?" Anne regretted telling Misty about the one with the young woman being forcibly married to the old nobleman.

"Don't try to bullshit me. When were you going to tell me that one of the heads was yours?"

"It wasn't important."

"Giving yourself a MEG overdose? Not important?"

"I couldn't let him get brained by the C-arm."

"It wouldn't have taken but an extra second to shut it down first. Instead, you get yourself zapped and start having all sorts of weird …"

"Misty, please, I don't need this."

"Sorry." Misty paused for a minute. "So, how are you feeling?"

"Fine. Just fine."

There was no need to tell Misty about the few flashbacks she's had—they seemed to be abating. Certainly no point in confessing about how she heard a woman crying in the middle of the night, and woke up in the morning with a cold wet spot on her pillow.

"How's the other patient?"

"What patient?"

"The other head."

"It's Sasha, the woman I work with. She seems OK, and I didn't want to bring anything up. Don't want to alarm them unnecessarily."

"Or give them reason to think that there are problems with the MEG itself. Good thinking. Anyway, any aftereffects should disappear in a week or two."

"Or sooner!" Anne was happy that Misty had come to the same conclusion.

"Just be careful, you dope!" Misty chided gently.

"How's Miles?" Anne asked to change the subject.

"Your pesky feline scratched the hell out of my couch."

"I'm so sorry. I'll make it up to you."

They talked for a few minutes about Misty's patients and her latest love interest, Ramman the Moroccan plumber.

"Same guy for three days in a row?" Anne teased.

"Slowing down, I guess," Misty laughed. "How's your love life?"

"Who needs a love life? I have chocolate," Anne answered glibly.

"Come on, all those Russian bears and you haven't found one you want to hug?"

"No, I haven't."

Something in Anne's voice made Misty skeptical. "What about Boboday?"

"Who?"

"Bobo-something. The guy who gave you a tonsil massage at the wedding."

Anne couldn't help laughing. "Volodya. And it was just a traditional kiss."

"Whatever."

"He seems interesting," Anne said.

"Ah-ha!"

"Intellectually interesting, Misty."

"Go on."

"There's nothing to go on about."

She told Misty about her discussion with Volodya about his work with memory transmission, and her disappointment when she realized how unscientific his experiment was.

"Don't be so narrow-minded," Misty said.

"I'm not narrow-minded," Anne exclaimed. "It's pseudo-science. A waste of time. And then he called me a pragmatist."

"I see he got you angry. That's good."

"Nothing good about it."

"Anne, you intimidate the shit out of most men. At least this guy seems to stand his ground."

"He can keep standing."

Misty sighed. The woman was brilliant. Yet emotionally, she was a klutz. "How come you're trying so hard to hate him?"

"Quit analyzing me. I'm not trying to hate him. I was disappointed that here's this man, so passionate about his work ..."

"A kindred soul?"

"Yes, but scientifically he's a quack."

"There must be something in him you found attractive."

Anne wanted to tell her how electrifying this man's touch was, how his blue eyes seemed to see right into her soul, how whenever they were in the same room, his attention, his energy, his whole being appeared to be completely focused on her. *And his lips …*

"Well?"

"OK, I admit it. There *is* something attractive about him. He likes playing with mice."

"Mice?" Misty exclaimed. "Why mice?"

"That's what he's using for his memory research."

"He must be a Scorpio. Is he a Scorpio?"

"How should I know?"

"Ask him! It could tell you a lot about whether you are compatible or …"

"Misty, please!" She changed the subject. "Do you know a book called *A Change of Heart*?"

"I do. It's about cell memory."

"And what did you think?"

"Far-fetched but fascinating."

"Tell me more."

"Well, the author, Claire Sylvia, undergoes a heart-lung transplant, the donor being an eighteen year old guy who crashed on his bike. And immediately after the operation, she starts to see changes in herself."

"What kind of changes?"

"Oh, I can't remember it all now, but things like colors, for example. She started to like reds and oranges instead of pastels."

"And beer?"

"Yeah, I think beer. How did you know?" Misty asked, surprised.

"Never mind. Go on."

"She also had behavioral changes. She became more aggressive … Why are you asking me about this?"

"Just tell me about the book."

"Fine. So after the changes … here's where it gets really bizarre … she had a dream about meeting some guy … To make a long story short, the guy in her dream turned out to be her heart donor, whom she had never met before."

"And what was the explanation?" Anne asked, wondering how the book referred to cell memory.

"In the last chapter, she reviews her theory."

"Which is?"

"Hey, you're really into this all of a sudden."

"Tell me her theory."

"Systemic memory. Memories can be stored in any part of the body, not just the brain."

"That's where you lost it, right?" Anne asked.

"Hm-m-m, not really. I can see the part about storing memory in certain types of cells, recorded on DNA."

Anne was silent.

"Like the DNA that 'remembers' to make your hair red." Misty clarified. "Or your eyes green."

"Can you send me the book?"

"Sure," Misty said, surprised. "I think you'll like it. I didn't want to mention it, because I was afraid you'd think I was weird, reading stuff like that."

"Hey, I already know you're weird," Anne laughed. "Thanks for looking at the scan."

"You owe me. And Anne?"

"What?"

"Go play with Vodolya's mice. It'll do you good."

40

Anne had braced herself for yet another confrontation with Baldyuk over the Namordin issue, but two days went by and he didn't show up. Although she was glad he hadn't come, she was hoping his absence was not due to loss of interest in the MEG.

Sasha, on the other hand was working as enthusiastically as ever, and when Anne saw the schedule, she was relieved to see that every slot was filled for the next three weeks. The MEG was still on track.

But Anne's contentment with work was marred by her concern about Sasha's behavior. Several times she had noticed Sasha staring into space, speechless and motionless. The episodes were probably a side effect of the MEG overdose.

She wondered if Sasha was having weird dreams too. *But Sasha would have probably said something ...* Based on the intensity of her own nightmares, Anne was convinced that it was her head that had gotten the most exposure, not Sasha's.

Perhaps she should talk to her anyway, Anne wondered. *But then she would have to share her own symptoms. How do you discuss a bride rape dream with a total stranger?*

Besides, as long as no ablation had been done, the memory-enhancing effects of the MEG were totally harmless and would clear in time.

Anne decided to give it a few days.

Her thoughts drifted to Volodya. She hadn't seen Volodya for two days. *What did Misty call him? Boboday.* She wanted to ask him about Abby's pregnancy. How big would her litter be? Was there such a thing as mouse prenatal ultrasound? Maybe she could bring up the issue of cell memory and show him that she was more open-minded than he thought.

But "Boboday" was nowhere to be found.

During one of their breaks, two days after Namordin's failed treatment, Sasha turned to Anne. "Do you like the ballet?" she asked.

Anne tensed at the thought that Sasha might be asking her out. "I have a busy week at home..." she started to say, as Sasha pulled a ticket out of her pocket.

"Here, take this," Sasha said. "I had a ticket for Swan Lake at the Bolshoi Theater tonight, but I can't go. My Mom is ill. You know how these old people get," she added, rolling her eyes.

"Can't you resell it?" Anne suggested, reluctant to accept the gift.

"Take it. You'll love it. You need a break from that hotel room."

Although Anne's evenings alone gave her a chance to catch up on medical reading, the prospect of seeing one of the world's most famous ballet companies in their home theater was irresistible.

"Let me pay you for it," she said.

"Don't insult me," Sasha exclaimed, forcing the stub into Anne's hand. "Next time we'll go together, and I'll let you pay."

At 5:00 p.m., with one patient still to go, Sasha turned to Anne. "You'd better go. They start at seven sharp, and they won't let you in if you are late."

Anne glanced at her watch, calculating the time. *She could get dressed fast.* "Let's finish this one together," she said.

The case, a young woman with ornithophobia, went smoothly, and a half hour later the attendants wheeled her back to the recovery room, her fear of birds gone.

"OK, run," said Sasha, holding up Anne's coat so she could slip into it. "I'll turn everything off."

"One more second …" Anne stepped back to the console and exited out of the ablation program. *Her rule was never to leave the MEG in ablation mode unless she was physically in the room. No exceptions. The rest, Sasha could do.*

"Hope your mother feels better. Thanks again for the ticket," she said hurrying out. "I'm very excited," she added with a smile.

"Have fun," Sasha smiled back.

As soon as the door closed, Sasha's smile vanished. She marched up to the phone and paged Sergey, the computer whiz.

There was work to be done.

41

Anne hurried into her room, shedding her work clothes on the go. She wished that she had time to relax, dress leisurely, perhaps enjoy a glass of wine. But it was 6:15, and all she had time for was a quick shower.

She turned the faucet on and let the scalding water cascade through her hair and down her back. She felt the heat penetrating, relaxing her shoulders. She hummed a few bars from the Tchaikovsky masterpiece she was about to see. It was going to be a good evening.

Her wardrobe options for evening wear were limited. She settled on the inexpensive but functional dress she had brought along for festive occasions. It was the proverbial "little black dress" but it was woven through with fine silvery strands. Under bright lights the strands sparkled like sequins, making the dress look very elegant. The material clung to her body, but a conservatively high neckline kept the dress from appearing too provocative. "I'm so jealous!" Misty had said when Anne was trying the dress on in Boston. "You look like a million bucks, no matter what you wear."

Anne added a stunning set of earrings and a necklace—diamonds, hanging like water droplets from silver strands, accentuating her beautiful neckline. *Amazing what $25 of cubic zirconium could do for one's appearance*, she chuckled. She wrapped herself in the thick black shawl that had served her well through every Boston winter, and walked out.

Although the Bolshoi was less than half a mile from the hotel, Anne asked the concierge to order one of the hotel cars to make sure she would be on time.

The driver, a thin young man in thick glasses, did a double take as she emerged from the lobby.

"Matvey. For your service," he mumbled, saluting like a soldier, his jaw hanging in midair as he held the car door open.

Minutes later, they pulled up to the entrance.

From the outside, the Bolshoi Theater, world-renowned for its ballet company, was totally unimpressive. The simple façade of white marble columns supporting a classical Greek roof was no match for the ornate Le Palais de L'Opera, or the imposing La Scala, or even the simple lines of Lincoln Center. But there was a mystique about the building that Anne couldn't explain.

Anne worked her way through the smoking men and women crowded on the short stairs leading to the entrance.

The entryway itself was through a door so small that people went through it one by one. *Probably to cut down on heating bills,* Anne figured, as she stepped from the chilly Moscow night into the hot, steamy vestibule.

The lobby, surprisingly small, was packed. Germans in mismatched sport jackets, Americans in jeans and parkas, French women in designer floor-length gowns, Russians in gaudy, ill-fitting, festive best. Everyone was pushing and jostling and babbling.

She joined the crowd funneling toward the entrance. The usher tore the stub off her ticket and said something in Russian.

"*Ne ponimayu,*" Anne said, shrugging her shoulders. She wondered why the woman took her for a native, until she realized that with honey blond hair and green eyes she could easily pass for one of the newly-rich Russians.

The usher pointed toward a set of stairs. "Down. Go down."

The stairs brought Anne to another crowd in front of the coat-check area. The attendant handed her a numbered plastic tag, then pointed to a cheap set of binoculars.

"*Shesdesat rublei*, two dollars, one pound sterling, two euros …" she recited, covering the most likely possibilities.

"*Nyet, spasiba.* I don't need binoculars."

"Have binoculars, no line to get coat when theater finish. Not have binoculars, big line." She thrust the binoculars into Anne's hand.

Still mystified, Anne took the binoculars and handed over the money.

She went up another staircase, squeezed her way through a narrow door and stopped. The majestic interior of the theater took her breath away.

The Bolshoi was far more sumptuous than she had imagined. Five levels of balconies surrounded the orchestra, their railings decorated in ornate gold baroque design, the wide handrail covered in rich red upholstery.

Opposite the stage, at the back of the theater, was the imperial loge. It extended the full height of the five balconies and was flanked by red curtains that mirrored the curtains of the main stage. She could practically see Nicholas II and Alexandra and their glittering entourage applauding a Dyagilev premiere a century ago. Or the Bolsheviks, holding a 1920s post-revolution rally, sprawled irreverently in the orchestra seats. Now the place was flooded with visitors from the world over.

She looked around, mesmerized, wishing that Jack or Misty were there to share the experience.

She found her place and settled in. In contrast to the majesty of the theater itself, the seats were conventional wooden chairs held in place by a beam nailed to the floor.

She had a great location—sixth row, only a few seats off the center aisle. The two Asian women in front of her were short, and she had an unobstructed view of the stage. On her left, the seat was empty. Most of the seats in adjacent rows were filled with tour groups. At exactly seven o'clock the lights dimmed. The conductor entered and bowed, to loud applause.

As the hall settled down and the first chords sounded, Anne felt someone slide into the seat next to her.

"Very sorry I was late," a familiar voice whispered into her ear.

She spun around. Volodya's face was inches from hers. His hair was combed back in an attempt to control the curls. He wore a dark wool jacket, stretched open by his broad shoulders, a white shirt with a collar that was too tight, and a dark blue tie tied in a clumsy knot.

Anne felt her heart racing. *Was this an intentional setup? Volodya's idea? Sasha's? Weren't the two of them an item? It made no sense ... Or was the explanation simple—Sasha had gotten tickets for herself and Volodya, but she had to drop out at the last minute because of her mother's illness?*

She felt his breath on her ear again. "Sasha told me, 'Make sure Dr. Powell is not lost'," he whispered, as if reading her thoughts.

Actually, his instructions were to make sure Anne had an enjoyable night out and stayed away from work. If for some reason Anne decided to leave early, Volodya was to call Sasha and let her know immediately. When Volodya raised his eyebrows, Sasha told him that Anne had been working too hard, had made a few mistakes, and needed a restful evening away from the hospital, whether she wanted it or not.

Anne was about to ask him what he was doing there, but the angry stare from the woman in front made her reconsider. The explanations could wait. She tried to concentrate on the ballet.

Dozens of perfectly matched, elegant ballerinas spun effortlessly to the sounds of Tchaikovsky's music, imitating swans flying down and settling on a lake, their beautiful white shapes silhouetted against a midnight blue backdrop.

To a burst of applause, a new ballerina floated onto the stage, a tiny diamond crown on her dainty head setting her apart from the rest of the flock. Her arms moved with such incredible grace, it was impossible to tell where her joints were. *She had truly captured the essence of a swan,* Anne thought, wondering how a human body could move with such fluidity.

Anne glanced at Volodya. He was leaning forward in his chair, intently following every movement. He noticed her look.

"Magnificent, yes?" he whispered.

"It is," she whispered back, surprised by the excitement in his voice.

Another wave of applause drowned the orchestra as a male dancer exploded onto the stage, his graceful leaps defying gravity.

"He is hunter. He will meet swan," Volodya whispered.

But the eloquence of the dancers' movements needed no explanation. Anne sat, mesmerized, watching as the hunter and the swan met, fell in love, and were separated by the rising sun.

The curtain dropped for the intermission.

"Hello," Volodya said, grinning, as the lights came up.

"Hello."

"This is surprise for you?"

"It's so beautiful," Anne said, unsure whether he was referring to his presence, or the beauty of the ballet. "I wish I knew more about the story."

"Come, we eat something and I tell you story."

He took her by the arm and guided her through the crowd. Again, as at the airport and during their first encounter in his lab, she felt the heat of his touch spread through her body. *I'm like a Pavlovian puppy*, she thought, disgusted at her automatic reaction to him. What was it about this man that gave him such a direct connection to her nervous system? She had decided to stay away from him. Yet here they were, strangers plastered against each other in the crowd, sharing one of the most romantic experiences she had had in years.

They got into the long line of people, almost all of them Russian, waiting to buy food at the counter, where salami sandwiches, caviar on crackers, smoked fish, and pieces of pastry were piled side by side.

When finally they were served, Anne opted for mineral water and a dish of apple slices. Volodya took a glass of Georgian cognac and a ham and cheese sandwich on black bread, copiously smeared with butter.

"Before, white swan was woman," he started to explain, "but now swan is under power of ..." Sandwich in hand, he was gesticulating impatiently. "How you say, person who can do things, special things, only he can do?"

"Magician? Sorcerer?"

"Maybe sorcerer, I do not know. So swan is under power of sorcerer."

"Under a magic spell."

"Yes. She can be woman again only if some man loves her very much. In beginning, hunter prince falls in love with white swan. Then black swan—bad woman who belongs to sorcerer person … then, I don't know how to say …"

He was completely frustrated by his inability to find the words.

"It's OK, I understand what you're saying." Anne touched his arm. "Only love can break the sorcerer's spell."

"Yes, yes, yes. You make sound very easy. Then …"

He pantomimed how the prince and swan fell in love, then separated. Even in the confines of the crowd, his movements were expressive and passionate. Anne couldn't take her eyes off him. It was like watching the prince on the stage making love to the swan all over again.

"Then, black swan makes prince fall in love with her. So prince forgets white swan." He waved sadly.

Suddenly an image flashed through her mind: *Anytchka being carried out of the carriage by Grudskoy, going past Vovka, their hands touching, the farewell wave …*

"You understand?" Volodya asked.

Anne nodded, her mind lost in her reverie.

The second act was even more moving than the first. At the moment when the white swan realizes that all is lost, that the prince had fallen in love with her foe, Anne and Volodya looked at each other, at the same time. Their eyes locked, sharing the incredibly poignant moment, a wordless communication, each somehow aware that the other knew the pain of separation.

Anne had an urge to lean against him, to feel the comfort of his body next to hers. She wondered if he could see it in her eyes, and if he felt the same.

"This is so beautiful," she whispered, neither of them sure whether what was beautiful was on the stage or between them.

On the stage, true love prevailed. The prince realized his error, and, drawing his bow, shot the black swan. As the evil bird fluttered to her death, the white swan was released from the spell, and now, as a woman, ran into the prince's arms.

After numerous curtain calls to a standing ovation, the lights went on and everyone headed for the exit. Anne and Volodya lingered behind, both knowing, and neither admitting, that they wanted the magic moment to last.

It wasn't until the hall emptied that Volodya took her hand and said quietly, "We should go."

42

ergey, a jovial, totally bald man in his forties, had worked with the Mir Space Station program until seven years ago, when funding for the project dried up and the pride and joy of Communist technology literally fell out of the sky. He was no stranger to complex equipment. But the slick, ultramodern lines of the MEG, and the intricacy of its design made him scratch his balding head and whistle.

"It's either for mixing bread or flying in space," he said, circling the unit, his fingers caressing the control panel. "So what is it that you want me to do here?"

As Sasha explained, a grin spread over his face. Sergey loved a challenge, particularly when it involved American products.

He poured over the MEG blueprints, tracing circuits with his fingers. "Mm, *da. Da, da, da,*" he mumbled periodically, nodding his head.

Finally he looked up at Sasha. "Any way we can get hold of the maintenance manual? I need more details."

Sasha shook her head. "Everything is going through Boston. Part of the deal, until we get approved to use this thing."

"It's not going to be easy ..." Sergey sighed.

"It's American, Sergey. I know you can do it."

Despite his bulk, Sergey slid easily between the main pedestal of the unit and the wall.

"Let me get in here first, then we'll see," he said, unscrewing the fasteners on one of the panels.

Much of the computer technology used in Russian space programs over the past two decades was based on American products. Sergey was second to none in reverse engineering—disassembling a product and using the information to duplicate it. *But this little assignment was going to be a stretch, even for him.*

Sasha was happy that they didn't need to rush. Volodya hadn't called, which meant that he and Anne were safely away at the ballet for the next several hours.

The thought of the two sitting side by side, enjoying Swan Lake together, drove her crazy. Ever since the soccer game—or was it even before that, when she saw Anne and Volodya kiss at the wedding?—she had bouts of insane jealousy. Unexplainable jealousy. She had never resented Volodya's numerous liaisons. In fact, she enjoyed ferreting out details of his escapades from him. She even fantasized about watching him with other women.

But with Anne? The image made her temples pound.

Gut wrenching as the decision was, Volodya was her best choice for keeping Anne away from the Institute for a few hours. *Right now time was more important than jealousy.*

43

The coat check attendant hadn't misled Anne. Instead of getting in line behind a hundred people, Anne and Volodya simply walked up to the area reserved for those who were returning binoculars and retrieved their coats.

Volodya held Anne's coat. She slipped into it, aware of his hands as they lingered briefly on her shoulders. Then they headed out into the chill of the night.

"I do not have car tonight. Alternator broken. I took it out yesterday, but need to find part to fix. Maybe in two days," Volodya said. "May I walk you to hotel?"

She welcomed the offer. She had neglected to tell Matvey to come back to get her, and getting into a strange cab had no appeal. *Besides,* she admitted to herself, *she would enjoy a few more moments with him to discuss the ballet.*

"Thanks, I'd appreciate that," she smiled.

He held his arm out for her, and, as if it were the most natural thing to do, she put her arm through his.

They walked arm in arm, their steps in perfect synchrony. Still glowing from the magic of Swan Lake, neither of them felt the need to talk.

As they negotiated icy patches, Anne steadied herself against

Volodya, acutely aware of the warmth of his body and the rock hard muscles in his forearm.

She realized that they were walking slower, prolonging the time.

Halfway to the hotel, Volodya stopped abruptly. "Did you have dinner?"

"An apple," Anne said. "And a Luna," she confessed with a giggle.

"Fruit and chocolate! Is not enough. How you will be strong to play soccer?" He shook his head disapprovingly. "Would you like *real* Russian food?"

She knew she should turn him down, go home, get some sleep. But she heard herself saying, "That would be nice." *What was the harm in sharing a meal with him? Besides, she owed him an apology for her rudeness during their last encounter.*

They dashed across Tverskey Street, dodging six lanes of cars that whizzed by even at this late hour, then walked up Nagatenskaya Street and turned right into a narrow, dark alley.

Anne started to feel uneasy. *Where exactly was he taking her?*

They entered the deserted lobby of an office building and took the elevator up to the nineteenth floor. The hallways were dark and gloomy. Just as Anne started to wonder how she could back out of this situation, Volodya opened an unmarked door and stepped in.

Immediately, the smell of garlic and fresh bread filled Anne's nostrils. As her eyes adjusted, she made out a small room, with a dozen tables, dimly lit by oil lamps.

A waitress ran up to greet them. "*Volodya, privet!*" Completely ignoring Anne's presence, she gave him a lusty kiss on the lips, then helped them with their coats.

"*Vodky khochish?*"

Volodya held up three fingers. "*Trista gram.*"

The waitress nodded and disappeared into the kitchen.

Completely at home, Volodya led Anne to a table by the window. "This is best place for looking," he said, pulling the chair out for her.

Indeed, the view was magnificent. The entire Kremlin lay at their feet. Beyond it, the skyline of brightly lit buildings was dominated by an imposing cathedral, its white walls and five golden domes illuminated by spotlights.

"*Sobor Christa Spassitelya. Spassat* means 'save'."

"Cathedral of Christ the Savior," Anne guessed.

"Yes. Was finished in 1883, to commemorate that Russian army beat Napoleon's army," Volodya said. "You know story, yes? Napoleon army was very very strong, and so they come very close to Moscow. Next day, maybe Napoleon will take city." He became more animated. "That night, Russian commander made decision: We do not fight! We burn Moscow!"

"Burn it? Why?"

"Ah-ha! I tell you. Big sacrifice, but ..."

He paused for a moment, and Anne could see how proud he was of his Russian heritage.

"Russians set fire to all buildings in Moscow. Next morning Napoleon march into Moscow, very happy. And then he sees. No houses. No food. Nothing. Not even machines for—how you say?—to stop fire?"

"Fire fighting equipment."

"Yes. We burn everything. And it was winter. French soldiers died. When Napoleon must return to France, Russians make attack from back, and destroyed French army."

He made sounds of explosions, then hummed something. Recognizing Tchaikovsky's *1812 Overture*, Anne chimed in. They completed a few bars together and broke into laughter.

"So, to mark victory, church was build," Volodya continued. "With money given by people, not by government. Then, during Communism, Stalin destroyed church and tried to build government office building, but earth did not hold."

"What do you mean, earth did not hold?"

"Not hold weight of building. It sink into ground. Engineers very confused, many think it was sign from God. So Stalin built place for swimming instead."

"A swimming pool?"

"Yes, swim pool. And now ..." He pointed toward the cathedral. "We build church again. Very fast. Only two years. With big concrete walls." He indicated a four foot thickness with his hands. "And see, no problem, earth holding weight very well," he smiled. "And we bring new bells from a broken church in Siberia. They sound *so* beautiful," he added wistfully, his eyes sparkling. "So very, very beautiful. Maybe someday I can play them."

Anne listened, enraptured by this man's passions—his dancing, his work, his appreciation of ballet, music … his love for his country, his openness with his feelings. She could feel his energy flowing into her, rejuvenating her.

The waitress appeared with a quart-sized carafe half-filled with a clear liquid, a basket of thinly sliced rye bread and a bowl of marinated mushrooms.

"In Russia we order vodka by weight."

"That's enough for five people!" Anne exclaimed, the memory of her drinking experience at the wedding still quite vivid.

"Is nothing. Only three hundred grams."

Ten ounces, Anne calculated. *Her share was enough for a royal hangover.*

Volodya filled their glasses.

"*Na zdorovye!*" she said, raising her glass. "Is that how you say it?"

"*Na zdorovye!*" he smiled.

She held her breath and swallowed. The liquid burned its way down her throat, less painfully than the first few times. Following his lead, she put a piece of bread and a mushroom in her mouth and was impressed by how well this combo soothed the burn.

"Tell me where you learned to ring church bells," she asked chewing heartily on a slice of bread.

He explained how his grandmother had tried to preserve the Russian Orthodox faith in their family. Under Communism, that was a daunting task. When Volodya was a child, she would often sneak him into one of the few churches that were allowed to remain open under the atheistic regime, exclusively for the use of the elderly. He loved the pageantry, the smell of wax candles, the singing of the choir. And particularly the bells.

When Volodya was five, his father hung scraps of metal of various sizes from a line strung between two chairs, and young Volodya spent hours tapping at them, trying to imitate the melodies he had heard in church.

Once he started school, his parents discouraged any association with religion, knowing that it would end any career aspirations he might have. As an adult, he stayed away from religion. But when churches started to reopen after the 1991 coup that deposed the Communist party, Volodya volunteered to ring bells at the local parish. There was practically no one trained in the dying art, and his services were gratefully accepted.

"Now, every big holiday, people in church say I must ring."

"I can see why. You do such a wonderful job."

He beamed. "Breath taking?"

"Yes, breathtaking." Anne smiled. *His vocabulary was expanding nicely.* "Are you religious?"

He thought for awhile. "Yes, maybe something exists, some, how you say, force ..." He waved his fingers through the air as if trying to capture the word. "Energy. And we are part of it. Same energy, we use, then return to pool."

Anne tried to visualize his world. Where was the energy contained? How was it divided among people? Could you transfer it? What made it individual?

"And you?" he asked. "What do you believe?"

The question startled her. *"Nothing" would be accurate.*

"I guess I believe in the four-minute brain," she said quietly.

"What is four minute brain?"

"Four minutes after the heart stops, the brain dies from lack of oxygen."

"And then?"

"And then, nothing."

"Everything person learned? Feelings, memories, all become nothing?"

"I guess so."

"So you believe we save nothing of us, to give to others?"

"We can write articles about our research, for example."

He looked sad. "Articles?"

She shook her head, bracing herself for another biting comment, like "You, pragmatist."

"I know," he said. "It is difficult to believe without proving, without understanding. But I say to myself we can accept now, then maybe later we understand."

"I don't like not understanding," Anne said, envious that she could not share the simplicity of his philosophy.

The waitress returned with a tray full of appetizers. Smoked salmon, marinated eggplant, tiny hard-boiled quail eggs, another bowl of mushrooms.

"Where is your family from?" Anne asked, loading her plate, happy to change the subject to something less introspective.

"Ah! My grandfather had farm. Fifty thousand sheep. When Communists came …"

The conversation took off.

When they first got to the restaurant, Anne felt apprehensive that he would flirt with her, then surprised that he didn't. Now, she forgot about the issue entirely and enjoyed the company.

He wanted to hear in detail about how she conceived the MEG idea. Anne had had to field similar questions in the past, but his were different. He seldom asked, "How did you do it?" dwelling more on the "Why?" and "What were your hopes?" and "How did you feel about it?". Not accustomed to describing her feelings, Anne felt pleasantly challenged.

He enjoyed watching her ponder the answers. He sensed that he was dwelling in territory where no one had dared venture before, and it made him feel special. *This woman had so much hidden within her, so much protected by her shell.* He saw the cracks, the vulnerability, the desire to share it all with the right person who dared ask.

Their conversation flowed easily from topic to topic. Medicine, history, philosophy, art. Anne adapted to his vocabulary, learning to understand him with a few words, responding in unconventionally structured sentences, or dropping articles, Russian style.

During lulls in their dialogue, they simply looked out the window or at each other, comfortable with the silence.

Anne noticed that sometimes, for no apparent reason, he would stop in mid-paragraph, stare in her eyes, smile and say, "Hello, Anne." It made her feel that for him, at that moment, there was no one else in the world. It was a struggle to keep her mind from racing off into fantasy.

At one point, noticing how uncomfortable his tie was, she reached forward, pulled it loose, then slipped her fingers inside his collar and unbuttoned it.

I can't believe I did that, she thought immediately. But he just rolled his head, relaxing his muscles, and kept talking as if it had been the most natural thing for her to do.

Many topics later, Anne felt someone standing behind her. She turned. It was the waitress, holding their coats and smiling apologetically.

"Is time for closing," Volodya said.

For the first time the entire evening she glanced at her watch. She gasped. It was almost three in the morning. They had talked for four hours.

"We must go to work soon," Volodya grinned.

He split what was left of the vodka between their glasses.

"To the white swan," he said, raising his glass.

"To the prince," she replied, her head spinning.

They strolled, arm in arm, oblivious to the frigid gusts that swept across the now deserted streets.

He stopped at the hotel entrance, their breaths shimmering under street lamps.

"So …" *So, this was the real Dr. Anne Powell. Interested and interesting, curious and opinionated. The shell so hard, and yet so thin. And inside, a kindred lonely, passionate soul. She was more than he could have imagined in his wildest dreams.*

"How do you say? It was good to make your acquaintance," he smiled.

She nodded. *It was good indeed. Many layers had been peeled back.*

Perhaps too many.

"Your ears are frozen," he said suddenly.

Pulling off his gloves, he cupped his hands over her ears, not touching them, letting the warmth build. She felt the heat spreading across her face, into her scalp, down her neck.

"*Spokoynoy nochy,*" he whispered.

"*Spokoynoy nochy,*" she whispered back. "May the peace of night be with you." Despite herself, she leaned toward him, his lips close enough to kiss.

But he turned and hurried away.

44

"**D**r. Powell," the night attendant called out as Anne walked past the front desk to the elevators. "Your husband called. He instructed me to ask you to call him as soon as you got back."

Halden. At this hour? Did something happen to Misty? Or to a patient? Maybe the Feds decided to approve the MEG after all.

The phone was ringing when she walked into the room.

"Good evening. Or shall I say good morning?"

His tone grated on her nerves as much as the words "your husband" had when the concierge said them.

"Jack! Is everything all right?"

"Of course." He paused. "Late night, uh? I was getting worried."

"I was out."

"How nice. Did you have a good time?

"I had a great time. We saw *Swan Lake,* and then …

"Ballet. Excellent. With whom did you go?"

Listening to him now, while she was still glowing from her evening with Volodya, was like being dragged out of a warm sauna and thrown on cold concrete.

"I went with a colleague."

A colleague. Halden cringed. *She was being too evasive.* "Male?" he asked, sitting up in his bed but trying to sound casual.

"I can't believe you're asking me that!" her voice burst from the receiver.

He clenched his teeth. *She was out with a man. On a date. Until the wee hours of the morning. Well after any opera would have ended.*

"What am I supposed to think? You're not home at four in the morning, you …"

"You're supposed to think I'm having a good time, and will be back safe and sound."

He crunched the bed sheet in his fist. *Having a good time. With whom? Why? What was she doing? Laughing? Dancing? Or … He felt bile backing into his throat.*

Not that she had ever given him reason to doubt her … But she was thousands of miles away now, completely out of his control. Anything could happen. She was a beautiful woman, soon to be rich. Somebody could get her drunk, seduce her, blackmail her and ruin the whole MEG deal. To say nothing of their relationship. It was precisely the situation he feared when she decided to go to Russia.

"Anne?"

"What?"

"You are our company's ambassador. Don't do anything that would embarrass us."

She was so furious she couldn't speak for a long time.

"I'm going to sleep now." Her voice was quiet. Almost a whisper. "So I can be efficient tomorrow and not embarrass anybody," she added, hanging up.

She yanked the phone off the hook and marched into the bathroom. *Embarrass the company? He calls in the middle of the night to check up on her because he's worried about the company's image? Being questioned about an accidental outing with a colleague was demeaning enough. But for him to worry about what impression it would make on others?*

She climbed into the bathtub and closed her eyes. One by one, tears started to roll down her cheeks. Tears of disappointment in Jack, tears of frustration that she couldn't let herself go, tears of sadness that she didn't feel free to look forward to another evening with Volodya.

Another evening just like this one had been, until Jack called.

Her few hours of sleep were tortured by nightmares. She dreamed that she was MEGing a patient. A man. His scan looked not like a brain, but like a tunnel. She turned up the power. A white glow appeared at the far end, beckoning. She walked up to the patient and kissed him on the lips. Without even seeing the face she knew it was Volodya. His arms came out of the MEG restraints and he reached up and drew her closer. His breath had the scent of honey. Sweet honey that comes from wide-open sun-drenched fields of summer flowers. She felt herself melting in his arms.

Suddenly Baldyuk barged into the room brandishing a bloody ax, and rushed toward them. Anne tried to stop him, but he shoved her aside and grabbed Volodya's curls. She realized that it wasn't Baldyuk at all. It was Grudskoy.

Anne heard hoof beats. Giant horses, thundering toward her.

Grudskoy's booming voice: *This is the price you'll pay, whore.*

Someone's severed head rolled up to her feet.

She was so terrified that she willed herself awake. Her heart was racing. Her nightgown was soaked in sweat. The familiar gnawing pain was tearing at her pelvis.

She sat up and turned on the light.

There was no denying it. Her nightmares about the young bride being raped, the severed head, the fires—they were all related to her pelvic spasms. And to being in love.

Instantly she felt herself closing, like a disturbed sea anemone. She wanted nothing to do with Volodya. She had to get him out of her mind. Never see him again.

It was just like when she left Peter. The same dream. And the following morning the sweetest love of her life was replaced by uncontrollable fear.

"No, damn it!" she exclaimed, bounding out of bed. This was no way to live life. If she was ever going to love a man, she had to figure out where these dreams were coming from.

It was time to face it, process it and let it go.

ven though Anne got to the Pavlov half an hour earlier than usual, Sasha was already there and the MEG was powered up. "You and I have a full day ahead of us," Sasha announced cheerfully.

"I'm rested and ready," Anne fibbed. Her two hours of tortured sleep would have to do.

She walked up to the console and started to key in the start up sequences. As her fingers ran over the keys, she stopped and frowned. *Strange.*

She completed the sequence and went to inspect the repaired restraint. It had been days, but the lock washer had not been delivered yet, so Anne checked every day to make sure the bolt wasn't coming undone.

Satisfied, she started to turn away, but something on the floor caught her eye. She picked it up. It was half-an-inch of blue plastic tubing, the kind used for wire insulation. She was positive it wasn't on the floor the day before. *What the hell was going on here?*

"We had a problem with the room wiring," Sasha said, anticipating the question.

"Anything I should know about?"

"The MEG is drawing more power than these old circuits can

handle. I had engineering replace some of the wiring from the junction box all the way to the main transformer downstairs. Poor guy was here most of the night."

"I guess he likes to work in a steam bath," Anne mumbled.

"Why do you say that?"

"He must've had the room heat full blast the whole time."

"Why do you say that?"

"Usually it takes hours for the console to get this warm."

Nothing gets past this woman, Sasha thought.

"Did the Bolshoi live up to your expectations?" she asked to change the subject.

"Oh, what a treat it was!" Anne exclaimed.

"I gave the other ticket to Irina, but she backed out at the last minute. I hope you didn't mind that Volodya showed up."

Mind? It was the best part of the evening, Anne thought. "I'm glad Volodya was there to explain, or I would've missed the story entirely."

"Hope it wasn't a long explanation. He can be a real bore."

What's with those two, Anne wondered. They looked like a well-matched couple when she first met Sasha in Volodya's lab. Now, the man had obviously fallen out of her graces.

As hard as she tried, she couldn't help thinking that she was not unhappy about this development.

"Well, I've something even better for you." She dangled a set of keys on a monogrammed silver key fob.

Anne gave Sasha a puzzled look.

"Our dear professor must be feeling very contrite, because he invited you to his *dacha* for the weekend. Don't worry, he won't be there," Sasha laughed, seeing Anne's expression. "I think he's really trying to do something nice for a change." She touched Anne's arm. "Wait 'til you see it. The place is incredible. Three hours by car from Moscow, but worth every minute. Eighteen rooms, five fireplaces, sauna, a kitchen to die for. Not that you'll need to go in it. He has two full-time maids and a cook."

"Sounds like a castle."

"Huge grounds. Stables. Horses. Do you ride?"

"I don't care for horses." Actually, Anne was petrified of them, ever since she could remember. Even the smell of them made her freeze up.

"Anyway, there's plenty to do. Or just sit and be pampered. You'll love it. I wish I were invited," she added wistfully.

"Tell the professor I'm very grateful, but I have to work this weekend."

"You're kidding! Bring your work along. He has a fully equipped office …"

"I'd really rather not, Sasha," Anne said firmly. The research she planned to do had to be done in Moscow.

Sasha bit her lip. If she couldn't get Anne out of town for a few days, Sergey's wiring would be wasted.

"You're missing a once-in-a-lifetime chance to live like a Russian princess," Sasha said.

Anne shrugged and smiled apologetically. Right now, the life of a Russian princess was exactly the issue she was preparing to face.

46

"Natalia, where can I find a library around here?" Anne asked, walking up to the concierge desk the following morning.

"It's not far," Natalia said, producing a map. "It's called the Russian Government Library, but since our government doesn't have money to change the sign, it's still labeled Lenin Library. You can't miss it," Natalia added handing Anne the map. "And it's easy to use—just go in and ask for what you need. All the librarians speak English. It is required to get a job there."

Standing in the rocking subway car, Anne formulated a plan of action. Do a word search for the name "Grudskoy" in the computer. Cross-reference for the mid-1400s to get a first name. Look up the full name. If it ever figured in any major literary work, or in a film, it would turn up. Then she could review the story and perhaps find the ending that she was so afraid to remember. Face her demons in order to conquer them. And then she would be able to chase the nightmare out of her system forever. It worked for Misty's patients, why not for her?

It sounded reasonable, but inside her a voice was whispering, *"Don't do it, don't go probing. What if you find something you don't want to know?"*

Nonsense, her rational self assured her. *She was a scientist. Doing a search was the scientific way to approach the challenge.*

The former Lenin Library had a definitely Leninesque grandeur—an imposing angular edifice, fronted by giant square columns of black granite, surrounded by trees and fountains, both dead for the winter. A sign—*Biblioteka Lenina*—dominated the façade, the giant bronze letters covered with pigeon droppings.

She entered through a small door with an impossibly strong self-closing mechanism that took all of Anne's strength to force open. Russians are really protective of their warm air, she thought. No winter blast was going to force this door open!

The coat check attendant was a man in his seventies, a row of war medals prominently displayed above his name badge. Noticing that Anne was looking at them, he puckered up proudly to give her a better look. There were several red stars, a couple of hammer-and-sickles, two parachutes, and half a dozen other insignia. *The man had paid his dues.*

"*Voyna?*" Anne asked, remembering the word for war.

"*Da, voyenye medally. Bylly Guitler.*"

He traded her coat for a numbered plastic chip and pointed her toward another line.

Anne noticed that everyone here had a small green booklet that was politely presented to the uniformed female guard stationed at the head of the stairs.

Anne produced her passport.

"*Nyet, nyet. Noozhen propusk,*" the guard snapped, as if Anne had insulted her personally. "*Pro-pusk.*"

Anne tried her Boston Library card. *She wasn't going to be checking the books out, so why couldn't she just go in?*

The guard was implacable. "*Propusk.*"

The people in line shuffled impatiently. Anne fumbled with her purse. *Would a driver's license do?*

"*Nyet,*" the guard barked, directing her toward the exit.

Anne gave up and returned to the coat check. The veteran smiled, surprised to see her again so soon.

"*Vse?* All done?"

One more try, Anne decided.

"*Izvinite pojaluysta gde ...*" Her Russian ran out. "Excuse me, do you speak English?"

The man's mouth spread into a giant smile, revealing ill-fitting dentures.

"*Ein bischen Deutsch, un poco Italiano, un peux Francais*, little American. I fighted everywhere, speak everything."

"I want to learn about Russian history," Anne said, trying to keep it simple. "How can I get inside?"

"Room one-zero-seven," he rattled off crisply, as if calling out a compass heading. "There." He pointed toward the back of the lobby and gave Anne a little salute.

In room 107 a pasty-faced matron handed Anne a two-page form to fill out and scrutinized her passport with the diligence of a border guard. Then, with great pomp, she produced a credit card-sized booklet, bound in green cloth and embossed with gold letters: *Biblioteka Lenina.* Very carefully she wrote in Anne's name.

"Good one week," she said sternly, hammering several stamp marks across the *propusk* and handing it to Anne.

Holding the pass as if it were a trophy, Anne returned to the line. The guard let her through without any sign of recognition.

Anne walked up the wide marble staircase flanked by enormous granite columns that reached toward a majestic high ceiling, wondering how she would find and use a computer terminal in this bureaucratic labyrinth.

She reached the mezzanine and stopped. There was not a computer terminal in sight. The entire floor was filled with rows upon rows of old fashioned card catalogs. It was a sight that reminded her of the tour of the public library she had in kindergarten.

Anne wandered up and down the long rows of cabinets, their wood polished to a fine patina by thousands of users over half a century, each drawer carefully hand-labeled with Cyrillic letters.

So much for "just go in and ask," Anne thought.

She approached a group of teenagers clustered around one of the drawers. "Excuse me, can you help me?"

The youngsters exchanged puzzled glances.

"We shall try," a red-haired teenage boy articulated.

"I am looking for information on a man named Grudsky, or Grudskoy," Anne said. "He was from Novgorod."

"Probably Grudskoy. If from Novgorod, then is Russian name," the boy corrected her. "Grudsky is Polish."

"He may have been mentioned in *War and Peace* or *Anna Karenina*," Anne added.

"No Grudskoy in *Anna Karenina*," said one of the girls. "Is sure," she added with finality.

Anne wondered how many times the girl read and reread this beautifully romantic, heartbreaking story about a married woman who ruined her life by falling in love with an officer who later abandoned her. It had been one of her own favorites in college.

"*War and Peace*, perhaps?" Anne asked.

The teenagers smiled apologetically.

"We only read *Voina y Mir* little bit," one of them confessed.

"Can you tell me how I can look it up? I don't see a computer …"

"Perhaps you ask, how you say, *bibliotekarian*?" the red-head suggested. "In that room," he added, pointing to a door at the back of the mezzanine.

The librarian, a woman in her thirties, dressed in casual street clothes without any identification, greeted her warmly.

"My name is Yureva, Marina," she introduced herself, giving her family name first, in formal fashion. "What can I do?"

"I am looking for information on a man named Grudskoy, from Novgorod. Could you help me?"

"You know occupation, or year when born?"

"A war leader of some sort, I think. From around the mid-1300s."

"Could you be more specific?"

"I only know that he was probably important in his time."

"Let me try the boyar families genealogy … Perhaps we are lucky."

The librarian disappeared into the stacks and returned with an old tome with tattered binding.

"Every boyar family is listed here, from late thirteen century."

"Boyar?"

"Boyars were Russian nobles. Like barons in other countries," the librarian explained. "And above *boyar* is *knyaz*. More like prince."

Marina leafed through the book while she continued her recitation.

"Boyars owned large pieces of land. More land, more important *boyar*. Some land they received as gifts from Tsar. Other land they bought from neighbors, or simply took. With soldiers, you know? Also they took the men and women who lived on land. Peasants were serfs. They worked all life for *boyar*, received only food and a little land, and were at his mercy, to do what he pleased. Also peasant women. For example, when peasant girl was married, *boyar* had right to have wedding night with her and take her virginity. Then second night, she was given to husband. The most powerful *boyars* spent some time on their lands, some time in Moscow at the court with the Czar…"

Anne tried to stop the tirade as politely as she could. "I think Grudskoy was from Novgorod. Do you see anything listed?

"Novgorod means New Town. But it is one of the oldest cities in Russia," Marina continued in her singsong monotone, like a tour guide. "Novgorod was founded in the seventh century. It is near St. Petersburg. The area was covered in forests and was very rich in animals. Furs were traded for food and tools and for gold from the south. Because area was so rich, villages were frequently attacked by Tartar hordes."

Anne looked over Marina's shoulder as she scanned the pages.

Marina continued the recitation. "Tartars were fierce warriors. At peak of their power in mid-1300s, Tartars controlled most of country. To ensure peace, towns like Moscow, Novgorod, Kiev and others had to pay tribute to Tartars—gold, furs, wheat. Tartars liked to humiliate Russians. One time Russian Czar had to wait on his knees, in snow, for several days outside Tartar khan's imperial tent, before entrance."

Anne's patience was being strained. "Did you find Grudskoy?"

"Nothing so far."

Anne sighed. "Maybe I made a mistake. It could be a fictitious character. Thanks, anyway." She started to get up.

"Ah-ha. Wait. Here!" Marina exclaimed. "Grudskoy."

She turned the book so Anne could see and translated the text.

"Very long family. The first Grudskoy fight against Tartars almost six hundred years ago. Last Grudskoy fight against Bolsheviks sixty years ago. In fifteenth century, circa 1430, one Grudskoy unified most of Novgorod province, et cetera, et cetera ..."

She scanned the text further.

"The Grudskoy family was very powerful during reign of Czar Ivan the Terrible, as you call him in English. In Russian is 'Ivan Grozny,' which means 'like tempest', not 'terrible'."

She glanced up at Anne. "Oy! What is matter?!" she exclaimed.

Anne was staring at the drawing of a stocky man on horseback, with a full beard, wearing chainmail armor on his bulging chest and a tunic resembling a Scottish quill. It was the image she remembered from her dream. She had no trouble deciphering the caption: *Alexandr Grudskoy.*

"You do not feel well?" Marina asked, concerned.

"I'll be OK," Anne answered, trying to regain her composure. "Did he ... did he look like that?"

"Who knows. This is only artist's idea. From old paintings."

"Is there anything else about him here?"

The librarian turned the page. "Not much. Very ruthless man. Took many lands from weaker neighbors. Was very successful fighting Tartars ..." She reread a passage. "Had one captured Tartar woman as concubine. Very interesting. Just what Tartars used to do to Russian women. Had three daughters, one son. As special honor, for uniting lands and serving the Czar, this Grudskoy was buried in Sergyeva Lavra. It is very old monastery, started in 1345 by St. Sergius. It is a very important monastery, because it never was closed. Not when Tartars invaded Russia, not in French war, not even under Communists. When monastery was most important, it housed ..."

"Where is it?" Anne interrupted, her voice trembling.

"Not far from Moscow. Is very beautiful. You should visit perhaps."

As she rode the Metro back to the hotel, Anne could think of nothing but the picture in the book. *The resemblance was striking.*

But what did it mean?

If that was the picture of the man in her dream, what had she proven? That she had seen that picture before? Where? In a history book? Maybe at some traveling Russian art exhibit that she had forgotten about? Besides, did it really matter?

She knew it did. She had opened Pandora's box. Now there was no way not to look inside.

47

The hotel's Mercedes, its gilded "Hotel National" logos on the doors glowing like royal crests, inched agonizingly through rush hour traffic. Torturing an unlit cigarette between his teeth, Matvey the driver glanced nervously at his watch.

"Maybe change visit to tomorrow, Doctor?" he asked, gripping the wheel more tightly.

"Let's keep going."

"I must return to Moscow at seven o'clock."

"We'll make it. I don't need a lot of time there."

It took an hour to reach the city's outskirts, but once on the highway the car picked up speed. Fallow fields, dilapidated factories and deserted junkyards flashed past Anne's window. Here and there she saw clusters of small wooden houses, their steep snow-covered roofs, ornate ewes and elaborately carved porches seemingly straight out of a fairy tale.

It was after four o'clock by the time they turned off onto a two-lane road and entered a small village.

"Sergyeva Lavra," Matvey announced.

A massive white wall, interrupted by looming guard towers, emerged slowly out of the bluish mist.

The car coasted up to a wooden gate. Matvey pointed to his

watch, showed five fingers and gestured toward the highway. The body language was clear: *At five o'clock, I'm out of here.*

"*Khorosho,*" Anne agreed. *Finding what she was looking for shouldn't take long.*

Anne fought her way through a rowdy group of French tourists trying to crowd into a bus, hurried past a line of vendors who were packing their wares, and rushed toward the outhouse-sized ticket booth adjacent to the gate. Just as she reached it, the small window slammed closed. Anne knocked. Nothing happened. Anne knocked again. An obese woman emerged from the side door of the booth.

"*Zakryto.* Closed," she said gruffly, buttoning her coat.

"I only need ten minutes," Anne pleaded. "I want to see Grudskoy's grave," she added, pulling out a slip of paper where the librarian had spelled out the name in Cyrillic.

The woman squinted avariciously at Anne's clearly American outfit and pointed to the small sign posted over the window. *Foreign visitors—6000 rubles,* the sign said. That was equivalent to twenty dollars. *Ruskye grazhdany—600 rubles.* A ten-fold markup for being a foreigner. But this was not the time to discuss the inequities of the price structure. Anne reached for her wallet.

"Photos? More six thousand."

"No photos, only look," Anne answered, counting out the money. The woman pocketed the bills and waved Anne through the gate.

Anne walked up the narrow cobblestone path, past straggling visitors hurrying toward the exit. She passed through the short tunnel that traversed the thick wall and entered the confines of the monastery itself.

The enclosure was occupied by four churches, the largest one topped by three beautiful, blue, onion-shaped domes adorned with silver stars.

Anne continued along the road, past the churches, wondering how to find the cemetery. She smiled as two bearded clerics in long black cassocks passed her, talking quietly.

"Please, where is this grave?" she asked, pointing to her paper.

The monks paused, exchanged a few words, then silently pointed toward a narrow alley behind the main church. Anne felt like an intruder. Admission charge notwithstanding, this was still a real monastery, with real monks and real churches. *And real relics.*

Rounding the corner, Anne found what she was looking for—several hundred graves surrounded by a rusted iron fence. She pushed open the metal gate and started up the uneven path, trying to avoid icy patches.

The tombs were of various ages. Tall crosses, some in stone, some in weathered wood, topped many of the graves. Others were marked by small headstones barely sticking out of the snow. In many places, the markers were overgrown by bushes or trees.

This was like looking for a needle in a haystack. Daylight was fading rapidly. She would have to come back another day.

As she turned, she noticed a metal plate engraved with the plan of the cemetery. A few of the tombs were labeled with names and dates.

Grudskoy's tomb was not on the map, but Anne noted that the graves were clustered by dates. Taking a few moments to get oriented, she walked down the main path, turned left and headed toward the back of the plot where the tombs from the 1400s were supposed to be.

The uneven surface made walking treacherous. She had to keep stepping off the path to examine the grave markers, their Cyrillic inscriptions worn shallow by centuries of weather.

1440-1498, 1370-1394, 1456-1468. It was strange to be so close to people who had died before anyone in Europe even dreamed of sailing off in search of the New World.

Her heart started beating faster as she found a stone marked 1389-1434. She concentrated on the name, but it had none of the letters she was looking for.

She moved up to another one.

Nothing.

Two more.

The light was growing dimmer. She hurried from marker to marker. 1480s, 1500s, 1550s. *She was going in the wrong direction.* She stopped, frustrated that time was running out and she should be heading back.

"Just one more set," she told herself, then she would go. As she took a step back, her foot slipped and she crashed on her side. An intense pain pierced her left elbow.

"Damn!" *How could I be so clumsy,* she wondered, examining the blood oozing through the shredded fabric.

Slowly, she flexed the joint. *At least nothing was broken.* She sighed with relief. She leaned on her right hand to push herself up. The snow burned her fingers and she cursed herself for not wearing gloves.

As she rubbed her fingers to warm them up, her eyes fell on the spot where her hand made an imprint in the snow. There, in the weathered granite, she saw the unmistakable outline of a Cyrillic "G." Anne remembered it easily—"G" for gallows, which the letter, shaped like a Latin "F" without the crossbar, clearly resembled.

She rolled to her side and dusted the snow off the stone, revealing a "P" for the Cyrillic "R." The rest was covered with ice.

Pulling a coin out of her pocket, she started scraping away frantically. She felt her heart pounding as the inscription emerged.

Grudskoy, Aleksandr. 1373-1448. There was also a Russian cross, with two extra crossbars unevenly carved into the rock.

Suddenly, she heard a voice. "I found you!"

Anne gasped and spun around. Sasha, wearing a short black leather jacket, blue jeans and heavy boots, stood behind her. Her cheeks were red. She was smiling.

"What are you doing here?" Sasha asked cheerfully.

Anne wasn't prepared for the question.

"I wanted to … A friend of mine …" she stammered.

Sasha squatted down next to Anne. "Hmm. Grudskoy."

Sasha ran her fingers over the aged rock, pitted by centuries of rain and ice. "Somebody special?" she asked.

"A friend of mine wanted me to look up this grave. Apparently her grandfather was related to this Grudskoy …" Anne mumbled as she stood up awkwardly.

"She can trace her ancestors five centuries back?" Sasha said skeptically.

"Evidently …"

"What happened?" Sasha exclaimed, noticing blood seeping through the tear in Anne's jacket.

"It's nothing," Anne said, flexing her elbow, happy to change the subject. "I fell."

"You need to get this cleaned up."

"I'll take care of it when I get home," Anne said, starting toward the main path, gingerly avoiding stepping on slippery slabs. "What are *you* doing here?" she asked Sasha.

"I've been calling you all morning. Couldn't figure out where you could possibly be. So I stopped by the hotel and asked Natalia."

Anne winced, irritated by the concierge's indiscretion. "She told you?"

"Why not? I've been there a few times now. They're starting to think we're related or something!" Sasha chuckled.

As they exited the gate, Anne realized that the parking area was deserted and dark. The vendors were gone. The buses were gone. The hotel car was gone.

"I can't believe this!" Anne exclaimed. "My driver said he'd wait."

Sasha shrugged. "He probably figured he missed you, since everyone else is gone."

"There's supposed to be a train. I guess I'll take it," Anne mused.

"Don't be silly. You want to spend three hours crammed in with smelly people and their smelly chickens?" Sasha laughed. "Come on, I'll give you a ride."

There was no elegant way out of this one. Whether she liked it or not, Anne was about to spend some alone time with Sasha.

48

Anne followed Sasha around the corner and found herself in front of a huge red MottoGuzzi motorcycle.

"I've never been on a motorcycle before," Anne said, eyeing the machine suspiciously.

"Ah-ha! A bike virgin," Sasha exclaimed, pleased.

The bike, a souvenir of a stormy relationship with an affluent Italian psychiatrist who did a fellowship at the Pavlov a couple of years ago, was her pride and joy. MottoGuzzis were powerful and exotic machines, and hers was probably the only one in Moscow. In fact, it was probably the only motorcycle, of any brand, on the road in this weather.

She glanced at Anne. "I can't believe you walk around like this. No hat, no scarf, no gloves." Shaking her head disapprovingly, Sasha took off her own scarf and wrapped it around Anne's neck. "We're a lot closer to Siberia than to Florida, you know."

She swung her leg over the bike and thrust the key into the ignition. The bike roared to life.

"My people, the Tartars, practically lived on horses. I guess you can say this is the urban equivalent," she laughed, revving up the engine with a flick of her right wrist. "Climb on."

Anne unbuttoned the bottom of her coat, pulled up her skirt and struggled onto the seat behind Sasha, mentally counting her blessings for having at least worn thick hose.

Without warning, the bike surged forward. Anne felt herself pulled backwards by the acceleration. By reflex, she grabbed Sasha's waist.

They bounced through a couple of potholes, muddy icy water splashing up to her calves.

Anne felt the bike banking steeply as Sasha rounded the corner. It was a frightening feeling of being totally out of control.

"Relax and lean with me," Sasha yelled over the noise of the engine. "Don't fight the turns."

Relaxing was out of the question. Anne tried to concentrate on the leaning.

"I have to go a little slower here. Lots of ice patches," Sasha yelled again. "We'll make up the time on the highway."

Anne stole a glance at the monastery's walls receding into the evening fog. She could still feel the icy slab under her finger tips and see the letters on the inscription. No matter how much she twisted her thinking, trying to rationalize her find, there was no denying that the man she had seen in her dreams was buried behind those walls. She wanted to be alone in her hotel room, to sort out her confusion. Instead, she felt herself pressing harder against Sasha's back as they hurtled through the frigid air.

"Is this like Boston?" Sasha shouted over her shoulder.

"Much colder," Anne shouted back.

"Do you miss home?"

"A little."

"Do you miss your fiancé?"

It wasn't worth it to discuss the fact that they were not engaged. *How did Sasha know, anyway? Probably Jack said something to Baldyuk.*

"We talk on the phone," Anne replied, ending that line of conversation.

Did she miss Jack? She missed the Jack she thought she knew.

He had called twice to apologize about questioning her the other night. But the damage was done. She had come to terms with the fact that their relationship was nothing but a fragile house of cards, held together by their crippling fears of commitment.

A coupling of convenience, predicated on respecting each other's protective shells. He overstepped the boundaries. The façade had crumbled. The connection they had was broken. Some time soon she would have to tell him that she wouldn't be moving in.

She sighed, anticipating how the breakup would leave her, once again, staring into a sea of loneliness.

The motorcycle accelerated, merging with the highway traffic. Sasha shouted something, but Anne couldn't understand her. The noise of the wind, hum of the engine, and roar of passing trucks was deafening. The frigid wind penetrated every seam of her clothing. Within minutes, her fingers started to stiffen and she tried to pull them into her sleeves for protection. Her elbow ached. Her legs were spread uncomfortably, cold air blasting between them. Her face and eyes were burning, bombarded by snowflakes slamming against her skin. She didn't know how she would last the trip.

Even through her thick leather jacket, Sasha could feel Anne shivering. Skillfully balancing her bike with her hands off the handlebars, she reached behind herself, grasped Anne's hands and slipped them under her clothing, against the skin of her own belly.

"You need to keep them warm!" she yelled, turning her head slightly toward Anne.

Anne tried to pull her hands away, but Sasha squeezed harder, holding them in place with her elbows.

"Keep them there or you'll get frostbite!" Sasha yelled. Anne's frozen fingers burned her belly. But it was the most exquisite feeling that Sasha had ever felt.

The burn spread through her body.

Suddenly a young couple materialized in the middle of the road. The woman's long blond hair was blowing in the wind. They were clinging to each other, kissing passionately. Before Sasha could swerve, the motorcycle blasted through the couple.

The image vanished.

Sasha felt droplets of perspiration oozing down her back.

They hit traffic on the outskirts of town and even with the maneuverability of the motorcycle, their progress became painfully slow.

Anne was so cold she could barely hold on to Sasha. "Are we almost there?" Anne managed to ask. Her whole body was numb, her mind unable to think of anything except warmth.

When they stopped at a traffic light, Sasha glanced back and saw Anne's face—pale, drawn, her lips blue.

Without a word, she gunned the engine, and, narrowly missing a truck, made a U-turn, the bike bouncing violently over the center divider.

"Where are you going?" Anne managed, her jaw frozen stiff.

"In this traffic, it'll take another hour to get to the hotel," Sasha yelled back. "Let's stop and warm up at my place!"

Anne was too cold to protest. "Is it far?" she mumbled.

Five minutes later they pulled into an alley behind a row of boxy, gloomy apartment buildings. *Just like low-rent tenements in the outskirts of New York, only grayer,* Anne thought.

Sasha drove the bike over the curb and stopped under a set of concrete stairs. Everything was suddenly very quiet as she shut the engine down. A dog barked somewhere.

"Quick, let's get you inside," she said, pulling Anne toward the entrance. Anne followed on stiff legs.

They rode to the tenth floor in a tiny elevator that smelled of fried fish.

"My neighbor," Sasha said apologetically. "You can always tell what's for dinner."

At the end of a dim corridor, they stopped in front of a metal door. Sasha unlocked three locks and pushed the door open.

"Please, come in."

They walked into a short narrow hallway. A dozen wooden crates, several oily motorcycle parts, two metal barrels and a punching bag were laid out against the wall.

"Please excuse. This is my vestibule. I think you call it mud room in the States?" Sasha corrected herself.

She unlocked another door. Anne felt a welcome wave of dry hot air sweep across her face and body.

"This is home," Sasha said, spreading her arms as they walked into a large open space divided by a single partition.

Anne heard a bark, and a giant husky rushed toward them.

"*Volk, molchi,*" Sasha said, barely loud enough to hear. The animal came to an abrupt stop. Sasha patted it, then took Anne's hand, and guided it toward the dog's head. "Friend."

Anne ran her numb fingers through the thick fur. The dog sniffed her hand and walked away.

"First of all, let's get you out of your wet clothes and into a warm bath."

"I'll be fine, really," Anne protested.

"Don't argue," Sasha said sternly. "I'll get you something dry from my bedroom," she added, disappearing behind the partition in the center of the room.

Moments later she reappeared with a terry cloth robe. "This should work until we get your clothes dried."

The tiny bathroom was dominated by an old-fashioned bathtub on short legs. In bizarre contrast to the old ceramic, the gleaming chrome faucets were of ultra-modern design.

"You make do with whatever you can get," Sasha explained. She adjusted the water and turned to Anne. "Good. The boiler downstairs seems to be working. Now, get out of those wet clothes while I make us tea," Sasha said, and squeezed out the door.

Anne pushed the door as closed as the old hinges would allow. A sizable crack remained. She ducked into the far corner and began to undress.

Sasha crossed the room and went into the alcove that passed for a kitchen. Trying not to think about Anne standing naked just a few feet from her, Sasha busied herself making tea and setting the small table.

She pulled out a package of Belgian cookies that she had been saving for a special occasion, and a jar of homemade strawberry jam she had bought from a woman at the subway entrance. Satisfied with her preparations, she went back to her makeshift bedroom, pulled off her clothes and slipped into sweats.

When she heard the water draining, Sasha walked up to the bathroom door. "Done?"

"Almost."

"Feeling better?"

"At least I can feel my body again."

Sasha tapped on the door. "You left the bathrobe …"

The door moved, and the crack widened. Sasha caught a glimpse of a long thigh, a muscular, well-rounded, shoulder. Her heart began to pound.

A swooshing sound overwhelmed her ears. The room filled with steam, and she saw the outline of a naked woman standing in front of her. Young, tall. Her sinuous body curved elegantly as she stepped out of a wooden tub. Two teenage girls appeared and started rubbing her skin with oil. The young woman's face was hauntingly beautiful.

"Thanks," Anne said taking the bathrobe and pushing the door closed again.

Sasha's vision vanished. Seconds later, Anne emerged wrapped in the bathrobe.

"I was able to get two small apartments instead of a large one," Sasha explained as they strolled around her pad sipping tea. "So I took down a couple of walls and joined them. What do you think?"

The area was airy and light. The screen that partitioned off the bedroom area was decorated with an odd assortment of artwork. A poster of St. Basil's Cathedral against a sky full of fireworks, celebrating the 850th anniversary of Moscow. A picture of Lenin's statue irreverently suspended by the neck from a helicopter. Two icons. And a postcard of snow-capped mountains.

The center of the room was occupied by two wooden armchairs and several bookcases neatly packed with books.

One side of the room was clear of furniture. A gym mat lay on the floor in front of a set of iron weights.

"My exercise area," Sasha said.

"What is this for?" Anne asked, running her hands over a thick wooden board propped against the wall. The board had a life-size outline of a human body painted on it and was pockmarked with holes and dents.

"For target practice," Sasha replied.

"What do you shoot?"

"Not shoot, throw," Sasha said, pointing to two axes—a long one, with a bayonet-like tip, and a short one, with a glistening, curved edge. "These were used by Russian warriors in the fourteenth century. They're replicas, of course. The originals are at the Hermitage Museum in St. Petersburg. They dug them up from villages in northern Russia."

"Fascinating," Anne said. "Why do you have them?"

Sasha shrugged. "For fun. The little one is perfect for throwing. I just started, so I am not very good. But let me show you."

She stepped back a few feet, aimed, and hurled the ax at the board. The ax whistled thorough the air, and, with a dull thud, the blade sunk an inch into the wood, right across the throat of the human outline.

"Feel it," Sasha said proudly, extricating the weapon from the wood.

Anne ran her fingers over the blade. It was cold and razor sharp.

"Where did you learn to throw?"

"Trial and error," Sasha laughed, pointing at several gouges in the wall.

The hobby was new—in fact, she had just started. But already she was a better marksman than any of the instructors. "Was your dad a lumberjack?" they teased her, amazed at her instant success and unerring aim. "You were born knowing how to use axes!"

Anne leaned to pick up the other ax. Volk perked his ears, growled and leaped toward her.

Sasha's hand shot up. Volk froze in mid-movement, his bared fangs inches away from Anne's hand.

"It's OK," Sasha said softly to Anne. "Just back away, slowly."

Holding her breath, and trying not to spill the tea from her cup, Anne inched back toward the center of the room.

"That's his private little area. And he's very territorial," Sasha said, sinking into one of the armchairs and draping her leg over the armrest. "Ah, territoriality. The most powerful instinct known to man or beast."

"I thought it was sex," Anne laughed nervously, still shaken.

"Not at all! What good is sex drive and procreation, if you can't feed your offspring? If you control territory, you can hunt. That means food. It's a must for species survival."

"I never looked at it that way."

"Why do you think the Bosnians and Croatians were killing each other over a couple of villages? Or why your people and my people almost blew up the world over a lousy island? It's all about controlling territory. It's in our genetic code." She picked up the teapot. "More?"

Anne put her hand over her cup. "I should be going."

"Wait. Don't go yet. Tell me about your fiancé."

Anne shrugged. "Not much to tell."

"Young, old? Handsome?"

"Early fifties. Average-looking."

"Is he a good ..." Sasha stopped herself. "What does he do?"

"He works for Sidens."

"What exactly?"

"Heads up the MEG project."

"Ah!" Sasha said, giving Anne a long look. "Figures. An alpha male."

"What do you mean?"

"Alpha male. The strongest male in ..."

"I know what an alpha male is. What do you mean by 'figures'?"

"Women are always attracted to power."

"I'm not attracted to his position!" Anne bristled. "Besides, that's a ridiculous generalization."

"Oh, come on! Tell me women don't go for power—muscles, dollars, or rank."

"The shallow ones, perhaps." Anne was beginning to resent Sasha's cynicism.

Sasha leaned back in her chair and sipped her tea.

"Power means survival," she said patiently, as if explaining a simple fact of life to a child. "Females of every species try to choose the most powerful male of the group to mate. You've seen those National Geographic programs—crocodiles or mountain goats fighting to their death for the favors of the most fertile-looking female. And she picks the strongest, because if she mates with a runt, the offspring won't be competitive, and that line will get weeded right out of the gene pool."

"I'd like to think human selection criteria have progressed beyond animal."

"Progressed?" Sasha chuckled. "'Suppressed' is more like it."

"We're more enlightened …"

"Look, females have been choosing the strongest males for millions of years. It's not a matter of choice. That would make the outcome too unpredictable. This behavior is … is hardwired. Like body temperature control, like maternal instinct. What makes you think you can educate it away, in a lousy few thousand years of so-called enlightenment?"

"Plenty of women choose men who are not powerful."

"Maybe with their heads. But not with their instincts. It's all a façade. Look at Baldyuk. Fat, old and ugly. But women find him attractive. Why? Because he's powerful."

"Career advancement."

"Not true. I'm talking women who don't work at the Institute, who have nothing to benefit. Or take Volodya. There isn't a woman at the Pavlov who is not lusting after him. And it's not because some find him handsome."

"Why then?" Anne asked before she could check herself, revealing more curiosity than she wanted to show.

"Why? Because he makes each woman feel like she's the most important thing in his life and he would walk through fire to protect her. It's your basic primordial formula for gene survival. Tell me that's not the most potent aphrodisiac!"

"That's so … such a … clinical way to look at it."

"Clinical but real. Look, it makes all the sense in the world. Can't you see it happening?"

Sasha stood up and started pacing, her arms painting the picture as she spoke. "A vast Siberian plain. A small group of our ancestors, maybe a male and three females, foraging for food." She slumped her shoulders in a credible imitation of a Cro-Magnon man and grunted. A low, guttural sound. Volk perked up his ears.

Sasha picked up the short ax and crouched behind the chair. "Suddenly, a male from another clan leaps out of nowhere …"

She jumped and growled, the ax poised high above her head. Volk sprung to his feet and growled back, the hair on his neck bristling.

"The stranger has caught the smell of estrus." Sasha's nostrils flared. "He knows one of the females is ready to mate. He dashes toward them."

Sasha's lips were open, her body a steel coil, her eyes wide open. She stared straight at Anne. Anne looked away, a shiver running down her spine.

"The male turns. He tries to fight, to protect his females. But the intruder is stronger." Sasha swung the ax, striking the board so hard that the floor vibrated. The blade sank into the wood where the human head was outlined. "The newcomer wins."

Anne watched, mesmerized. The veins on Sasha's arms bulged as she rocked the ax back and forth to extricate it from the wood.

"The females scream and scatter. He grabs the largest one. She fights. He tries to mount her. She resists …"

Sasha paused, breathing heavily.

"But she doesn't really resist." Sasha's voice dropped to a whisper. "She's genetically programmed to give in to a stronger mate. He'll make better babies. Stronger babies. Babies that will thrive. A female has to be selective. Pregnancy will put her out of commission for months. She can't guess wrong. She must go with the strongest, whose offspring is most likely to ensure the survival of her genes."

Sasha had a dreamlike look on her face, her mind somewhere else. "Gradually, she lets him subdue her. She's his now. He enters her."

Sasha's eyes were staring at some image from the distant past.

"When it's all over, they wander off. She's carrying his seed. The smaller females follow obediently, awaiting their turn. Their former male companion is left to the buzzards. Dead-end for the gene pool of the weaker. Long live the genes of the stronger. It is the bio-behavioral imperative."

Anne was speechless. Finally, she spoke. "OK, so maybe that's what happened to our prehistoric ancestors. But we have reason, laws."

"Oh, so now things are different?" Sasha asked sarcastically.

"Of course."

Sasha laughed. A joyless laugh. "Is that why every romance novel has a strong, handsome male forcefully taking the heroine?"

"What does that have to do with anything?"

"Don't you see? It's the old formula in a modern version. The same recipe for survival that's hardwired into us! It's part of our gene pool, like fear of falling, or maternal instincts. Reason and laws can make us behave differently," Sasha continued, "but they can't change our animal nature. It is behavior that's passed on from parent to progeny, generation after generation, century after century. It's going to take a lot more than a millennium or two of enlightenment before there are no more rapes or wars."

"So what's your point?" Anne asked.

"Like it or not, deep down inside …" Sasha lowered her voice to a whisper and leaned close to Anne. "We are what we were. That's the point."

Sasha stood up and walked toward the stove. "I'll make more tea," she said, her voice husky.

"I'd better be going," Anne replied.

"Stay for dinner?"

"Maybe next time."

"Up to you," Sasha said coldly. "I'll call the hotel and have them send a car for you."

When the car came, Sasha rode down in the elevator with Anne.

"Thanks again for the ride," Anne said, getting into the hotel Mercedes.

"My pleasure," Sasha replied. She started to close the door, but stopped. "By the way, if you want to find out more about the Grudskoy family, ask Volodya. They are practically related," she laughed. Then she added more seriously, "Allegedly, his great-great-grandmother seduced and married one of them. I guess being crafty and seductive runs in the genes," she couldn't resist adding. "She was from a lowly family, so the Emperor—this was of course way before Communism—stripped him of all his titles and lands. The man died a pauper."

She smiled. "It's amazing what people will do for love. Or lust." She gave Anne a quick kiss on the cheek, the lips barely making contact. "I'll see you at work. Sweet dreams."

In bed that night Sasha dreamed about a pair of muscular hairy arms grasping a woman's body, digging into her soft flesh, the skin paling under the pressure. The more the woman resisted, the more forceful the arms became. Probing, exploring.

She was enjoying the dream, until she felt a warm wetness between her thighs and realized that she was awake. Her body was filled with a sweet ache. She rolled on her stomach and felt the slippery liquid oozing out. She touched her lower lips, now parted, aching.

As an intense orgasm swept through her, she could feel Anne's body fluttering underneath her.

49

Anne was awakened by the insistent ringing of the phone. She reached for the receiver, but stopped. Was Halden checking up on her again? The thought was infuriating.

The ringing continued. Misty calling? A medical problem? She picked up. The voice at the other end was Volodya's. "We're parents!" he shouted.

For a second, still in her sleepy stupor, Anne wondered how they could be parents. They hadn't had sex, she wasn't pregnant ...

"Parents." Volodya was excited. "Abby made offspring."

"You woke me up for this?" She rolled over, her eyes only half open, and smiled. "What time is it?"

"Late. I mean early. Very early." Anne focused on the clock. It was 5:00 a.m.

"Please come to see them?"

"Now?"

"If parents are not there to baptize offspring, is very bad luck."

"You make this up as you go along?"

"Sorry, what?"

"Another Russian tradition?"

"No. This one I invent," he confessed. "But please come."

His intensity was irresistible. "Give me half an hour to wash up and get dressed."

"Half hour? Ten minutes, I pick you up!"

Lena was visibly disappointed when she saw Anne come in with Volodya.

"Dr. Powell, please let me present Lena Sokol, my very good helper."

Anne read Lena's expression like a book, and felt a twinge of jealousy that she tried to suppress. *What did she expect, anyway? Volodya's life was filled with women.*

Lena gave Anne's hand a half-hearted shake and turned away. It was bad enough having to hide her affection from Sasha. And now this newcomer, and a foreign one at that, was obviously the center of Volodya's attentions.

"You took too long picking up the Americanka. I already delivered three," Lena said in Russian, throwing Volodya an accusing look. "There's another three or four in her. Maybe *she* can help you now," she added, nodding in Anne's direction. "I'm going home to get some sleep." She walked out and slammed the door.

Abby was sprawled on the floor of her cage, three tiny mice jockeying for position at her nipples. They were no larger than a thumbnail.

"They're so small!" Anne smiled.

"We must dry them, or they will catch cold," Volodya said concerned. He slipped on a pair of latex gloves, picked up a mouse and gently wiped it with a piece of cloth. Then he placed it on a scale.

"Eight grams. Good."

He put the animal in a small box padded with rags, then opened a notebook and wrote in the animal's weight.

Without prompting, Anne slipped on gloves, picked up the next mouse and wiped it, handling it as gently as Volodya. She put the mouse on the scale.

"Seven point four grams."

Volodya recorded the weight and transferred the mouse to the box. In the meantime, another mouse was born.

Wipe, weigh, box. They moved like a team.

"So now will you tell me exactly what Abby is doing here?" Anne asked.

"A few more days. Then you'll see. And you will pay."

"What?

"Remember, we made bet? You must dance with me."

An image of his body dancing next to hers flashed through her mind, but she chased it away. *He wasn't safe. There were entirely too many women in his life.*

The weighing completed, Anne and Volodya watched the newborns nestled comfortably against Abby's side.

"So, are they properly baptized?" Anne asked.

He smiled. "Yes."

"Can I go back to sleep now?"

"Yes." He glanced at his watch and thought for a second. "No, cannot sleep," he exclaimed. Grabbing her hand, he pulled her toward the door. "Come with me. I will show you beautiful thing."

Volodya hurried down the deserted hallway, Anne in tow. Opening an unmarked door, he started up a narrow, dark staircase.

"Quickly, or will be too late."

Puzzled, Anne did her best to keep up with him as he ran up the stairs, flight after flight.

"Where are you taking me?" she panted between flights.

"You will see."

The stairwell became dimmer. She wanted to stop, to catch her breath and get oriented.

"Volodya, wait." He was putting her runner's lungs to shame.

"We are almost arrived."

One more flight, and he stopped on the dark landing. Anne could see a faint light seeping through the outline of a small door.

"We here," Volodya announced. With a firm shove of his shoulder, he forced the door open. A blast of cold air made Anne gasp.

"Careful, step," he said taking her hand again.

They were on the roof of the Pavlov, among the ducts, pipes and enormous metal structures that housed the ventilation units. They stood side by side, panting, the steam of their breaths blending with the clouds of vapor spilling from the vent shafts. The morning was eerily quiet, except for the low-pitched cooing of a flock of pigeons roosting under an overhang.

Volodya guided her through the maze of air heating equipment, toward the knee-high banister at the edge of the building.

"Look. Moscow is at your feet."

She saw a strip of orange clouds on the horizon, and outlines of distant buildings. Way below them, within the walls of the Kremlin, onion-shaped church domes loomed like magical chess pieces.

"It is so beautiful," Anne whispered.

"Yes. Quiet. Peace. All is in balance."

They stood silently, their shoulders touching, listening to the gentle cooing of the pigeons, watching as the sky gradually turned orange, then golden yellow.

Anne was so enraptured that she didn't notice when Volodya took his sweater off and gently draped it over her. Nor did she notice that his hands remained wrapped around her shoulders.

"Now, new beginning, new day," he whispered as a ray of sun shot out from behind the horizon. "*Na voskhode solntza vse stanovitsya ...*"

Anne turned her head, her face inches from his. She couldn't take her eyes off his lips, enraptured by the melodious cadence of his whisper. She sensed that the poem he was reciting was about love and sadness, about something terribly dear and important to him, something that mere words couldn't communicate.

He continued whispering as the sun emerged over the horizon, its rays arching up into the sky, turning silhouettes into shapes, gray into color, cold into warmth.

The cooing of the pigeons stopped abruptly. An instant later, Anne heard the sound of distant church bells, and with it the flock exploded into the air, filling the sky, obscuring her vision.

The flapping of wings grew louder and louder, dominating everything. There were no more vents, no buildings, no Volodya. Only a flurry of wings. Closing her eyes, Anne felt as if she, too, were flying through the air.

Suddenly she saw a pigeon settle in front of her. She looked down and realized that the bird was perched on a wooden windowsill. Beyond the window, outside was a blue sky and dense woods. Part of her mind tried to understand where she was, but couldn't.

She took the bird into her hands. A miniature bouquet of tiny wild flowers was tied to its foot. Blue, red, yellow. A beautiful harbinger of springtime.

Anne turned around and realized that she was in a spacious room with a low ceiling and whitewashed rough walls. Both the ceiling and the walls were painted with a pattern of intertwining branches, bright green leaves artfully interspersed with red flowers. An icon with gilded edges was hanging in one corner. An ornately carved wooden dresser stood against one wall. Next to it, a tall bed, its thick down comforter covered with a colorful quilt.

Nyanya, a shapeless dress covering her strong body, stood next to her.

"What, Anytchka?" Nyanya asked, and Anne knew she was talking to her.

"Look. Another one!" Anne heard herself say, but the voice was young. And spoke in Russian.

Anne's mind reeled in confusion. She knew if she reached out, she could touch Volodya. But as Anne, she could not move. She tried, but her mind drifted, and Anne ceased to exist.

She was Anytchka.

Two young chambermaids stood at her side—girls no older than twelve or thirteen. One was combing out Anytchka's hair, the other held a silver wash basin.

"It is the work of the devil!" exclaimed the second girl when she saw the flowers tied to the bird's feet. The basin slipped out of her hands and landed with a deafening crash. The water seeped into the wooden floor.

"Nonsense!" Anytchka answered firmly. "How can something so

beautiful come from the devil?" She untied the flowers and released the pigeon. It sailed out the window, toward the forest.

"It is not right, these flowers ..." the other girl mumbled.

"Work of the devil ..." the first one repeated, gathering the basin.

"We should tell Aleksandr Ivanovitch ..."

Nyanya clapped her hands. "Quick, you two! Go fetch more water."

"But we have more here ..."

"Don't argue, go."

The youngsters hurried out. Anytchka put the bouquet on her dresser, next to several others just like it.

Picking up the comb, Nyanya ran it through her mistress' hair. "He loves you very much," she said suddenly, her voice almost a whisper.

"What are you talking about, Nyanya?" Anytchka exclaimed, blushing.

"I am talking about the man who comes to you every night in your dreams," Nyanya answered softly.

Anytchka held her breath.

"The man who cannot live without you," Nyanya continued.

"How do you know all that?" Anytchka asked, trying to keep her voice steady.

"I cannot say, my lady," Nyanya answered, shaking her head. "But I know who he is. And I know he loves you."

Anytchka turned toward the window and stared at the rising sun, the warm rays bathing her face.

"I want to see him," she said firmly.

"No! You mustn't," Nyanya exclaimed, throwing her arms up. "It will mean certain death for both of you."

"And this is life?" Anytchka spun around. "To be beaten and humiliated every night?" She pointed to the bruises on her neck and chest.

"I know Alexandr Ivanovitch can be rough ..." Nyanya said, "but it is your ..."

"No, you don't know!" Anytchka interrupted her. "He's an animal, a monster …"

"I *do* know, child," Nyanya repeated quietly.

Anytchka looked at her, confusion giving way to revulsion.

"Oh, my God!" she gasped, raising a hand to her mouth.

Nyanya lowered her eyes. "I was young, attractive. He … used me … whenever it was his pleasure …"

"Animal!" Anytchka whispered.

"He was the master. I had no choice. When I became pregnant, he found somebody else. And I wasn't alone. There were many others. Even a Tartar woman that he captured during one of the raids. Oh, how she suffered from him. One day she stabbed him, and ran away."

"Where is she now?"

"Who knows. Some say the wolves got her and her unborn child. Others think maybe she found a home somewhere, and her child will grow to be strong and will come back and kill him. That would be just vengeance."

"Sometimes I want to kill him too," Anytchka whispered.

Nyanya put her hand on Anytchka's shoulder. "You're his wife. You must accept him. It's God's will. Your *sudbah*."

"To hell with *sudbah*!" Anytchka exclaimed, shaking off Nyanya's hands.

"Oh mistress! Don't!" Nyanya crossed herself.

"*Sudbah* is nothing but a challenge that God gives us. A challenge we can fight."

"I beg you. Don't say that," Nyanya pleaded, terrified. "It's blasphemy."

"I do not accept my *sudbah*, Nyanya!"

"How do you get such ideas in your young head, child?

"Because I think. And I know God wants me to fight, to strive for something better. Otherwise, what good is that free will that Father Aphanassy preaches every Sunday?" She grasped Nyanya's hand and brought it to her chest. "Please, Nyanya. I have to see him."

"Don't do it, child!" Nyanya pleaded.

"I want to," Anytchka said firmly.

"No good can come of this, Anna Yurievna. My heart aches, my soul cries. I see merciless fury. I see death. A terrible death."

"You see love, not death."

"I beg you …"

"Will you help me or not?"

Nyanya stood still, tugging nervously at the black scarf double-knotted around her neck. Tears welled up in her eyes.

"Nyanya?"

The older woman nodded slowly.

Anytchka squeezed her hand. "Thank you!"

"God help us, child," Nyanya whispered, freeing her hand and making a cross over Anytchka's head. "May God help us all!"

"Anne?" Volodya's voice came from somewhere in the distance.

Anne forced herself to focus. "Volodya?" *Where was he? Was she sleeping? Did she dream the whole thing? Where was Nyanya? The flowers?*

Volodya was behind her and she was still wrapped in his arms. She felt an intense anxiety overpower her as she realized that what she just had was not a dream. Anne's heart was racing. She could hardly breathe. She wanted to run, hide, to pretend that what she just saw hadn't happened.

Volodya sensed her panic. "You are like bird in cage!" he said softly, drawing her closer.

"Please don't!" She struggled out of his embrace.

"But … I thought it was pleasant for you?"

"It is … but … I can't …" she stammered. "I need to go."

She jerked his sweater off her shoulders and hurried toward the stairs.

50

Stumbling through snow drifts, her shoes filling with snow, Anne hurried home.

Now what, Anne Powell? No demons in your caves, you say?

She tried not to think of her vision. *Or whatever it was.* She had to accept that it wasn't a dream. She remembered being wide awake, standing up, and she could pinpoint the moment she stepped from one reality … or at least one frame of mind, into another.

She couldn't bring herself to call it a hallucination. *Her patients had hallucinations. And then Misty or somebody hospitalized them and treated them and people called them "crazies" behind their backs. How could* she *be having hallucinations?*

She reached the hotel and made her way to her room. She had to talk to someone.

Misty.

But what would Misty think? *Hello, Misty? I'm seeing these little visions from five centuries ago. But that's OK because I'm going to see my lover soon. He just sent me a pigeongram.*

That just wasn't going to go over very well. Anne was supposed to be the rational one, the one who always had the "brain watch." But Misty was her only choice.

She braced herself and placed the call.

"Hi there! How's the magnetic maiden?" Misty asked cheerfully.

At the sound of Misty's playful voice, Anne's inclination to discuss her crisis vanished.

"Oh, just fine. Enjoying the effects of my magnetized personality," she tried to joke back.

"Did your magnetized personality attract any sexy Cossacks yet?"

"Tons of them! Can't beat them off with a stick!"

"Great! So you're calling for love advice?"

"Actually, I was wondering ... how's Miles?"

"Miles? He's fine."

"Good. How's work?"

"Hey, it's me you're talking to. So, no bullshitting."

"What are you talking about?" Anne tried to sound innocent.

"What's up, girlfriend?"

Anne hesitated, then told Misty what had happened on the roof of the Pavlov.

"So, the saga continues," Misty said cautiously after Anne finished her story.

"And I didn't just dream about this Anytchka. I felt what she felt. Her pain, her anger, her longing for her lover. It's like I *was* Anytchka."

"That's heavy stuff, Anne."

"How could I be remembering someone else? Someone from five centuries ago?"

"Sounds like you're doing more than remembering. You're reliving," Misty said quietly. When Anne didn't protest at this suggestion, Misty took a quick sigh. She could only imagine the havoc that this experience was probably wreaking in her friend's logical brain.

"And there's one more thing I didn't tell you," Anne volunteered.

"Don't hold back now."

"I went to look up this Grudskoy guy ..."

"And?"

"He's buried near here."

"For real?"

"I sat on his grave."

Misty digested that information. "Sure it was him?"

"No question. I looked up the dates. Misty, how do I deal with this?" Anne exclaimed.

"Well, if you believe Brian Weiss ..."

"Who's he?"

"The psychiatrist who wrote *Many Lives, Many Masters.*"

"Trust you to come up with a reference I've never heard of."

"He claims he can regress patients beyond their childhood. To past lives."

"A nut case."

"I knew you'd say that. Actually, he's a credible guy. I went to a lecture of his once. We talked afterwards."

"About past lives?"

"About Julie and Pedro."

"Who're they?"

"Two patients of his. Apparently, as he worked with them, he realized that they had known each other in their past lives. There was some unfinished business. Infidelity, or something. So he regressed them and ..."

"How?"

"The conventional way. Psychoanalysis."

"But that works only for what's stored in the subconscious."

"Who knows what we drag around with us?"

"Dead people's memories? I don't buy that."

"Well, their stories matched up pretty well. He was working with them separately, so there was no way one could know what the other had said."

"Isn't it a bit of a coincidence that both turned out on his couch?"

"That was my first thought, too. But there is something called synchronous potentiention. The energy fields in patients' current relationship evoke their past."

"Definitely weird."

"It's like the effect a woman's scent might have on a man," Misty continued unperturbed. "If she smells like cinnamon buns, the guy might think of his grandmother. If she smells like Chanel, he might visualize his mother."

"And if she smells of car exhaust, he'll think of his Chevy. Misty, please ..."

"I know, it's a tough sell to us scientists."

"Spare me the sarcasm."

"None meant. I can see how you may question his work."

"It's a preposterous concept."

"Of course, that's what they used to say about your MEG ..."

"But past lives ... There's no scientific basis whatsoever."

"No proof, therefore impossible?"

"It's a ridiculous comparison—MEG and past lives! First of all, with the MEG we have case studies. Patients' stories, witnessed, documented, recorded..."

"You seem to be telling a pretty compelling story yourself, with all those dreams fitting together rather neatly ..." Misty interjected.

"Second, we know how the MEG works." Anne pretended she didn't hear. "We have microscopic images of synapses, before and after ablation. You see the results. I see the results. It's not some metaphysical mumbo-jumbo."

"Who's to say the MEG can't take you as far back as there is anything to remember?"

"Exactly! That's where the 'past lives' thing falls apart! There's no way a memory record can be passed from a previous life into the present."

"No way that *we* know of," Misty agreed.

For a while, Anne was silent.

"It's all so bizarre," she said finally, sounding exasperated. "These people in my dreams—they seem so real. If the whole concept weren't utterly impossible, I could swear I actually knew them. Somewhere, sometime," she added.

"Well, there are lots of people in the world who'd say you're having a very normal experience."

"Even you?" Anne asked tentatively.

"Let's just say I'm more open to this possibility than you are," Misty said softly.

Neither said anything for a few moments.

"Misty?"

"What?"

Anne's voice was barely audible. "I'm scared."

"I know, hun, I know. I'd be totally freaked out by now! But listen, try not to worry about it. Whether it's something you read, or dreamed, or lived through ... it's just memories. They can't hurt you. It's not like you're going to actually run into these people, for heaven's sake," Misty laughed, trying to lighten the moment.

"I know. But still ..."

"Just keep reminding yourself—'It's all in my head, and in my past'."

"Right."

"Face it, process it, and let it go."

"I'll try," Anne said quietly, as she tried to chase away the vague fear that was slowly seeping into her brain. A paralyzing fear of what else she would have to face.

51

When Anne got to The Institute the following morning, Sasha wasn't there. Anne turned on the MEG and ran through the calibrations. Just as she was finishing, Sasha walked into the room, followed by Baldyuk. Both looked depressed.

"Don't bother," Sasha said without a greeting.

"What's going on?"

Sasha hopped onto the patient table and dangled her feet impatiently. "Ask the Professor."

Baldyuk walked up uncomfortably close to Anne, his wheezing louder than usual. "We have problem," he grunted.

Anne felt her stomach turn. "Something with the patients?"

"Yes." Sasha answered. "Something with the patients. We can't treat them anymore."

"What?!"

Baldyuk looked away. "Red tape problem."

"It appears that the Professor neglected to apply for your work permit." Sasha spit the words out with disgust. "In one of his drunken stupors, no doubt," she added so only Anne could hear.

Anne breathed a sigh of relief. "I thought it was something serious!"

"It is serious. No permit, project cancelled," Baldyuk barked.

"So how can I get one?"

"It'll take a trip ..."

"Where?"

"Farther than you think," Sasha said.

"No problem, I'm pretty good with the Metro."

"You have to go to St. Petersburg."

"St. Petersburg? Are you kidding? Can't we do it by mail?"

"We need it done in the next twenty-four hours or they'll ask you to leave the country."

"You are kidding, right?"

"I wish I were."

"Can't we fax it?"

"They want originals, signed in person," Sasha said.

"No alternatives," Baldyuk confirmed. "You must go to St. Petersburg. Tonight. Have good trip, Dr. Powell. I am sorry," he added with a forced smile.

"Thank you, Professor," she blurted.

"When do I leave?" Anne asked when Baldyuk left.

"There're only two non-stop trains to Peter. And the morning one left two hours ago."

"I'm going by train? Aren't there flights?"

"Believe me, you don't want to fly on a Russian airline if you don't have to," Sasha chuckled. "Don't worry, the train is nice. You'll get there first thing in the morning, so you won't waste the day traveling."

"Still a waste. And I thought our feds were a pain," Anne sighed.

Sasha nodded. "I apologize for what is left of our Communist bureaucracy."

"Old habits die hard."

"Old habits don't die at all, Anne," Sasha replied. "They just show up in different form." After a pause, she added, "I cancelled the day's patients. We'll make up the time when you get back. Now go home, relax."

Anne lingered. "I need to make a couple of adjustments," she said, glancing at the MEG.

"I'll wait and give you a ride back."

"No, you go ahead. This may take a while."

Reluctantly, Sasha left.

Ten minutes later, Anne followed, a contented smile on her face.

52

"Anne's a big girl. Why couldn't she go alone?"

Volodya sat in the cafeteria, polishing off a huge bowl of borscht. It wasn't as wonderful as the thick vegetable soup, deep red from beets that his babushka made, but it wasn't bad for institutional food. Sasha was sitting across from him.

"We couldn't just put her on a night train by herself, could we?" Sasha snapped back.

Something had changed between them in the past week or two. Sasha was aloof. Normally, she would've visited him in the lab after hours or dropped by his apartment. But she had stayed away. *Just as well,* Volodya thought. Anne had been on his mind more than he cared to admit. Being with Sasha, or with any other woman, would feel like betrayal.

"Why not? You sent her to Razdin Four by herself," Volodya replied. "If I hadn't shown up, heavens knows what would have happened to her up there."

"Don't exaggerate," Sasha said dismissively.

Volodya fished out a small chunk of meat, covered it generously with horseradish and put it into his mouth. He was saving the bright red beets for last. Concentrating on the food helped him think.

A few days ago he would have welcomed the opportunity to spend time with Anne. After the ballet he started feeling something for her that he hadn't felt in years. But her behavior on the roof of the Pavlov astounded him. He wondered if he could ever figure her out. *One thing he knew for sure: he was not about to let himself feel anything for a woman who did not reciprocate his feelings. There had been enough pain in his life. He would never again let anyone hurt him.*

"You will meet her at her hotel at ten tonight," Sasha was saying. "The hotel car will take you to the station."

Volodya took his time searching for another piece of meat in the bowl. "So why am I the guide?" he asked finally.

"I wanted Katya to go, but she let me down at the last minute. You're the only other one who speaks English well enough."

"Why don't you go?"

Sasha took a deep breath. "Because Baldyuk ordered you."

She wasn't about to explain to him why she couldn't go. She wasn't happy about sending Anne off with Volodya, either, but it was better than sending her off alone or with a stranger.

"I know. My research is not important."

"Look, it's only one day," Sasha said in a conciliatory tone.

She handed Volodya an envelope. "You'll be on the Red Arrow, leaving at midnight, arriving in Peter at ten after seven in the morning on Thursday. Go to the Ministry and take care of the paperwork right away. The address is in here, too. Baldyuk already called them with instructions. The return tickets are for the same night, also on the Red Arrow."

"That's a lot of traveling for a signature," Volodya said.

"It's not your concern."

He shrugged his shoulders.

"What are we supposed to do the rest of the day?"

Sasha hadn't thought about it. "Whatever."

"Maybe I can take her around, show her St. Petersburg," Volodya suggested.

"Fine. Just don't let her out of your sight," Sasha said sternly as she prepared to get up.

"Don't worry," Volodya replied with a twinkle in his eyes. "I'll have my arms around her the whole time."

Sasha's eyes froze.

"What did you say?" she hissed, leaning toward him.

He regretted the flip remark. There was no need to get Sasha irritated. Even though she had never been jealous of his flirtations before, the soccer game bruise that was still on his shin reminded him that her attitude toward his interest in Anne was different.

"I said, I'll take care of her," Volodya replied flatly.

Sasha felt the room starting to spin. Blood rushed to her head. Her muscles coiled into knots. She could no longer control her thoughts. Images of hands grabbing a woman's body flew past her eyes. "Mine, mine, mine," a voice screamed within her.

Frightened by her reaction, she forced herself to breathe deeply. Moments later, she was in control again.

"I'll see you when you get back," she said.

Then she saw Volodya's hands and inexplicably the blood went racing back through her head again, pounding her temples.

"Keep your hands off her," she mumbled, leaning close to his ear.

"I'll try …"

"*Try?*" she whispered. Sasha's hand made a barely perceptible motion. The curved blade of her knife flashed and disappeared.

As Sasha straightened up, Volodya felt something warm running down his cheek. A trickle of blood landed on his white shirt.

"*Akh ty, sooka!*" he exclaimed, pressing the napkin to his face. You, bitch!

"You should be more careful," Sasha replied, smiling sweetly as she turned toward the door.

"You spilled borscht all over your shirt."

53

The hotel car brought Anne and Volodya up to the main entrance of the Leningradskaya station.

The station turned out to be even more chaotic than the airport. Even at midnight, the street was teeming with arriving and departing passengers, porters, taxi drivers. Anne noted several shady characters that seemed to be following them.

"Gypsies," Volodya explained. "Be careful, hold your purse." He sounded impersonal, distant.

Just as well, Anne thought. *Obviously, neither one of them wanted to dwell on Anne's panicky escape from the roof the other night.* She almost wished Sasha had assigned her some other escort. *Or sent her alone, for that matter.*

The façade of the station was an enormous, imposing structure, and Anne was expecting to see an equally impressive interior. But once they passed through the main doors, she realized that there was no interior at all—only dozens of tracks under an open gray sky. *Just like a movie set,* she thought. *All show, no substance.*

They headed toward the Red Arrow that was hissing on Track 16, and walked along the platform until Volodya found their car.

"*Tchert pobery,*" he cursed. "This is not sleeping car."

He approached the conductor. Anne saw them arguing. Moments

later, Volodya returned.

"We were supposed to be in sleeping car, but there was mistake. So, we must sit whole night," he said, obviously distraught. "I am very, very sorry."

"Don't worry about it," Anne shrugged. "I can sleep standing up."

Their compartment was already partially occupied by two German students, snoring by the window. Anne and Volodya settled across from each other on the door side.

"I am very sorry," Volodya repeated.

"Forget it!"

No sooner did the train start moving, than Anne closed her eyes and fell asleep to the rhythmic clacking of the wheels.

Volodya sat, his eyes lingering on her beautifully contoured face, her soft hair, her full lips, partly opened. *Even asleep she looked full of life.* He thought of the wonderful evening they spent recently after *Swan Lake. Truly no one had ever made him feel so alive, so connected.*

He got up and gently slipped a pillow under her head. She mumbled something but didn't wake up.

"*Spokoynoy nochi.* May your night be peaceful," Volodya whispered.

He turned off the remaining lights and curled up in the corner across from her. Watching her beautiful face, he dozed off.

Even though they arrived an hour before opening time, the line at the entrance to the Ministry already reached halfway around the block.

"Wait here please," Volodya said, placing Anne at the end of the line and disappearing.

Twenty minutes later, he returned. "Everything normal. I found short way. No line. Please come."

They walked down the block, entered the building through a small door, meandered through several corridors, and finally came to a door marked with a sign that was worn beyond recognition. Volodya knocked.

"*Da,*" a raspy voice yelled from inside.

Volodya and Anne entered. The tiny cubicle reeked of stale cigarette smoke. Still holding his newspaper in one hand, the obese man behind the desk grabbed a batch of papers.

"*Podpissyvay*," he said brusquely, shoving the forms toward Anne.

"Sign please," Volodya translated.

"What am I signing?"

He did his best to help Anne decipher the forms. "Your title; name of patent owner; permission to import; work experience."

The man behind the desk glanced at Anne. "Doing business with Americantzi!" he said in Russian, giving Volodya a contemptuous look. "We need Communism back, is what we need."

"Bite your tongue!" Volodya replied.

"At least then we had stability. And now? Look, a new form every day." He waved at the papers in front of Anne. "Can you imagine? We got orders to print these yesterday, specially for her. And why Moscow couldn't handle it, I have no idea."

"She could have done this in Moscow?"

"Like all the other foreigners," he spat, turning away.

Volodya stared at the old man, his mind racing. *Was Anne's trip here arranged deliberately? And if so, why? And by whom?*

"*Khorosho*? Good?" Anne asked, pushing the forms toward the man. But the old civil servant was already deeply engrossed in his newspaper.

Back on the street, Volodya turned to Anne.

"Was easy, yes?"

"Hardly worth the trip."

"What is Sasha doing with MEG today?" Volodya asked casually.

"Nothing. She can't use it when I'm not there."

"Hmm."

Volodya wasn't convinced. *The whole trip, planned so suddenly. The new documents. What could Sasha and Baldyuk be up to?* He was not privy to the operations of the psych department—Sasha was not one to engage in pillow talk. But he knew something was going on that involved Namordin. And with Namordin, one could expect trickery, bribery and crime. Anne, with her typical American naiveté, probably didn't even suspect anything. He didn't want some Russian political plot to broadside her and her MEG.

"You have something electronic, maybe code for protection, so MEG cannot be used without permission, yes?" Volodya asked.

"Something like that," Anne replied vaguely.

"Very good." He felt better. *It was obvious that the manufacturers would have installed a means of locking out unauthorized users. Hopefully, it was up to Russian decode technology.*

They stopped at an intersection. Volodya looked around.

"Now what?" Anne asked.

"Returning train is only at midnight. I can show you Hermitage Museum." Volodya suggested.

"Sure," Anne said, trying to muster enthusiasm. The Red Arrow hadn't been as comfortable as the Boston-to-DC Metroliner, and her spine ached from a night spent sitting up. As exciting as the prospect of seeing one of the world's largest museums was—Anne had read somewhere that if one examined every object there for only one minute, it would take thirty-five years to see the entire collection—all she wanted right now was a place to stretch and a cup of Starbucks.

Volodya read her mind. "No Hermitage. I have better idea."

54

Anne's arm comfortably tucked into Volodya's, they walked down the ice-patched Morskaya Ulitsa, crossed a foot bridge over the Moyka Canal, and emerged on the bank of the Neva River, its granite ornaments reminiscent of Paris and the Seine. Within another block, they came to something that looked like a bus stop anchored to the bank.

"So where exactly are we going?" Anne asked as Volodya purchased two tickets. The lead-gray sky and the penetrating frigid breeze were not ideal conditions for a cruise.

"Very nice place. You will see."

"Volodya, you're teasing me ..."

Turning toward her, he gently placed a finger on her lips. "This will be surprise," he said, smiling. "Very important place for me," he added mysteriously.

Moments later, a ferry pulled up to the pier. It was a modern vessel, with a streamlined glassed-in cabin bristling with antennae and radars. They boarded with a dozen other people and the boat cast off immediately.

"We stay outside," Volodya suggested. "Better seeing."

The wooden deck vibrated as the diesel engines revved up and the vessel headed up the Neva. The cold, humid wind hit Anne's face. She ducked behind Volodya and pressed her body against his broad back.

"Sorry, but in this Titanic scene, it's you who gets to be in front."

He threw a puzzled glance at her over his shoulder.

"*Titanic*, an old movie," she explained. "There is a famous scene where the couple stands on the prow. Did you see it?"

"Ah, the couple who is in love, yes?" *There was the teasing twinkle in his eyes again, just like at the wedding.*

"No, the couple where she is engaged to the other man," she corrected him. "And quit turning around, because you're letting the wind through."

Anne watched in fascination as the boat glided past sites that she recalled from reading *Anna Karenina*. St. Petersburg was built by Peter the Great, from the ground up in less than ten years, in his attempt to emulate the palaces he had visited and admired in Paris. The result was so European, so Baroque, so different from Moscow … To Anne, the city seemed to be from a different culture entirely.

They passed an island with an imposing fortress, the low-lying winter sun reflected in its golden spire.

"This is St. Peter and St. Paul Fortress," Volodya said. "Peter the Great built it, to protect city. But fortress never used, because no enemy come close to city. Too cold," he added by way of explanation.

"And this is Winter Palace, with Hermitage Museum," he said pointing to an elegant building on the opposite shore, its lime-green walls and white columns extending for at least a mile. "Maybe next time we see from inside, yes?"

Volodya was shielding her from the wind, but Anne was starting to shiver.

"We should go in," he said. "Trip will take one hour."

He wished it were summer, when the bus-boats operated in hydrofoil mode: at a safe distance from shore, the engines revved up, accelerating to 40 or 50 km per hour. This made the boat rise above the surface of the water and glide on the wing-shaped pontoons attached to the keel. It was an exhilarating ride. But in the winter, with the Neva frozen, the boats had to stay in narrow lanes cleared by icebreakers and keep their speeds low. A high speed collision with even a small piece of ice could rip the pontoons off and sink the boat. So this trip, which normally took 30-40 minutes, would now take twice as long. *But it would be certainly more interesting for Anne than going by car*, Volodya thought.

From the warm comfort of the glassed-in cabin, Anne watched as the character of the surroundings changed from churches and palaces to gray apartment buildings and factories, and then to clusters of small wooden houses surrounded by patches of snow-covered pine trees.

"Long time ago, before city was built, this was important area, very rich, because had many ... how you say, animals to make coats, warm coats."

"Fur coats."

"Fur. Thank you. So, many times Tartars made invasion here. To take furs and gold. And sometimes Russian women," he added.

The ferry blew a shrill warning to a small fishing boat that was bouncing on the waves.

"Is not far now," Volodya said after a while. "We're in Novgorod Province."

55

Sasha was in a rage.

"What the hell do you mean, a part is missing?"

Sergey leaned on the MEG and calmly pointed to the circuitry that he had exposed an hour earlier.

"Right here, see?" He poked his screwdriver at an empty space on the circuit board. "The damned integrator is missing."

"Are you sure?" Sasha asked, starting to pace. "Maybe you're wrong?"

"No, I'm not wrong."

"Now what?"

Sergey shrugged his shoulders. "She may as well have taken the whole machine with her. Without the integrator, I can't turn this bucket of chips on for you."

"Then you have to build one," Sasha announced.

"Build an integrator? And how the hell am I supposed to do that?"

"Just follow the diagram."

"And parts?"

"Get them."

"From Germany?"

Sasha grabbed the first thing her hand landed on—a screwdriver—and flung it across the room. The tool stuck into the wooden bookshelf like a lance. Sergey backed away a few inches.

"How big is this integrator?" Sasha asked, her mouth suddenly parched. A fine tremor started in her right foot and spread up her leg.

"Hmm, probably like so." Sergey made a walnut-sized circle with his fingers. "What difference does it make?"

Sasha didn't answer. She summoned all her willpower to chase away the fear that was beginning to paralyze her. *A failure at this point would cost her more than her career.*

Her mind raced through the possibilities. *Anne would not run the risk of taking the integrator with her on a trip. So she probably hid it. The question was where.*

She began opening the drawers where Anne kept her paperwork, but stopped.

"Call Baldyuk," she said, turning to the engineer, "and tell him we won't be ready 'til later. Give me an hour," she added, grabbing her leather jacket and heading out the door.

Yakov, the night concierge at the National, greeted Sasha like an old friend.

"I swear, these American women are impossible," Sasha said rolling up her eyes in mock exasperation. "Guess what Dr. Powell forgot this time?"

"What?" asked Yakov, leaning closer to Sasha.

"Her lipstick. Her *very special* lipstick," she added sarcastically, touching Yakov's hand.

"Listen, you don't have to tell me about foreigners. That's all I have to deal with the whole day."

"I feel for you." Sasha smiled at Yakov, her hand still on his. "And of course, she also forgot to give me her keycard …"

"That we can fix," Yakov said, quickly imprinting a new card and handing it to Sasha. "Listen, perhaps next time we can have a drink …"

"That would be great."

"Room one-six …"

"One-six-seven-five, I know," Sasha said, disappearing into the elevator.

She let herself into Anne's room. Her heart began to race as she inhaled the familiar scent of Anne's cologne. There was something erotic about exploring Anne's private space.

Anne's papers and files were stacked neatly on the small desk. Her bathrobe was carefully laid out on the bed.

There were several post-it notes and a photograph of a cat pinned to a small bulletin board propped on top of the desk. There was another piece of paper ...

Sasha walked closer and peered at a photocopy of a man's head.

She felt a rush of adrenaline. *Volodya face! What the hell was Anne doing with a Xerox of Volodya's face?* Sasha had an impulse to tear it to shreds, but forced her anger under control. *It was only a Xerox. It meant nothing ...*

Anyway, there was work to be done.

She started with the obvious—the desk drawers—opening each one carefully, making sure not to disturb the contents.

Then she checked the closet, but found nothing except neatly hung clothes. There was nothing on the shelves above.

The suitcases. Empty.

Sasha went to the chest of drawers and explored the contents, her hands sliding carefully between layers of sweaters, blouses, jeans.

The lingerie drawer. Sasha felt a shiver as her hands penetrated the contents. Bras, panties. Some cotton, some silky. Several colorful thongs.

Completely losing track of her task, Sasha pulled out a silky emerald-green nightgown and held it at arm's length, imagining how it looked on Anne.

Closing her eyes, she brought the soft garment to her cheek. She had never lusted for anyone, let alone a woman, like she did for Anne at that moment. *It wasn't natural, it was bizarre, there was no reason for it, she told herself ... But, oh, how sweet it was to be here in this room, imagining that Anne would come in at any minute ...*

Suddenly Sasha felt the headache returning. Starting from the back of her head, the pain moved forward, intensifying, drilling through her temples. Her vision blurred. She steadied herself against the dresser.

Then everything turned to darkness.

Several candles flared up in the corner of the room, outlining a woman's body. Tall, poised. A white silk robe draped elegantly over the curves of her body. She just stood there, as if waiting to be taken.

Sasha felt the blood rushing to her face, burning, the heat spreading slowly to her throat, down her chest, to her groin.

She opened her eyes and found herself looking into the bathroom mirror, clutching Anne's nightgown. *What the hell was that?* she wondered, her head suddenly clear. *If it weren't for the very pleasurable images, she would say she just had an* absence *episode—those brief seizures ...*

Her eyes went to Anne's toiletries, neatly arranged on the marble counter. She picked up a perfume bottle and inhaled deeply. *It was pure Anne.*

She put the perfume down gently, like a precious relic, and picked up a jar of hand cream. She unscrewed the top and slowly dipped a finger into the smooth cream. The finger struck a rough edge. Sasha pushed her finger deeper and pulled out a small plastic bag.

Inside the bag was the integrator.

56

The boat docked, and Volodya and Anne stepped ashore with a few of the other passengers. The quay was nothing but a wide wooden platform bobbing precariously on empty oil drums and connected to the shore by a narrow walkway. Instantly, the wind, colder and stronger than in the city, swept through Anne's coat, sending a chill down her spine. She clung to Volodya.

A dirt road led to a cluster of wooden houses. Their steep roofs were covered with snow, and icicles were hanging from the eves.

Holding on to each other, sliding on icy patches and laughing like school children, Anne and Volodya negotiated the steep slope. Panting, they approached one of the houses on the periphery of the settlement. Volodya walked up the stairs to the minuscule porch and knocked three times.

Almost immediately, an old woman opened the door. Anne was struck by her appearance. The face was covered by wrinkles that seemed centuries old. Her white hair contrasted with her jet-black eyebrows. The piercing eyes smiled even when the lips didn't. On top of her simple dark gray dress, she wore a black scarf tied with a double knot.

The old woman swept Volodya into her arms.

"*Volodychka, meelinky ...*" She could hardly contain herself.

Anne watched, surprised and touched, as Volodya tenderly held the old woman in his arms, gently rocking her.

Finally, she pushed Volodya away, wiped her eyes, and looked at Anne. Anne felt that it was a stare that could see right into her soul.

"Dr. Anne Powell, please meet my *babushka*. My grandmother," Volodya said.

"*Ochen pryatno*. Nice to meet you," said Anne, stretching her hand for a handshake. But Babushka pushed the hand aside and hugged her like a long-lost relative.

"You. Are. Vell. Come," she said, struggling with the pronunciation, smiling proudly because she could muster enough words to greet her guest.

Following Babushka in, Anne found herself in a small room, its ceiling low enough to touch, the walls paneled with plywood darkened by time. There was a small round table against one of the walls, and a narrow bed neatly covered with a beautiful hand-knit afghan.

Through a narrow doorway partially covered by a faded curtain, Anne could see a kitchen with a wood burning stove. The heat emanating from the brisk fire made the air warm and comforting.

Babushka fussed, helping Anne with her coat, shaking her head and mumbling something.

"She thinks your coat is not warm," Volodya explained. "And she wants to know where are your gloves."

Ducking into a closet, Babushka produced a pair of worn sheepskin slippers and gestured for Anne to put them on.

"*Teplaye*," she said smiling at Anne.

"Warmer," Volodya translated.

"*Spasibo*," Anne answered, the slippers making her feel at home.

Satisfied that her guests were comfortable, Babushka ducked into the kitchen, all the while lecturing Volodya about something.

"Babushka is very angry—I bring guest and not tell her, so she has not prepared food," Volodya said.

"I didn't want to impose," Anne exclaimed. "Please tell her I'm not hungry."

Volodya laughed. "You do not understand. Is not possible to come here and not eat. Not possible," he repeated, shaking his head as if the idea were totally preposterous. "Babushka would not let you out."

"*Volodychka!*" Babushka called from the kitchen.

"I must go help," Volodya said. "Please, be like in your house."

Anne took stock of the room, admiring the touches that made it so inviting. A small carpet with a red and yellow flower pattern hung on the wall adjacent to the bed. A set of mismatched dishes was carefully stacked on a dresser, next to a cloth bag with knitting needles.

In the corner facing the entrance, a votive oil lamp burned in front of an icon. The icon, the size of a small book, showed an image of a man wearing a long, jewel-encrusted robe and a royal crown topped by a halo. In his right hand he held a cross with two crossbars.

One corner of the icon was burned to charcoal. *Probably the result of a votive lamp gone astray,* Anne figured.

A brief image flashed past Anne's eyes: a woman in a white dress, surrounded by fire, the icon on the floor, burning.

The image vanished so fast, Anne wasn't sure she saw it.

Anne tried to read the gilded inscription at the bottom of the icon, but it was in the ornate, calligraphic font that she had seen in churches, quite different from modern Cyrillic. All she could decipher was an "A," an "L," and perhaps an "E."

Volodya appeared in the doorway behind her, looking very domestic with an apron tied around his waist, a knife and a loaf of dark brown bread in his hands.

"Do you like icon?" he asked, noticing what Anne was looking at. "It is in our family for many generations."

"What happened to it?" Anne asked pointing to the burned corner.

Volodya shrugged his shoulders. "Nobody knows, not even Babushka." He sliced the bread with a few practiced strokes, arranged them in a basket on the table and ducked back into the kitchen.

Anne turned to the several framed photos hanging on the wall, the most impressive being one of a handsome, austere man in military uniform.

"Volodya, who is the man in the big photo?" Anne called into the kitchen.

"My grandfather. He was officer in army during time when Leningrad was attacked by Hitler."

"Where is he now?"

"He died," said Volodya. "Defending city."

"I'm sorry …"

"He earned medal, Hero of War." Volodya peeked out of the kitchen. "You know, every one in city of Leningrad received medal. Because so brave against Hitler. Three years, surrounded by Germans, did not give up. One million people died. But most of them, not from guns."

"So why?"

"Because no food in city."

Volodya went back into the kitchen.

"How about this postcard?" Anne asked noticing a small card with the familiar old Manhattan skyline. The Twin Towers were still there.

"Babushka has—how do you say, not sister but … cousin of cousin—in New York," Volodya answered, reappearing in the doorway with a tray piled high with food.

He placed the tray on the table, took a slice of bread and handed it to Anne.

"Bread and salt," he said, handing her a saltshaker. "This is tradition for first time guest."

Babushka brought in a bowl full of pickles and a small jar of mushrooms marinated with cloves of garlic.

"Babushka prepares mushrooms herself," Volodya said.

After several more trips to the kitchen, the table was covered with pots, bowls and serving dishes with a variety of foods. Cabbage soup, smoked herring, rice-stuffed peppers filled the room with a mixture of aromas that made Anne's mouth water.

"*Pojaluysta*," Babushka said with a smile, gently steering Anne toward the table. "Please sit down," Anne figured out, gratified that her Berlitz language tapes were bearing fruit.

"Volodya, tell her this is too much food."

"Is better you try to eat, or Babushka will be hurt," Volodya said.

Babushka said something, wiping her hands on her apron.

"Babushka says please excuse, but no meat. It is, how you say, *pohst.*"

"It's what?" Anne couldn't venture a guess of what *pohst* might be.

Volodya tapped his forehead in frustration. "How you say, not eat, because soon is Easter?"

"Ah! Lent! It's called Lent. Fasting before the holiday."

"Yes, yes, yes. Lend!" Volodya exclaimed cheerfully, his message understood. "So, no meat on table. And no vodka. Babushka is lending." He winked. "But you and me, no need to lend."

He disappeared into the kitchen. Anne heard the back door open, and, moments later, Volodya returned wiping snow off a bottle of vodka.

"When is winter, we keep vodka outside, so is cold," he said topping off two shot glasses. The chilled vodka flowed like thick syrup.

"You remember, yes? All one swallow, then eat piece of bread." Volodya handed her the glass. "Or better, eat piece of herring. Babushka makes herself."

Resolved to be open-minded, Anne piled a piece of smoked herring on a slice of dark bread. Babushka nodded approvingly.

"*Na zdorovye,*" Volodya said, toasting the women.

"*Na zdorovye,*" Anne echoed. The ice-cold vodka percolated down her throat, leaving a burning trail. She followed with a bite of herring, the salty taste soothing the burn and enhancing the after-taste of the alcohol. Perhaps there was something to this Russian method after all, she thought.

As they munched their way across the table, Anne made an effort to communicate with Babushka without Volodya's translations.

"*Krassivyî?* Or is it *krassivaya?*" she asked, pointing to the afghan on the bed and wondering if she would ever grasp the permutations of Russian adjectives, which differed on the basis of whether the object was judged to be masculine or feminine. Was that a pretty she-afghan, or pretty he-afghan?

"*Ochen kras-sy-vo-yeh pokryvalo,*" Babushka corrected her. A very pretty it-afghan. So much for object gender. Afghan was neutral.

"*Kak delaet?*" Anne asked, pantomiming knitting motions, hoping Babushka would reveal her technique.

Babushka retrieved her knitting bag and gave her a demonstration for the next few minutes. Anne guessed that at that rate, even though the old woman's arthritic fingers moved with unexpected speed and coordination, the afghan must have taken Babushka several months to knit.

"*Da, otchen dolgo,*" Babushka said, as if reading Anne's thoughts, her hand making circling motions portraying the passage of days. Then she pushed the bundle of wool into Anne's hands. "You try it."

To her total surprise, Anne realized that her fingers were moving as if she had been knitting all her life. Yet she had never even seen it done until that moment.

She looked up, still knitting, and found herself staring into Babushka's black, unblinking eyes. Probing, wondering, searching her.

"Bravo," Volodya exclaimed, walking in from the kitchen. "You are more Russian every day!"

When Babushka got up to clear the dishes, Volodya brought in a large urn-shaped brass vessel and placed it on the table.

"This is samovar," he announced. "For making tea. You have samovar in Boston?" he asked.

"I have a coffee maker." Anne laughed. "Does that count?"

"Samovar is from words 'samo,' means self, and 'varit,' from word cook. Self-cook. Make tea very fresh and very hot. By itself."

Bending down, he blew on the coals in the bottom of the samovar, sending sparks flying dangerously close to his face.

"Careful," Anne exclaimed, instinctively pulling him back. "You'll burn yourself!"

"Is no problem, I keep eyes closed," Volodya said, amused by her reaction.

Picking up the small ceramic teapot nestled on the top of the samovar, he poured a little of the concentrated tea into the cups.

"This is very strong. When samovar boils, we put hot water to make tea," he said.

This was hardly a self-cooking setup, Anne chuckled to herself. "Now, honey," Volodya said, disappearing into the kitchen again.

Suddenly, there was a blast of cold air and a young woman burst through the front door.

57

The woman was in her late twenties, long-legged and pink-cheeked. She seemed perfectly at home here, but noticing Anne, she stopped dead in her tracks.

"*Zdraste*," she said, examining Anne as if assessing a job applicant.

"*Zdraste*. Hello," Anne replied.

The hint of a smile that passed over the young woman's lips made Anne feel that she had been written off. *Was she too old? Too foreign? Not Volodya's type?*

"Volodychka!" the girl exclaimed in Russian, throwing her arms around Volodya as he returned from the kitchen. "I saw you arrive a little earlier. You stayed away so long, you louse!" she added kissing him juicily on the lips.

"How are you, Katya?" Volodya asked, gently pulling away.

"What's the matter, you weren't going to come visit me at all?" Katya chided him without letting go.

"I'm here for only a few hours."

She slid provocatively closer. "I remember when even a few minutes was enough."

Babushka poked her head out of the kitchen. "Go on, go. We have a guest!"

"And who is the guest?" Katya asked.

"A colleague," Volodya said, glancing uneasily toward Anne.

"Oh, a colleague," Katya mimicked him mischievously. "Why don't you ditch her?"

Anne didn't understand the exchange, but the body language was clear. She felt an uneasy stirring in the pit of her stomach and realized that she was jealous.

"Katya, leave him alone," Babushka said sternly, steering the young woman toward the door.

"Volodya, stop by. Just for a few minutes," Katya said cheerfully, stealing another kiss from Volodya on her way out. "I'll make it worth your while." She smiled sweetly at Anne, chirped "Bye, bye," and fluttered out.

"Don't let me get in the way," Anne said as Volodya locked the door behind Katya.

"She is just old friend," Volodya replied dismissively.

"A friend in every port," Anne said.

"Sorry, what?" Volodya asked.

"Just an expression. It means you have women everywhere," Anne blurted out.

Volodya shrugged, as if apologizing. "And I love them all."

"Quite an accomplishment! I have trouble loving even one person," Anne replied with thinly-disguised sarcasm.

"To love only one, and lose her, is like … like to be ripped in pieces," Volodya said simply. "To love many is safe. Because with many, there will never be pain of being alone."

Anne glanced at him. His eyes spoke chapters.

"I loved one woman once," he said. "Too much pain."

He wanted to tell her about Svetlana, the love of his life when he was twenty-two. They had fallen in love at first sight during a soccer game where Volodya played forward. They started seeing each other and soon became inseparable.

But Svetlana was the daughter of a prominent general, a card-carrying party member who was not about to let his daughter waste her life on a man with no connections.

Volodya and Svetlana continued meeting secretly whenever and wherever they could, making love and making plans to elope. Volodya gave up his job at the factory and his apartment in the city, and obtained a permit to move to Kharkov, 1,200 miles away.

They picked a weekend when Svetlana's father was supposed to be traveling. Late in the evening, Volodya pulled up to her house. Svetlana dashed out with two small suitcases, jumped in and kissed him.

"To a new life, my love," Volodya said, turning the ignition key. At first the motor refused to turn over, and it took a while to get the car started.

As he shifted into gear, Svetlana put her hand on his. "Wait," she said softly. She sat for a long time, looking at him, then at her house.

"I forgot something," she said, flinging open the door and jumping out. "I'll be right back." She smiled cheerfully, but Volodya saw tears in her eyes.

She ran up the driveway and disappeared behind the huge doors. Volodya sat in the car, waiting.

"I loved her very much," Volodya said to Anne.

"And?"

"I was hurt," Volodya said, looking away. "Very hurt," he added quietly, rubbing his left shoulder, the fingers digging deep, as if trying to crush the joint and subdue an unseen enemy.

Anne waited for him to elaborate but he said nothing, staring into the distance, trying not to feel the pain he felt that night.

He had waited for a long time for Svetlana to return. After what seemed like hours, he could stand it no longer. He got out of the car, went up to the house and knocked. There was no answer. He knocked again. Suddenly, the doors opened and two huge men appeared.

"You're not welcome here," one of them said.

"I am waiting for ..."

Without warning, a fist landed on his jaw. Volodya heard the bone crushing. He staggered and fell backwards, rolled over, got back up and lunged at the men.

But they were stronger and better trained. He fought back as well as he could while their fists pounded his face, his chest, his belly. Finally, one of the men grabbed his left arm and wrenched it behind his back. Volodya felt the searing pain as his shoulder ligaments snapped, one by one.

Just before he fell on the ground for the last time, unconscious, he glimpsed Svetlana at the top of the stairs, held back by her mother.

He was almost dead when he arrived at the hospital. It took two abdominal surgeries and weeks of convalescence before he was able to go home. A letter from Svetlana awaited him. "I was not strong enough to go through with this. *Ne sudbah.* Forgive me if you can."

Since then, hardly a day had gone by when he hadn't thought of the pain. Not the physical pain of the beating, or the pain of humiliation because he was not good enough for the general's daughter. He thought of the pain of Svetlana's betrayal. He had let her into his heart. She ran away. The void she left behind gaped like a chasm. He was determined that it would never happen again.

"Did you see her again?" Anne asked softly.

"Yes. In pictures."

A few weeks after Svetlana dropped out of his life, Volodya came across a newspaper clipping. Svetlana was wearing a wedding gown, standing next to an older man who was dressed in military uniform. The clipping was dated just three weeks after their planned elopement.

His powerful shoulders drooped. "It was not to be," he sighed.

Anne started to reach out to him, but he got up.

"Honey. I forgot honey," he said, disappearing into the kitchen. He didn't want her to see the tears in his eyes.

58

The samovar came up to a boil, with a cloud of steam rising from the top. Volodya reappeared with a container that reminded Anne of Winnie the Pooh's jar of honey. His eyes were smiling again, the painful memory buried away.

"Ah, tea is ready now," Volodya said opening a stop-cock at the bottom of the samovar. Scalding hot water and steam sputtered out, filling the glasses.

With loving care, he helped Babushka into a chair, placed a cup of tea in front of her, dipped a spoon into the honey jar and put it into the tea.

"*Spasibo, milenky*. Thank you, dear," Babushka said, looking at him tenderly.

Volodya pecked her on the cheek.

"This is how she likes," he explained, noticing Anne's look. "Not too much honey, very hot tea."

Anne smiled, touched by the gentleness and caring between grandson and grandmother. She felt more at home with these two people who were practically strangers to her than she had felt with almost anyone.

A clap of thunder tore through the idyllic scene. Lightning flashed outside, followed by more thunder. The bulb in the ceiling flickered and went out.

"Oy, *Boje moy!* My God," mumbled Babushka, more in resignation than in surprise. Since the nuclear plant outside St. Petersburg
had been shut down, the electricity for the village was being supplied
by an ancient oil-powered generator. She was used to power outages.

By the light of the stove fire, she found her way into the kitchen
and returned with a candle and matches.

Volodya planted the candle onto the top of a teacup turned upside
down. The light shimmered, magnified in the polished brass of the
samovar.

"Who needs electricity?" he grinned. "Nicer like this, yes?"

Anne took a sip of tea.

"Ouch!" she exclaimed, as the liquid burned her lips.

"Careful. Water from samovar is almost boiling," Volodya said.
"Let me show you." He poured his tea into the saucer, and, bringing
it to his lips, slurped the hot liquid.

"Maybe too much noise, but does not burn lips."

Anne picked up her cup and did the same. "Like this?" she asked,
slurping loudly.

Volodya grinned approvingly. "Yes, you do it very Russian."

Suddenly a blast of wind knocked the window open and blew out
the candle. Volodya rushed to close the window while Anne groped
for the matches.

Babushka glanced around, making sure neither of them could see
her. Then she quickly leaned over Anne's saucer and squinted, examining the tea leaves floating on the surface. The red coals in the
samovar cast an eerie glow on her wrinkled face.

She leaned closer, frowning at what she saw. It couldn't be ... She
didn't want to believe it. Not about this sweet young woman. *Could
she be wrong? It wouldn't be the first time ...*

But the message in the leaves was very clear.

Babushka blew gently across the surface of the dish. Some of the
brown specs sunk, others reassembled into an even more ominous
pattern.

Maybe she was overreading because she was too close to Volodya, too afraid to see him hurt? But there was no denying it. The sudbah *was clearly spelled out.*

Babushka jumped up, almost knocking over the table.

"*Proch, proch.* Be gone!" she exclaimed, waving her arms.

Anne and Volodya stared back, stunned.

"Babushka, *shto takoye?*" pleaded Volodya. "What happened?"

The old woman backed toward the kitchen, crossing herself over and over with her arthritic fingers, pointing at Anne and repeating something in Russian.

Volodya tried to put his arms around her. "Babushka, let it be." But Babushka broke lose from his grip and still mumbling, rushed into the kitchen.

"What's going on?" Anne asked.

"Nothing, nothing."

"Did I do something wrong?"

"No, no. Is OK. Don't worry. She thinks she can see person's *sudbah* in tea leaves. That is all," Volodya said. "Sometimes what she sees is strange," he added.

There was no need to upset Anne with Babushka's bizarre statements. Besides, it was the second time Babushka had made the same prediction. Nothing happened after the first one. Nothing would happen after the second one either.

"What did she see?"

"Nothing. People in her generation believe strange things. Not worry. Here, I will play something for you," he said, trying to change the subject.

Anne watched as he lined up half a dozen glasses on the table and poured different amounts of vodka into each. Taking two spoons, he struck each glass several times, listening to the sound they made, pouring off or adding vodka until he was satisfied with the pitch.

"Now, ready," he announced. He paused for a moment, concentrating, then began playing his makeshift xylophone.

Anne listened, awed by how melodious this simple setup sounded, and how enraptured Volodya was by his music. Soon she recognized the church bell motif that she had heard on her first day in

Moscow, and again during the wedding.

"I can name that tune," she grinned.

Delighted, Volodya smiled back.

"Hello. I am Quasimodo of St. Basil's," he said, pantomiming the hunchback of Notre Dame. Then he puckered his lips and added mischievously, "Would you like to kiss Quasimodo, Anytchka?"

Anytchka.

Anne jumped up. The blood drained from her face.

Anytchka. The word reverberated in her head like a gun shot in the mountains.

Anytchka.

"Why did you call me that?" she asked, her voice trembling.

"Anytchka? It is Russian, how you say, love name. Little Anne. Annie. Anytchka."

Trying to control herself, Anne got up and walked away.

"You do not like it?" Volodya asked, perplexed.

Anne leaned on the windowsill and peered into the darkness, her breath fogging the cold glass.

"Anne?"

She didn't want to answer. She didn't want to think. She didn't want to be reminded of the visions.

Her head was spinning.

A flash of lightning illuminated a grove of snow-covered birch trees along the river bank outside. Anne saw a small church perched precariously over the river. The church had a small belfry topped with an onion-shaped dome, painted a pale blue.

"That church … I've seen it before!" she gasped.

"What church? There is no church there."

"Right there, on the shore."

Another flash of lightning. The church was gone.

"Maybe you were looking at bus station …"

Anne stood in silence, her mind spinning, confused, not knowing which of her senses she could trust.

"There was church here, but burned many centuries ago, during Tartar attack."

"Volodya, I saw a church. I know I did," Anne mumbled. "It had a green dome …"

Volodya watched her, perplexed. Babushka claimed that there was a local saying about some girl's eyes being as green as a church dome or something. He had never paid attention to it. How could Anne have seen it?

"Volodya, what did Babushka say, about my *sudbah*?" Anne asked suddenly.

"Nothing," he said, averting his gaze. Then he added cheerfully, "She said not enough chemistry between us."

Grabbing two of the fullest glasses from his makeshift xylophone, he handed one to Anne.

"Let us drink to chemistry," he exclaimed, raising the glass. "May it protect us from our *sudbahs*."

59

The password "M-E-M-O-R-I-E-S" appeared on the tiny screen of the decoder.

"Got it!" Sergey groaned, working his way out from behind the MEG. "You can fire it up."

Sasha flicked on the main switch. The C-arms started to turn.

"I'll send for our patient," said Baldyuk heading toward the door.

Sasha stopped him.

"Let's make sure first," she said, tapping in "M-E-M-O-R-I-E-S."

The MEG beeped. PASSWORD INVALID appeared on the screen.

"What the shit!" moaned Sergey, staring at the decoder, cold sweat starting to bead on his beefy forehead. "It's right here! M-E-M-O-R-I-E-S. Try again."

Sasha's fingers were trembling on the keyboard.

M-E-M-O-R-I-E-S was rejected again.

Sasha felt her face blanching. She was a drowning woman, going down for the proverbial third time.

"*Sooka amerikanskaya!*" Sergey blurted out. American bitch.

They huddled around the MEG, tapping in the useless password and checking and rechecking the decoder.

"I don't get it," Sergey kept mumbling in utter frustration. *The damn Americanka's sole purpose in life was to make him look incompe-*

tent. "I guess we're screwed," he said finally. "You need me to stick around?" Sergey added, hoping the answer was no. This looked like a good time to drop off the radar screen.

"Not tonight, nor tomorrow. In fact, we won't need you again. Ever." Baldyuk barked at the technician.

Then he turned and leaned into Sasha's face. "I was counting on you!"

She felt like a wolf cornered by hunters.

"I don't know what happened ..." she stammered.

"You wasted my time!"

Sasha's fear turned to rage. *The pompous ass, he had no idea what it had taken to get this far. Without her, Namordin would have been sent back to the loony bin right after the second MEGing.* She wanted to hit him.

Baldyuk continued his ranting.

"Why did I even think of trusting you with this? This was a man's job. A responsible man's job."

Be patient, Sasha, she told herself. *Be patient. Your time will come ... Just wait until you and Anne are in charge.*

"One hour. I need one more hour," she said firmly.

"For what?"

"I'll make it work."

"Oh, and how do you propose to do it?"

"That's my business," she snapped back, trying to sound more sure than she felt.

She needed time to try her last hope for figuring out the password. But Anne would be back in less than ten hours. Her jaw set, she faced Baldyuk.

"One hour."

Baldyuk walked out without a word, but his glare left no doubt. This was the last ten hours of Sasha's career—at the Pavlov, or any-where else.

Alone in the room, Sasha stared at the MEG. Slowly it dawned on her that it was not Namordin she was concerned about.

She had other plans ...

60

Pausing between rounds of vodka, Volodya and Anne realized to their surprise that it was after ten. Their Moscow-bound train was leaving in less than two hours.

"Quickly," Volodya exclaimed, grabbing his coat and ducking out of the door. "Put your coat on. I'll find car."

The ride back was long, dark and uncomfortable. Anne sat in the back seat of the tiny Zhiguly, hanging on as the car bounced over potholes. Volodya sat in front. Somehow he had sweet-talked Katya, the woman who visited them earlier, into driving them to St. Petersburg.

They ran up the platform with only minutes to spare. Volodya flashed their tickets at the conductor—an attractive, short-haired brunette, her figure neatly outlined by the immaculate, tight-fitting uniform. When she pointed him toward the back of the train, he launched into an animated discussion.

Gradually the conductor's face changed from official apathy to friendly attention, and then to a warm smile. After a minute or two, she wrote something on the tickets and motioned them toward the sleeper car.

"*Spasibo.*" Volodya grinned, and, leaning forward, planted a kiss on the conductor's cheek. The woman giggled and pretended to push him away.

Grabbing Anne's hand, Volodya helped her up the stairs.

"Now where are we going?"

"I asked conductor to give us more comfortable seats."

"And she did? Just like that?"

"I said we just got married, so we need sleeping train," he grinned.

The train wheels beat out their monotonous rhythm as the Red Arrow hurled across moonlit hills and valleys.

Volodya and Anne were settled in one of the luxurious sleeper compartments for which the Red Arrow was renowned. It was a cozy enclosure with wide, soft benches on either side, already made up as beds, each with a warm wool blanket, immaculate white starched sheets, and two plump pillows.

Under the window, a tiny fold-down table held two bottles of mineral water and two ceramic mugs engraved with the railroad's logo. On the adjacent wall, there were several controls for the various lights: reading, overheads, night-lights. All the luxuries of a home on wheels.

Anne and Volodya sat on the beds facing each other uneasily, like two teenagers contemplating spending their first night together.

"This will be more comfortable for you," Volodya said.

The train started moving precisely at midnight, with no warning whatsoever. Shortly thereafter, the conductor knocked twice on their door and walked in without waiting for a reply.

She smiled at Volodya as if they were good friends, then spoke to both of them. Her English was good, probably honed on the countless foreign travelers who chose this safer alternative to Aeroflot's planes.

"If you need bathroom, please go now. During the trip, please do not leave the compartment."

She handed them a small device made of hardened plastic. "And keep door always locked," she said demonstrating how to install the device over the door latch so it couldn't be forced open from outside.

Noticing Anne's raised eyebrows, she added casually, "Sometimes, bandits try to break in between stations."

So much for safety, Anne thought. She looked at Volodya, who remained totally unperturbed. "In second class was safe, no bandits want poor people. But here we are with the rich," he grinned. "so we lock door very well."

After it passed the suburbs of St. Petersburg, the train picked up speed. Fatigue from the night before, the rhythmic beat of wheels, and the dim lights made Anne sleepy, but she didn't know how to get in bed. *Should she lie on top of the blanket wearing all her clothes? Or ask Volodya to turn around while she undressed?* The prospect of spending the next eight hours so close to him was unnerving enough. The intimacy of disrobing was absolutely terrifying.

Volodya took the lead. He stood up and turned the lights off. Then, facing the wall, he unbuttoned his shirt and took it off. As the occasional outside lights flashed in the window, Anne couldn't help stealing glances at the outlines of his muscular back and arms.

Then she heard the clicking of a belt buckle and the unmistakable sound of a zipper. She stared at the ceiling, concentrating on taking slow, deep, quiet breaths.

He steadied himself against the window frame to slip off his pants. The train passed a crossing, street lights spilling into the cabin for a brief instant. Anne caught a glimpse of the muscles rippling across his powerful thighs, the rounded outline of his buttocks. *Soccer players' legs,* Anne thought.

Slipping under the covers, Volodya let out a contented sigh, "Much better than sitting, no?"

Anne didn't answer. She was still savoring the vision of the cutest buttocks she had ever seen.

Retreating into the shadows, Anne took off her blouse and skirt, letting them fall to the floor next to her so she wouldn't have to stand in the window light to hang them up. Then she peeled back the covers and quickly slid between the sheets, their cold starched surfaces rough against her skin.

"Yes, it is much better," she agreed echoing his sigh.

Suddenly, she wasn't sleepy anymore. She found that if she raised her head by folding the pillow in two, she could see outside. As her eyes adjusted to the darkness, she started to discern stars. Thousands of them. Unlike anything that she could ever see in Boston, where the sky was spoiled by the glare of city lights.

"Maybe later we will see moon," Volodya said, as if guessing what she was looking at.

They lay quietly, listening to the beat of the wheels, and to each other's breathing.

"Thank you for a wonderful day," Anne said quietly. "I really enjoyed meeting Babushka. She seems like a great woman."

"I love her very much."

"Tell me about your parents, Volodya."

"What to tell?" he said quietly.

"Whatever you remember."

In his broken English, he did his best to describe his mother's disappearance when he was still a child, and his life with his father, until he died of alcoholic cirrhosis of the liver when Volodya was barely fourteen.

"Brothers, sisters?"

"Nobody. My family is Babushka," he said. "And you?"

"I have an uncle in Philadelphia."

Then she told him about the abusive relationship her parents had had, the sleepless nights, the worries about her mother.

"Did she leave him?"

"Yes, she did," Anne replied in a choked whisper.

She heard Volodya turn toward her. They were barely an arm's reach from each other, separated only by the space between the beds.

"Was it painful for you?"

She held her breath, wondering whether to go on.

"Once I walked in when my father was ..."

She stopped, and he heard her take a little gasping breath.

"He was ... was beating and raping her, Volodya. Like an animal."

Anne felt tears welling up in her eyes.

"I hated what he did to her. But I hated what he did to me even more. I needed him to love me. I longed for his touch, for a kind word. He never touched me. Never said anything nice. Other dads came to school, watched their daughters perform in theater. But all I got was, 'Did you study? Did you finish your homework? Don't disappoint me'."

She was sobbing now, no longer able to suppress the painful past simmering below the surface.

"He was not with you when you needed," Volodya whispered.

"No, he wasn't. And maybe that's why I couldn't stand up to him and defend my mother—I was so afraid to anger him, so afraid to lose whatever tiny fragment of affection I imagined he had for me."

Memories were coming back, furious, painful. She poured them out without restraint, without editing, sensing that with him, her feelings were safe. It was the most open she had ever been with another human being.

"He beat her and raped her, and I could have done something, but I didn't. And now I have to live with this ... with this sin, Volodya." She paused as tears choked her.

"Sin?"

"A few days after my sixteenth birthday—it was Valentine's Day—my father had been away for a week, at a business meeting or something. He was due back that night, so my mother sent me to spend the night at my girlfriend's house across the street. My mother didn't want to ruin Valentine's Day for me."

Anne sobbed. "I woke up because I heard sirens and then, through my window, I saw this orange glow. I looked ..."

Anne sobbed harder. She had never shared this part of the story with anyone. Never let it surface from the deep recesses of her memory.

"I looked out and I saw our house. It was burning. I'll never forget it. It was like a giant torch, reaching toward the sky."

Anne paused, the painful memory raking her insides.

"I ran out, and tried to run to the house, but the firemen wouldn't let me. And I just stood there, as it burned, and burned. Oh, Volodya, it hurt. It hurt so much ..."

"I know, Anytchka," he said quietly.

"And then, when there was nothing more to burn, the firemen went in, and found their bodies. My mom and him. My father. And they told me ... they told me ..."

She had to stop again, her sobs choking her. "They said that my mother had set the fire. She killed herself, Volodya, to get out of her nightmare. And I had the chance to help her, and I didn't do anything. I could've called the police, I could've made her leave him. But I did nothing ..." An unbearable upwelling of guilt blocked any words.

She felt his arm reach across the gap between the beds.

"I am so sorry, Anne," he said touching her wet face.

"I should've done something. But in some weird way I loved him too much, I needed his love, and I was afraid to anger him ... I have to live with that for the rest of my life."

"It was their *sudbah*, Anne," Volodya whispered. "No one can change *sudbah*."

She covered her face with the pillow, trying to muffle her sobs. *Stop it, Anne,* she tried to tell herself. *Stop the memory. Too much pain. Too many regrets.*

A roar filled the cabin as the train blasted into a tunnel.

Anne tried to breathe slowly, willing her brain to rest, her muscles to relax. Willing the demons away.

The roar died, and she started seeing bursts of light. She uncovered her face and realized that the train was now speeding through a town, the street lights flashing like strobes. In their light she could see glimpses of Volodya's face, as if lit by lightning, turned toward her, staring into her eyes.

The wheels clacked their unrelenting rhythm.

Another tunnel. The car banked precariously. *So close to the walls.* The metal wheels screaming around the curve.

Suddenly, all was absolutely quiet and she was floating on a slowly flowing river blanketed by morning fog. In front of her were two figures: Anytchka and Nyanya, both wearing peasant dresses, standing huddled on the prow of a small ferry-raft. The simple craft, made of tree trunks tied together and reinforced by wooden cross planks, glided down the glassy water, propelled by the boatman's pole.

Anytchka, her face concealed by a scarf, glanced nervously back at the boatman—an old man wearing a dirty, crude caftan. As he forced his weight against the long pole, his weathered face strained, revealing a row of decaying teeth.

Gradually, the opposite bank emerged from the fog bank. Moments later, the ferry ground ashore. The boatman helped the women off, without missing a chance to peek under Anytchka's scarf. Nyanya paid him, and she and Anytchka walked away, soon disappearing in the grove of birch trees at the river's edge. Glancing back one last time, Anytchka saw the boatman poling his ferry back toward the opposite shore.

She followed Nyanya as the woman expertly picked her way through the tree branches and undergrowth. Nyanya stopped next to a downed pine tree, its trunk eaten by beetles into sponge-like consistency.

"I will meet you by the riverside at dusk," she said. "May God protect you." She made a sign of the cross over Anytchka's forehead and hurried off into the forest.

Anytchka stood still, holding her breath, listening. A light breeze, scented with the smell of clover, caressed her face and whispered in the birch trees. Soon she heard a branch crack, then faint footsteps approaching. And then Vovka appeared in the clearing. He was thinner than when she last saw him after her wedding, four months ago, but his body seemed just as powerful.

They ran toward each other and Anytchka buried her face on his chest.

"Oh, Vovka, my darling, my lover, my life …"

They stood rocking tenderly, lovers reunited, his gentle hands exploring the contours of her back, her arms, her neck, as if to ascertain that it was really her, really his beloved Anytchka, in his arms again after he had given up all hope of ever seeing her.

After a long time, Vovka turned her face up … and recoiled, horrified. Her beautiful features were marred by the black and blue marks of a recent beating.

"Anytchka, what has he done to you?"

She tried to hide her face against his chest, tears of shame welling up in her eyes. The bruises were not the worst part of her life with Grudskoy.

"I'll kill him!" Vovka whispered, choking. "I will kill him," he yelled at the top of his lungs, the cry piercing the silence, tearing through the forest, echoing back from the distance, dying.

He held her again in his arms, gently kissing her lips, her eyes, her bruises, whispering, "I love you, I will kill him, I love you, I will kill him."

She pressed her fingers to his mouth, silencing him.

"Don't talk. Just love me. Kiss away my nightmare. Make this moment last a lifetime."

She stepped closer to him and slowly untied the belt holding his caftan. Concentrating as if trying to commit every sweet moment to memory, Anytchka opened his caftan, pulled it off his powerful shoulders, and let it fall around their feet. Vovka stood in front of her, unable to move, his heart beating faster and faster.

Anytchka leaned closer and inhaled the familiar scent—that indescribable blend of aromas—beeswax, sage and honey, and something else that was only him, something that kept her awake by night and dreaming by day.

Her hands slipped under his shirt, the feel of the rough linen cloth bringing back the memories of the moments they shared when Anytchka was still unmarried, still with her parents. Those were the memories that gave her life meaning. The first time she walked past the new barracks, where the garrison that Grudskoy left behind was stationed, and saw Vovka, as handsome as the day he saved her from the Tartar. The first time they ventured off for a walk along the river edge. The first time they confessed their love to each other, under a moonless, star-studded winter sky. Until this instant, all those moments seemed so distant, so hopelessly lost.

Grasping the edges of his shirt, she pulled it over his head, down his muscular arms.

Her fingers slid over the hard body that she had longed for, for so many months. The body she thought she had kissed for the last time. She stroked the thick curly hair on his chest. She felt his nipples harden as she touched them, and saw his eyes close, his chest heaving. Resting her hands on his shoulders, she sunk slowly to her knees, drawing him down with her, then easing him back onto the soft carpet of leaves and moss.

Still on her knees next to him, her hips hot against his, she began loosening her own clothes. One by one, she cast aside her garments, keeping only a thin camisole of fine silk, a gift her father brought her from a trip to Novgorod when she was fourteen.

Vovka held his hands up, palms toward her, his eyes still swimming in hers. Her hands came toward his, fingers spread, closer, not touching, closer still, the heat streaming across the narrow gap that separated them.

Then softly, like a butterfly landing on a petal, their fingertips touched one by one, each connection sending a wave of energy through their bodies, the energy building until they could no longer stand it, their interlaced fingers blanching with the power of the grasp.

Vovka spread his arms like a bird taking flight, drawing her body down toward his, her full breasts embracing his chest, their lungs matching rhythms, breath for deep breath, legs sliding against each other, resenting the few garments that still kept them from blending into one single body.

They kissed again, moistening each other's lips, their tongues exploring, their minds lost in the moment, drinking in every sweet sensation.

They raced to rip the remaining clothes off each other, and she felt his hardness against her, as his fingers gently exposed her wetness.

And then neither of them could wait any longer, and his breath turned into a fierce moan that shook her entire body as she slid over him, welcoming the exhilarating fullness.

As Vovka entered her deeper and deeper, Anytchka felt the gradual healing of the horrible scars that Grudskoy had inflicted on her body, mind and soul. It was like a soothing balsam that erased the pain of the last four months.

They drank their pleasure for hours, postponing the final ecstasy, pausing occasionally to listen to the insects buzzing lazily in the trees, or to watch the clouds colliding in the blue sky.

Finally they let themselves be swept by each other's passion, their voices blending into one deafening cry, their union now complete.

Afterwards, she cried quietly, feeling free, if only for a few moments, of the painful yoke of her horrible marriage.

Later, they laid side by side, the sinking sun casting shadows across their naked bodies.

"We'll run away ... to Novgorod. No one will find us there," Vovka was saying.

"Look around, Vovka," Anytchka replied, sweeping her hand toward the horizon. "All this belongs to my husband. Four days on horseback, in any direction, all his. We'll never make it out of here. He will hunt us down like animals."

"Then I must kill him," Vovka said with determination.

She clamped her hand over his mouth. "Don't ever say that. You'll die trying."

"I don't care ... I can't bear it, Anytchka." There were tears of pain and anger in his voice.

"You must bear it," she said firmly.

"What have we done to deserve this *sudbah?*"

"I knew it would be like this the night I gave myself to you," she said quietly. "And I would do it again, any day of my life. Here on earth, or beyond the grave."

Her lips touched his. "My *sudbah* is to be your lover. Forever."

The pounding Anne heard was not the wheels of the train, it was her heart beating. Vovka was no longer there. Anytchka was gone too. Anne could still feel the sweet kiss and salty tears on her lips. A deep longing permeated her body, tempting, tantalizing, tormenting.

She heard her own breathing, shallow, guttural, catching in her swollen throat. Her heartbeat, accelerating.

From his bunk, in the dim light of the moon shining through the window, Volodya saw Anne's arm inching toward him. Slowly, tentatively, fingers barely open.

He reached toward her. One of her fingertips brushed ever so gently against one of his. An electrical spark passed between them.

Street lights flashed outside like lightning, revealing glimpses of his face, eyes wide open, lips parted, nostrils flaring. Freeze frames of a moment they would never forget.

Their fingers explored each other, fluttering like butterfly wings. A gentle touch more intense than the strongest embrace.

Anne saw two bodies pulsating against each other. Anytchka and Vovka, their hearts beating like one. Faster. Faster. Faster.

Anne's fingers grasped Volodya's hand. Her lips, open, longing for his. A sweet burning spread from her fingertips, where Volodya's hand touched hers, up her arm, through her chest, swelling in her breasts … A new feeling, frightening, intoxicating. The longing raced to her belly, down to her groin. She felt the heat and wetness building like never before.

And then, with the roar of the train reverberating off the tunnel walls, Anne felt the waves of agonizing pleasure drowning her, blanking out her thoughts …

"Volodya …" she cried out as the overwhelming climax swept her away. A climax like she had never experienced, never dreamed of, never knew could happen.

Over the beat of the wheels, she heard him whisper, "I love you, Anytchka."

Her fingernails dug deeply into his wrist.

"I love you, too, Volodya," she whispered back, so softly even she couldn't hear it.

The train blasted out of the tunnel onto the wide open plain under the wide open sky, studded with fading stars.

61

Locked away in her little office, Sasha reviewed what had happened. The modulator was plugged in where it belonged, and the unit started up without a problem. The decoder supplied the password to access the ablation mode. Where was the problem?

In a fit of fury, Sasha rammed her elbow against a cabinet. The thin metal door warped and flew open, spilling books, folders, videotapes and office supplies onto the floor. Now even angrier, Sasha kicked the pile, her powerful soccer leg scattering everything across the room. A videocassette arched through the air and landed on her desk. The cassette was labeled "M. F." *Marussya's treatment.*

When the video cameras were installed in the MEG room, one of them was aimed at the console. When Sasha set off in pursuit of the password, she had reviewed all the tapes, but found that Anne's arm obstructed the view of the keyboard. That is when she resorted to the decoder.

Somehow, she had missed Marussya's recording. As a last ditch effort, she shoved the video into the VCR and played it.

On the monitor, Anne input the password, but, like all the other times, all Sasha could see was part of the keyboard and Anne's right elbow.

Dead end.

She closed her eyes. *Now what?*

She heard the soundtrack, with Anne's fingernails clicking on the keyboard. *A practiced rhythm. Steady patter, interrupted by a tiny pause.*

Sasha opened her eyes and replayed the segment. *There definitely was a stumble in the middle of the pattern. And there seemed to be too many keystrokes.*

She counted them.

Ten.

But MEMORIES only had eight characters.

Sasha hit Play again, eyes glued to the screen. Anne was wearing a short-sleeved shirt. Her beautiful arm …

Sasha forced herself to concentrate. *Ten strokes.* She couldn't see the fingers. *Except the right pinkie …*

That was it! How could she have been so stupid? It was so low-tech! Sergey, with all his KGB training—he should've figured it out!

Minutes later, Sasha and Baldyuk were back at the control panel and Namordin was immobilized in the MEG unit.

Sasha turned the unit on, and the C-arms started spinning around Namordin's head. The image of his brain appeared on the screen, the two distinct clusters of memories clearly delineated.

"I'm going to show you how to rewrite history," Sasha announced, selecting the ablation mode.

"To hell with history. I care only about next week," Baldyuk smirked.

The unit beeped and the message ENTER PASSWORD appeared on the screen.

Confidently, Sasha tapped in M-E-M-M then corrected herself— a break in the rhythm, a tiny pause as her right pinkie flew up to hit the "delete" key. Then the rest. O-R-I-E-S. Ten strokes in all. It even sounded the same as when Anne did it.

The unit beeped. A red light flashed on the panel. The ablation mode was on.

"But that's what you had last time," Baldyuk said, confused.

Sasha couldn't help smiling. *She wasn't about to reveal how simple the solution was. The password was the entire entry, including the back-space. Sergey's decoder was designed to read only the final input. Low tech beat out high tech, but persistence prevailed.*

Now came the hard part.

"Sing *Suliko*," Sasha ordered Baldyuk.

"What?"

"Sing. The first bars will do."

"But …"

"Don't argue, damn it."

No sooner had Baldyuk started humming the tune than Namordin joined him. The two men's voices, hoarse and off key, singing an old love song, sounded bizarre in this room full of space-age equipment.

A hot spot appeared on Namordin's scan, identifying the memory cluster.

The MEG arms spun like a runaway Ferris wheel. Sasha aligned the ablation beams.

"Here we go," she breathed.

With bold strokes, she started carving out her masterpiece. One by one, large portions of one of the memory clusters faded and vanished from the scan.

"Should you be cutting all that off?" Baldyuk asked, concerned. *That's not what he had seen the Powell woman do.*

"Keep singing."

She worked the red beams with surgical precision.

Slash, slash, slash.

Namordin's voice grew stronger, the words to the song more intelligible.

Sasha felt excitement welling up inside her.

Slash, slash.

She wielded the joystick with consummate confidence.

Layer by layer, she stripped away every cell that was not part of the song-related cluster. Every memory that did not belong. Every synapse that stood in the way of her reaching her goal.

"And now I give you …" A few more passes with the red beams.

"Not Namordin …"

Then she punched the stop button. The C-arms stopped. Sasha pushed another button and the restraints popped open.

"Not Namordin," she repeated, "but your beloved leader himself." Namordin sat up and blinked. Then he raised his hand and wiped his mustache.

Baldyuk's jaw dropped. *That little gesture, the thumb and forefinger coming down the thick bush of hairs over the upper lip, then converging into a pinch at the bottom. To anyone who grew up on propaganda films, that was pure Stalin.*

"Come on, we have work to do," the new Namordin exclaimed, with a thick Georgian accent. He leaped off the table and headed toward the door. Alert, smiling, confident.

His bodyguards gasped.

"Walks like Stalin …"

"The man himself, in the flesh …"

The third guard, a much older man who had actually seen the infamous leader in person, crossed himself over and over as if he had seen a ghost.

"What are you waiting for?" Namordin-Stalin yelled at the guards. "Let's go."

The group marched out, the bodyguards barely keeping up with their leader's fast, short steps.

As the door slammed closed behind them, Sasha threw her head back and laughed hysterically.

It was so simple.

By erasing one set of memories, she had allowed another set to surface. With the dominant personality gone, the alter was free to take over. Namordin was dead. Stalin was back.

It took several minutes for the implications to sink in, and a boundless panorama of future opportunities to unfurl before her eyes.

She had gone back two generations to get to Namordin's grandfather Stalin. *But why not regress three, four, five generations, erasing memory record after memory record? Peeling off the layers of the onion, guided by the MEG image?*

Incredible possibilities were now within her grasp.

"But how does it work?" she heard Baldyuk mumbling.

"What?" she snapped, her reverie interrupted.

"How are the memories from past generations stored in the brain?"

"Who cares?" she spat contemptuously. "It works."

Baldyuk rubbed his pudgy hands in anticipation. "This is marvelous. As soon as we get rid of the Americanka, we can ..."

Sasha felt the familiar pounding in her head and saw red circles floating across her field of vision. The onset was so sudden she wondered if she was having a stroke.

This pitiful excuse for a director wanted to move in on her territory, a territory that she had carved out for herself, single-handedly. Not only that, he wanted to send Anne away. Anne wasn't going anywhere. As a matter of fact, now that the conversion of Namordin into Stalin proved to be an astounding success, Sasha had big plans ...

"Are you referring to Dr. Powell?" Sasha's head felt like it was going to explode.

"We don't need her anymore. No point sharing the money and the glory."

"I have a better idea. How about we get rid of you, and I get the money and the glory? And the Americanka," Sasha added.

Baldyuk frowned, trying to figure out whether she was serious.

She approached and stood on tiptoes so her face was closer to Baldyuk's. She was going to tell him to get out of her sight, but she felt her hand clenching into a fist. All by itself, as if the hand belonged to another person. Without warning, the fist rammed into Baldyuk's belly.

The old man staggered and fell backwards, hitting his head against the MEG.

"You bitch! You're finished," he groaned, struggling to his knees.

Slowly, reality caught up with Sasha, but she didn't really care what she had done. "Without me, it's you who are finished," she snapped back. "So here's the deal. For now, we'll pretend that you are

the head of the department. But if you as much as think about sending Anne back to the U.S., or interfering in what we do—in any way
at all—I'll screw you up so bad, your head will spin. Do you understand?"

"You can't …"

"I can and I will. Do you want me to tell your sponsors how you
botched up the operation, and how I had to save you at the last
minute?"

Without a word, Baldyuk staggered to his feet.

"Now, get out of here," Sasha barked, "and go set up a time to collect the balance. And remember, I want to be there at payoff time."

Baldyuk started to object, but reconsidered and limped out.

On her way home, Sasha stopped at the Hotel National to put the
integrator back into the jar of cream. The sight and smells of Anne's
suite brought a new surge of feelings. But this time she didn't linger.
The object of her fantasies would be back soon.

She rode the motorcycle home, recklessly weaving in and out of
the heavy traffic, crossing intersections against lights and gunning the
bike at hapless pedestrians. Suddenly her vision turned red in one eye,
then blurred completely.

She was on horseback, surrounded by Tartar warriors. She was leading them on a raid. They were galloping through smoke, swinging
their curved swords, foot soldiers scattering under their onslaught.

Just as inexplicably as it had appeared, the image vanished. Sasha was
back on her motorcycle. But the street was unfamiliar. She had missed
a turn. Tires screeching, she spun her bike around, drove over the center divider—sending pedestrians scrambling in all directions—and
leaped to the other side.

Nothing will stop me, she thought. *Nothing.*

As she entered her apartment, Sasha glanced in the mirror and caught
a glimpse of her bright red lipstick. Disgusted, she wiped it with the

back of her hand, smearing it all over her face.

She went behind the partition into her bedroom, pulled off her dress and held Anne's emerald-green nightgown against her bare breasts.

All of a sudden, Anne walked into the room. "I came to you," she said in a soft voice, her lips open in a balmy smile.

But before Sasha could run up to her, Anne's face dissolved into a kaleidoscope of blurred images. Candles, icons, a church service. A troika galloping across snowdrifts under a starlit night.

Sasha tried to clear her head, but the images spiraled faster and faster.

A woman in a peasant dress being ravaged by someone whose face Sasha could not see.

A small infant lying on a grassy field, smiling at the blue sky.

A chapel perched on a river edge; inside the chapel, two young lovers, hiding.

The ruins of a barn burned to the ground.

Sasha could smell the acrid smoke, mixed with the odor of burned flesh.

Suddenly, her entire body was flooded with pain. The excruciating pain of realizing that something has gone horribly wrong, and can never be fixed.

Clutching her head in anguish, she collapsed on the hard floor.

62

The Red Arrow pulled into the station just as the sun was coming up.

Pausing on the platform, Anne and Volodya kissed good-bye. A light kiss. Neither wanted to risk disturbing last night's magic by discussing what happened, or kissing with the full passion they were now feeling for each other.

After a brief stop at the hotel to change clothes and to retrieve the integrator, Anne headed for the Institute.

Sasha awaited Anne's arrival with great excitement. Her heart raced when she imagined how she would take Anne to her home, make her comfortable...

Reality hit. *She couldn't take Anne home. First, she had to show Anne how things were meant to be.* Sasha had no idea how she was going to do it. She just knew it wasn't going to be easy.

"Welcome back." Sasha could hardly contain herself when she saw Anne walk in earlier than expected, but she forced herself to keep the conversation casual. "Thank you so much for taking care of the paperwork!"

"No more surprises like that, OK?" Anne said. "So who do we

have today?"

"Only four cases. I didn't think you'd want to work hard after a sleepless night," Sasha said.

"Just as well, I'm dead tired," Anne confessed.

"We'll be done by three. And then I have a special treat for us," Sasha said, a teasing smile on her face.

"I'm going to pass. I need to go home and rest."

"But what I've planned is restful! Trust me, you'll feel like a new person!"

The health club was an odd combination of modern amenities and old-world architecture. The building, once the opulent palace of one of the members the Romanoff imperial family, was now converted to serve the needs of a different upper class.

A uniformed doorman inspected Sasha's I.D., checked Anne's passport, and called upstairs for authorization before admitting them. Sasha and Anne ascended the wide curving marble staircase to the mezzanine level, where they were buzzed into another lobby, all chrome and glass and decorated with pictures of athletes and movie stars. Several young men in flashy clothes were lounging around. Anne had already learned to identify them as the newly minted millionaires who were everywhere in the city. The men gave Sasha and Anne lazy, arrogant looks and went on with whatever they were doing.

A stunningly attractive young receptionist greeted Sasha with a respectful smile, immediately ushered them into the spa area, and turned them over to yet another attendant. *It paid to have Baldyuk make the reservations,* Sasha noted. *Power spoke. Soon she, too, would be powerful. Her time would come. Soon.*

"Hello, I am Janna," the pink-cheeked attendant said in English. "You have private cabin tonight, yes?"

Sasha nodded.

"Follow me please."

They crossed the lobby. A group of people gathered around the TV were engaged in an animated discussion of what was on the screen.

"Something happened?" Sasha asked in Russian.

Janna shrugged her shoulders. "It's some political rally again."

Bypassing the ladies' locker room, Janna led them down a wide hallway and unlocked one of several doors.

"Is there anything you need?"

"We're fine, thanks," said Sasha.

"Please enjoy," the attendant said, disappearing.

The large room had a sitting area covered with a plush carpet, a tiny rock-lined pool, and a wood-paneled enclosure separated from the room by a thick glass door.

"What do you think?" Sasha asked, visibly pleased by Anne's reaction.

"Amazing," said Anne shaking her head. Russia's rich seemed to have wasted no time acquiring a taste for Western luxury.

"Make yourself at home," Sasha said, quickly stripping off all her clothes and wrapping herself in a thick terry cloth robe embroidered with the image of St. George on horseback slaying a dragon. "I'll see you in there," she added, pointing to the sauna.

Anne changed into the other robe, hanging her clothes next to Sasha's. She was starting to look forward to a relaxing evening.

Anne enjoyed occasional sessions in saunas during her day trips to spas in Boston, but she wasn't prepared for the heat that blasted her as she entered the *banya*. The thermometer registered 92 degrees Centigrade. That was 198 degrees Fahrenheit. *Practically boiling,* Anne thought. The heat seared her nostrils with every breath.

"Try the bottom shelf," Sasha said laughing. "It's cooler down there."

Anne settled down, gradually adapting to the temperature. For a while they lay in silence. Anne was starting to enjoy the hot wood of the bench heating and relaxed her back muscles.

"How did you like Peter?"

"Peter?"

"St. Petersburg."

"Well, we didn't see much of it."

"Oh?" said Sasha tensing up at the way Anne said *we*. "So what did you do all day?"

"Volodya took me to visit his grandmother."

Sasha held her breath. She felt the headache starting up again.

"And what did you think of Babushka?" she asked, trying to sound casual.

"You know her?"

"I met her once. I think the woman is a fruitcake."

Sasha climbed down from her bunk, leaving her bathrobe behind. Sweat covered her entire body and her skin glistened as if oiled. Anne was surprised by how muscular Sasha was, and how small her breasts were.

"Damn, they didn't give us any whisks!" Sasha exclaimed, looking around. She pushed the intercom button and said something in Russian.

"What whisks?"

"To open up the pores. You can't go to a sauna and not use whisks!" Sasha laughed, perching on the edge of the bench next to Anne.

"Anyway, a few months ago I was having tea with Volodya and his Babushka. She's into reading tea leaves. And suddenly, she snatched the cup out of my hands and told Volodya that the tea leaves showed that I was going to kill him." She glanced at Anne. "Crazy, isn't it?"

Anne lay still, remembering her first conversation with Volodya. "*I shall be killed by jealous husband. Babushka saw it in the tea leaves,*" he had said.

Then she thought about Babushka's outburst during her visit. *Was the old woman really going crazy?*

Janna knocked politely, and, sticking her hand into the sauna, handed Sasha two whisks made of birch branches.

Anne welcomed the brief blast of cold air that wafted in from outside, but the door closed again.

"Let me show you," Sasha said, and without waiting pulled Anne's robe down, exposing her back. Before Anne could protest, Sasha struck her lightly with the whisk.

"This is called *venyk* in Russian," Sasha explained. "It improves circulation and opens pores."

The room filled with the pungent odor of eucalyptus oils. Anne found that the whisk really did enhance the sensation of heat.

"It's getting dry in here," Sasha said. She picked up a ladle and splashed water on the hot rocks. Sputtering and hissing, then a cloud of steam filled the room, obscuring everything.

Anne felt the heat building beyond her tolerance. The room started shrinking. Anne began to panic.

"OK, now do me," Sasha said handing over the *venyk* and turning her back to Anne. "Do it hard!"

"I'm sorry, it's too hot," Anne exclaimed, leaping off the bench. She clutched her robe and ran out.

Trembling, sweat cascading off her entire body, she sat on the edge of the pool and dropped her legs into the ice-cold water.

"Wimp!" Sasha laughed, strolling out of the sauna, the bathrobe draped casually over her shoulders. She walked to the edge of the pool, let the bathrobe fall, and slid into the frigid water, a contented smile on her face.

A minute later she surfaced. "OK, back in."

They went back into the sauna again. When they came out again, Anne followed Sasha's example and dove into the pool with her. She never imagined that frigid water could be so delightful.

The third time was easy.

"Now, the grand finale—the mud baths," Sasha announced, leaping up on the edge next to Anne and wrapping herself in the bathrobe.

"I really think I should be going."

"Nonsense," Sasha said firmly. "It's the best part. If you liked the steam, you'll love the mud."

Sasha got up and held her hand out to Anne. "Let's go." She said it cheerfully, but Anne heard a steel-hard edge that defied objection.

Anne was relieved to see that mud treatments were done in individual rooms, and that she was alone with the therapist.

The small enclosure was lined from floor to ceiling with aquamarine ceramic tiles. A vat of black mud stood in the middle of the room, next to a tall, narrow, wooden table. There was a drain in the middle of the floor. *For easy hosing off,* Anne figured.

The fat, morose therapist greeted her and motioned her to lie down on the table. After covering Anne's eyes, cheeks and forehead with seaweed, the therapist had her roll over, and positioned her face in the face cradle. The therapist dipped a thermometer into the vat and checked the temperature. Satisfied, she scooped up a gallon of the black, viscous substance and deposited it on Anne's back.

The warm mixture ran down her back, her sides, tickling her neck. Another ladle-full landed on her buttocks, the mud slowly oozing between her legs. Anne opened her eyes, but the sheets of seaweed covering her face allowed only a diffuse green glow.

As the therapist's hands began spreading the mud over her body, Anne took a deep breath, closed her eyes, and finally relaxed. The panic of the sauna slowly gave way to the warmth of the mud covering her body. Her mind floated to the train ride with Volodya. She heard his voice, felt his touch.

At some point during the treatment, she realized that the pattern of the hand strokes had changed. The fingers dug deeper, the hands traveled lower.

She wanted to move, but the hands held her firmly down, still massaging around her shoulders, then moving down, gliding toward her buttocks.

Then she heard Sasha's voice, whispering. "Don't fight it, Anne."

Anne struggled to get up, but her body felt paralyzed. Even though her eyes were closed, she saw a vivid image of a man's hands kneading a young woman's breast, grasping the nipple so hard that it turned pale.

"Don't fight it," she heard Sasha's voice again. "It's our *sudbah.*"

Anne felt the hands sliding along her body. *Up. Down. Slowly. The thumbs slipping, ever so lightly, toward the top of her buttocks. The mud oozing on her skin.*

"Who are you?" Anne whispered.

There was no answer.

"Who are you?" she repeated, her terror growing, her voice faltering as conflicting images raced before her eyes: Grudskoy's face pushing Anytchka down; Vovka's handsome profile against the blue sky, his body naked, making love to her.

She heard Sasha's voice, like the guttural rumble of a gathering storm. "I can be anybody you want me to be. You and I, we're meant to be together. The rest doesn't matter."

Anne heard a woman screaming.

Everything went black.

Anne bolted upright and ripped the seaweed off her face.

She was alone. The room was empty.

63

"**A**nne, slow down, slow down! You're not making sense," Misty was saying as she raced around the kitchen with a cordless phone pinned against her shoulder, trying to follow a recipe for lamb tajine with couscous and apricots she was preparing for dinner for Ramman. "Just slow down and tell me the whole story again," she said, trying to sound as calm as possible.

After the mud treatment, Anne had gotten dressed and hurried out of the spa, petrified that she would run into Sasha. The big *M* of the Metro station glowed just on the other side of Tverskey Street. Anne made several suicidal attempts to cross the eight lanes of erratically moving traffic, almost getting killed by a speeding Mercedes. Then she spotted the underpass.

She ran down the stairs, past the old ladies selling their wares, past the kiosks with cigarettes, liquor and blaring bootlegged CDs of American music. People stared as she pushed her way through the crowd. She realized that her clothes were stained with black mud. Her face probably was too. She couldn't remember whether she had showered before leaving. In fact what little she remembered seemed more like a nightmare.

She saw a row of public telephones and rummaged in her purse for the phone card that Natalia had given her. She tried three phones before she heard a dial tone. She punched in the access code.

"USADirect, may I help you?"

A Texan accent never sounded so good. A few minutes later, she had tracked down Misty.

"Misty …" Anne's voice was trembling.

"Anne, darling, what happened?" Misty put the tajine down and leaned against the counter.

"Sasha … Something's wrong with Sasha."

"The woman you work with?"

"I think she's having the same halluci… the same visions."

"If memory serves, she got an even higher dose, so it's to be expected …"

"I think we were lovers."

Misty's jaw dropped.

"You had sex with her?"

"No! In the past."

"But you just met her!"

"As Anytchka."

"But that's crazy!" Misty blurted out before she could check herself.

"I'm not crazy!" Anne shrieked.

"Not you crazy. The notion …" Misty was trying to sound calm, but little red flags were popping up in her mind. *Was Anne having more serious after effects from the MEG overdose than they originally thought? Was she having a psychotic episode? Was she on drugs?*

"Just slow down, and tell me what happened."

Deep breath, Anne told herself. Take a deep breath.

"Sasha was massaging my back."

"Why was she massaging your back?"

"We were in the sauna together. She had been acting weird for a while. Volodya and I just came back from Peter."

"Who is Peter!"

"St. Petersburg. I was tired. She invited me to the spa. And she said—I think it was her—that we were meant to be together. Misty, I think she's ..."

Anne screamed as she felt a viselike grip on her shoulder. Dropping the receiver, she gasped and swung around.

"American, you want candy?" An unkempt young man shoved a half-eaten chocolate bar in her face. His speech was slurred and he was unsteady on his feet.

Anne backed away, unsure whether to kick or run, but two of the man's buddies grabbed him by the arms and marched him away. "Excuse please, very sorry," one of them said. "Vodka."

Her heart still racing, Anne retrieved the receiver.

"What happened? What happened?" Misty was frantic at the other end.

"Somebody just attacked me," Anne said in an unsteady voice.

Jeez, now she's getting paranoid, Misty thought. "Listen, get yourself someplace safe, where we can talk. How far away are you from the hotel? Can you take a taxi? Is there someone you can call?"

"Don't worry," Anne said, regaining some of her composure. "I'll manage. Just help me think this through. If what I am remembering are snippets of a past life ... I can't believe I'm even saying this!"

"It's OK, just go on."

"So is it possible that the MEG made Sasha remember... It's just too much of ..." Anne's thoughts were racing far ahead of her ability to articulate them.

"Too much of a coincidence?" Misty finished the sentence. "Not according to the theory of synchronicity. If people are close in this life, they regress on parallel tracks."

"If you believe that stuff! Besides, the gender is wrong. Sasha is a woman."

"Gender switching is not unusual in past life experiences."

"Stop calling it past life experiences! I'm just having ... I don't know what I'm having. I just need it all to go away! Soon!"

Misty never heard Anne sound so agitated. Even in the hairiest medical emergencies.

"Anne, listen to me." Misty summoned her professional voice. "Right now what you need is a good night's sleep. Go home. Get in bed. Visualize yourself in a peaceful …

"I know the drill, Misty."

"Good. Go do it. Tomorrow we'll sort all this out. Call me the minute you wake up, you hear?" Misty said, hoping she was sounding firm enough.

Anne hung up and hurried up the steps on the other side of the underpass. The *M* was just a short walk away now, down a narrow street.

She walked along the dimly lit sidewalk, her steps muffled by a layer of fresh snow that reminded her of the thick carpet in her granduncle's house when she was a little girl.

Gradually, she was able to force her racing brain under control.

She had to admit that she was seeing images from a life that wasn't hers. But there has never been a scientifically plausible explanation for past life experiences. So there was no way that she could be having them.

Except that she was.

And how did Sasha fit into this? She wasn't in the mud room when Anne looked up. Probably wasn't, anyway. And why images of Vovka and Grudskoy? *Her mind was playing tricks on her, that's all.*

She heard light footsteps behind herself, and picked up the pace. The footsteps got closer. Her heart pounding, she broke into a run.

"Anne!"

She turned. It was Volodya.

"I was looking every place for you," he said as he caught up to her, panting. "What happened?" he exclaimed, gently wiping a smudge of mud off her cheek.

"I forgot to shower," she answered.

"You must come to Pavlov. Something very important happened."

64

A nne examined the six photos labeled A-1 through A-6 that Volodya laid out in front of her. They showed images of tiny X-shaped structures, each made up of four sausages-like parts, about fifty to a page.

"Chromosome sets," she said, recognizing the classical image of genetic material contained within each living cell.

"Yes. Mouse chromosomes." He picked up a stack of computer printouts covered from edge to edge with letters. Anne saw row upon row of sequences of four letters—A's, T's, G's and C's—that were used to describe genetic information encoded in genes.

"I ran sample of DNA from Igor's sperm cells through sequencer."

"Who's Igor?"

"Ah!" Volodya reached into one of the cages and pulled out a white mouse. "This is Igor, champion in running maze," he said, stroking Igor's back. "Sequencer shows mutation in Igor's DNA," he said, pointing out where two of the printouts differed in the order of letters.

"A mutation."

"Yes, mutation. I labeled mutation with radioactive cytosine so we can see on the picture. Little dark spot, right here, yes?" He indicated the spot on one of the prints.

"OK." Anne had no idea where he was going with this.

"This mutation is from learning to run maze."

"Hmm," Anne grumbled skeptically. Genetics 101 was coming back. Random mutations were a dime a dozen and they were seldom traceable to a specific outside stimulus. "And how do you propose to prove it has anything to do with learning the maze?"

"Very simple. It was not in sperm sample before Igor learned."

"Come on! That's not proof enough. Something else may have caused it."

"Is true, but wait to see more." He walked over to one of the cages. "Remember fertilizing Abby?" he asked.

How could she ever forget? *Day one, his knee pressing against her thigh. Had it been three weeks?* It seemed like yesterday. And like an eternity ago.

"We used sperm from maze champion Igor to fertilize Abby."

Volodya opened the cage and pulled out a tray with six small mice each labeled from A-1 to A-6. "And here are offspring that we baptized. Four boys, two girls."

They had grown a lot in just a few days.

"Last night I took samples of cells, and studied gene sequence," Volodya continued. "Offsprings A-1, A-2 and A-4 do not have mutation, but A-3, 5 and 6 have, yes?" He compared the pictures.

"Go on." In all living creatures, half the genes come from the father, and half from the mother. An offspring has a 50-50 chance of inheriting a specific gene from one of the parents. Hence the 50-50 split of mice with and without the mutation. *So far it was plausible.*

"Now, for maze test, I must use males only, because reward only works for them."

"What reward?"

"I use fluid from female mouse in estrus—how you say?"

"In heat."

"Yes, in heat. Because smell from hot mouse is very attractive to male."

Clever approach, Anne thought. Pheromones were highly odorous compounds produced by a wide variety of species, from insects to mammals, to attract mates. Pheromones had been part of the mating process for millions of years. In early times, when the animal kingdom was just evolving and population densities were low, it was difficult for widely scattered males and females to find each other for mating purposes. Scent traveled faster and farther, and was a far more reliable signal than mating calls.

Pheromones could be turned on and off by simple physiologic changes, like ovulation, making the timing more precise. In most species the male's response to pheromones was hard-wired. They were born programmed to be attracted to a fertile female that was sending out the right pheromones. The beauty of the reward Volodya had chosen for his mice was that it was simple to find and one-hundred-percent reliable.

Volodya took the mouse labeled A-1 and placed it in the starting gate of the maze. He sat down at the controls and turned a dial. The mouse started shuffling restlessly.

"I found last year that just mutation is not enough. Now I send very low-voltage current through mouse feet, to make depolarization in brain. So synaptic threshold lower, mouse remembers better."

"Fascinating!" Anne mumbled, now even more intrigued by the experiment. When she was developing the MEG, she had briefly worked with electrical currents applied externally to the skull to help patients access memories. Eventually she chose the much more precise magnetic waves to generate the needed currents.

"Thirty seconds, is enough," Volodya said turning the dial back to zero. The mouse settled down.

"Now maze memory, if there is in mouse brain, is active." Volodya flipped a switch. The door of the starting gate snapped open. The mouse stuck its nose out, sniffed, scurried down one of the branches of the maze, turned back, ran around a corner, started down another path, ran into a wall ...

"You see?" Volodya asked.

"Yes, I do. It's lost."

"Yes. Means no maze memory. And no little dark spot on chromosome picture. No mutation." He craned his neck to look in Anne's eyes to ascertain that she was keeping up. "Now look."

Volodya removed A-1 from the maze and placed A-3 into the starting gate.

He pointed to the picture of A-3's chromosomes, with its telltale dark spot. "This offspring has mutation."

The depolarizing current went on, and the mouse repeated the shuffle. Volodya flipped open the gate. A-3 stuck its nose out, crawled out into the maze, and stopped.

The mouse glanced in both directions, sat on its hind legs and licked its front paws.

Anne looked at Volodya.

"He's lost too."

"Wait," Volodya said.

Suddenly, A-3 took off like a racehorse. Right, left, left, right. The creature dashed along the narrow passages of the maze, taking the turns as if it were on rails. Once, it missed a turn but backtracked instantly and continued on course.

Twenty seconds later, A-3 crossed the finish line, ran up to the tiny hole from where the scent was being released, and shoved his nose into it, panting.

"You see!" Volodya exclaimed triumphantly.

"He learned fast," Anne conceded.

Volodya put his arms on her shoulders and looked into her eyes. "Anytchka. This mouse has never been in that maze," he said quietly.

She glanced up, startled. "Then how did he …"

"Because his father, Igor, knew maze very well."

"And A-3 has never even seen another mouse run the maze?"

"No. Before I called you, I made him run, only once, and already he knew. He did not learn. When he was born, he knew," Volodya repeated.

The implication of this result reached Anne's brain with difficulty, like a fish struggling up the rapids.

"But that means the mouse actually inherited the knowledge from the father. The memory of the maze pattern was somehow transmitted … That's impossible," she mused.

The science of genetics was built on a solid principle: Acquired characteristics were not inherited. No matter how many generations of Dobermans had their ears and tails clipped, they were still born with long ears and long tails. And Volodya wasn't talking about a single trait, like different eye color. He was dealing with a complex behavior pattern that was somehow transmitted, apparently by a genetic change.

The closest to such a phenomenon that she could think of were experiments done in the '60s where mice were trained to run mazes, then their brains were fed to other mice, and these mice learned the maze patterns faster. But that was attributed to increased levels of a memory-enhancing enzyme in the brains of the trained mice, and not to any genetic transmission of knowledge.

"Yes, they know maze because changes in chromosomes passed memory to offspring," Volodya confirmed, grinning from ear to ear like a kid on Christmas morning.

"Impossible."

"Other males with mutation, A-5 and A-6 had same results."

"Coincidence."

"Statistically, chance to reach end of maze that has twenty turns, with only 3 mistakes is ..." Volodya referred to a table, "about one in 400,000. Chance of three mice doing same ..." He whistled, dismissing the possibility. "So, not coincidence!"

"Why hasn't this experiment been done before?" Anne asked, her brain still refusing to accept what she was seeing.

"Many people tried. But nobody tried with depolarizing current."

"Why hasn't somebody thought of that?"

Volodya shrugged his shoulders. "Why nobody think of MEG?"

She couldn't help smiling. The point was well taken. In science, for every "Eureka!" there was always a "Why didn't we think of this before?"

She was willing to admit that the mice's performances were pretty persuasive. But this brought up the next question.

"OK, so tell me this," Anne asked. "How did learning the maze cause the chromosomal mutation in the first place?"

"Pheromone reward had effect on brain and formed new connections in synapses."

"Like Pavlov's dogs that learned to salivate when the bell rang because it signified food was coming."

"Correct."

"But how would a change in the synaptic pattern cause a genetic change?"

"Ah-ha!" he exclaimed enthusiastically.

"Yes?" Anne asked expectantly.

"That I do not know," he confessed.

"Well then. Aren't your conclusions a bit premature?"

"Not premature. Only unexplained. In beginning, did you know why magnetism helped your patients remember?"

"Well, not really, but I had a good feeling ..."

"You, feeling?" he teased.

"A theory. Then we were able to show how synapses became depolarized."

"When, 'then'?" he persisted.

"Months. Maybe a year later. Maybe more ..." she admitted.

"You see. In time I know I make explanation also." But he sensed her skepticism. "There are many examples in nature, how animals pass information. Think of—what you call white birds, always live near ocean, eat fish and shells?"

"Seagulls?"

"Yes, seagulls. How seagull know to pick up shell, fly high, and drop shell on rock to break it, so he can eat inside?"

Anne remembered seeing the birds do that when she went to the beach as a little girl. She never thought to ask her dad how they knew to do that. She shrugged her shoulders.

Volodya raised a finger. "I think one time, long ago, one seagull flied up and dropped shell accidentally. Shell broke. Seagull became very excited when he discovered that shell was now open, and he could eat it. Excitement released neurotransmitters, which caused change in his chromosomes."

Anne nodded appreciatively. "A mutation that spelled out 'Drop shell to get food!' And the mutation was passed on, generation after generation. So that became standard behavior for all future seagulls. Hmm!"

He looked at her triumphantly, knowing his logic was irrefutable. "It is not different: Transmit knowledge to make correct turns in maze, or knowledge to drop seashell on rock."

She stood still, processing the information.

"Another example: Cats are born afraid of dogs, monkeys are born afraid of snakes."

Anne looked at him. "Same principle?"

"Possible, no?"

Anne imagined the primordial monkey, hundreds of thousands of years ago. The monkey squats on the ground of the forest, picking berries. A giant snake slithers up to him. The monkey has never seen one before, and continues munching peacefully. The snake springs forward, its coils encircling the monkey. The animal struggles, unable to breath, its brain unleashing a flood of adrenaline—the fight or flight hormone—and other hormones and neurotransmitters.

With a final effort it manages to slip out of the deadly embrace and struggles up the tree, the snake in close pursuit. The monkey, terrified, uses his last strength to leap to a small branch. The snake follows. But the branch breaks, the snake crashes to the ground. The monkey is safe.

The terrifying encounter would certainly cause a surge of neurotransmitters that would leave a permanent imprint on the brain, and would in turn lead to a mutation in the genes, recording the lesson. The reward: survival.

Anne broke out in a smile. "Volodya, if you're right, this is truly a remarkable breakthrough. You should be very proud."

His face lit up. "Thank you," he said quietly. "I am happy you are first person I tell this."

She too was happy to be sharing the excitement of the momentous findings.

"And you know what this means?" Volodya asked.

"That you need to have this study published, immediately. Then get funding and ..."

"No," he said with a twinkle in his eyes.

"What then?"

"Means you lose bet, so you must dance with me!"

He opened his arms. She walked up and leaned against him.

"I will, Volodya, when you teach me."

He kissed her gently.

"Come, we go home now."

"How can you think of going home? This is an amazing discovery! I'd think you'd stay here, and, I don't know, just work or something."

Volodya laughed. "But then we miss last Metro! Is better we celebrate—*po rusky.*"

65

"In the States, if you proved that genetic memory existed, they'd at least give you a car that worked," Anne joked about Volodya's chronically malfunctioning vehicle, as they ran down the escalator into the Metro.

They rode in silence in an almost empty subway car, their knees and shoulders touching as the subway car screeched around the steeply banked corners.

Anne glanced at Volodya out of the corner of her eye. He was deep in thought, but still had the contented smile on his face.

He had all the reasons to be smiling. Of course, the experiments would have to be repeated and confirmed by other researchers. Nothing with such deep impact would be readily embraced. But there was no denying that the main discovery was a milestone. She was happy to share in his afterglow.

She heard coins rattling in a tin cup. A wrinkled old man in ragged clothes stuck his cup toward Anne and droned something.

"*Ookhody pojaluista,*" Leave please. Volodya tried to wave him off.

Anne reached into her pocket and dropped a fifty-ruble note in the man's cup. It was almost two dollars, and would have been appreciated even by the most jaded Bostonian panhandler. But this man looked angrily in his cup, then at Anne.

"*Bolshe davai,*" he crowed.

"I can't believe! He wants more," Volodya said.

As the train pulled away from the station, the man rocked unsteadily on his feet and leaned into Anne's face. His puckered lips, covered with white ulcers, exposed his rotting teeth. His breath made her gag.

She closed her eyes and turned away, but inexplicably the man's face was still there. This time she felt the vision coming, like an epileptic feels an impending seizure.

The grinding of the train's wheels became painfully loud. The noise changed into the squeaking of a rope rubbing against the side of the river ferry as it rocked on the waves at the dock.

Anne was not in the subway car, but on the shore of a river, in a torrential downpour. A flash of lightning lit a cluster of birch trees, bent low by gusts, their leaves tearing and vanishing into the darkness.

The boatman leaned toward Anytchka.

"It's too rough. She'll have to wait," he shouted to overcome the noise of the wind, pointing to Nyanya. "She will sit under the tree. I'll take you across, then come back."

He grasped Anytchka's arm and hoisted her aboard the bucking raft.

Nyanya watched as the ferry slipped into the darkness, bouncing like a cork on the waves. She covered her head with her black scarf and ducked under a tree.

Anytchka crouched on the prow steadying herself against the rigging as best she could, peering ahead into the darkness.

Suddenly she realized that the ferry was no longer moving forward. She turned around and found herself staring into the boatman's face.

He bowed with exaggerated politeness. "Begging your forgiveness ... but are you not Anna Vassilyevna?" he asked, his voice hoarse.

Anytchka tried to turn away, her knees weakening. But lying would be futile. The man knew.

"I am," she answered proudly.

The boatman hid a crooked smile. "Begging your forgiveness, Anna Vassilyevna …" He bowed again. "Does Knyaz Grudskoy know where you were?"

"I was visiting Nyanya's family," Anytchka answered as firmly as she could, her voice unsteady, the blood draining from her face. "What business is it of yours?"

"I am your husband's devoted slave. His business is my business."

He hesitated for a moment, as if gathering courage, then stretched his hand toward her, palm up. It was callused and part of the thumb was missing.

"I will not tell His Excellency where you were," he croaked glancing from her to his empty hand and back.

Anytchka's temper flared, but she knew she was in no position to negotiate with this man. She reached under her caftan and dropped a few coins into the boatman's hand.

The man grinned. He leaned even closer to her face and leering expectantly, hissed, "And I will not tell His Excellency what I saw."

Anytchka was infuriated by the man's greed. "That's all I have," she said firmly, determined to stand her ground.

"No, I saw. You have other … things …" The boatman drooled brown saliva and wiped his chin with his sleeve.

"What other things?"

"Things," he repeated reaching for her chest.

"How dare you!" She shoved him away, but he grabbed her cape and wrestled her down.

"Please, Anna Vassilyevna, I just want to smell you," he hissed, burrowing his rough face in her neck.

Anytchka felt the drooling lips trying to kiss her skin.

"If you let me smell you, I won't tell His Excellency about Vovka."

Anytchka's heart missed a beat. *How did he know? He cast off right after he let Nyanya and her off on the shore, and couldn't possibly have seen her and Vovka making love.*

Unless he came back later. Oh God, Anytchka thought.

Sensing her hesitation, the boatman forced his hand under her garments. His callused fingers groped around until he found her breast.

She turned away, disgust and fear etched on her face, afraid to resist, realizing that a few words out of this man's mouth could cost her and Vovka their lives.

"Yes," he hissed, roughly grasping her nipple. "I won't tell His Excellency ..." He fondled her other breast, then started to pull up her dress.

"Or maybe I will." A flash of lightning lit his leering face.

Anytchka lay still, but her hand groped around the decking, searching for anything that she could use in self defense. Her fingers connected with a fishing knife nestled between the beams of the raft.

She felt the boatman's hand reaching between her thighs, tugging at her hair.

Another bolt of lightning lit the blade as it flashed through the air and plunged into the man's chest. The boatman reared up and screamed, spewing saliva mixed with blood. Anytchka braced herself and, gathering all her strength, heaved him off the raft.

The boatman's body splashed into the river. In the next flash, she saw him floating away, face down, a bloody red trail streaming behind him, mixing with the muddy waves.

Anytchka collapsed on the deck, her sobs blending with the rhythmic sound of the waves lapping at the aimlessly drifting raft.

"Anne, we must get off," she heard Volodya's voice next to her.

She shuddered, sprung to her feet and headed for the door, her legs moving stiffly, like tree trunks.

The subway car ground to a halt. As she stepped out onto the platform, she staggered and started sinking to the floor. Volodya leaped forward just in time to catch her.

"Are you all right?" he exclaimed, supporting her gently.

"I'm sorry, I'm a little dizzy."

"You look terrible! I must feed you."

"Forget it, I'm fine ... I must have gotten dehydrated in the sauna, so when I stood up suddenly ..."

He put his finger against her lips. "Shh," he whispered. "Let me be doctor tonight."

She leaned on him and they blended into the crowd of commuters inching toward the exit.

Volodya led her to the hotel and into her room. He propped her up in bed and poured her a glass of bottled water. While she drank, he unlaced her boots and carefully pulled them off.

She felt better and realized that she was indeed hungry.

"Let's eat," Volodya said.

Anne pointed to the desk. "The room service menu is in the top drawer."

He smiled. "Real food. Ten minutes," he said going out the door.

Anne felt restless. Memories of the train ride, of the mud bath, of the attempted rape on the ferryboat, raced through her mind. She started pacing.

She walked around the bed, up to the little stairs, around to the window and back to the bed. Around and around, trying to think of nothing, anxiously awaiting Volodya's return.

She didn't even need to think about the pacing—her feet adjusted to the pattern and she took the turns automatically.

Like a mouse running a maze. Genetically hardwired to take the turns that would lead to the expected reward.

Somewhere in the mouse's brain the blueprint of a certain behavior pattern was written in stone. Or in genes. When something activated it, it surfaced. Like a combination that opened a safe, revealing an old map. A map to be followed again...

We are what we were.

She stopped pacing. She knew she had found the missing piece. She felt an odd vibration—as if her whole body were reverberating with a new truth.

She looked at the clock. It was past midnight. In Boston it would be only a little after six in the evening. She picked up the phone and tracked down Lucia.

"That's right," Anne repeated when Lucia thought that she misunderstood due to the phone static. "I want you to cancel all upcoming MEG patients."

"What happened?" Lucia exclaimed.

"Let's just say, a puzzling technical development. And Lucia … Keep this down for now." *Halden would freak out at the thought of what putting the program on hold would do to sales, to say nothing of the FDA approval process.* Anne didn't want his ranting to affect her judgment.

"Dr. Powell, somebody's bound to wonder about all the blanks on the schedule. Mind if I write in some fakes? Then they'll just be 'no-shows'."

"Do what you need to do," Anne said. "I'll tell you more when I know what we're dealing with here."

"Take care, Dr. Powell."

After she finished her calls to the patients and fixed the schedule, Lucia left Halden a brief voicemail. She was sure that Anne's admonition to "keep it down" couldn't possibly have included the chief of the MEG project.

66

The electronic door lock clicked open.

"I know how past life experiences happen," Anne blurted out the instant Volodya appeared in the door, carrying several bundles.

"Past life?"

"Genetically transmitted memory. I know how it happens."

"Is that good?" He still had no idea what she was talking about.

"It sounds too simple." Anne was bubbling with excitement. "Hear me out."

Volodya set the bags of food on the coffee table. "I am hearing."

She took a deep breath. "If your theory is right, certain stimuli make the brain release neurotransmitters, which cause changes in genes. And these changes become a part of the genetic record, and are passed on to the next generation."

"We saw it tonight in mice, yes?"

"In the offspring, the new pattern in the genes creates a memory record in the brain."

He nodded. "Like memory record to 'make strong legs' or 'make green eyes' or 'turn right in maze'."

Anne raised her voice. "Why does it have to be limited to behavior patterns like running a maze? Why not lifetime experiences?"

"Whole life?" Volodya asked.

"Or at least large pieces. Clusters of memories dealing with the same event. Maybe segments a few months long, or even a few years."

"Not years," he corrected her. "In mice, few years is whole life."

"I wasn't thinking mice. I was thinking people."

Volodya ran his hand through his blond curls and exhaled heavily.

"Must eat, before food becomes cold," he said absentmindedly, unpacking the bags of food, his hands moving jerkily, like a robot. Eating always helped him think. He sensed this new twist on his findings was going to take a lot of eating.

The comforting aroma of freshly baked bread filled the room.

"The question is whether there's enough room on the genes?" Anne asked, pinching off a warm, crispy piece of crust.

"Because transmission is not only one life?" Volodya understood her concern. "Every generation add new record?"

"Exactly. It'd be cumulative. Information would be recorded generation after generation, and passed on like a family diary."

As Volodya's mind tackled the scientific challenge, his hands unwrapped skewers of juicy lamb alternated with lightly charred vegetables. "Shish kebab," he explained.

He carried the food to the coffee table, then sat on the floor, cross-legged, and pulled Anne down next to him.

"*Mm, da,*" he mumbled. Twenty-three pairs of chromosomes. Each chromosome with maybe three million sites. I think more than enough," he concluded. "Please try this," he added, depositing a skewer in front of her.

"Isn't shish kebab Greek?" Anne asked, slipping several pieces off the skewer, letting the juice drip on her bread.

"Greek, Tartar, Russian. Everybody eats them. It is all mixed," Volodya replied, dishing out a generous portion of tiny parboiled potatoes smothered in butter and garlic.

"So, enough space on gene. But is enough space in brain, to carry memories from so many people?" he asked skeptically.

"We use so little of our brain capacity, there's plenty of room,"

Anne said confidently. "Maybe all those blank areas on the brain scans are not so blank after all."

Besides, not every memory would have enough impact to cause a neurotransmitter surge, she mused. And of course there would be attrition, when later mutations erased parts of old records. That would open up room for other information to be stored. Even in ideal cases, there may be only a handful of recoverable past life memories stored in anyone's brain, and many of those would probably be fragments at best.

Volodya continued chewing heartily. He seemed to manage to enjoy the taste of the food while concentrating. "So when we give electrical current …" he began.

"Or a blast of magnetic energy," Anne chimed in, "the memories…"

"*Da!*" Volodya stopped chewing, completing her sentence in his own mind: *The stimulus would unlock a memory from a past life and make it real in the present.*

"Yes, very much possible," he exclaimed.

Anne glanced at him. *He had no idea how "very much possible" it really was. She was living proof of it!* The MEG overdose had awakened one of the memories that had been handed down to her through her parents' and their parents' genes.

She wasn't crazy or psychotic after all. It was just a past life experience.

What am I saying? she thought. "Just" a past life? Sure, some people took past lives for granted. But she was a scientist, for heaven's sake! How could she admit that she was experiencing something completely contrary to everything she had been taught, everything she and her colleagues believed in?

So far she had managed to treat her visions with denial. After all, there was no known way that past memories could be transmitted. Without a mechanism, the concept could be conveniently dismissed.

But now, the evidence that such a mechanism did exist was staring her in the face. If it could happen in mice, it could happen in higher mammals. The differences between remembering the turns in a maze, the trick of breaking shells against rocks, or the details of a relationship were simply a matter of degree.

Suddenly, all the *deja vu* experiences, the love-at-first-sight episodes, the past-life memories that some of her patients claimed to have had—suddenly they all made sense.

And so did all her visions and nightmares. Anytchka, Grudskoy, Vovka were no longer figments of her imagination.

She didn't know whether to be relieved or terrified.

Volodya had mixed the pieces of lamb with grilled peppers, onions and tomatoes, and doused everything with the garlic yogurt sauce.

"Try this," he said, gently slipping a juicy chunk of lamb between Anne's lips.

She bit into it slowly, enjoying the exquisitely rich mix of flavors.

"So why everything not come back, all mixed? Maybe three, four lives?" Volodya was saying, his mind exploring the ramifications.

He had a point. Why didn't al l past lives come tumbling out, like an avalanche of books from overturned library stacks, burying the hapless researcher?

Volodya picked up a full skewer and twirled it. "Because memories are like shish kebab," he answered his own question.

"The records are linked," Anne added. It made sense that various memories from the same life would be anchored to each other, like scenes in a movie.

That brought up another issue. Why didn't a past life memory just take over, like a very engrossing movie?

Volodya echoed her thought. "If person remembers past life, will he follow past life, like my mice follow new mutation?"

For a second, Anne pictured what it would be like to stop being Anne and become Anytchka. She shuddered.

"I'm sure it wouldn't happen," she replied quickly. The brain was designed to protect the sense of "self" at all costs. The present self. In most people, most of the time, that was the only self that existed.

Unless they were schizophrenics.

Or had somehow ventured into their past.

They continued talking, completing each other's sentences, their minds racing ahead in different directions, then converging and working side by side, wrestling jointly with logical stumbling blocks, asking each other, "What if?"

At one point, Volodya paused. "I am thinking," he said staring out the window.

"*Molodetz*," Anne teased. Good boy.

"What if two people who knew themselves in past, meet today."

Anne glanced at him. "Slim odds. People move around."

"Maybe. But in Russia is not like in America. In my country we live in same places for many generations. We love lands where our parents are born. And their parents. Like my Babushka—her people live in same village for three, four centuries. Maybe more."

"I don't know, Volodya …"

In terms of numbers, a meeting was not unlikely. Even assuming that most lifetime records would be erased or damaged over the years, there would still be a number of people whose memories could be a match. She remembered Misty's story about the Yale psychiatrist and the young couple whom he regressed to their respective past lives.

A thought tore through her mind, like a meteor across a black sky. *Sasha! What was all that "We belong together" in the spa?*

Whatever memory Sasha's brain got launched into by the MEG, she was going to live it out all on her own. It had nothing to do with Anne. And, like Anne, and all the other MEG patients, she would soon be over it.

She shook her head and changed the subject.

"So, how about a Luna for dessert?"

Sometime during the evening—neither of them noticed when—they pushed the coffee table off into a corner, shut off the lights and opened the curtains so they could see Red Square. Sprawled on the floor, their backs against the bed, they argued ardently or sat quietly while thoughts crystallized into words.

Neither had ever felt so in tune with another person, so energized by another mind. It was a mental and emotional ballet of two, exhilarating and gratifying.

Late into the night, Volodya laid his head across Anne's outstretched legs. For a while she hardly noticed, continuing to talk of synapses and neurotransmitters and mutation rates.

Finally, she fell silent, enjoying the weight of his head on her thighs. Her fingers absentmindedly traced the outlines of veins on his muscular forearms, touching ever so lightly. She followed the blood vessels, so firm and exposed on his lean body, naming them in her mind with the names she had learned in anatomy classes.

Gradually she became aware of his face lying at her left breast. She felt her nipples swelling, and wondered whether he could feel them through her thin blouse.

She leaned back against the bed and closed her eyes, letting the longing spread through her body.

Suddenly she realized that she was not afraid of being drawn to this man. She could love him, and make love to him, and be in love with him, and she was open, and ready, and nothing was in her way. It was a liberating experience that made her heart race. Maybe for the first time in her life, she could love without running.

Perhaps remembering her past—her very remote past—helped her resolve the fears of her present.

Volodya felt Anne's heartbeat speeding up. Her hand was running through his hair, her hard fingernails gently scratching his scalp, sending shock waves down his spine.

A new realization hit him: he didn't want to just make love to this woman. He wanted to be in love with her. To need no one else, ever.

They looked at each other and he could read his feelings reflected in her eyes. The protective shells, that each had constructed so carefully over the years, were crumbling.

Anne heard a very faint sound, almost a vibration. It grew louder and more melodious. It was Volodya singing. Even without understanding the words, Anne knew it was a love song. About a sad and unrequited love.

"*Ya Printsessa Alloy, s zolotystoy kossoy, oobegala taykom is dvortza ...*"

The rhyme flowed beautifully, the words so soft. "Translate for me, Volodya," Anne whispered.

"I am Princess Alloe, with golden hair. I run away from my castle, away from guards, away from old husband, to hear my lover singing. He sings with his heart, he sings …"

He trailed off into singing again.

Her eyes closed, she let her fingers slide toward his mouth, touching his lips, exploring them gently.

After a while, he stopped singing. His lips caught her fingers. She let it happen, finding the tip of his tongue, caressing, teasing, wet.

Anne heard the sounds of a church choir coming from somewhere in the distance, somehow finding its way through the double-pane window.

An oil lamp appeared in the corner of the room. *Why didn't I see it there before,* she wondered.

When she turned, she saw that the faint flickering light was casting bizarre patterns across two nude bodies, lying side by side on the ground, bales of hay piled high around them.

Oh, no! The cursed dream.

Anne wanted to scream. But words didn't come.

She held Volodya's face in her hands. "*Ya tebya looblyu,*" she whispered. "I love you. From the moment I saw you, I knew that I've always loved you!"

"I love you too, Anne," Volodya whispered back.

He rolled off her legs and pulled her up so they were kneeling face to face, their lips drifting closer. Tentative, then hungry, opening, welcoming. Their tongues joining in a passionate dance.

She undid his shirt, then her own. He fumbled with her bra, frustrated by the unfamiliar front hook. She helped him. Her breasts, finally released, longed to be touched.

Her hands slid up his arms to his shoulders, the touch so soothing. Then her nipples brushed the hair on his chest, and he pulled her closer until there was no more space between them, no more skin, no more barriers.

"Anytchka … *solnyshko,* my sunshine …"

Still holding each other, they eased onto the floor. Slowly she rolled him on his back. She straddled him and forced his arms up above his head.

"Let me love you," she whispered. "I want to love you like I've never loved anyone."

"Yes, please be my only love."

She leaned forward, against his aroused flesh. He gasped as he felt her wetness against him. Slowly. Engulfing. Welcoming.

Their low moans blended into one as she lowered herself fully onto him. It was a union as delicious and unforgettable as it had been centuries ago. Finally, they were one again.

They didn't sleep. The night flew by, too short to satisfy their hunger. In the morning, Anne walked Volodya down to the street, pausing at the hotel entrance to give him a long kiss.

"*Do svedanya*, Anytchka."

"I'll see you soon, my love," she said, sliding her fingertips along his. "I'm glad I found you." *Again*, she added to herself.

67

Anne sprinted up the entire sixteen floors back to her room. Around and around, up the dimly lit stairwell. By the time she reached her floor, her lungs were bursting and her legs were on fire, and there was a radiant smile on her face.

She walked down the hall feeling a little dizzy, and opened the door to her room.

The room had changed. The walls were whitewashed, the ceiling was much lower, and decorated with a fine line of winding vines. Instead of the tall glass doors overlooking the Kremlin, there were several small arched windows with panes of opaque glass.

Two young girls in white linen dresses were sitting in a corner spinning lamb's wool into yarn.

An older woman hurried toward Anne and took her by the hand. "Hello, mistress. I've been waiting for you."

Nyanya led Anne to a wooden stand supporting a large piece of embroidery. It was a beautiful design—a young woman and a young man meandering across a meadow. As Anne sat on the small wooden stool, she noticed Grudskoy.

He was sprawled on a huge carved wood chair, clad in a loose woolen robe edged with ermine fur, a necklace of large pieces of amber hanging around his neck. With his boot he was stroking his favorite hunting dog, sprawled at his feet. Occasionally, Grudskoy glanced lasciviously at the young women. Anne felt her skin creep and her pelvis tighten at the prospect of sharing the bed with him tonight.

Anne couldn't figure out how she had gotten into this room. *She had just spent the night with Volodya …*

But she loved Vovka. She was Anytchka. Who was Volodya?

"Mashka, more wine." Grudskoy waved a silver cup at one of the girls. The youngster obediently dropped her distaff and scurried over. Grudskoy's hand explored her buttocks appreciatively as she refilled his cup from a clay pitcher.

All of a sudden, the door swung open. Anytchka saw two guards holding up an old man, his dirty clothes tattered, his shoulder bandaged with a bloody rag.

Anytchka glanced up and squinted, trying to remember where she had seen the man before.

"We found him crawling outside, Your Excellency," said one of the guards. "We were going to throw him back in the river but he says he has something important to tell you."

"Speak," Grudskoy nodded, barely paying attention.

The old man staggered a few steps into the room and sunk to his knees.

Anytchka gasped. The blood drained from her face. She gripped the embroidery stand to keep herself from falling. She recognized the boatman who tried to rape her.

"I'm your lowly slave, Your Excellency," the boatman whined, bowing to the floor.

"Just speak," Grudskoy grunted lazily.

"Your beloved dove, the woman who shares your bed …"

Anytchka's heart stopped in mid-beat.

"She has sinned with another."

Grudskoy's nostrils flared.

"What?"

"She was with a man …"

Grudskoy heaved his body up from the chair and groaned like a wounded animal.

"Liar!"

"Begging your mercy, Your Excellency! I saw her with my own

eyes."

"No, no!!"

"She was with your lieutenant, Vovka Ermakoff ..."

"No!" Grudskoy staggered forward, his massive frame dominating the room.

"I took her across the river ... I didn't know ... Then I saw them in the birch forest." The old man wiped the brown saliva drooling from his lips. "They were naked, Your Excellency."

Grudskoy grabbed the wine pitcher and hurled it at the boatman. The pitcher shattered, splashing red wine high up the whitewashed walls.

"I'll kill him!"

As she slid to the floor, losing consciousness, the last thing Anytchka remembered was the red wine streaming down the walls, like rivulets of blood.

Then she was in her own bed, and Nyanya was bending over her, placing cold compresses on her forehead.

"Are you all right, my lady?" the kind woman asked, leaning closer. "Please speak to me."

"She will speak!" bellowed Grudskoy as he crashed through the door, several of his henchmen close behind.

Shoving Anytchka's feet to the side, Grudskoy sat down on the edge of her bed. "We can't find your lover anywhere."

Anytchka looked at him, hatred in her eyes. "And you never will," she whispered.

Taking a deep breath, Grudskoy suppressed his rage.

"I have to find him," he said patiently. "Or the whole province will be laughing at me."

"You deserve it, bastard."

Grudskoy's hand flew up but he suppressed the urge to hit her.

"I'll make it easy on all of us. Tell me where he's hiding ..."

"Never!"

Grudskoy tried to sound calm.

"I'll make you a deal."

"Why should I deal with you?"

"Because you know that sooner or later I'll find him. And if it's later, I won't be as lenient."

Anytchka glanced up at him.

"So what deal?"

Nyanya wrung her hands nervously. She knew Grudskoy well. Leniency was not in his heart. It was a trick. She wanted to warn Anytchka but didn't dare interfere.

"If you tell me where he is," Grudskoy said patiently, "I'll sentence each of you to five lashes of the whip in the village square. You'll give up my name and title, and you and your lover will be exiled from my lands. Forever."

Anytchka hesitated. "Five lashes?" She had seen men and women who lived through ten, fifteen, even twenty. It took more than thirty to kill a man. She and Vovka could take five.

"A child's punishment," Grudskoy said casually, as if reading her thoughts. He sat motionless, holding his breath like a predator waiting out his prey.

"And we can go away together?" Anytchka asked.

"I'll give you food for two weeks," Grudskoy assured her.

It seemed to be too good to believe. "Why are you doing this?"

"You disgraced me. You are my wife, so I cannot kill you. But I want you gone."

Nyanya sat, head down, afraid to look at either of them, her insides screaming, Don't do it, Anytchka, don't do it!

"You give me your word?"

"Upon my mother's grave."

Anytchka took a deep breath. *Maybe her dreams would come true after all and she would spend the rest of her days with her beloved. The urge was too strong to resist. She had to take the chance.* Gathering her courage, she blurted out, "You'll find him across the river. He's hiding in the belfry of the old church."

Grudskoy smiled. "You made the right decision," he said leaping to his feet and hurrying out, not bothering to close the door.

Anytchka breathed a sigh of relief.

"I'll see him soon."

She turned to Nyanya and gasped. Nyanya's face had aged by a hundred years. Her eyes were lifeless. Tears were rolling down her drawn cheeks.

"Nyanya!"

"God have mercy on you," Nyanya whispered, her voice trembling. "Oh, please, may God have mercy ..." Her sobs muffled her words.

"What? What have I done?" Anytchka exclaimed, a horrible tightness beginning to strangle her chest.

"You killed him," Nyanya whispered softly, shaking her head. "Your love killed him."

Anne stifled a scream and collapsed onto the bed. She was back in her hotel room: the desk, the nightstand, the curtains, all in place, the noise of traffic streaming through the tall glass windows.

Volodya's voice sounded in the distance. "*I will be killed by a jealous husband.*"

"No!" Anne breathed. "I can't let it happen ..."

She tried to command her brain to stay on the memory. Back. She had to go back to the past. She had to find out what really happened. How did her love kill Vovka? What was going to happen to Volodya? How could she keep the cursed pattern from repeating itself?

Anne fixed her eyes on the domes of St. Basil's, barely visible through the falling snow. She had to get back to Nyanya and Anytchka.

But the vision was gone.

She sat on the bed for a long time. Gradually her head cleared and she started thinking more rationally. *That love triangle was just a memory. Grudskoy, Vovka, Nyanya, they were all gone. Somehow the conflict was resolved. The details weren't important. She had faced her past, left it behind, and she was now free to love Volodya. Love him the way she wanted to love. With her whole heart, her whole body.*

She took a quick shower, got dressed, and hurried to the Pavlov, smiling at the anticipation of working side by side with the love of her life.

68

Sasha twisted her ankle as she leaped out of bed. It had been only two days since she had purchased this antique and she was not used to the new height. The four-poster was so beautiful, she paid whatever the old woman at the Ismailovo Flea Market asked, without even bargaining.

While the electric teapot warmed up, Sasha splashed cold water on her face and fed Volk the leftovers from last night's dinner.

Then she started the favorite part of her day. Exercise always made her feel powerful. She loved the feeling of pushing herself physically until her limbs hurt and her lungs begged for mercy.

Lately her muscles had gotten bulkier, and she felt stronger. Even her aim with the ax throw was improving daily. Perhaps it was because her adrenaline level had been sky-high for the past week or two. She had been feeling so energized, so self-assured, so in control. It was wonderful.

She looked in the mirror, admiring her bulging triceps, glistening with sweat, as she powered through her twelve reps of one-armed push-ups.

Up. Down. Up. Down.

She moved faster, her teeth clenched.

Up. Down.

The exercise gave her a pleasure that was almost sexual.

She had given up on finding a reasonable explanation for her attraction to Anne. Now she was just reveling in her feelings, letting her imagination take her to places she never knew existed. It was lust, it was craving, but mostly it was an overwhelming desire to possess the woman.

"Mine, mine," she would whisper, laying awake in the middle of the night. "I want her to be mine."

As she let her mind wander, she felt Anne's body, so soft, so delicate, so vulnerable, right next to her. *She ran her fingers through the blond hair ...*

Sasha shuddered and opened her eyes. She was lying on the mat face down, panting, sweat running off her back and down her sides.

She started another set of push-ups.

Faster and faster. Her body completely stiff, her face expressionless.

Suddenly a sound broke her concentration. She stopped. There was a loud knock on the door.

"What?" she yelled, flinging the door open, furious at the interruption.

It was Baldyuk. He winced. He had expected a more cordial reception. After all, it had taken him a huge effort to subdue his pride and come to Sasha, hat in hand.

"What are you doing here?" she snapped.

"May I come in?"

Sasha stepped aside.

"I've been knocking for five minutes."

"I was exercising."

"Have you seen the news?"

"I don't watch the news."

"Our patient had another appearance this morning."

"And?" Sasha asked carefully.

"The crowds love him. Our clients are happy."

"I told you, your clients would kiss my feet and think that I've pulled off a miracle."

"He's even more charismatic than before. He has another rally later today."

She wanted to humiliate him like he had humiliated her in the past. To make him grovel, to show him whose turf he was playing on now.

"We're meeting them tonight to collect the balance," Baldyuk said. "They wanted to meet tomorrow evening, before Easter Mass, but I told them you were busy." He chuckled. "Going to confession."

"I'll see you then."

"Till tonight then," he said cordially. *And by then I'll figure out how to get rid of you, you sooka,* he added to himself.

As Baldyuk headed for the door, he caught a glimpse of Sasha's bed behind the partition. It was not the bed he remembered from previous visits.

"Interesting," he said, examining the four posts, hand carved out of solid oak, and the massive canopy. A provocative dark green nightgown was tangled in the sheets.

"What happened, Volodya got tired of the old bed?"

Sasha glanced at him but said nothing.

Baldyuk grinned, looking at the posts. "So, now you can tie him down to keep him from running to the Americanka." The dig was too tempting to pass up.

Sasha jerked as if he had struck her.

"What?"

"Oh, you don't know?" Baldyuk asked innocently. "I hear he spent the night with her."

Sasha felt the blood rushing to her head. Her vision went red. She could no longer see Baldyuk. In his place was a young couple, their nude bodies locked in an embrace. Then a church, precariously perched over a river bank. A handsome young man standing inside the church, defiantly facing armed guards rushing toward him.

Sasha grabbed the first thing underhand—her ax—and hurled it at Baldyuk.

"Get out of here, you liar," she screamed. The ax whizzed past Baldyuk's head and splintered the doorframe.

After Baldyuk left, Sasha forced herself to complete her exercise routine. But one thought kept drilling through her head: *If her plans were to succeed, she had to act now.*

69

nne entered the sepulchral lobby of the Pavlov and headed straight to the basement, down the now familiar corridors. Volodya looked up as she stepped into his lab without knocking. Smiling, he walked toward her and wrapped her in his arms.

"Did you miss me that much?" she laughed, holding him close and kissing his lips.

"One hour without you is eternity."

"And one hour with me?" she teased.

"Eternity in paradise."

"We have an eternity to catch up on," she said, letting go of him.

They spent the day comparing notes, looking for parallels in their work.

Late in the afternoon, as they huddled over Abby and her litter, preparing them for another run through the maze, Anne was startled by a familiar voice.

"Ah, there you are!"

She spun around. Halden was standing in the doorway, elegant in his casual traveling clothes—a camel hair jacket over jeans, pastel-blue shirt unbuttoned at the collar. He was cleanly shaven and neatly combed.

"What are you doing here?" Anne exclaimed.

"I thought I'd drop in and ask you the same question," he replied coldly.

He might still have been in Boston, blissfully ignorant, had it not been for Lucia's dedication to him. She even booked his Moscow flight.

"So, how's it going?" Halden asked casually. He walked up to Anne, put his arms around her. Before she could turn away, he gave her a quick kiss on the cheek. "And who is your colleague?" he asked, staring at Volodya, not letting go of Anne's shoulder.

"Volodya, I want you to meet Jack Halden, the CEO of Sidens." Anne said, shrugging Halden's arm off. "Jack, this is Volodya Verkhov."

"Pleased to meet you," Halden said, Anne's impersonal introduction telegraphing a message he dreaded hearing.

With ill concealed animosity, the two men shook hands.

Halden was startled by the strength of Volodya's handshake—*a weight lifter,* he thought. *Or a former laborer.*

"Well, shall we?" he said, motioning Anne toward the door. "I would love to see where you put our MEG."

"You go ahead, I'll catch up," she said quickly. "Just take the elevators at the end of the hall and …"

"I'll wait outside. Hopefully you won't be long," Halden said curtly. "Nice meeting you, Mr. Vodoya," he added with a perfunctory nod, walking out the door.

When Volodya's eyes locked with Anne's, his look spoke volumes: shock, pain, disappointment, anger.

"You didn't tell me you had man in your life," he said, walking away from her toward the other side of the lab.

"He's not in my life. It's over," Anne protested.

"He does not think so."

"I haven't had a chance to tell him yet. Things have moved so fast here …"

"And why does he treat you like property?"

"Volodya, stop. He's history. I'll explain ..."

"Why did you not explain before I fell in love?"

"Sweetheart, come here!" She came around the bench and wrapped him in her arms. "Listen to me. I did have a relationship with him. But it's over. It had started falling apart the instant I saw you, the instant I felt your touch. It was so sudden, between you and me. I haven't even talked to him on the phone. I had no idea he was coming."

His look softened. He held her.

"Please do not leave me. The pain to lose you would be too much, Anytchka."

"Don't worry. It took too long to find you," she smiled. "I'm not about to lose you again." She touched his lips, and walked out.

"Jack, there's something we need to discuss," Anne said as she joined him at the end of the hallway. "Volodya and I ..."

"Spare me," he said coldly. "What is going on with the MEG?"

She glanced at him, surprised and hurt. "OK, I'll tell you about the MEG."

As they entered the MEG room, they ran into Sasha. Anne introduced them. "Sasha is the Acting Chief of Psychiatry," she added as a reminder.

"Yes, of course, I remember. You two are coming up with very interesting results, it seems," he added pointedly, intending to get to the reason for the patient cancellations as soon as possible. But the look on Anne's face told him to go no further.

Sasha noticed the subtle exchange. She glared at Halden. What did Anne see in this plastic excuse for a real man, anyway?

"Perhaps you can brief me later?" Halden suggested, glancing at Anne, then at Sasha.

Sasha felt her blood pressure rising. *The newcomer wanted her gone! The audacity! He was now on her turf. Or didn't he figure that out yet? And he was fast outstaying his welcome.*

"You two go ahead," Sasha said forcing a smile that bordered on a scowl. "I'll catch up on paperwork."

As soon as she left the MEG room, Sasha hurried to her office, found the key to the observation gallery and headed back.

"What the hell is going on, Anne?" Halden blurted, as soon as the door closed.

"What are you referring to?" Anne stalled, trying to figure out how much he knew.

"Well, first you're getting great results. Then you cure a VIP. Next thing ..."

"Cure a VIP?" Anne's eyebrows shot up. "If you are referring to Namordin, we failed."

"That's not what I heard. The Russians couldn't be happier. Good work!"

"From whom did you hear that?"

"From Baldyuk. And Namordin's recovery has been on the news since yesterday."

"I had nothing to do with it."

"Oh, come on!"

"Really, I didn't. We tried a couple of times, but it was useless."

"What's the difference? The man is as sharp as ever. You made us look good. And now you want to blow everything up and cancel patients?"

Anne hesitated for a moment. "We're coming up with unexpected side effects—at least in the very high dose range. I need to figure out why before we can go on," she said simply.

"You should've let me know as soon as you suspected something!" Halden exclaimed. "I'm not just the CEO, I'm your friend," he added, taking Anne's hand in both of his.

"There are things about the MEG that I'm not prepared to discuss with you yet."

"It's a joint project. We should have no secrets."

"When I'm ready."

"I'm responsible to a board of directors. I need to know. Everything."

She had to tell him, sooner or later.

"You want everything? I'll give you everything. What would you say if I told you my little encounter with the MEG made me remember that five hundred years ago I was married to an old Russian nobleman? And that ..."

"What the hell are you talking about?"

"... And that I ran away with my young lover?"

"Oh, boy. You did go off the deep end, didn't you?!" Halden exclaimed.

Keeping the lights out, Sasha eased herself into the observation gallery and peeked over the banister through the glass. She heard faint voices coming from below through the public address system. She searched for the audio panel in the dark and located the volume control.

"Want more?" Anne continued. "I now know that whatever happened back then made it impossible for me to love anyone now. And I am so confused and scared and lost, that I do feel like I've gone off the deep end."

She paused, fighting back tears, relieved that she was able to at least verbalize her confusion.

"What does it have to do with your work?"

"Don't you see? The high dose somehow unlocked a connection to a past that I didn't know existed."

Halden looked at her as if she were one of the patients.

"Anne, it was probably some aberrant effect. Let's keep going with the program and see ..."

"We are talking past lives, Jack! So, please forgive me if I feel that I should look into this a little deeper, before we go exposing any more patients."

"Are you out of your mind? You want to derail the whole project because of this psycho experience of yours? My job is to make sure the units sell."

Anne glared back at him. "You seem to forget that I have the final say-so in clinical matters."

"Anne, please understand, I can't let you jeopardize the success of this project."

"And I can't let you endanger patients." She stared him down.

"Anne, I beg you to reconsider!"

"Jack, I can't. We are stopping."

His jaw set. "That may be an issue for our attorneys," he replied coldly. "In the meantime, I'll have the Russians take you off the project and ship you back to the U.S."

"You can't do that!" Anne snapped back, but there was no conviction in her voice. Both of them knew that she was here simply at the pleasure of her Russian hosts. And nothing would give Baldyuk more pleasure than to get rid of her.

Without reveling in his victory, Halden spun on his heels and walked out.

Sasha felt the hair stand up on the back of her neck. *This pathetic puppet was threatening to ship Anne back? Over her dead body!* She hurried out of the observation gallery, ran down the narrow stairs and positioned herself at the elevator. *No one was going to send Anne home. She had to deal with him.* A wave of uncontrollable rage swept through her.

Suddenly she was on horseback, brandishing a sword. Three warriors were galloping toward her. Her weapon connected with the first. The man flew off the horse in a fountain of blood. The next came charging. With a single swing, Sasha decapitated him. The third rammed into her.

Sasha had to hold on to the wall to keep from falling. She took a deep breath, willing her mind to focus. The battle vision vanished.

As Halden stormed toward the elevators, Sasha intercepted him.

"Mr. Halden?" she said, forcing a semblance of a smile, "I've noticed strange things about Anne's behavior. Perhaps we should talk."

Halden raised his eyebrows. *Did everybody already know that something was wrong except him?* He was tempted to tell her to go to hell, but reconsidered.

"Go ahead, I'm all ears."

"Not here. How about I meet you on the second floor, at this elevator, around seven tonight? Then we can find some place quiet …"

"I'll be there," Halden said without hesitation. If his damage control was to be effective, he had to find out who knew what.

70

As soon as Halden left, Anne went back to Volodya's lab. Volodya wasn't there. She realized that she didn't even know how to get hold of him. She walked around the lab for a while, looking at the mice.

She heard someone walk in.

"Oh, excuse me." It was Lena.

"Hello. I think we've met. I'm Anne Powell."

"Lena," the young woman mumbled.

"Lena, do you know Volodya's phone number? Phone number. *Telefon Volodya.*"

"*Ya ponimayu.*" She understood. She just didn't know if she wanted to give it to this *Americanka* who kept showing up at the lab at all the wrong times.

"Please, I need to find him." Anne looked desperate.

Lena sighed. *Her love for Volodya was in vain. He would never love her like she loved him. They could have been so happy! She would cook... What was the use?*

She took a pencil, wrote down Volodya's number, and handed it to Anne.

"*Spassibah,*" Anne exclaimed, hurrying out.

She tried calling as soon as she got back to the hotel, but there was no answer. A vague discomfort began building inside her. In a few minutes, she tried again. No answer. He was not home.

She slipped into her jogging clothes and took a few laps around the brightly lit Red Square, determined to think about nothing except breathing and running. She returned physically refreshed but even more worried. There was still no answer at Volodya's.

She took a hot shower. As she dried herself, she felt a wave of panic sweep through her body. Her knees buckled, and she had to sit on the edge of the bed to keep herself from falling.

She heard noises in the hallway and, without a knock, the door opened and the room filled with strangers. Guards, peasants, monks.

Not again, not another one. Would these visions never end?

The monks huddled in the far corner with Father Andrei, the highest-ranking ecclesiastic in the entire Novgorod area.

Sitting on one of the few benches in the room, Anytchka could see Grudskoy slumped casually in his massive chair, presiding over the assembly.

Vovka appeared, flanked by two soldiers.

Anytchka stifled a scream. Vovka's face was bloodied, his caftan was torn, and rough ropes bound his wrists behind his back. He could barely walk. Four more guards followed close behind.

"Look what we found in his house, Your Excellency," one of the soldiers said placing several cages on the floor. The cages, made of interwoven twigs, held several pigeons, a few mice and two ferrets.

Grudskoy smiled a crooked smile. Vovka was his now.

"So," he said, glancing at Anytchka with a triumphant scowl. "You didn't tell me your lover is a witch."

A gasp swept through the crowd.

"Witch, witch!"

Grudskoy scanned the room, letting the words sink in.

"Is that how he seduced you? With witchcraft?"

"He didn't seduce me," Anytchka snapped back defiantly. "I fell in love with him."

"In love? With a witch?" Grudskoy smirked. "Are you a witch

too?"

"Witch, witch!" the crowd hissed.

"I'm not a witch!"

Grudskoy turned to the monks. "How do we deal with witches?"

The monks crossed themselves, mumbling in unison. "We burn them." "Fire to the death." "Burn!"

Father Andrei tried to intercede. "Alexandr Ivanovitch, perhaps there is another explanation."

"Another explanation?" Grudskoy scowled. "Who else would keep such animals? Mice? Ferrets? And for what, except to do the devil's bidding? No, Father Andrei, I tell you, the man is a witch. And witches must burn!" he added, slamming his fist on the table.

Nyanya dashed forward and fell at Grudskoy's feet. "Alexandr Ivanovitch, I beg you, listen ... There's something you must know ..."

At Grudskoy's glance, the guards dragged Nyanya away.

"You gave me your word!" Anytchka exclaimed leaping to her feet.

"My word?" He spit the words out. "What about your marriage vows, you whore?" He turned to the monks again. "And what do we do with whores?"

The monks crossed themselves again. "God have mercy on her soul," they mumbled.

"She's innocent," Vovka yelled, struggling to break free. "She's completely innocent. She never loved me. I cast a spell on her!"

"It's not true!" Anytchka screamed, "It's all my fault."

Grudskoy leaned back, smiling. "So, whose fault?" he asked, enjoying the moment.

"Mine. I am a witch! I made her do it," Vovka exclaimed, struggling against his restraints. "Let me go. I'll prove it."

Grudskoy hesitated, then nodded to the guards.

Moments later, Vovka was untied. He moved his right arm, flexing his muscles, wiggling his fingers to restore circulation. The left arm, injured during the struggle earlier that day, hung uselessly by his side. He massaged his left shoulder, grimacing with pain.

Grudskoy shifted uneasily at the sight of Vovka unrestrained. The man was superbly trained. He didn't pick him to be his lieutenant for nothing.

"Get on with it!" Grudskoy barked,

The crowd backed away deferentially as Vovka walked over to one of the cages and removed the peg that held the gate closed.

He reached in and took out one of the ferrets. A gasp of consternation swept through the room as the animal perched itself peacefully on Vovka's shoulder. It was well known that ferrets were vicious creatures that wreaked havoc in chicken coops and inflicted ferocious bites on anyone who tried to capture them. No one had ever been able—or willing—to handle the pests, let alone allow them to sit on their shoulder.

Vovka lifted his right arm, pointed a finger at Grudskoy and whistled softly. The ferret scurried down Vovka's clothes, jumped on the floor and dashed across the room. Before Grudskoy could react, the animal scrambled up his leg and disappeared under his kilt. Grudskoy leaped to his feet, flailing frantically, trying to chase the animal away.

Vovka whistled again and the ferret returned, settling on his shoulder. An amber button from Grudskoy's shirt was in its mouth.

The crowd recoiled, murmuring, "Witch! The devil! He must die!"

"You're going straight to hell, witch!" Grudskoy screamed.

"You and I will burn together, monster," Vovka replied.

"But you'll meet the devil sooner," Grudskoy hissed. Turning to his guards he yelled, "Prepare him. Tonight at midnight, justice will be done."

Father Andrei rose to his feet. "Alexandr Ivanovitch, you cannot execute a man because he was with your wife ..."

"He's not a man, he's a witch."

"I am not sure ..."

Grudskoy scanned the crowd, an accusing finger pointed toward Vovka. "He consorts with wild animals. He casts spells on honest women. What more proof do we need?" He turned to Father Andrei. "Do we tolerate witches now?" he asked with a quiet threat.

"Tomorrow is Easter Sunday. At least wait 'til after Ascension ..." Father Andrei said quietly.

"No! There's no need to wait. The evidence is before you. The man sold his soul to the devil. He will die tonight at midnight, just as Christ is resurrected," Grudskoy crossed himself piously. "Tonight," he repeated, raising to his majestic height and marching out of the room.

The door slammed.

Anne realized that she was lying on the floor of her room and Father Andrei was leaning over her.

"Forgive me, I have sinned …" Anne heard herself whisper. "Only God can forgive adultery, my child," said Father Andrei making the sign of the cross over her head.

"No, not the adultery. That's not the sin that I'll burn for, Father Andrei. My sin was my desire to be reunited with the one I love." She stared absently into the distance.

"What are you saying?"

"My love killed my lover," she whispered.

"Are you delirious?" The voice grated like a rusty rasp.

Anne opened her eyes. The figure leaning over her wasn't Father Andrei. It was Halden.

He had persuaded the concierge to let him in by claiming to be Anne's husband. He was glad he did. She looked sick.

"You're talking gibberish. Did you take something? Pills? Speak to me."

Anne forced herself to sit up and focus.

"No drugs." She shook her head. "Just the past."

"What past?"

"I tried to tell you." She felt very tired. "My past life."

"You're not well," Halden said firmly. "As soon as I get you home, I'm sending you for a complete workup. CAT scan, EEG, the works."

"I can't leave 'til I unravel this," she said, her voice very quiet.

Halden started to say something, but her look stopped him.

"I need to find out what happened. In my past. Or no relationship will ever be right for me."

"I didn't think there was anything wrong with ours," Halden commented, barely hiding the sarcasm.

"Yes, it was a good relationship. But it's over, Jack. I'm in love. In the kind of love I've always longed for, but never thought I could find."

"With that peasant in the lab?!"

She gave him a reproachful look. "I'm sorry. I wish I'd had the chance to tell you before you came," she said quietly, turning toward the window.

Halden stepped forward and put his arms around her from behind.

"Anne, your head is clouded from the MEG overdose. Don't make any decisions now. Let's wait 'til you get better." He guided her head toward him, his mouth searching for her lips. "I need you ..."

With an explosive twist, Anne shoved him away. "No. The answer is no, Jack. I'm in love with Volodya."

Halden's jaw set and his face went ashen. Without a word, he turned and walked out. *Anne wasn't in love. She was sick. And he had to figure out how to nurse her back to health, back into their relationship, and back to the MEG project.*

71

Anne was awakened by a loud knock. Morning light was just beginning to seep through the heavy draperies.

She looked through the peephole. It was Volodya.

"I am very sorry I run away," he said as soon as Anne opened the door. "I was afraid I lost you ..."

She didn't let him finish. "You haven't lost me," she whispered, wrapping her arms around him.

"Where is your man?"

"He's not my man."

"I am here to take you back!"

Anne smiled. He sounded like a teenager. "No need to take me back. I didn't leave."

He looked at her, standing there, disheveled, in her wrinkled flannel pajamas, white with little red roses ... Suddenly he started laughing.

"What?"

"I always imagine you sleep in beautiful gown. Maybe silk."

"Maybe I like flannel," she made a fake pout and threw a pillow at him. "And if you don't like the flannel, maybe you should try to take it off," she suggested, her eyes sparkling.

With a grin, he moved toward her and slipped his hands under her top, cupping her breasts.

"Yikes!!" Anne shrieked. "You're totally frozen. Come to bed," she ordered. "Right now!"

She helped him undress, and they slid under the covers. Laying on their sides, her back pressed firmly against his front like two spoons, they felt warmth and happiness flowing between their bodies.

"Volodya?" Anne asked suddenly. "I want to know what Babushka said about my *sudbah*." She had been curious for a long time. Now it felt safe to ask.

"What *sudbah*?"

"From the tea leaves, when we visited."

"Nothing ... I don't remember."

"Volodya! The truth."

He paused for a moment, then answered.

"Babushka said your love will kill me."

The words exploded in her head. She saw Vovka and Anytchka in an animal barn. Anytchka was holding an oil lamp.

"No! God, no!" Anne whispered.

"Do not worry, it was only superstitious woman talking."

Just as she heard his words, Anne saw Anytchka hurling the oil lamp into the hay, the lamp crashing, the oil spilling in a ball of fire, flames engulfing everything.

Pushing Volodya away, Anne leaped out of bed toppling the night stand, sending the clock, books, glasses and Luna candy bars scattering in all directions. Clutching her flannel top she dashed to the opposite side of the room.

"We can't be lovers," she screamed, her chest heaving with sobs.

"What are you saying?" Volodya asked, trying to follow her.

"Don't touch me. Don't love me." She backed further into the corner, her extended arm warding Volodya off, as if he were a ghost.

"Anne! You cannot believe what old woman says!"

"She was right!"

"It was tea leaves! You are scientist!"

"Scientist or not, I'm scared ..." She was quiet now. "Volodya, believe me, I cannot love you."

"Babushka was wrong. Confused. Crazy." Volodya tried to reason with her. "Remember, she also said I shall be killed by jealous husband. And you're not even married!" he added, forcing a laugh.

"Volodya, please. There are things … things in my past I did not tell you."

"I do not worry about your past," he said.

"You don't know, Volodya …"

"I know you are first woman I am not afraid to say, 'I love you'."

"Be afraid!"

"Why?"

The image of flames flashed in her mind. This time it was her parent's house, burning with her mother and father inside. She heard Sasha's words, "We are what we were," echoing in her mind. It all made sense. Death by fire was in her genes. Anytchka burned herself and her lover. Anne's own mother did practically the same thing. What else could Anne expect?

"Please tell me why?" Volodya pleaded. "Why I must be afraid to love you?"

"There was a man in my past. Long ago."

"You loved another man?"

"No! Yes. I don't know!"

Words were failing her.

"With this man … What happened?"

"You won't understand."

"How you say, 'Try me'?"

She buried her face in her hands.

"I killed him."

"Sorry, you what?" Volodya knew he hadn't heard right.

"Killed him. Dead. Finished. I burned him, and me. You mustn't love me. My love is fatal. I know it will happen again. *Ne sudbah,*" she added softly.

He wrapped her in his arms. "Anne, you have delusion. We will fix it. Together."

"We can't be together."

"Anne, I will not give away on you."

"Please, just trust me."

For a long time, Volodya stood still, too stunned to speak. Then, slowly, as if he had aged thirty years, he bent down, picked up his shirt and fumbled with it, looking for the sleeve holes.

"You know what I think, Anne?" he asked as he started to button up. "One of two things. Maybe something very wrong with your head, and I must help you find doctor …"

"I don't need a doctor. I know what I'm doing," she said firmly.

"Then, you are afraid to love. And you invent excuses."

"It's not an excuse. I feel it."

"You feel? You have no feelings," he exclaimed, his resentment mounting. *The first, the only woman to whom he could give himself entirely, was abandoning him. And for what?*

"I think you'd better go now," she said softly, as a voice inside her screamed, *Please understand, I love you, I would die for you, I must protect you from your sudbah.*

"I am going," he said. "I hoped maybe you change. But you are same what you were. So is OK. Follow your habits. Always run in same circles. Round, round, round. Like mice!"

"Volodya!" she mumbled, tears welling up in her eyes.

"Yes, never try to change. Always do what is easy. What is safe. What gives no pain."

He paused at the door. "For me, to have you and then to lose you, is too much pain. Good bye, Anne."

He raised his hand slightly and waved. That tentative flick of the wrist. Anne had seen it before. *How long ago was it?*

The door slammed shut.

He was gone.

Anne sank to the floor and started to cry.

She had found the man she could truly love. She was in love. She thought she had faced her demons and subdued them.

Over the years she learned to live with the memory of her abusive father, and of the fire that her mother set to the house. A fire that killed both her parents. Moments ago, she had faced another fatal memory, the fiery death that consumed her lover and her. *Wasn't that enough? Wasn't that how it was supposed to work? Face your past to fix your present, and all that?*

Instead, the nightmare was back. All her fears revived. And once again, she had run away from her love.

Why wasn't she at peace? What else did she have to face to expiate her sins and finally be free to love?

"Damn it," she cried out. "Damn it all!"

She stood up, her teeth clenched, her face drawn. It was time to go find her demons, every last one of them, wherever they were.

She picked up the phone and dialed.

"Sasha? It's Anne. I need you to help me with something."

72

Asking Sasha for help didn't come easily for Anne. But she had no choice. There was no one else who could do what she needed done.

To Anne's disappointment, Sasha couldn't meet her until the evening because she was going to be tied up in some important meeting.

Anne considered going running to kill time, or calling Misty and sharing her plans. But nothing felt right. She didn't even want to venture out of her room for fear of running into Halden, or missing a call from Volodya. So she sat on the floor, leaning against the bed, looking out the window, like she and Volodya did just two nights ago. One by one, she ate every single remaining Luna bar in her stash.

Late in the afternoon, as she was preparing to go and meet Sasha, the phone rang.

Anne leaped up and grabbed the receiver.

"Volodya?"

"Anne!" It was Misty. "Thank God I found you!"

Anne was struck by how upset Misty sounded. "What's going on?"

There was a moment of silence, then Misty's voice, speaking softly. "You ... you don't know?"

"Don't know what?"

"Jack ..."

"Yes, that was a real surprise. He just showed up."

"Anne, listen ..."

"What?"

"He killed himself."

"What?!"

Anne sunk back on the bed, her mind refusing to believe what she just heard.

"Jack killed himself?"

"Oh, honey, I'm so sorry."

"How ... how did it happen?"

"They said he jumped off the roof of the building."

"What building?" Anne focused on meaningless details. Anything to deflect the impact of reality.

"Your institute."

"But why?"

"Who knows."

"How did you find out?

"The Moscow police notified the consulate and they called his office."

Anne's mind was reeling. Jack, dead? Jack killed himself?

"Maybe it's a mistake. Are they sure it's him?"

"I'm afraid so."

"But I was just with him yesterday! We argued, but ..."

"Anne, I'll fly in."

"Don't. I'll be all right."

"You need me to ..."

"No. Please. I'll call you."

"You sure?"

"Yes," Anne said, hanging up.

Almost immediately, the phone rang again. The coroner wanted her to identify Halden's body and the police had a few questions. It was just a formality, he assured her.

73

Sasha rode home on her motorcycle, the triumphant smile on her face pulled even wider by the blast of cold wind. *Her meeting with Halden was a success. She had defended her turf. Nothing would stop her now.*

Turning a corner, she discovered that her regular way home, past Tversakaya Boulevard, was blocked. So was the next intersection. And the next. She would have to go all the way around the backside of the Kremlin. In the distance she saw red banners fluttering, and a giant crowd filling the entire west side of Red Square. *It must be Namordin,* she realized.

She had heard in the news that the man was actively campaigning and rapidly gaining popularity, but she had been too preoccupied with her thoughts of Anne to take the time to see her star patient perform in person.

She slowed down her bike and eased it into an alley leading toward the square. Deftly maneuvering among ruts, garbage bins, and shuttered vending carts, she made her way toward the gathering. As she reached the crowd, she pulled up to a hydrant, chained her bike and proceeded on foot toward the center of the gathering.

The crowd blocked her view, so she elbowed her way up the stairs of the old KGB building. Barely fifty feet away was Namordin, stand-

ing on a makeshift podium, surrounded by bodyguards, red banners
fluttering all around him.

"It is time for change. It is time for Russia to return to the power
and glory, when my grandfather ..."

"Spit image," an old man next to Sasha mumbled, to no one in
particular.

"What?" Sasha asked.

"Just look," the man perked up, happy to have an audience. "Do
you hear the accent? Do you see the way he strokes his mustache? The
arms—look, look." He pointed, his deformed fingertips poking
through the worn-out mitt. "I tell you, it's pure Yossif Vissarionovich,
God rest his soul." The man crossed himself. "Where is our beloved
tovarishch Stalin, I used to say. But maybe our prayers have been
answered. May his grandson be as great a man ..."

But Sasha was no longer listening. She was heading back.

Namordin turned out to be an unmitigated success. She felt like
a sculptor who had carved a beautiful body out of a shapeless hunk of
marble.

But Namordin was just a dress rehearsal.

As Sasha started on her way back to the Pavlov, the roar of her
motorcycle covered up the sound of gunshots coming from Red
Square.

74

The coroner's car picked Anne up at the hotel entrance and drove her to the city morgue—a new building not far from the Pavlov Institute.

Even before they reached the impeccably clean autopsy room, Anne recognized the familiar odor of blood and freshly cut flesh that she remembered from her days as the pathologist's assistant.

The coroner glanced at her—was she ready?—and pulled back the sheet covering Jack's body. Anne braced herself. The body looked intact except for the strange angle at which his neck lay. An expression of surprise was frozen on his face.

Anne touched his forehead.

"It's him," she said simply. "How did it happen?"

"He went to roof of Pavlov and jumped."

"Jumped?" she asked. "Did he leave a letter?"

"We are looking, Dr. Powell."

"If you don't mind, I want to be alone with him for a minute."

"Of course," the coroner said, hurrying out and closing the door softly behind him.

Anne leaned against the gurney and held Halden's cold stiff hand in hers, tears welling up in her eyes. She knew now that she had never been in love with him. But they had spent so many days working together, so many years sharing a common goal.

And now he was dead. A suicide? Of all the things she did not expect Halden to do was end his own life. He was too pragmatic for that. *What did she miss? When they parted company yesterday he was angry, but he didn't seem despondent.*

Perhaps the realization that the MEG project had failed, at least as a commercial venture, spelling an end to his career ambitions, was too much for him.

Or was it their breakup?

Suddenly she felt nauseated.

Your love will kill. Your love will kill.

"Very sorry about your loss, Dr. Powell," the coroner said as she walked out.

"I want to go now."

"One more minute, yes?"

He took her to a small room, sparsely decorated with a worn couch, a table with a couple of chairs, and a refrigerator. In the corner an old black and white TV played something, the volume muted.

Anne sat quietly, staring absentmindedly at the screen, waiting for the coroner. The sitcom on the TV changed to something that looked like the Russian version of Jeopardy.

Anne started pacing.

"Your love will kill," kept running through her mind. *She didn't really love Halden, but what if that was all it took? Her* sudbah. *Typhoid Mary. Lethal Anne. Maybe there was something to Babushka's predictions.*

You're going crazy, Anne thought. But she couldn't get her brain to think rationally and dismiss the possibility.

She tried to recall what happened to Anytchka after Vovka's trial but the memories refused to return. *If she wanted to be free to love again, if she wanted to avert another fatal outcome, she would have to recall every painful detail.*

She was glad she had made plans to meet Sasha.

As she stopped pacing, Anne's eyes caught a familiar face on the TV screen. It was Namordin, stroking his thick mustache as he spoke to a reporter. A newscaster appeared, his stiff lips moving silently. Anne tried to find the volume control, then remembered that she probably wouldn't understand anyway.

The screen cut to shaky footage of Namordin surrounded by bodyguards, preaching something, with the Kremlin in the background.

Suddenly, Namordin grabbed one of the guards by the lapels, reached inside the man's jacket, pulled out a gun and started shooting. The image bounced, went to snow, then resumed. Namordin was still shooting at the crowd, his movements jerky, a deranged look distorting his face. Moments later Namordin staggered and fell backwards.

Then there was a close-up of him being loaded into an ambulance by the bodyguards. Without sound, the images looked even more bizarre.

"Terrible, yes?"

Anne was startled by the coroner standing in the doorway.

"What happened?" she asked.

"I just heard it on radio. Namordin—do you know him? He is …"

"I know who he is," Anne interrupted impatiently. "What happened?"

"He got in argument with man in crowd. The man criticized him … So Namordin shot him. Also four others. A tragedy. The Communist party is finished. And I will be doing autopsies for the rest of week."

Anne stood speechless.

"Is anything I can do for you?" the coroner asked.

"Yes. Get me to the Pavlov."

75

By the time Anne got to the Institute the building was cold and deserted for the holiday. For a moment Anne thought about how nice it would be to be seeing the Russian Easter mass, away from here, away from her troubles, away from what she was about to do. She could almost hear Misty. "Are you out of your cotton-picking mind?"

She could turn around and go home. But the little voice kept whispering: "Your love killed Jack. Your love will kill Volodya." *She had to find out what had happened to Anytchka. Face the demons and break the pattern.*

Anne walked into the MEG room.

"You're here!"

Anne turned.

Sasha was standing close behind her, smiling. "I wasn't expecting you for another hour," she said cheerfully. "But I'm ready when you are."

Sasha was ready. Very ready. Ever since Namordin's successful treatment, Sasha had been wondering how to take the next step. And suddenly Anne came to her with a story of needing help to get over some weird dreams. Anne didn't elaborate, but Sasha didn't care. Anne would be within her reach. Clearly, it was *sudbah!*

"Thanks for coming, Sasha. You know what to do. Just a quick jolt. I can almost do this myself, but I'll feel better with somebody at the panel."

"You want me to ask questions?" Sasha asked, trying to sound casual.

Anne shook her head. "No need. It'll come back by itself," she added, as if reassuring herself. "Set it really low, at half-tesla, and I'll take it from there."

Double-checking that the ablation mode was disabled, Anne walked over to the MEG. She hesitated for a brief instant, then hopped onto the table and laid down.

Her heart pounding with expectation, Sasha took one of Anne's wrists and started to open the restraint clamp.

"You don't need them," Anne said pulling back.

"But what about positioning?"

"What for? We won't be ablating anything." She wanted to say, No demons in my caves, but that certainly had proven to be a lie. "I can hold still enough for a quick depolarization. No clamps."

Hiding her disappointment, Sasha went behind the panel.

Anne watched as the C-arms started to spin, their pods so massive and intimidating from this angle. She took a deep breath. *It's not brain surgery,* she tried to reassure herself. *I do it to patients all day long.* She would face the last demon, whatever that may be, and then she would be free of her ordeal.

The C-arms spun up to full speed, their blue beams crisscrossing the room. Anne closed her eyes and tried to visualize the last thing she remembered—the trial, Grudskoy's rage, his plan to execute Vovka at the stroke of midnight.

Almost immediately the images returned, more detailed than Anne had ever seen them.

It was night. The gigantic moon had just risen above the horizon. A cluster of birch trees cast long shadows onto a small wooden barn. Grudskoy's estate loomed in the distance, outlined by festive torches.

Anytchka skulked toward the barn, hiding in the shadows, cursing herself for having worn a white dress. She saw the sentinel silhouetted against the sky.

She froze until the guard passed, then rushed toward the barn and searched for the door. Precious moments passed as she worked the padlock trying to unlock it, the sentinel's footsteps returning.

The padlock yielded. She cracked the door open, slid inside and pushed it shut.

It was pitch black and quiet. The familiar smell of sweaty saddles and dry hay permeated the air.

"Vovka?" she whispered. "Are you here?"

She thought she heard a hoarse whisper, then nothing.

She fumbled under her cape and pulled out a flint stone and a small oil lamp. After a few tries, the wick flickered to life. As her eyes adjusted, she saw him.

Vovka was laying on the straw-covered floor, completely naked, his face and body bruised, his wrists and ankles bound with coarse ropes. As he recognized her, his cracked and bloodied lips spread into a weak smile.

"Anytchka! My sunshine!" he muttered in a hoarse whisper.

She hurried toward him and resting the oil lamp on the ground, knelt at his side. Carefully, she cut the ropes.

"My darling man, what have they done to you?" she whispered. She leaned over him, her fingers caressing his face, her tongue sliding gently over his dry lips, wetting them.

"Beloved, you must leave," Vovka said, his parched tongue struggling with the words. "If he finds you here, he'll kill you."

Anytchka pressed a finger to his lips. "Shhhh. It doesn't matter anymore."

From under her robe she pulled out an icon. "May St. Alexei have pity on us," she said, making a sign of the cross over Vovka, then crossing herself. She kissed the icon, then held it up to his lips.

He turned his head away. "St. Alexei abandoned us."

"It is not his fault, my darling," she said gently. She propped the icon up in the corner, in front of the oil lamp, and settled on the floor next to Vovka. She held his hand. "Forgive me, lover. It's I who brought this upon you."

Wincing with pain, Vovka reached up with his right arm and

covered her lips. "I'm not afraid to die. It's the thought of leaving you with him that is unbearable."

"He won't have me. I'm yours. Only yours. Now and forever."

Slowly she started to undress herself.

He reached to touch her belly, bulging ever so slightly.

Anytchka smiled. "That day in the forest. The time was right. Do you think it's a boy?"

"Don't! I can't bear the thought of what could have been."

"Then let us think of what is. Now. One more moment."

Oblivious to the sharp straw and coarse gravel that ground into Vovka's wounds, they embraced, their naked bodies blending into one, passionate kisses turning into frenzied lovemaking, their lips devouring each other, forgetting all, wishing that moment to be their last memory.

Then they lay in each other's arms, listening to the choir coming from the chapel, the mournful chants of a pre-Easter mass.

"It will be midnight soon," Anytchka whispered, both knowing what that meant.

"You must go before they come for me," Vovka whispered, forcing himself to push her away.

"I must do what I must do, my love," Anytchka replied softly.

Leaning over, she picked up the oil lamp.

"Farewell my love …"

"Anytchka, don't!" he shouted in his hoarse voice, realizing what she was about to do.

"I can't live without you. Perhaps, beyond the grave, we will meet again," she whispered.

Their lips touched for a final time.

Anytchka stood up, the curves of her body silhouetted by the light, as she lifted the lamp high above her head.

With a gut-wrenching cry, she hurled the lamp at the wooden wall.

The lamp shattered, oil spilling, exploding into a ball of fire, spreading, engulfing the straw, smoke filling the barn, lapping the roof, the sentinel shouting outside.

"Beyond the grave," they repeated, clinging to each other, choking, hoping it would all end soon, no longer able to hear the words over the roar of the flames, the blaze scorching their nostrils, the red ambers searing their naked skin, pain flooding their minds ...

As Anytchka's brain began to shut down, she was aware of a huge figure crashing through the inferno, and a voice thundering, "You can't take the easy way out!"

Anytchka's last memory was of Grudskoy as he swept both her and Vovka's lifeless bodies into his arms, and dragged them toward the door.

Anne opened her eyes and saw Sasha leaning over her, the blue lights spinning behind her head.

"Sasha!" *What was Sasha doing here? She should be at the panel. Had something gone wrong?*

Sasha was holding a large syringe in her hands. A drop of thick syrupy fluid was hanging from the point of the needle, but the syringe was empty.

That's the syringe we use for injecting C-14 labeled glucose, Anne mused. When we are preparing to treat the patients. Before she could process the thought, Anne saw Sasha's lips. Coming closer. She could feel the heat of Sasha's body. She could smell her hands. Metallic, rusty. A familiar, revolting smell, long forgotten.

Anne tried to push Sasha away, but her arms wouldn't move. She felt the restraints gripping her firmly. Her head was immobilized.

"Sasha, what are you doing?"

"Relax, my sweet one."

Anne felt a wave of panic wash over her. "Let me go!"

"We're not done yet."

"Yes we are. I've changed my mind. I don't want to be MEGed," Anne said trying to sound calm. "Release the clamps please!"

"Oh, no. Don't you see? You and I, together, forever. It's our *sudbah.*" Sasha's lips came closer.

"I've wanted you for a long time," she whispered.

"Stop it!" Anne shouted trying to turn her face away.

"I remember how it felt, touching you ... don't you remember?" Sasha's fingers slid gently over Anne's breasts, along her neck, then moved up to explore her face, tracing her lips, evading Anne's teeth as she tried to bite.

"I don't remember anything," Anne lied, as vivid images of Volodya's hands caressing her body flashed through her mind.

"You don't?" Sasha said mockingly. "Look at your scan," she added glancing at the monitor screen filled with Anne's brain pattern. "It's lit up like a Christmas tree." She smirked. "No, my dear, it's all there. We just have to release it."

Craning her neck as much as the restraints would allow, Anne tried to see the screen. Her own brain was in the center, but Sasha's head was on the scan too. Way off the center, near the periphery.

That's how we got the overdose, Anne remembered suddenly. That day, the first time they treated Namordin, both their heads were way off center, where the doses were enormous. Without realizing it, Sasha was getting blasted again. *If only Anne could keep her in that part of the field a little longer. Eventually the extreme depolarization would take its toll and she would be able to talk Sasha down.*

"Look, if it's sex you want …" Anne said, trying to prolong the conversation.

"Oh, yes, sex and love, and … and everything. But all that will come later. First, I'll help you become what you were: mine," Sasha was saying. "Mine. You're going to be mine."

"What does that mean?"

Sasha stopped abruptly. "What?" she snapped.

"What does that mean, yours?" Anne's brain was racing, trying to figure out what Sasha knew, how much of the past she remembered.

Sasha frowned, concentrating. "Mine," Sasha repeated, a confused look on her face.

The magnetic field is affecting her, Anne thought.

"Yours as in your girlfriend?" Anne was stalling for time, but, to her disappointment, Sasha moved away and out of the field.

"I don't remember," Sasha mumbled incoherently as she stumbled up to the console and flipped several switches.

"What are you doing now?" Anne exclaimed fearfully.

"Oh, just getting ready to do a little ablation. Nothing drastic."

"You know you can't get in," Anne said. "It's password protected."

"Memories, right?"

Anne felt the blood draining from her face. She had guarded the password so diligently. How did Sasha find out? She thanked her lucky stars for building in that extra mistyping trick ...

Sasha was enjoying the moment. "I believe it's spelled funny. With two m's."

To her horror, Anne heard the beep as the password was accepted and the ablation mode was enabled.

"And now, let me help you forget everything that you don't need to know."

The blue lights turned to red.

"Sasha, stop. You'll never be able to hide this. Jack will be here any second. I asked him to meet us ..."

"Oh-oh, Jack is coming?" Sasha let out a short laugh. "The Jack you just checked in the morgue?"

"How did you know?"

"I also know the autopsy will show that he jumped. I do have friends everywhere. Even in the city morgue."

Anne's mind was reeling. Jack didn't jump? Sasha knew about his death?

"What did you see in a guy like that?" Sasha smirked. "For a big guy, he was a pushover. No pun intended," she added, laughing hysterically.

Anne felt a clump of vomit in her throat.

"You ... You killed him?"

"He wanted to send you back to the States!" Sasha exclaimed. "Big mistake. Should've just let you and me do our work. OK, now be still and let me concentrate," she added seriously, continuing to work the controls.

"You can't do that!"

"Oh, yes I can. I just need to strip away all this extraneous stuff ..." The tip of her tongue stuck out between her lips as she worked the stick. "I'll just trim it up a little."

Out of the corner of her eye, Anne could see the cross-hairs homing in on her brain. Smoothly, efficiently. *She had taught Sasha too well.*

"And then we can be together, and fulfill our *sudbah*."

Anne made another effort to wrestle out of the restraints.

"Sasha, think this over. You're acting crazy."

"Crazy? What's crazy about wanting you?"

"Why do you want me, Sasha?" Anne mumbled, almost to herself. "Why me, why now?"

"None of it matters." Sasha's face glowed in the light of the control panel. She felt like she could almost remember how she was connected to Anne, and why she wanted her, but memory failed.

"You're mine!" Sasha shouted. "Don't resist."

"Sasha, please stop, you don't know what you're doing!" Anne screamed.

"What do you mean? I've experience!" she announced indignantly. "Look at Namordin."

"What did you do to him?"

"Simple. I just ablated some of his present, and let his grandfather's genes take over. I wish you'd seen how he turned out," she announced proudly. "Stalin in the flesh."

"Oh, Sasha!"

"What? That's what they wanted. He's sure to be elected now."

"Namordin just went berserk."

"What?" The MEG beeped as Sasha's hands faltered on the controls. The red beams went spinning erratically across the room.

"Look out!"

"I've got it." She readjusted the controls. "What about Namordin?"

"He went crazy and shot someone."

"But I just saw him ..."

"I did too."

"You're lying. You weren't there!"

"On TV, Sasha. He shot a bunch of people. They took him away..."

"Damn it!" Sasha rammed her fist against the glass partition. All that work. Well, I'll do better this time. You'll turn out perfect, I know it."

Sasha continued to fiddle with the controls, her frustration mounting. "Anne, stop wiggling, I can't get alignment."

It was no use. The woman was determined.

Out of nowhere, Misty's words flashed through Anne's mind. *"Don't worry about your memories. It's not like you're going to run into these people."*

Anne realized that she just did. Very slowly, against the protests of her rational brain, she began to face who Sasha was.

She shivered as the familiar pain began to invade her pelvis.

"Sasha?" She paused. "Alexandr Ivanovitch?"

Sasha froze. "What did you call me?"

"I think you're Alexandr Ivanovitch Grudskoy. Used to be."

"I don't care who you think I am. I just know you're mine." Sasha was desperately trying to concentrate on the ablation controls, but her mind flashed to the cemetery. Grudskoy's grave.

"You married a young woman against her will, many centuries ago," Anne continued.

"Grudskoy …" Sasha's movements slowed down. Random images started tumbling past her eyes, like a bizarre montage of old movies.

She was on horseback, fighting off a band of Tartars. Victory. A half-burned house. The family. A beautiful maiden. She slapped him.

She heard Anne's voice. "Does the name Anytchka mean anything to you?"

Sasha was at a wedding. The crowd chanted, "Gorko, gorko." She saw herself sweeping the veil off her bride's face. The maiden Anytchka was now his, to give him what he wanted. An heir.

Sasha tried to stop the avalanche of images, but couldn't. Somewhere in the distance Anne was saying, "But she was in love with another man. They tried to run away from you …"

An old man—Grudskoy's boatman—he was prostrate on the floor, saying something horrible about Anytchka. Then a barn on fire. Horses.

Sasha rammed her fists into her eyes. It was too horrible to remember.

"Sasha, you don't have to be Grudskoy. See, it frightens you. You don't have to …"

Easter meal. But not joyous like they used to be when he was young. More of a wake. Only a few people around the table. *Anytchka.* Her hair was gray, her face marked with deep wrinkles. But she sat as proud as ever.

Two young girls. *My daughters,* Sasha realized. *The daughters Grudskoy and Anytchka had. Good looking, dark-eyed youngsters, the image of their father,* she noted proudly.

And the son. Blond, sultry boy, about eight. He sat close to his mother and never looked up. Grudskoy didn't like him. The male heir he longed for felt foreign.

But someone was missing. The older son, a young man now, wasn't with them. He was not Anytchka's son.

Why wasn't he there?

Sasha felt a painful memory bubbling up to the surface, like lava from a volcano. Something horrible had happened on Easter day many years ago. That's why the older son was missing.

She recoiled as a human head rolled up to her feet.

A wave of excruciating pain swept through her body. Steadying herself against the MEG, Sasha leaned to pick up the head, but it wasn't there.

She struggled with the mix of present and past, unable to tell which was which.

"You tricked the young woman into telling you where her lover was hiding," Anne was saying.

"How do you know all this?" Sasha grunted, her voice thick.

"I was Anytchka once," Anne replied quietly. "Your claimed wife."

"I knew it!" Sasha exclaimed, her lips curling into a grim smile. "We were meant to be together."

Her head began to clear. It was all so simple. "Well, at least now I know I'm not crazy," she laughed. She stepped out from behind the console and approached Anne.

"When I first saw you in Volodya's lab, there was something ... I couldn't place it. You looked familiar ... And then, when we were treating Namordin ... you were looking at me, with those huge wet green eyes, and it was like a hand reaching in and grabbing me." Sasha touched herself on the cheek, where Anytchka's slap across Grudskoy's face burned as if it had just happened. "I just had to have you."

Sasha staggered but forced herself to focus.

"And then at the wedding ... Volodya kissed you."

Sasha felt the stabbing pain in her temples returning. She saw herself as Grudskoy, ripping off Anytchka's wedding gown, forcing her down on the bed.

"Vovka took your virginity," Sasha yelled. "He'll pay."

Anne tried to sound calm. Her only hope was to talk Sasha through this.

"He did pay," Anne said as gently as she could. "Remember, you sentenced him to death?"

Sasha saw a young man being locked in a barn. She couldn't wait for the execution. Sweet revenge was at hand.

The vision didn't come.

"So how did he die?" Sasha asked.

"He burned in a fire. Anytchka died with him. She doesn't belong to you."

Wedding. Gorko, gorko, gorko.

"But we were united in holy matrimony," Sasha mumbled.

"Only 'til death did us part."

"So Anytchka saved herself from me by dying in a fire?" Sasha sounded resigned.

Anne saw a glimmer of hope.

"Yes, Alexandr Ivanovitch. Anytchka burned. She's gone. Forever."

Sasha exploded. "You're lying! We were married for a long time. You gave me children."

For a moment Anne was confused. "What children? I loved Vovka. I was carrying his child. That's why I set the fire—to save us all."

"You? His child?" Sasha whispered, bewildered. "The blond boy at the Easter table. He was Vovka's son?"

"There was no son. Anytchka and Vovka died in the fire. Anytchka and Grudskoy, you and I, we don't belong together. Now let me out."

"We don't belong?" Sasha repeated. Slowly, she walked up to Anne and began unbuckling the first restraint.

Then she stopped. "But I love you," she pleaded, tears in her voice. "And you love me."

"Sasha, how can I love you?" Anne asked as gently as she could. "I love Volodya. I was meant to be with him. Let me out. Please. We'll…"

"No!" Sasha yelled. "No Vovka. He's gone." Sasha's voice suddenly became hoarse and guttural like a man's. "Vovka is dead, and you're mine."

"Sasha, concentrate. Not Vovka. I love Volodya."

"That bastard! He stole you again."

"He didn't steal me …"

"Slut! Whore!" Saliva was drooling out of Sasha's curled lips Adulteress!"

Sasha ran back to the panel and jerked the joystick.

"I'll make you forget all of them," she yelled, trying to realign the ablation beam.

Her vision blurred. Random images flashed past her eyes. A huge crowd, blood-thirsty faces. Horses, prancing, ready to run. An old woman. Sasha recognized her. *It was Nyanya. An old concubine? Anytchka's servant?* Sasha couldn't remember. Nyanya was screaming something. Sasha let go of the joystick and squeezed her temples, the searing pain now unbearable.

"Sasha!" Anne could see the woman's sanity unraveling.

"What?" Sasha barked.

"The only way to make me forget Vovka, or Volodya, is to let me say good-bye to him. Then I could be yours."

Sasha stopped, like a bull confused by a red cape.

"You're lying!" But she didn't sound sure.

She's lost it, Anne thought with renewed hope.

"Take me to him," Anne continued. "So I can say good-bye." If only she could persuade Sasha to let her out of the MEG! "Think about it! You're a psychiatrist. You know I need closure. A proper farewell."

Sasha scowled. "You want closure? I'll find him."

Anne began to breath a sigh of relief.

"And then I'll tear his head off, with my bare hands. And I'll bring it to you, on a silver platter, like Salome did John the Baptist's."

An image flashed through Anne's head: Grudskoy, holding Anytchka by the hair, the guards dragging Vovka away.

"Spare him, Alexandr Ivanovitch," Anytchka cried out. "I beg you. I'll do anything you want"

"I know you will," Grudskoy grunted back.

"Sasha! Please," Anne pleaded. "I'll do anything …"

"I have to kill him. I'm protecting what's mine. Look, I'll show you his head. You can say good-bye …"

A head rolled up to Anne's feet. "No!" she screamed

"And then we'll both know that Vovka is out of our way. Closure. Forever."

"It'll never work!"

"Of course it will. You'll love being with me. Did I tell you about our new bed?" Sasha looked lovingly into Anne's eyes. "It's ready. A soft mattress. And curtains all around. Servants will bring us wine. You like wine?"

Without waiting for a reply, Sasha headed for the door.

"Take me with you," Anne exclaimed, seeing her last hope dashed. "You need me to tell you where he is."

Sasha laughed. "But you already did. He's in the chapel by the river. Or somewhere …" Her gaze wandered as she tried to refocus on the present. "I'll return soon. And then I can enjoy you. The way it was meant to be."

The lights went out and the heavy metal door slammed closed.

Light beams slicing the room, the C-arms continued spinning, whistling like a breeze in a birch forest.

76

Anne tried to move her arms, but the clamps held her like vises. She could still hear Sasha's words reverberating in her head. "*I'll tear his head off with my bare hands. And I'll bring it to you.*"

She saw Vovka's face, his lips coming closer to her. She was Anytchka again, and she was in love, and Vovka's touch was the most delicious feeling she had ever experienced.

Then the image faded, and her eyes focused on the C-arms spinning overhead. Her thoughts were becoming more disjointed, her memories tumbling out of their neat little pigeonholes, where they had been kept safely out of sight for her entire life.

She heard Sasha's voice. Or was it Grudskoy's? "*Who fucked you? I'll kill him.*" Then came the searing pain in her pelvis, her sphincters going into spasm as if bracing against the onslaught that she knew would tear her flesh. Then Grudskoy's hands, grabbing her hair, throwing her on the bed face down.

Forcing herself back into the present, Anne struggled against the clamps, the hard plastic digging into her flesh. It was useless. She stopped, trying to think.

The door of the little barn was locked …

She had to get in to see Vovka.

Focus, Anne!

Locked.

Lock washer. The Russian repaired the clamp that Namordin ripped out. Anne was concerned because he didn't have a lock washer. Without a lock washer the nut could come undone again ...

Anne started twisting her arm back and forth, with a steady, rotating motion. The clamp yielded slightly. Anne continued, faster. She knew that given enough time, she could loosen the nut. The question was, did she have the time?

The sentinel was coming around to the barn. Get in ...

Get out. Anne pulled up on the restraint as she twisted it to the right, and relaxed as she twisted it to the left. Working feverishly back and forth, she finally got the nut loosened enough to create some play in the restraint. She reached under it. Grasping the nut awkwardly between two fingers, Anne was able to give it a few final twists.

Moments later the entire restraint popped out, bolt and all. With a gasp of relief, Anne reached across the table, fumbled under the edge and found the release button. The remaining clamps sprung open.

Anne rolled off the table, banging her hip as she fell to the floor, panting, her heart racing. She slithered under the C-arms and limped out of the room. There was no time to shut the unit down. She had to find Volodya before Sasha did.

Anne raced down the corridor, oblivious to the pain in her hip. She slipped as she turned the corner toward the lab, but managed to catch herself.

Now that she was out of the magnetic field, her head was clearing.

She reached the doorway to Volodya's lab and froze.

The lab had been trashed. Overturned benches, broken cages, shattered bottles. She was too late. Sasha had gotten there before her.

Surveying the damage, Anne noticed a trail of red spots. Then patches. Puddles.

"No, please, no. Volodya!" The sight of the blood—Volodya's blood—made her gag.

Further in, everything was covered with blood. But Volodya's body was nowhere to be seen. Then she saw the source of the blood.

Mice. Beheaded mice. Dozens of them. The heads chopped off with something sharp.

She bent down and picked up a tiny decapitated body that bore the initials A/B inscribed on its back. Gently, she deposited Abby's body on the counter.

Suddenly Anne heard Sasha's voice. *"Babushka told me that I would kill Volodya. How preposterous."*

Then, Volodya's voice. The same thing he said the day they met. *"I will not be killed by car. I will be killed by jealous husband."*

The room filled with the rumble of galloping horses.

Volodya's voice again. *"Babushka said your love would kill me."*

It was all coming together ...

Horse hooves flashed past Anne's face.

A woman screamed.

Frightened out of her wits, Anne stumbled out into the hallway and leaned against the cold wall to steady herself. *She had to find Volodya. Where was he?* It was the night before Easter Sunday. A big holiday for Russians. Bigger than Christmas. Family time.

Babushka. He went to see Babushka, the only relative he had. He was probably there. Anne guessed that Sasha would have no trouble coming to the same conclusion.

It was 11:35 p.m. If she hurried, she could make the midnight Red Arrow. Perhaps she would even find Sasha on the train. If not, she would need lots of luck to find transportation and get to Babushka's before Sasha did. Perhaps she could call ahead, alert the police. She had all night on the train to figure out what to do.

She dashed out onto the street. A lone taxi was lingering in the driveway in front of the institute. Anne leaped in.

"Pojaluysta, vokzal. Train station."

"Shto?" the driver droned.

Why couldn't this man understand what she wanted? "Train. Choo-choo. Fast please. *Bystro, bystro!"* She tried to use body language to get the man to move.

"Kakoy vokzal?"

"St. Petersburg. Choo-choo."

"*Ah, Leningradsky vokzal! Noo, poekhaly.*"

The dilapidated vehicle was old and reeked of smoke. Anne rolled down the window and leaned her head out to avoid the stench.

The driver, clearly drunk, sped recklessly down Tverskey Street and turned left onto Shiroky.

As they passed St. Gyorgy's church, where Anne had gone to see the wedding, she heard bells ringing. A rich, melodious motif.

"Stop!" she yelled. "Stop."

The driver screeched to a halt. Anne threw a fistful of rubles on the front seat and jumped out of the cab.

The bells were still ringing. It was the familiar syncopated tune that Volodya had played for her at Babushka's.

he crowd of parishioners spilled out onto the street.

"*Izvinite*, excuse me, very important ..." Anne mumbled as she forced her way past dirty looks and angry shoves, scanning the crowd for any sign of Sasha.

The bells rang again. At least she was not too late.

The image of Anytchka's wedding to Grudskoy floated into her mind again. She recalled vividly how she stood next to the old man, holding back tears, convinced that she would never see Vovka again.

The memory stopped her in her tracks, and Anne had to force herself to focus before she was able to continue.

The main door was closed. Anne yanked at the huge rings that served as handles, until a woman steered her toward the side entrance. Inside, the church was almost empty. A handful of old women were scurrying around, removing the black shrouds draped around the icons and replacing them with white ones. It was close to midnight— the transition from mourning to celebration. The Easter Sunday Resurrection Mass was about to begin.

In the central nave, twenty or thirty priests, clerics and altar boys holding banners and icons lined up behind the archbishop, as the old man prepared to lead the procession. He had a long white beard that spilled over his gold embroidered garments. On his head, he wore a massive crown encrusted with precious stones. He stood facing the main entrance doors, leaning on his staff, two deacons supporting him by the elbows.

There was no sign of Sasha. The bells were still ringing.

Anne approached one of the old women.

"Volodya? Verkhov? Ding-dong," Anne said, making the motion of pulling on an imaginary rope.

The old woman snarled, irritated by the interruption. But seeing how distraught Anne was, she softened. She took Anne by the arm and led her to a small door in the back of the church, on the left side of the nave.

"*Toodah idy, tam kolokolnya. Dzin-bom,*" she smiled, mimicking Anne's ding-dong.

At that moment the choir started singing, the altar boys picked up the banners, the main doors swung open, the archbishop glided forward and the procession began to file out.

Anne opened the small door and found herself at the bottom of a narrow circular staircase. She hesitated, then started climbing.

As she felt her way up the dark shaft, the scent of incense and wax that permeated the church changed gradually to the odor of dust and bird droppings.

She saw herself in the dark dungeon of Grudskoy's castle. And she saw Vovka, surrounded by guards with torches. His wrists and ankles were bound again with coarse ropes. Parts of his body were covered by burns from the barn fire, pieces of blackened skin hanging in sheets.

A priest held an icon to Vovka's lips.

"Repent," the priest intoned.

"I have nothing to repent for," Vovka answered proudly. "I would do the same again if I had a chance."

Anne stumbled and almost hit her forehead on the edge of the step.

"Concentrate," she told herself, trying to chase the terrifying images away. "Just concentrate. Up. One step at a time. To the belfry. You must find Volodya."

Below her the procession had filed out and the interior of the church was now completely deserted. As the last parishioners exited, Sasha appeared in the doorway.

She looked tall and poised. Her black boots, black leggings, wide black skirt, and black leather jacket festooned with silver buckles, gave her a military appearance.

The bells started ringing. Sasha grinned triumphantly, walked toward the back of the church and ducked into a small door on the right side of the nave.

Anne continued up the stairs. The stairwell was now pitch black and the ringing was deafening. She must be near.

Something soft brushed against her cheek, then her neck. She felt, rather than heard, the flutter of countless wings.

Suddenly she was engulfed in a swirling tornado of shrieking bats. She screamed and covered up her face. The creatures, now awake, were circling in the confined space, their cold membranous wings brushing against her face and arms, their tiny hairy claws grasping her hair and clothing.

Anne flailed, trying to chase them off. After an eternity, the flock flapped past her and disappeared toward the top of the belfry.

Shaken, Anne continued to grope her way upward. Moments later, she ran into a flat cold surface. Door. She felt around and found the door handle. She pushed. The door creaked open.

Anne emerged onto a small platform under a cluster of bells, hanging motionlessly. Volodya was nowhere to be seen.

Several dim spotlights outlined the onion-shaped domes towering above. Right in front of her, a narrow walkway led from the north belfry to the south belfry. There were no handrails, no banister.

Far below, the procession was circling the church, the archbishop blessing the crowd, the priests swinging their incense burners, banners fluttering in the wind.

Anne breathed a sigh of relief when she heard bells coming from the opposite side. She started across the walkway, concentrating, afraid to look down. Her knees were shaking and she hoped that one of her visions didn't throw her off balance.

At the end of the walkway her progress was blocked by a wall with a small metal grate door. Thick rusted bars. An old padlock, crusted over with layers of rust and pigeon droppings.

On the other side, fifty feet away, was another landing. Volodya was standing there, his back to her, ringing the bells. She called out to him, but her voice was drowned by the ringing.

Suddenly, a wooden door opened at the far end of the landing, and Sasha appeared. She stood behind Volodya's back, watching him work the ropes. Slowly she circled around, like a predator stalking her prey.

Cold sweat beaded on Anne's forehead.

"Volodya!" she screamed again, grasping the metal bars, tugging, trying to open the gate. "Volodya!"

But the bells were overwhelming, and he couldn't hear her.

Still ringing, Volodya took a step toward the edge of the landing and leaned over to get a better view of the procession. The bells had to be timed precisely, because, at the end of the third circuit around the church, the procession would go inside and he would need to change the rhythm so that ...

As he turned, he came face to face with Sasha. There was a disruption in the familiar motif as Volodya faltered. Anne saw Sasha yell something, her face contorted with anger. Volodya said something back.

Anne forced her face against the bars, as if she could will her way through.

Lightning fast, Sasha's fist struck Volodya's chin. Still holding on to the bell ropes, Volodya tried to protect himself, but the next blow crashed into his left eye.

The ringing turned into a cacophony.

Volodya backed toward the edge of the roof.

Sasha followed and swung again.

This time Volodya was prepared and the deflected punch landed on his left shoulder. Crying out in pain, he let the ropes go.

Far below, parishioners and priests looked up in confusion as the bells died down.

Sasha swung her leg high, and her boot crashed into Volodya's jaw. He staggered and fell face down, his head slamming hard against the brick ledge.

For a few moments, Sasha stood over his body, then walked away. Anne's relief changed to horror as Sasha approached a wall-mounted fire-fighting box and rammed her elbow into the glass. Shoving aside the shattered fragments, she pulled out the fire ax.

"Volodya!" Anne yelled, her voice shrill with terror.

With the bells silent, they both heard her. Volodya opened his eyes and rolled out of the way just as the ax came whistling past his head, sinking an inch into the oak floor.

Livid, Sasha struggled to pull the ax out of the planks, yelling, "You'll never have her. She's mine. It's her *sudbah*."

As Volodya tried to get up, Sasha's boot struck him in the temple. He fell back, limp as a rag, unconscious.

Sasha succeeded in extricating the ax and started to raise it again.

"No!" Anne screamed. "Sasha, come to your senses!"

Sasha scowled. "Shut up, whore. He won't be fucking you again. You're mine now. You belong to me. You and everything else. See, there, in the distance? The institute. It'll be mine, too. And him." She prodded Volodya with her boot. "He'll be out of our way. Forever."

"Sasha, wait, let me explain ..." Anne said, trying to sound calm, to buy time, as her mind searched desperately for some way to open the gate. "What's happened to you?"

"Happened? Nothing. Thank you for helping me figure things out. I love who I am. And I love having you. But there is no room for him in this life." She rammed her boot into Volodya's side.

Out of the corner of her eye, Anne spotted a short piece of rusted pipe. Reaching out with her foot, trying not to attract Sasha's attention, she rolled the pipe closer to herself.

"He'll be gone and then everything will be the way it was supposed to be," Sasha continued.

"But it's not Volodya, it's Vovka you must eliminate."

"Volodya, Vovka, what's the difference," Sasha yelled. "All bastards…" She turned her back to Anne, and bent over Volodya's body.

Anne wedged the pipe into the lock and heaved. The lock snapped. Elated, she leaned against the gate … But it still wouldn't yield. Anne felt her muscles stretching to the tearing point, her temples throbbing …

Somewhere in the distance Anne heard Sasha yelling. "Roll over, you bastard, I need to get to your neck."

Then a bright orange light. Torches. A crowd. Grudskoy …

God, not again, not now, her mind screamed, as a sea of torches filled her vision. She was in the town square. The crowd was restless with anticipation. Many of the men and women were crying.

Grudskoy and his retinue stood on an elevated spot, lit by two giant fires. Two of Grudskoy's guards held Anytchka by the arms, her mouth gagged with a rag.

Anne was still struggling with the gate. *Or was she Anytchka, struggling with the guards?*

Suddenly, the crowd grew very quiet. Anytchka heard hoof beats and five horses pranced into the square, each led by a stable boy. Guards appeared, leading Vovka, heavy ropes tied to his limbs and neck. They forced him toward the horses.

Anne watched, confusion giving way to horror as the ropes tied to Vovka's limbs and neck were connected to the horses' harnesses, one rope to a horse.

The macabre cavalcade approached Grudskoy.

A priest lifted a cross above Vovka's head, and droned, "Confess your sins. Renounce the devil."

"My sins are between me and God," Vovka spat back.

A chill raked her flesh as Anytchka realized what was about to happen. She struggled desperately to dislodge the gag, but her attempts were futile, her screams reduced to unintelligible groans.

"*Ubyitza!*" Anne heard herself yell, as if she knew what Anytchka was trying to say. "Murderer!"

"Prepare," Grudskoy barked.

The horse handlers steadied the horses. Suddenly there was a commotion at the back of the crowd.

"Alexandr Ivanovitch! Please, wait!"

It was Nyanya, fighting her way toward Grudskoy. "You must hear me out!" She pushed and shoved, panting, out of breath, frantically trying to reach him.

Sasha was struggling to roll Volodya over so the back of his neck would be exposed. It was the only way to be sure that a single strike of the ax would sever the head off cleanly. The front of the neck was soft, and the ax would lose momentum, and she would need a second strike and …

Grudskoy raised his hand. "Burn in hell, antichrist!" he thundered, as he swung the hand down.

The handlers cracked their whips.

The horses blasted off. Each in a different direction.

"No!" Anne screamed as she heard the rumble of hooves, thundering like her heart.

Vovka's scream blended with her own. A whirlwind of dust and horses swept past her. The ropes snapped tight.

Slowly, Vovka's body lifted off the ground and flew into the air. Anytchka heard the sound of flesh tearing, tendons snapping. The smell of blood seared her nostrils, as parts of Vovka's body separated, his severed head flying up, then crashing down, rolling up to her feet, lying on its side, his handsome features distorted, eyes locked with hers in a last farewell.

The stunned guards released her and Anytchka sunk to her knees next to Vovka's head, clasping it in her trembling hands, caressing the face, kissing the bloodied lips, as if trying to breath one more instant of life into him.

Their gaze stayed locked until his eyes glazed over and froze.

And at that instant, her pain stopped, her soul frozen too.

Anne saw that Sasha had succeeded in rolling the still unconscious Volodya face down and was preparing to raise the ax.

Then she heard another blood-curdling scream, as Nyanya reached Grudskoy. Before the guards could intervene, Nyanya's nails dug into his throat.

"Monster!" she screamed. "You killed your son!"

Slowly, very slowly, Grudskoy turned from Nyanya to the remains of Vovka's body.

"Your son! Our son!" Nyanya screamed again.

Grudskoy staggered. "My … son?"

"Yes, you monster." Nyanya collapsed next to Anytchka, sobbing. "Vovka, Vovka …"

Anytchka looked at Nyanya. "Oh my God," she whispered.

"You never told me …" Grudskoy mumbled, his voice hoarse. "Why …?"

"Because I didn't want him near you, you blood-thirsty animal," Nyanya spat back. "I didn't want him to grow up like you!"

Anne forced herself to focus back on Sasha, her ax poised high above Volodya's head.

"Don't!" Anne screamed, leaning against the gate with one last, superhuman effort.

Sasha hesitated.

"Why?"

"Don't kill him …"

"I must!"

The rusty gate yielding, Anne dove toward Sasha, but it was too late.

The ax whistled through the air.

"*On tvoy syun!*" Anne cried out suddenly. "He's your son!"

With a grunt, Sasha deflected the blow and let the ax sink into the wooden floor a hair's breath from Volodya's face.

"What?"

"He is the son you always wanted."

"You're lying!"

"No, Alexandr Ivanovitch," Anne said quietly as she approached. "Think back! When Nyanya was younger, she was your concubine. Then you got tired of her. But she was pregnant. "

Sasha started to moan. "Yes … Grudskoy … My son. Oh, God. Vovka was my son. I killed him."

Anne inched closer, her hand reaching for the ax, trying to ease it out of Sasha's hands.

Sasha wouldn't let go. "But I did it for you," she mumbled. Then with renewed vigor, she yelled, "You're mine," and lunged for Anne's throat.

They wrestled dangerously close to the edge. Sasha was far stronger, but Anne was fighting for her beloved's life and for her own.

Below, the procession completed its final circle. Midnight and the time of Christ's resurrection were near. The Archbishop raised the scepter and knocked on the church door three times.

"*Khristos voscresse!*" he shouted. "Christ has risen."

"*Voistinoo voscresse!*" the choir and all the people echoed back. "Indeed, He has arisen."

The choir broke out in a joyous chant.

"I want you!" Sasha yelled, her voice coarse and manly.

"You can't have me."

"I'm your master. You belong to me. You'll give me new heirs, so my name will live forever."

Anne saw the look in Sasha's eyes. They had the look of an animal defending its territory, fighting to the death for the survival of its offspring.

Anne knew she needed to stall for time. *Perhaps Volodya would regain consciousness and together they could overpower her.*

"You don't need me anymore. All that is over now," Anne said, her voice soothing.

"You'll be mine, or you'll be dead," Sasha hissed.

"You don't want me dead. Think back, Alexandr Ivanovitch. Think back. Why did you want me?"

"I saved you and your family from the Tartars," Sasha groaned.

"Why?"

Sasha's eyes rolled wildly.

"Because I wanted your father's lands."

"Yes. You wanted control."

"Yes. Lands. Possessions. You." Sasha reached forward but Anne stepped back.

"Keep remembering," Anne said quietly. "Why possessions? Why territory?"

Sasha's mouth spread into a wild smirk. "I ... always was ..."

Images flashed through her head. Young Alexandr Grudskoy slugging it out with another youth, striking him to the ground and stepping on his throat, the joy of victory, the urge to kill, adults running up and separating the combatants just in time.

Then Sasha saw her father, dead. He had died fighting the Tartars when Alexandr was barely three. She knew she was proud that her father died fighting. It was his *sudbah.*

The images flashed by faster and faster, racing through generations, men fighting, always fighting, to control. The mandate of the wild. The territorial imperative. *She had to follow it.* The joy that came from owning land, possessing, controlling territory. Hunting grounds. Food. And then mating. The females would know he was strong.

She laughed, leaning back dangerously, oblivious to the edge of the platform, inches from her boot.

The images spun faster. Her brain was melting down, millions of synapses firing. All the memories pried loose by the enormous magnetic overdose, tumbling out like books from overturned stacks, burying her.

"Stop," she wanted to say, but only a groan came out. Slowly, she sank to the floor, curled up into a little ball, her brain no longer able to process anything.

Anne finally heard the choir below in a joyous, edifying chant.

"*Khristos voskresse iz mertvykh, smertyu smert poprav* ... Christ has arisen, conquering death with death," they sang, as they filed into the church.

Anne felt an arm wrapping around her shoulders. Volodya was next to her, alive and well, except for his left eye, swollen shut.

Together they pulled Sasha away from the edge of the landing. She was panting but unconscious. Her body was trembling. Volodya slipped off his coat and covered her up. Then he and Anne slumped on the floor and held each other.

There wasn't much they could do for Sasha. The body was young and strong. The vital organs functioned perfectly. *But the brain ...* After the overdose and the meltdown they just witnessed, Anne could only guess. It took over an hour to get an ambulance for Sasha. It would have taken much longer had it not been for Baldyuk's influence. "My best scientist," he kept repeating. "She was my best scientist. What happened? We must give her best care possible. I'll see to it," he kept saying to anyone who would listen, as Sasha's comatose body was being loaded onto the stretcher.

If Sasha remained in her vegetative state, he could blame the whole Namordin fiasco on her. As a zombie she would make an excellent scapegoat. If she recovered ...

"Take her to the Institute," he ordered the ambulance driver. "We'll hospitalize her on Razdin Four. I will be personally responsible for her care."

As the ambulance rolled away, Anne and Volodya walked back into the empty church.

The stress of the past few hours had taken a toll. Anne felt drained. But despite the physical exhaustion, there was an overwhelming sense of relief. She had faced her beloved's violent death, a death for which she had felt responsible. This burden that she must have carried with her, unconsciously, for generations, was now off her shoulders. The last demon had been chased out of her caves.

They found an icon of St. Alexei, patron saint of lovers, and stood in front of it, shoulder to shoulder, their hands clasped.

Finally free to be together.

EPILOGUE

In the newly built genetic memory laboratory of the North Boston Medical Center, a white mouse was negotiating an elaborate system of corridors, wheels and bridges. Its every move and even its vital signs and EEG were tracked on a multi-channel monitor, analyzed by a computer, and displayed on a large color screen.

A young boy, in jeans worn almost through at the knees, and a T-shirt with Mickey Mouse on a surfboard, was leaning over the maze, mesmerized by the little animal.

"Papa," he said, "When I grow up, I want to do what you do. Play with animals."

Volodya smiled and picked Michael up. The boy was big for his four years, his body hard as rock.

"Let's go see Mama," Volodya said, giving Michael a peck on the cheek. "I want to hear her talk. We can come back later."

"Maybe she has a Luna bar for me," Michael exclaimed, his eyes big as saucers.

Volodya rolled his eyes. *Of all the Russian things to get the kid hooked on! A chocolate bar. Anne!*

They rode in the elevator up to the eighth floor, where a new amphitheater had been built with money donated by Sidens Medical

Systems. It was the least the corporation could do, considering the MEG profits—past, present and projected.

Clutching Michael with his right arm, Volodya tiptoed into one of the side doors, trying not to disturb the lecture.

"Wow, that's Mommy!" Michael whispered excitedly, as he recognized Anne's face on the giant screen dominating the auditorium.

Even in the dark, Volodya could tell that the auditorium was filled to capacity. Anne stood at the spot lit podium, stunningly elegant in her champagne-colored silk suit that accentuated her blond curls. She was nearing the end of her lecture, her crisp, clear voice echoing over the mesmerized crowd. "…It would have been impossible without the contributions of others. If I had to single one out, I'd say that it was the work of a Russian scientist, Volodya Verkhov, that made the crucial connection …"

Volodya smiled. *She never failed to credit his small contribution.*

"The other reason to single him out, of course, is that he's my husband. And I don't want to wind up sleeping on the couch tonight!"

The crowd laughed. Anne's disarming humor seemed to brighten even the most serious presentations.

A head turned toward them. Volodya recognized Misty and waved.

Of all of Anne's friends, Misty was by far his favorite. They connected from the first day, and soon became good friends. When the three of them were together, and the conversation turned to topics off the beaten scientific path and drifted toward the philosophical and metaphysical, Volodya usually argued on Misty's side.

She smiled and waved, then mouthed: "Your wife is awesome."

Volodya nodded, "I know!"

Father and son turned back to the screen.

Anne was continuing. "Most scientific theories are viciously rejected before they're embraced. Nearly two thousand years ago, when Galen boldly opened live patients to take out tumors, his contemporaries called him a witch."

The image on the giant screen showed a painting of men in white togas performing surgery in an amphitheater. The caption read "150 A.D.—Greek physician Galen credited with the earliest successful cancer surgery."

Anne continued. "And when Jenner infected people with serum from sick cows, the medical community was appalled."

The image on the screen changed to a black and white photo of a man. "1798—E. Jenner develops smallpox vaccine."

"And when Roentgen, shortly after he discovered X-rays, suggested that they could be used to see organs without performing surgery, his contemporaries promptly put the new invention to gratuitous use, X-raying feet in shoe stores, for a better fit."

A chuckle spread through the room. Some of them had heard that story from their parents.

"Every discovery meets with skepticism. Every innovation generates social conflict."

Anne scanned the crowd. Many were nodding.

"We need to look no further than the recent implant of a cloned heart, performed in South Africa. Those who think it was a moral calamity will never see eye-to-eye with those who consider organ cloning a life-saving breakthrough."

Anne lowered her voice, and continued with the slow, persuasive, cadence for which she had become known in her lectures around the world.

"Five years ago, if anyone had told me that I may be able to remember details from a past life, I'd have called them crazy."

She scanned the crowd.

"Believe me, there were many days when I'd have given anything to be wrong! But the evidence is incontrovertible: deep regression to the preconscious is indeed possible. Memories of past lives not only exist, but are accessible."

A brief pause. She lowered her voice even more.

"Is the MEG an affront to morality? An insult to those who are spiritually inclined? Or is it a discovery that will serve us well, like surgery, vaccination, X-rays, and cloned organ transplants?"

She raised her voice again.

"Like any tool, the MEG is what we, responsible scientists and moral human beings, make it to be. So I ask that you view our data with an open mind, and consider our work not as a frivolous venture into the metaphysical, but as a valuable psychotherapeutic tool. A tool that can unlock the past, so that our patients can live better in the present."

Enthusiastic applause drowned her last words. The crowd rose, row by row, into a standing ovation.

"Thank you," Anne said, as the big screen flickered off.

"Can we go visit Mommy's machine again?" Michael whispered.

"Sure we can," Volodya whispered back. "Let's wait for her, so we can all go together, OK?"

There was another wave of applause as Anne stepped off the podium, poised, elegant, smiling.

Volodya, still holding Michael on his arm, stood back and watched as people crowded around his wife to ask questions, to shake her hand or to just stand and admire the woman whose work promised to become a turning point in science.

It took Anne more than ten minutes to extricate herself from the circle of admirers and make her way back to where Volodya and Michael awaited her.

Much later, after Michael had his fill of watching as the new four-armed MEG did its octopus-like dance, the three left the building and headed to the parking lot.

"Papa, do the door trick," Michael exclaimed as they approached the sable-brown Lexus SUV.

Anne watched, smiling, as Volodya made a big show of mysteriously unlocking the door using the remote access key concealed in his pocket. It wasn't clear which of them was more fascinated by the technology, father or son. Even after five years of living in the United States, Volodya still got a child-like enjoyment from Western gadgets.

Volodya helped Michael scramble onto the back seat and fastened him in.

"Dr. Powell!" a voice came from behind them.

An elderly, stooped woman was hobbling toward them, a warm smile on her wrinkled face.

"I wanted to congratulate you," she said shaking Anne's hand.

"Thank you," Anne replied, straining to remember where she had seen the woman before.

Anne still couldn't place the woman.

"You treated my sister. When your machine first came out."

"How is your sister doing?" Anne asked, still unclear. There had been thousands of patients.

"She is doing well..." the elderly woman replied vaguely. "She's different," she added. "Sometimes she speaks of events that neither of us understands. But she is so happy now. Your machine did something for her. I hope it can help others too. That's why I wanted to come wish you good luck."

"But of course," Anne exclaimed remembering the woman who gave her the silver cross at the good-bye party, before she left for Russia.

Before Anne could thank her, the woman squinted at Volodya. "Haven't we met?"

"Only if you've been in Russia," Volodya laughed.

"No. Can't say that I have," the woman answered, shaking her head. "But my great-grandmother is from there. Her family were serfs under the czars. Somewhere up in the North, near a city called Novgorod, I think," she added, adjusting the double knot on the black shawl she wore over her shoulders.

Anne and Volodya exchanged glances, struck by the same thought.

"Would you like to come ..."

"I don't want to hold you up," the woman interrupted, her jet black eyes smiling, as they darted from Volodya to Anne. "It was nice meeting you. You're a lovely couple. God speed." She turned and walked away.

Holding hands, Anne and Volodya watched her disappear behind a corner. He held the door open for Anne, then walked around the car and got in behind the wheel. As they pulled away from the curb, a ray of sun swept across the metallic letters of the sticker that Volodya had affixed to the rear bumper:

HEY YOU, OUT OF THE GENE POOL.